ALL IS FAIR

Julie and Dicky Otterman arrive at Grundy's fair with an extraordinary new motorcycle extravaganza, The Wall of Death. This seemingly happy couple are the talk of the town, but all is not as it seems, and Dicky's dark and violent nature means Julie lives in constant fear.

There's always plenty happening at Grundy's fair: Gemma knows Velda's secret. Renata is finally with Donny. New member, the well-spoken Tom, catches the eye of Jenny, the Grundy's lost daughter who returned to the fair very recently . . .

Meanwhile, Sonny is away, angry and plotting. Amidst all the challenges the most worrying of all is betrayal from those closest to you.

ALL IS FAIR

ALL IS FAIR

by

LYNDA PAGE

Magna Large Print Books
Anstey,
Leicestershire

British Libarary Cataloguing in Publication Data.

A catalogue record of this book is
available from the British Library

ISBN 978-0-7505-4708-6

First published in Great Britain by Canelo in 2018

Published in Large Print 2019 by arrangement with
Canelo Digital Publishing Limited

LP

Magna Large Print is an imprint of Library Magna Books Ltd.

Printed and bound in Great Britain by
T. J. (International) Ltd., Padstow, Cornwall, PL28 8RW

1

The roar of the revving motorcycle engine reverberated deafeningly around the 32-foot-high wooden walls of the drum-shaped structure called the Wall of Death.

Julie Otterman — or Miss Jules, as she was known when performing — a very attractive, shapely 27-year-old platinum blonde, who was always being reminded of her resemblance to the American film star Lana Turner, clutched the shoulder of her husband's leather jacket, leaned over to place her lips against his ear hidden under the strap of his flying helmet and urged, 'Dicky, please don't do this. You know what the doctor — '

Before she could say any more, Richard Otterman — who performed under the name of Daredevil Dicky — had irritatedly shrugged her off and snapped angrily, 'For God's sake, stop nagging. If I say I'm ready, then I'm ready, got that?' He revved the engine even harder before adding, 'Now get out of my way.'

Julie sighed despondently. Dicky was not fully recovered from dislocating his shoulder only a week ago. The doctor had advised him not to ride for at least another three to give it proper time to heal, but Julie knew she was wasting her time trying to persuade him not to attempt what he was about to, as Dicky listened to no one but himself.

She stepped as safe a distance away as she could in the small space, watching intently as Dicky kicked back the stabiliser, revved the engine again by twisting the throttle on the handlebar several times, then set off at speed onto the incline of the structure, gathering pace as he went, continuing up onto the vertical side. Despite the rate at which he was travelling, Julie's sharp eyes never left him.

He had barely completed two circuits when to her horror she saw the front wheel suddenly slip and start wobbling dangerously. Dicky yelled out a string of expletives as he fought to regain control of the violently swerving vehicle. Sheer panic rushed through her, her hand clasped to her mouth as she helplessly watched him fighting to get himself out of this life-threatening situation. It all seemed to happen in slow motion — a frantic Dicky and the bike appeared to hang in the air for several long moments before they fell stone-like to the ground, landing with a loud crash that echoed around the high wooden walls. Then everything went deathly quiet.

Julie froze, staring blindly over at Dicky lying motionless on the wooden floor, the bike on top of him, its wheels still furiously spinning. She tried to move her feet to go over and check on him, but the fear of what she might find prevented her.

Then she saw one of his legs move, then an arm, and next his eyes were open and he was yelling at her, 'Don't stand there like a fucking idiot, get the bike off me!'

She dashed over, grabbed hold of the

handlebars and heaved the machine off him whilst worriedly demanding, 'Are you hurt, Dicky? You haven't caused any further damage to — '

He was on his feet now, rubbing his injured shoulder and bawling, 'Go and tell Frank or one of the other lads to bring the long ladder!'

She eyed him, confused. 'Ladder? Why — '

'For God's sake! What it is with you women that you need to question everything? Ladder. NOW.'

She spun on her heel and ran over to the door in the side of the wall, yanking it open and dashing through it.

Outside, the fairground was a hive of activity as the rest of the Grundy fair folk went about their business, readying the stalls, side shows and rides for opening in a couple of hours' time. Julie headed over to a brown Morris J-type van parked at the back of the Wall of Death that had been converted into a workshop for the repair and maintenance of the riding team's bikes. The back doors were wide open, and as she arrived, she could see Simon Jones — or Speedy, as he was nicknamed — working away inside in his oily overalls.

She called to him. 'Speedy, have you seen Frank or any of the other lads?'

At the sound of her voice, the five-foot-ten, pleasant-faced 24-year-old, with short fair hair beginning to recede at his temples, immediately stopped what he was doing and turned his head to look at her. As always, at the sight of her, his eyes lit up and a broad smile of pleasure split his face. Despite their four-year age difference, Speedy had fallen in love with Julie the first moment he had been introduced to her, when he had come to seek work with the Wall of Death team at the start of the season. His feelings were no secret to Julie, as despite how hard he tried, he could not disguise them from her. Other women might have taken advantage of this, teased him or led him on — even cheated with him on their husbands behind their backs — but not Julie. Her marriage was sacred and she wasn't the type to have fun at someone else's expense, especially a nice man like Speedy, who didn't deserve to have his feelings ridiculed or exploited.

He told her, 'Frank went off to town about half an hour ago to get some wheel bearings for number four bike, and Rod went with him to send a postal order off to his mother. Since his dad died, she relies on the bit he sends her each week. I've no idea where Harry is, but he's knocking off that woman whose husband owns the rifle range, so it's a safe bet he's sloped off for a bit of how's-yer-father with her while Dicky's back's turned. Can I help?'

'Dicky wants the long ladder.'

Speedy frowned as he wiped his hands on an oily piece of rag. 'What for? I thought he was testing out the new bike this morning. Though it's my opinion he should have let me do it, as he's hardly fit enough after dislocating his shoulder last week.'

In defence of her husband Julie said, 'I did try to persuade him not to, but he's put a lot of work

4

into modifying the bike and couldn't wait any longer to see how it performs. I've no idea why he wants the ladder.'

They both knew that since Speedy had been the one to make the majority of the mechanical improvements to the bike, the honour of riding it on its maiden run should have fallen to him, but as the boss of the team and by way of asserting his leadership, Dicky had claimed the right as his. To voice his displeasure would have more than likely resulted in Speedy getting his marching orders, so sensibly he had kept his mouth shut. He had joined this particular team for a specific reason, and until he had achieved his aim, he wouldn't give either the fair owner or Dicky any reason to get rid of him.

'I'll take the ladder to him,' he offered.

Smiling appreciatively at him, Julie turned and left.

She made to return inside the Wall of Death, to check that her husband had suffered no after-effects from his accident and also to satisfy her curiosity about why he wanted the ladder, but she changed her mind and instead went back to their van, situated amid a huddle of others at the back of the main fair arena. Smoking was banned inside the Wall of Death for both riders and spectators, and she felt the desperate need for a cigarette and a cup of sweet tea to calm her nerves, which were still jangling from the shock — albeit momentary — of thinking her husband was dead.

Not in the mood for conversation, she managed to avoid several potential way layers en route back to the van, and a short while later was sitting by the stove in a worn but comfortable armchair, alternately drawing deeply on a cigarette and taking sips of tea, her eyes riveted on a photograph in a plain silver frame that sat on the narrow mantel above the stove.

It was of herself and Dicky on their wedding day. It hadn't been a lavish affair; just themselves and a couple of witnesses grabbed off the street who'd been willing to oblige. To have had her family present would have meant the world to Julie, but no matter how much she had pleaded her case, her parents had been stolidly against her marrying a man she had only being dating for a couple of weeks, and her all-consuming feelings for Dicky had rendered her incapable of listening to their arguments.

She had only been eighteen, Dicky ten years older, when she had first met him in a dance hall in her home town and been swept off her feet by the handsome charmer who worked for a travelling funfair as a Wall of Death rider. He had assured her that his job was only temporary, as he had great plans to own his own Wall of Death ride in the not too distant future, and then she'd want for nothing.

He had let it slip one night early in their relationship when he'd had far too much to drink that his original ambition had been to become a speedway rider. He'd had the talent to possibly become one of the best in the country, but high-performance bikes cost money he hadn't got, so instead he had found a job with a fair as a stunt rider.

Despite living in primitive conditions on very little money, estranged from her family, amongst a group of people with ways and traditions alien to her, for the first few weeks of her marriage Julie had been deliriously happy, but that was all to change when she discovered just what her parents had seen in Dicky that her love-blinded eyes had not. The handsome face and outward charisma cleverly hid an ugly interior. Dicky was in truth a man who had to be in control, everything done his way with no compromise. He didn't take failure graciously, in his conceitedness never considering that his lack of success could be down to himself in anyway whatsoever, and he possessed a volatile temper that would erupt at the slightest provocation. He would satisfy his wrath via his fists, always on someone weaker than him, and since his marriage, that had mostly been Julie herself. He was very clever, though, never damaging her where it would show. To outsiders, the Ottermans' marriage seemed perfect: a devoted couple very much in love. Dicky might be happy with the way things were between them, but that was far from the case with Julie.

A tear wobbled on her eyelid before it fell off to run down her cheek as she remembered the first time Dicky had used her as a punchbag. Still getting used to cooking on a temperamental old gas ring in their dismal, damp and cramped one-bedroom 1930s caravan, she had burnt a tin of Irish stew she had been heating up for their dinner. That attack had left her with two broken ribs and extensive bruising on her torso. In his remorse afterwards, as he pleaded with her to forgive him, promising that nothing like that would ever happen again, Dicky had let slip that his violence was nothing to do with the ruined meal but due to his anger and humiliation that his boss had passed him over for promotion to lead rider on the grounds that another man had been with them longer. Julie later found out that the real reason was that the rest of the team had threatened to walk out if Dicky became their boss.

Over the last eight years, she had lived in fear of Dicky's unwarranted assaults, never knowing when they were coming and powerless to stop them when they did. She had lost count of the number of times she had had to make excuses to others for her injuries; lost count too of the times she had tried to plan a way to leave him. But to start a new life would take money, and as he held the purse strings, only handing her enough to pay for food and essentials, there was nothing spare for her to secrete away until she had enough to make her escape. The only place she could go was back home, but to do so would mean having to tell her beloved parents what Dicky had been doing to her, and she couldn't break their hearts like that, especially when they had begged her not to marry him in the first place. She had made her bed and now she must lie on it.

If it was any consolation, though, this last couple of years had seen a marked reduction in Dicky's attacks. It had come about through an idea of his that at first she been vehemently against, as what he was proposing terrified her witless. He wanted her to learn to stunt-ride. They'd been working for a seaside fair at the time, and his dream of becoming leader of his own team or owning a Wall of Death ride was no nearer to fruition than it had been when Julie had first met him. They had worked at five different fairs since they had married, each time leaving under a cloud because of Dicky's attitude; in fact, Julie suspected it wouldn't be long before they were ousted from the fair they worked for now, as she knew the leader of the team was getting sick and tired of Dicky's highhanded attitude.

Dicky had happened to overhear a conversation between two of the other riders as they were cleaning their bikes. They were discussing a Wall of Death act in America where the rider was a vivacious woman in her twenties. Crowds, particularly men, flocked to see her performing, and wherever she went she was treated with film-star reverence and had become very wealthy as a result. Dicky immediately saw the wisdom of Julie learning to ride. To his knowledge, there was no other woman performing on the Wall of Death in Britain. She was young, blonde and attractive, and their act would be unique and in great demand, with fairs vying with each other to hire them. This was just the edge he would need to get himself taken on as lead rider, and their share of the entrance money would all the sooner amass to allow him to buy his own ride.

Watching the men perform the stunts was terrifying enough for Julie, knowing that one false move could seriously harm them, possibly end their life, and she had no desire whatsoever to try it herself. Dicky, though, would not listen to her arguments, leaving her in no doubt that she was going to do what she was told. He didn't give her any time to get used to the idea, but immediately fetched one of the practice bikes, took her to a straight piece of quiet road and, with only a quick lesson on the workings, ordered her to take it for a spin.

Nearly two years later, she could still feel the sheer terror she'd felt at the time, sitting astride the bike for the very first time, the throbbing of the engine reverberating through her body, knowing that once she engaged the throttle and released the brake, she was in control of how fast it went and whether she stayed on. How long she sat there, frozen in fear, staring down the long road ahead, she had no idea, but finally Dicky's bullying tactics did the trick and she closed her eyes, revved the throttle and lifted her foot off the brake.

Next thing she knew, she seemed to be flying, the wind whipping through her hair. By the time she finally brought the bike to a stop a good half a mile down the road without so much as a wobble, the fear had been replaced by pure exhilaration. She was shocked to find she had enjoyed every moment of the ride and couldn't wait to repeat the experience. She now understood what riders got out of riding motorcycles at speed. Without any reservations whatsoever, she turned the bike around and rode back to Dicky.

From then on, she became his willing pupil, and within only a couple of weeks had mastered the rudiments of riding a motorcycle and was ready to tackle a few simple stunts. Six months later, she was performing alongside Dicky as part of a double act, and the crowds were flocking to see her. Not that Dicky ever praised her part in that, and neither did she benefit financially, as he pocketed her share of the entrance fee as well as his own, but she was prepared to accept the situation if it kept him happy. He might be a violent man, but he wasn't stupid, and now that they were working together, he generally managed to keep his temper in check, astute enough to know that if he incapacitated her in any way, she could not perform, and that would severely affect his pocket.

Dicky's belief that fairs would be fighting with each other to take them on now that he had Julie as his bargaining tool was proved wrong, as his reputation as a difficult man to work with preceded him, although it was down to her that he landed his first job as leader of a team — not that he gave her any credit, simply gloating that at last someone had recognised his prowess.

Through the fairground grapevine he had heard that Grundy's fair was on the lookout for a lead rider after theirs had decided to leave the dangerous profession to settle down with his new wife and work for her father as a mechanic in his back-street garage. Dicky wasted no time in putting himself forward as replacement.

Julie had taken an instant liking to Sam Grundy. His fair wasn't one of the biggest in the country, but nevertheless it boasted numerous stalls offering games of chance, skill and strength, several sideshows — boxing, magic and illusion amongst them — and many thrilling rides, supporting the livelihoods of over forty families as well as a dozen labourers and gaff lads. Sam himself had come across as a gruff, no-nonsense sort who didn't suffer fools at all, let alone gladly, but she had seen the twinkle of humour in his shrewd eyes and knew that behind his tough veneer was a kind, principled man, unique in her experience of fair owners in that he genuinely cared for all those who worked for him in whatever capacity and would be ruthless to anyone who brought harm to them or his business. She might not have known Big Sam, as he was respectfully called, for very long, but she was as shocked and upset at his accidental death only months after they had joined the fair as were the rest of the community.

During the interview for the Wall of Death team leader, though, Julie had sensed that Big Sam hadn't liked Dicky or his cavalier attitude. Not that she had ever hinted at the fact to her husband, for fear of repercussions, but Sam had intimated very strongly to her that the sole reason he decided to give Dicky the job was because he had taken a shine to Julie herself. He had foreseen the asset she would be to his business — the only female rider at present in the country — and if he wanted her to join his team, then he had to take Dicky too.

As with all the other fairs, she had worried that their time with Grundy's would be short-lived due to Dicky's behaviour, but so far none of the other riders had made any complaints about him, and she dearly hoped it stayed that way. At Grundy's she felt she belonged to an extended family who all looked out for each other. She had made good friends, especially Jenny, the owner's pretty 24-year-old daughter, and Ren, who owned the candy floss and confectionery stall, and she very much looked forward to the time they spent together. Like everyone else in the community, both Jenny and Ren were oblivious to what went on between her and Dicky behind closed doors, believing them a devoted, happy couple. Julie couldn't bear the thought of becoming the object of their pity and sympathy, so she kept that side of her life from them.

Taking a last draw from her cigarette, she stubbed it out into an ashtray and then smiled to herself. Jenny's mother, Gem, had roped Jenny, Ren and Julie, along with Fran, Jenny's aunt, into helping her organise a surprise birthday party for Velda, the fairground fortune-teller, who was turning 66 in a week's time. Although her actual birthday was on the Monday, the party was planned for the previous Sunday afternoon, when the fair was closed, so those attending could relax and make merry. If the weather was fine, it was going to be held outside Gem's van, and if not, then inside.

Gem, Fran, Jenny and Ren would be doing the setting-up and the preparation of the food and drink, and it was Julie's job to keep Velda out of the way whilst that was in progress then, at the allotted time, to get her to Gem's van. She was still not sure how she was going to keep the older woman occupied for several hours, but she still had time to come up with an idea, and a backup plan if that failed.

She was looking forward to the do, which promised to be fun. This was the first party hosted by the owners that she and Dicky had been invited to since they had joined Grundy's. She just hoped that Dicky behaved himself and didn't rile any of the other men with his supercilious attitude, or flirt with any of the wives as he had a habit of doing with a few drinks inside him.

She stiffened as the tall, dark-haired man in her thoughts arrived in the van. She didn't need to look at him to know that his mood wasn't a good one; she could tell just by the way he had thrust open the door and stomped inside.

Before she had a chance to explain her reasons for not returning to the wall after going off to fetch the ladder, he was furiously waving his arms about and shouting, 'Bloody imbecile could have killed me! I wish I knew which damn idiot it was and they'd be sorry after I'd finished with them. I knew it wasn't anything I'd done that caused the accident.' He slammed his hand on the dining table. 'There was a patch of grease on the wall that must have come off one of the bikes and wasn't cleaned off when the wall was given its once-over this morning. That was what caused my front wheel to slip.'

Julie jumped up and went over to him in a desperate effort to calm his rage before it reached a point of no return. 'It was just a mistake, Dicky,' she soothed. 'Any of us could have made it.'

Glaring darkly at her, he erupted. 'You insinuating it was my fault? It was me that left that glob of grease on the wall?'

To her horror, she saw him ball a fist. Fearing it was about to come her way, she hurriedly blurted, 'No, no, not at all, Dicky. I know you don't make mistakes like that. No, as I said before it could have been any one of us.'

His eyes narrowed menacingly as a thought occurred to him and he cut in. 'It was you. You put that grease there on purpose. Put a dollop of it on the end of a mop or something and smeared it on the wall. You want rid of me. That's it, isn't it? Got your eye on someone else, have you? Been playing around behind my back with him? Huh, it all makes sense now. That accident I had last week when I dislocated my shoulder . . . I knew I'd checked all the wheel bolts on the bike before I went out for a smoke. While I was gone, you loosened the bolt, you bloody bitch, so you could be with your new man.'

She gawped at him, appalled, and frenziedly blurted, 'No, no, how could you even think such a thing, Dicky? I would never look at anyone else. It's you I love. You know that.' He would never consider that the blob of grease might have come from his own bike, or that he hadn't tightened the bolts properly either. 'I remember now, I came out for a smoke with you and none of the other lads were with us at the time.

15

Speedy and Rod were in the repair van. Frank and Harry . . . I'm not sure where they were, but I'm positive it was only us two around the wall at that time. It was an accident, Dicky, it couldn't have been anything else. And what reason would any of them have to want to do away with you? You've had words with them all, but nothing serious enough for any of them to risk a long stay in jail.'

He sneered nastily as he grabbed her chin, squeezing it hard and pulling her up so she was standing on tiptoe. Pushing his face into hers, he snarled, 'Yeah, yer right. If they know what's good for them, none of the lads would dare cross me. As for you . . . If I ever as much as catch you looking at another man . . . ' He balled his fist and swung back his arm.

She froze in terror. His need to vent his wrath had risen to such a pitch now that it was stopping him thinking straight. She cried out, 'No, Dicky, no. I love you. No other man would ever compare to you.' Then she lowered her voice and, despite her inner turmoil, managed to say in a soothing tone, 'Listen, love, if you hurt me, I won't be able to ride for a while, and think how that will affect your share of the takings.'

He bawled furiously, 'You saying the punters only come to see you?'

Although she was not yet quite as accomplished as Dicky at performing daring and dangerous tricks, in truth she was the main draw, but nevertheless she vehemently insisted, 'No, no, absolutely not. I could never hope to perform as well as you. It's you that's the star, Dicky. You

16

have to be the best daredevil rider in the country. The crowds love you, especially the women. I'm so lucky that you're my husband and they can only dream of having you.' She lowered her voice. 'You're hurting me, darling. Please let me go.'

One hand still tightly squeezing her chin, the other balled and aimed at her chest, he glared manically at her for what seemed like an age, and then the wisdom of her words appeared to penetrate his anger. He released his grip, pushed her forcefully from him and smashed his fist down on the kitchen table so hard that the small caravan shook. Then he turned and stormed out of the van, slamming the door shut behind him.

She stood frozen for a moment, fearing that he might return and finish what he'd started. It was several minutes before she dared exhale in relief at her escape from a beating and sink down on a chair at the small kitchen table. She rested her arms on the top and stared blindly across at the wall opposite her, worrying thoughts tumbling around inside her brain. Despite his inexcusable behaviour towards her at times, she still loved Dicky. But if that was the case, why was it that as he had lain motionless after the accident this morning, just for a brief moment a feeling of great relief had surged through her that she was finally free of him? And as she had seen his eyelids fluttering, a sense of doom had replaced the relief that Dicky's reign of terror upon her was not over yet.

2

A week and a half later, outside a parked one-bedroom bow-top wagon, two women were sitting in wicker chairs sharing a pot of tea and a plate of Garibaldi biscuits whilst they chatted together.

Fortune-teller Gypsy Velda May, her large hands clasped over her mound of a stomach, was saying, 'It's not often I'm shocked. I've never been attacked before because someone didn't agree with what the cards were telling. He came into the tent looking every bit the gent in his suit, tie and bowler hat. I told him to sit down and asked what sort of reading he wanted — tarot, palm or crystal ball — but then the next thing I knew he had his hands around my neck and was screaming at me that I should be jailed as a marriage breaker. Nearly throttled the life out me before I managed to wrench his hands away.'

She paused long enough to issue a deep throaty chuckle. 'Then it was him that was shocked from the left hook I gave him. Knocked him flat to the ground and it took him several moments to realise how he'd come to be sprawled on the floor. I'm not a violent person as you know, Gem, but I'm not going to let anyone try and murder me and not defend myself.' She flashed a meaningful look at her companion before she added with a spark of humour in her shrewd brown eyes. 'Well, he certainly picked the wrong woman to have a go at when he picked on me, didn't he? I wish I'd had a camera and taken a photo of the look on his face when I knocked him flying.'

37-year-old strawberry blonde Gemma Grundy laughed as she eyed her friend with deep affection. The wife of the owner of the fair, Solly Grundy, her figure was still very shapely for a woman who had given birth to three children, and she wore a flattering pair of black slacks with a pink crew-necked jumper, a broad black belt circling her trim waist. Velda was dressed as usual in a flowing tent-like dress, which today was black with large red and yellow flowers embroidered all over it. A black scarf was tied gypsy-style around her head, a long greying plait hanging over one shoulder. When working, she would attach a string of coins across her forehead. She looked every bit a woman and acted more feminine than many women Gem knew, but the fact was she had been born male.

Velda had been Grundy's fortune-teller for over thirty years. Gem had known her for twenty-two of those, and never once had she or any of the rest of the Grundy community found reason to suspect that Velda was anything other than the woman she presented herself to be. That was until several months ago, when Gem had accidentally walked in on her whilst she was in a state of undress, and Velda had had no choice but to take her into her confidence and reveal her tragic history. Whilst listening to the

19

harrowing tale, Gem's initial disgust and hurt at Velda's deception, not only of herself, but of the community of people she lived amongst who had come to greatly respect her, turned to unadulterated sympathy, and to Velda's enormous relief, she agreed to keep her secret. Velda knew that Gem wasn't the type who looked for repayment for any favour she did, which in this case was a good thing, as the debt of gratitude she owed Gem for keeping her silence on such a controversial matter could never be settled.

With a dark scowl on her rotund face, Velda went on. 'What an insult to my profession to blame me for his wife chucking him out. I told him in no uncertain terms that an honourable clairvoyant would never tell a client what to do. We are just vessels for the spirits, and it's them that offer the guidance to those who seek it. In his wife's case she chose the tarot cards, and they informed me that she was a very miserable woman, and until she got rid of whatever it was that was making her unhappy, then she'd never know peace. He bawled at me that he didn't believe in all that bunkum, but as I told him, his wife obviously did, and as she'd gone straight home after her reading and thrown him out, it was clear that he was the reason for her unhappiness. He slunk off then with his tail between his legs. Oh, and a black eye to boot. Odious little man. I sensed that he was the sort that took great joy in making those close to him miserable, if you understand me. I really don't like to see any marriage break up, but she was a nice, unassuming sort of woman and I hope she finds herself a man who gets pleasure in making her laugh rather than cry.'

She paused for a moment and looked upwards. 'I don't like the look of that big black cloud heading our way. Hopefully it'll have done its worst and passed over before we open this afternoon. Not the most picturesque place, Grimethorpe. Hardly a tree to be seen, and surrounded by slag heaps. But the people are such a friendly lot. I look forward to when we first arrive to set up and the locals come out in force to wave and cheer at us as we drive through the town, with the Grimethorpe colliery band leading the parade.'

She pulled a grim face. 'I feel sorry for the womenfolk — it must be a constant battle for them against all the coal dust. It gets everywhere, doesn't it? No matter how I try to keep my van door closed as much as possible, and the windows shut tight, the coal dust still manages to get in somehow and invade every nook and cranny. As soon as we get to our next place, it's a good spring-cleaning of my van for me, and a launder of all my clothes. I can't imagine how frustrating it must be for the poor housewives to put out a line of white washing and find it covered in the black stuff by the time they come to take it in. I never do any washing while we're here, just save it all up until we move on. But in all the thirty years I've been coming here with Grundy's, I can't ever remember a time when for half the week it didn't rain, and when I say rain, I mean bucketing it down for hours on end. Having to deal with mud is bad enough, but mud mixed with coal dust is a nightmare to clean up.'

Gem readily agreed. 'Yes, it is. Like you, I'm sorry when it's time for us to move on, because the folk are so nice, but in other respects I'm the first in the queue. But I suppose it is only April, and April is well known for its showers, so it'll be a miracle if we get to the end of the week and we haven't seen any. Do you remember the storm we suffered while we were here the year before last, when we were worried the big wheel was going to buckle under the force of the wind? Your tent ended up wrapped around the top of the helter-skelter. Several times during that storm I thought we were going to end up like Dorothy in *The Wizard of Oz* and our caravan be sucked up and thrown down someplace miles away.'

Velda bellowed with laughter for a moment at the vision Gem had conjured up, before her guffaws died away and she said seriously, 'Didn't it rock your van so badly on one occasion that Robbie was thrown out of his bunk?'

'Oh yes, it did. My poor son was lucky he didn't break any bones, but he was covered in bruises. None of us got any sleep that night except for Jimmy who snored through the whole thing, oblivious to the mayhem going on around him. At least Robbie got off lightly compared to the poor Cramp and Evans families. The Evanses' van was almost destroyed when a rotting part of its roof disintegrated from the force of the battering rain and water poured in, and the Cramps' van was smashed to smithereens when the wind blew it into a tree.'

22

Velda pursed her lips. 'I did feel sorry for the Evanses, as they're nice people. We all pitched in to help them dry out the van and fix the roof, and had a whip-round to replace some of the furniture and possessions that the storm ruined, and how grateful they were: laid on a party by way of thanking us. Can't say the same for the Cramps. They have always been the money-grabbing type, and never volunteer any help to others in the community if they can weasel their way out of it. It was awful them losing their van and hardly anything inside salvageable, but Big Sam put up a sizeable donation himself and all the rest of us chipped in with whatever we could afford, and all Ada Cramp did was grumble that the living area in her new van wasn't as big as the last one, and Horace moaned that it hadn't got anywhere for him to fix a box to at the back to keep his tools in.'

Gem sighed. 'Yes, those two can be very selfish. I remember at one community party a few years back, I saw Ada acting very oddly. She sidled up to the food table, had a look round to make sure that no one was looking, then brazenly picked up a fruit cake and a plate of sausage rolls and handed them over to Fran as her own contribution.'

Velda gawped. 'What a nerve she's got. Did you let her know you'd seen her?'

'Indirectly I did. I said to her, 'Oh, what a coincidence that you've put glacé cherries on the top of your fruit cake just the same as I have on the one I made, and Elsie has cut a cross in the top of her sausage rolls exactly the same as you have too.' She never batted an eyelid, just stuck her head haughtily in the air, took a sausage roll off the plate and went off to get herself a drink.' Gem chuckled. 'There's good and bad in all communities, but thankfully Grundy's has far more of the good.'

'Yes, thank goodness. On the whole, I couldn't wish for a better bunch of people to be living amongst. Oh, talking of the Cramps, your Jimmy's got himself a new girlfriend, I see.'

Gem stared agog at her. 'Has he? He hasn't mentioned it. Mind you, on subjects like girlfriends, he never tells me anything. Who is she? And why has talking about the Cramps made you think of his new girlfriend?' Suddenly her face filled with horror. 'It's not their daughter Doreen, is it?'

Doreen was a sour-faced, dowdy girl who slouched around looking like she'd the weight of the world on her shoulders; she certainly wasn't the sort whose personality encouraged punters to spend their money on her parents' Derby horse-racing stall, and Gem couldn't for the life of her see her outgoing, fun-loving son taking a fancy to her. It wasn't the possibility of having Doreen for a daughter-in-law that horrified her the most, though. Her parents she could tolerate at a distance, but as her son's inlaws, the humourless, miserly couple would have an open invitation into her own family's life, having to be invited to any special occasion or social event Gem organised.

Before she could have her worrying question answered, a visitor arrived to join them. Renata

Shawditch was a midget at four foot three, but what she lacked in height was more than made up for by her bubbly personality. The 25-year-old, who owned the candy floss and confectionery stall, was a slightly built, pretty girl and a much-loved and respected member of the Grundy community. Her disability attracted much verbal and at times even physical abuse from ignorant types, but Ren never let those responsible see they had got the better of her, and any upset she did suffer was always expressed in private behind closed doors.

Ren had had her fair share of life's ups and downs. Having lost both her beloved parents several years back, she had then suffered intolerable heartache witnessing the man she had loved more than life itself since childhood being swept off his feet by another woman and marrying her. But then her grief was to turn to unadulterated happiness on the discovery that Suzie had only married Donny for the material benefits he could give her, and that since their marriage she had been unfaithful on numerous occasions in her mission to find herself a man who could give her an even better life. Her betrayal had served to show Donny that her clever manipulation had blinded him to the fact that it was only infatuation he felt for her, and that it was his lifelong friend Ren he truly loved.

Since Suzie had disappeared off the scene several months ago, Donny and Ren had been inseparable. Both would have liked nothing more than to marry, but with Donny unable to divorce Suzie until they found out where she was, they were content just to live together, regardless of what some narrow-minded people thought of them.

The tiny woman was giggling as she greeted Velda and Gem. 'Look at you two sitting there like you're on holiday while the rest of us are running around like headless chickens to be ready for opening.'

Velda replied drily, 'Well some of us are better at our jobs than others, so have more time for sunning ourselves. I expect you're rushing to get Donny's dinner.'

'Well, I am, but I've time for a — '

Velda cut in. 'You'd best not dilly-dally then. You don't want him coming in and finding his dinner not ready. I'll see you after work tonight as usual, and we'll have a catchup then.'

Ren looked both bemused and a mite hurt that the woman she considered her second mother was making it very obvious that her company wasn't wanted.

As she went on her way, Gem looked at Velda quizzically. 'Are you annoyed with Ren for some reason? You obviously didn't want her to come and join us.'

'Yes, I know I was short with her and I will explain why to her later. Knowing Ren as I do, she will be most understanding. But had she joined us, you wouldn't have got around to telling me what's worrying you, and you'd then have had an anxious wait until you could get me on my own again to ask me for my help. I think we've caught up with all the gossip now, so are you finally going to tell me what it is that's on your mind?'

Gem gawped at her. 'How did you . . . ? Oh, never mind. Your sixth sense, womanly instincts, psychic powers, whatever you care to call it, kicking in, I see.' She clasped her hands together and sighed heavily. 'There is something I'd like your advice on, please, Velda.'

'It's not to do with Jenny, is it?' the older woman enquired worriedly.

Jenny was Gem and Solly's eldest child. Gem had fallen pregnant with her when she was thirteen and Solly fourteen. Despite their youth and naivety, for both of them it had been love at first sight when Gem had sneaked to the fair with her friend behind her parents' back, and for the rest of the week they had spent as much time as possible together. When it came time for the fair to move on, the thought of not seeing each other again for a whole year was unbearable to them both. They had known it was wrong, but their need for each other had overridden all their common sense. Three months later, Gem's mother realised her daughter was pregnant. Despite her obvious anger, Gem was determined to keep the child, and adamant that she and Solly would become a family and raise it together when the fair returned the following year.

The pain of childbirth was unbearable for Gem, hardly more than a child herself at the time, but nothing compared to what she then suffered on being told by her mother that her much-wanted baby had died. Despite her resolve to tell Solly the truth when the fair returned and they reignited their relationship, the time just never seemed right, and anyway Gem was reluctant to put her beloved husband through the loss of their child when she had grieved enough over it for them both.

Twenty-two years later, to their utter astonishment, they found out that their baby had not died after all, but was very much alive, when she turned up unannounced to vent her wrath on the mother she believed had chucked her away like a bag of rubbish because she'd been an inconvenience. Only then did she discover that that was not at all the truth; that her mother had very much wanted her, but her selfish grandmother hadn't been prepared for the stigma of an illegitimate grandchild, and had had her whipped away for adoption straight after the birth. Shocked to the core to learn all this, Jenny had disappeared off for a while to come to terms with this turn of events, leaving Gem and Solly uncertain whether they would ever see her again. To their utter joy, she had turned up out of the blue at the end-of-season party last October, very keen to be part of her real family, and had been living with them ever since.

Gem smiled, her eyes softening tenderly. 'I've no worries over Jenny. She's settled in so well, it's hard to believe she's only been with us a few months. The boys adore her and she them. The way the three of them rib each other, it's hard to believe they haven't known each other all their lives. As you know, I was worried she wouldn't settle, as the life we live is far different from the one she had with her adopted parents, but she's taken to it like a duck to water. Anyone who didn't know her background would think she was a born show woman.'

Velda reminded her, 'But she *was* born a show woman, dear, just that she never had a chance to live the life of one until now, thanks to your mother. Anyway, if it's not Jenny you're worried about, then it's got to be one of the boys.'

Gem shook her head. 'Not either of my boys this time.' She paused for a moment, sighing heavily. 'It's Solly, Velda.'

Velda looked surprised. 'Solly!' She frowned. 'Now why would that lovely husband of yours be causing you worry when I have never known him give you a moment since you married him? Don't tell me you think he's playing around behind your back, because I won't believe it. There's only one woman for Solly, and that's the one he's married to.'

Gem smiled wanly. 'It might sound compla- cent of me, but I know without doubt that Solly would never betray me. Something is worrying him, though, and he won't tell me what it is. Every time I ask him, he tells me I'm imagining things and that he's fine, but I know he's not telling me the truth. Running a fair is far from easy, Velda, as I've no doubt you know, having been with Grundy's for over thirty years yourself. Solly wasn't expecting to be in charge; he thought Sonny would become ringmaster on his father's death. Suddenly being solely responsible for keeping the punters wanting to come to Grundy's and looking after all the people who work for us as well as his own family

. . . well, it's enough to cause the strongest of men sleepless nights. Not to mention coping with all the problems we face on a day-to-day basis and dealing with those who think us fair folk are the scourge of society and should be banned from entering their villages and towns.'

'So, you think it's the worry of being in charge that's bothering him?'

Gem grimaced. 'Yes . . . no . . . I'm not sure, Velda.' She heaved another deep sigh before she added, 'As you know, Solly was absolutely devastated over his father's death. How on earth Big Sam came to be on the helter-skelter at that time of night, and after the long journey he'd had that day, let alone fall off it, will always remain a mystery, but I thought Solly was coming to terms with it. He's got to the stage where he can laugh at some of the things his father did and said, and talk about him at length without getting upset.'

She eyed Velda meaningfully then and leant over to pat her hand affectionately. 'Not that you ever get over losing someone you love. Big Sam was the love of your life and he loved you back. If it hadn't been for the cruel hand Mother Nature dealt you when you were born, the two of you would have been together.' She sighed heavily yet again. 'But then I suppose Solly didn't just lose his father, but his brother at the same time.' She shook her head, eyes filled with bewilderment. 'How could Sonny do that, just disappear off leaving Solly to pay his debt to those gangsters and possibly facing a prison sentence had the police believed that he was involved with them too.' Her voice became harsh then, her eyes flaming in anger. 'If Solly hadn't been brave enough to help the police put those villains behind bars for a very long time . . . well, we could have lost everything that this father had shed blood, sweat and tears building.

'Big Sam would be turning in his grave if he knew what Sonny had been up to behind his back. In a way, I'm glad he's no longer here, because it would have broken his heart. I don't care how nasty this makes me sound, Velda, but wherever Sonny is now, I don't wish him well. I hope he's being kept awake at night by nightmares about the mess he left us in. But somehow, I doubt it. I bet he's living the life of Riley somewhere, and not one penny of what's paying for it would he have earned honestly. Selfish man that he is.' She paused and took a deep breath, shooting Velda an apologetic look. 'Sorry, Velda, I do feel very venomous towards my husband's brother.'

Velda smiled at her in understanding. 'It's just how I would feel if I was in your shoes. Sonny being Solly's brother is immaterial.' Her eyes glinted in amusement. 'I just hope he never shows his face around here again, or I fear he'll be finding out whether a right hook from you is as painful as the one I gave that woman's obnoxious husband. Now, enough of Sonny. It's why you're worried about Solly that's concerning me.'

Gem took a deep breath before she spoke again. 'Well, as I said earlier, he's not been himself for a few weeks now, ever since we

31

started organising the start of the season while we were still at the over-winter place. It's not just him still grieving for the loss of his father or worrying about keeping the fair running smoothly, but something more than that. You know how easy-going Solly is, takes a lot to make him lose his temper; well, now he snaps at the slightest thing and has become very distracted. Sometimes I have to speak to him several times before I can get a response. People are starting to ask me what's wrong with him, and several have told me that when he sees them coming over to ask him something, he pretends not to see them and shoots off the other way. If I didn't do the fair's books, I'd be worried that it was something to do with that, but although we're far from rich, we're managing to pay our bills and put some by towards buying some new rides and whatever, so it can't be that that's troubling him. But after what happened in the middle of the night, I knew I couldn't let this carry on, that I had to do something to help him.'

'What happened in the middle of the night?' Velda probed.

'Solly's always been a good sleeper, but he hasn't slept well for a while now. Last night he got up about one o'clock and I could hear him pacing around the kitchen. I went in and asked him if he'd like a cup of tea or Ovaltine to help him sleep. He flew at me, Velda. Told me to leave him alone and stop constantly asking him what the matter was when there was nothing wrong. He put his coat on and went out, didn't tell me where he was going. It was after three before he came back. I thought it best to pretend to be asleep after him having such a go at me earlier.' She wrung her hands, distraught. 'I'm at my wits' end with worry.' She looked earnestly at her friend. 'I don't like to ask . . . '

Velda was thinking that the behaviour Solly was displaying was not at all like him and she wasn't surprised Gem was concerned. She patted the other woman's hand. 'I'll do my best to get him to talk to me, dear, but of course I can't promise he will.'

'Oh, thank you, Velda,' Gem said gratefully. 'If anyone can get it out of him, it's you. You have a way about you that puts people at their ease and gets them to tell you anything.'

With a twinkle in her eyes Velda said, 'Well in that case I'll wheedle it out of him where he keeps his life savings and take myself off around the shops.' Her eye was caught by a woman making her way through the living-van area a short distance away, and she said, 'Now there's someone I don't envy for all her youth and good looks.'

Gem followed Velda's gaze to see Julie Otterman, dressed in her biking leathers, heading towards the Wall of Death. She must have sensed that someone was looking at her, because she glanced across, and when she saw Gem and Velda looking back at her, she smiled and waved as she continued on her way.

Gem frowned, puzzled. 'What do you mean by that?'

'Well let's put it this way. Many women might be jealous that Julie's nabbed herself such a good-looking husband, but it's no fun being married to a man with a roving eye, and I also have a suspicion that underneath that charming smile of his lurks something not so nice. My surprise birthday party week was the first time I'd seen them together socially since they joined Grundy's. As soon as they arrived, it was plain as a pikestaff to me that Julie was nervous. I thought at first it was because this was the first community do they had been to and they wanted to make a good impression, but then I very soon realised that wasn't the case. Dicky Otterman's eyes were on every woman but his wife, and Julie was obviously worried that the more he drank, the less likely it was that it was going to remain as just looking.

'I wasn't watching her all the time, but when I did, she was doing her best to keep tabs on him and how much he drank. A couple of times I saw he'd given her the slip and pounced on one of the women whose man wasn't nearby. He made a play for your Jenny, but don't worry, that daughter of yours ain't silly and gave him short shift, but Cassie Staybright isn't so smart and they disappeared off together for a while. If Julie was aware, then all credit to her, as she played dumb when he appeared again. But it's not just his womanising I'm suspicious of. A couple of times at the party, and also when I've come across them together at work, I've overheard him saying not very nice things to Julie.' She paused for a moment before she added, 'I think he's a bully and . . . '

'And what?' urged Gem.

Velda had a feeling that Dicky wasn't just a verbal bully to Julie, and even though she knew that what she was saying to Gem would not go any further, she had no concrete evidence. It wouldn't be right to brand someone of something without proof, even if she knew her instincts were right.

'And I hope she stands up to him, that's what I was going to say.'

Gem looked horrified. 'Oh, surely you're wrong, Velda. Julie's never once hinted to us that all might not be what it seems behind closed doors. I never heard her say a bad word against her husband. She's such a lovely woman. I'm in awe of her having the guts to do what she does. Surely someone who's brave enough to be a stunt rider on the Wall of Death wouldn't put up with being bullied by her husband. Trouble is, though, I've never known you be wrong about someone.'

Velda didn't think she was mistaken in this instance, but regardless she said, 'Always a first time for everything, lovey. I hope I am in this case.'

'So do I.' Gem got up. 'I'd best go and see to the dinner. I left a cheese and potato pie in the oven and it won't be far off done by now.' She leaned over and kissed the older woman on her cheek. 'Thank you again for offering to help.'

'Considering what you've done for me, it's the least I can do,' Velda replied with sincerity.

Gem walked a couple of steps away and then a thought struck her and she spun back around to face her friend. 'Oh, you never answered my question. Is Jimmy's new girlfriend the Cramps' daughter? Please tell me it's not. I can't bear the thought of having to welcome those awful Cramps into our family.'

Normally the mischievous side of Velda would have risen to the fore and she would have extracted a bit of fun out of the situation, telling Gem that she had overheard Doreen and Jimmy discussing a trip to the local vicar to arrange their wedding, just to witness her mortified reaction, but at that moment she felt it would be cruel to do such a thing when Gem was already worried enough about her husband. Instead she said, 'Jimmy's new girlfriend isn't Doreen. It's the daughter of the new family that joined us last week — the Davidsons, with their housey-housey stall. If I remember right, her name is Vivien. Pretty little thing. I say she's his girlfriend, but whether she is yet . . . Anyway, by the way they were acting with each other when I saw them, I would say there's a fancy for the other on both sides.'

Gem shook her head and said tartly, 'Well, he didn't waste any time, did he? Quite the Casanova. He seems to have a different girl every week. Not that me and his father ever get to meet any of them.'

'You will, lovey,' Velda assured her, 'when he meets the one he feels worthy of being introduced to you. Same goes for Robbie and Jenny too.'

Gem looked at her blankly. She had been somewhat miffed that neither Jimmy nor Robbie — or Jenny since she had come to live with them

— had brought any of their romantic interests home to meet her and Solly. It had even crossed her mind that they were ashamed of them. She hadn't given a thought to the fact that it was because they didn't feel the girl or lad in question wasn't special enough to meet them. Despite her worries about her husband, she felt a warm glow in the pit of her stomach that her children thought so much of their parents.

Much to the relief of the whole community, the wind suddenly changed direction, sending the dark cloud that had been heading their way to offload its cargo elsewhere, and at two o'clock, under a pale blue fluffy-clouded sky, a warm spring sun beaming down, the lights were switched on, popular music blasted through the speakers and crowds of people from the very young to the very old streamed under the arch with its brightly painted carved words:

WELCOME TO GRUNDY'S FAMILY FAIR. A GOOD TIME TO BE HAD BY ALL.

3

The voluptuous young woman serving behind the counter of the back-street corner shop couldn't have been any older than 17, though it was apparent from the clothes she was wearing and the amount of make-up plastered on her face that she was desperately trying to make herself look older. She eyed her customer with keen interest as she handed him the change from his purchases.

He was a sandy-haired, pleasant-faced young man in his middle twenties, casually dressed in market-quality dark trousers and thick jumper under a black three-quarter top coat. As he put the change safely away in his pocket, the shop assistant placed her hands on the counter and leaned forward to afford him a view of her ample cleavage bulging over the top of her low cut apple-green jumper tucked into a hip-hugging straight skirt, a black patent leather belt circling her waist.

'Ain't seen you around these parts before. Moved here, or just visiting?'

Picking up a heavy canvas bag from the floor and heaving it over his shoulder, Tom Stubbs replied, 'Neither. Just passing through.'

She pouted red-painted lips, disappointed. 'Oh, that's a shame. I'm not doing nothing particular tonight, so I was going to offer to show you the sights of our wonderful town.' She said the words sardonically, as the small mining town boasted little for the younger generation except a handful of pubs, a flea-pit cinema that only showed B-rated films, and a village hall that held the occasional dance. Then a thought struck and her eyes lit up. 'Oh, how could I have forgotten — the fair is here. I'm going with my friends, but they'll understand if I go with you. You can't want to leave town without a visit to the fair.'

Certainly not with this type of woman, who apart from being far too young for him wasn't his type at all. He flashed a smile at her. 'I appreciate your offer, but as I said, I'm just passing through.'

Her sulk of disappointment deepened. 'Oh well, if yer passing through again, maybe you'll stop a bit longer next time and look me up. You sure yer won't change your mind and come and have some fun at the fair with me now?' She eyed him meaningfully. 'I promise you won't regret it.'

Before he could again refuse her offer, a middle-aged woman dressed in a brown day dress with a faded floral wraparound apron and a scarf tied turban-style covering her greying hair came bustling through a door leading into the back of the shop. She looked suspiciously over at her customer, then gave a disparaging glance at the young woman beside her.

'What have I told you about wearing clothes like that when yer serving behind the counter? Get upstairs and change before yer dad sees yer, and wipe all that muck off yer face while yer at it.'

Head hanging, the girl scuttled off, mortified,

while her mother folded her arms under her matronly bosom and coldly addressed her customer. 'If my daughter goes to the fair, it will be with me and her father.'

He knew the woman was well aware that it had been her daughter who had propositioned him, and not the other way around; nevertheless, he smiled at her and said politely, 'I hope you all have a good time.'

The bell on the door jangled as he shut it behind him. Outside on the pavement he took a look around. The shop was situated at a crossroads. All the streets leading off it were of the back-to-back terraced type, disappearing off into the distance, the bricks blackened over the years through coal dust. He had arrived in the village earlier that morning in search of casual work, but none of the businesses he had approached had any jobs to offer or were prepared to take on a stranger. He'd been disappointed, as he had hoped to stay around here for a while. Grimethorpe wasn't the prettiest of places — in fact Tom felt its name was very apt, as it was decidedly grimy — but apart from the shopkeeper, everyone else he had encountered had been friendly enough, and he would have liked to become part of their community for a time. Hopefully he would have better luck at his next destination of Huddersfield. The journey by bus would take a couple of hours, and if he was to arrive there in time to find a place to stay for the night, then he really needed to start heading towards the bus station.

As he turned the corner to retrace his steps to

the village centre, his eyes fell on a striking colourful poster pasted on the shop window. It was advertising the arrival of the fair the shop girl had tried to tempt him into taking her to. He looked thoughtfully at it. He had never been to the fair. His father hadn't deemed such places suitable venues for his son.

The whole purpose of leaving his old life behind and embarking on this journey was to experience things that previously he'd been shielded from behind the high walls of the prison-like structure he'd grown up in. He had heard about fairs, circuses too, but only through stories told him by others, which was not the same as trying the thrills and excitement for himself. Did he really want to leave town and miss out on the opportunity to do exactly that? He could stay here tonight and journey on to Huddersfield tomorrow. If he couldn't find anywhere affordable to stay, he could always walk out into the countryside and pitch his tent.

His eyes glazed as a vision of his father rose before him. A big man all round, with a large ginger moustache and eyebrows to match, ruddy cheeks and humourless small grey eyes. What he had said went, and the punishment was severe for those who disobeyed. Tom wondered what he would say if he knew what his son was contemplating doing now. He quickly squashed that thought. His father was no longer here to dictate how he lived his life, and he was free to make his own decisions and mistakes.

He smiled to himself as a small thrill of anticipation ignited in the pit of his stomach.

Here he was at 25 years old about to pay his first visit to a fair. Out of all the new experiences he had promised himself, he was surprised at how much he was looking forward to this one. Having stopped a passer-by and enquired from them where the travelling fair was located, he set off jauntily.

The fairground was situated on a large area of waste ground on the edge of the village, black slag heaps rising high above it, an oasis of colour amid a sea of black. Tom was surprised that he seemed to be the only one heading towards it; from what he knew about fairs, people swarmed to them like iron filings to a magnet. He was soon to find out why, as a sign at the arched entrance told him that it didn't open until two. He looked at his watch. It was just after one. He could either stand around for an hour or return to the village and find a café to while away the time in. He was usually a patient man, but his curiosity to see all the stalls and rides got the better of him. He wouldn't be doing any harm if he had a wander around, surely?

He was making to walk through the arch when a loud voice stopped him short and he saw a man of around his own age crawling out from under the skirt of a children's carousel ride a few yards away. He appeared a rough sort, in oil-stained American-style blue jeans and white shirt open to his waist, showing a grubby vest underneath. His dark hair was styled in a quiff rising at least six inches from his forehead, face pockmarked and greasy. He looked most unsavoury, so Tom was rather surprised when he said to him in a very pleasant manner, 'We don't open until two, mate. Didn't yer see the times on the board outside?' He then noticed Tom's bag slung over his shoulder. 'Oh, if it's work yer after,' he said. 'It's Mr Grundy yer want to see then. He's the owner and does all the hiring and firing. He'll be having his dinner right now, same as everyone else. I was just finishing off a job and now I'm off to have mine.' He looked at Tom for a moment before he offered, 'Save you hanging about, yer can come back to my van. I'll share me beans on toast with you if yer hungry.'

Tom was extremely touched by such hospitality, but before he could point out that he wasn't after work, but just a customer arrived too early, the man was walking off and calling back, 'Come on. Dinner hour will be over before I've started mine.'

There were already two men eating from plates off their laps in the caravan. The bench seats had rumpled bedding on them, so it was apparent to Tom that two of the men slept here whilst the other occupied the bedroom at the back of the van. Just behind the door was a small kitchen area with a well-worn table on which sat a two-ring gas burner along with a packet of tea, a half-empty bottle of milk, a bottle of Camp coffee, a bag of sugar and the remains of a loaf. On one of the gas rings was a blackened kettle, steam billowing out of the spout, and on the other an equally blackened pan with a portion of dried-up baked beans inside. The van had seen better days, but it was obvious that the three men occupying it took pride in their accommodation, as it was

43

clean and for the most part tidy. Since Tom had set out on his journey he had seen some shocking hovels, and although this van was far from a palace, it was better than many of those.

One of the seated men spoke up. 'We've left your share of the beans in the pan. They might need heating up, though.' He then noticed that his van mate had a stranger with him, and eyeing Tom quizzically he asked, 'Who's yer friend then?'

The first man was over at the table using a petrol lighter to ignite the gas under the pan of beans. 'Come looking for work. I asked him to wait here till dinner time is over and I can point him in Mr Grundy's direction.' He looked at Tom. 'By the way, my name is Owen, and that's Marvin and Roger. We're all gaff lads. We do anything and everything to do with helping to keep the fair running.'

'I'm Tom. Tom Stubbs. I'm very pleased to meet you.'

They all looked at him open-mouthed before Owen said, 'You speak just like the queen, as if you've a stick up yer arse.'

Tom swallowed hard. 'Oh yes, I do sound rather posh, I know, but I can assure you I'm not.' He paused for several long moments before he added uncomfortably, 'My father was . . . er . . . a gardener for a big estate. I mixed with the master's children, even had some lessons with them, and that's how I picked up their accent.'

Marvin said drily, 'Well you ain't so special. I grew up on an estate myself.' He laughed before he concluded, 'A council-owned one in Leicester.'

'A two-up two-down rented back-street terrace in a Manchester slum for me,' added Owen.

Roger said proudly, 'Then I'm better than the lot of yer, because my dad was a coal man and owned the house we lived in and the yard he ran the business from. He had a dicky fit when I told him I wasn't going to hump coal all day for a living and wanted to see life and work for a fair instead. He ain't spoken to me since and ain't likely to either unless I go home like the prodigal son. I might one day, but for now I'm having too much fun.'

Next thing Tom knew, a plate with a chunk of bread spread with margarine and a portion of beans was being thrust at him, and he was told to put his coat and bag on the floor and sit next to either Marvin or Roger, who had both moved up to allow room for the other two men. He hadn't eaten since breakfast, and after all his fruitless traipsing the streets of Grimethorpe for work, he really enjoyed the simple meal and ate every last bean.

Owen collected the plates together and went over to the kitchen table to make a pot of tea. Taking a tin from his pocket and proceeding to make himself a roll-up cigarette, Roger said to Tom, 'You might be in luck with a job. Ronnie Biddle, one of the other gaff lads, got the sack this morning. The chap he was supposed to be helping found him asleep under a tarp on the back of one of the lorries and reported him to the boss.'

Tom went to correct Owen's mistaken belief that he had come to the fairground seeking work, but changed his mind at the mention that a job might be in the offing and instead asked keenly, 'What's it like working for a fair?'

It was Marvin who responded. 'Bloody hard work, mate, long hours and the pay hardly enough to keep a dog alive. As you can see, we don't exactly live in a palace or eat like kings. But then you get to see life in a different place every week and the main perk is the women. As long as you ain't fussy, as many as you can handle.'

Tom stared at him thoughtfully. It was not the prospect of abundant women that he was homing in on, but the fact that the fair folk visited a different town every week. He had embarked on this journey in order to see real life, something that had been denied him until his oppressive, narrow-minded father had died three months ago. Working for the fair would take him to places and show him sides of life that he might never experience otherwise. And the good thing was that when he'd seen enough, he could simply leave and resume travelling on his own. Or return home. The thought of what awaited him there made him shudder. He would have to go back sometime, he knew, but he was far from ready to yet.

He looked eagerly at Roger. 'Do you think your boss will consider me as a replacement for the man he sacked this morning?'

Owen plonked four tin mugs of tea on the table along with the bag of sugar with a spoon poking out the top. 'Only one way to find out,' he said. 'I'll take you to him after dinner time is finished.'

4

Solomon Grundy — or Solly, as he was affectionately called by his family and close friends — was a ruggedly handsome 38-year-old man, five foot ten and of medium build. He was easy-going and fair-minded but, just like his father, he would not stand by and allow anyone to cause hurt to those he cared for.

His easy-going nature was being put to the test when Owen and Tom found him just before two o'clock at the entrance to the fair. In the distance, a stream of excited, animated locals could be seen making their way towards the arch. Scraping a hand through his thatch of black hair, tinged with grey, Solly was shouting at another man. 'First job I asked him to do this morning was replace the dead light bulbs around the entrance. Where is he? Not the first time he's been asked to do a job and not done it. He's for the chop this time.'

Jonny Hiddles, a muscular man in his middle forties, at just under six foot an inch or two taller than Solly, was employed as a labourer and had been with the fair several years. In the meantime he had become engaged to Solly's deceased brother's widow, Fran, and they were getting married in a few months' time. Jonny placed a hand on the boss's shoulder and calmly told him, 'You already sacked the lad this morning when he was caught kipping in the back of a lorry.'

Solly slapped his hand to his forehead and groaned. 'Oh God, so I did.' He eyed the other man apologetically. 'Sorry for shouting, but I just get so frustrated when people don't do what you ask them. Look, I need to go and check a couple of things before the punter's start piling in. Can you sort out the bulbs?'

'Yeah, of course.' Jonny shot off to see to it as Owen and Tom arrived but before Owen could introduce Tom, Solly held up his hand in warning.

'Whatever it is, it'll have to wait. I'm up to my eyes at the moment.' He frowned at Owen. 'You're supposed to be helping Terry on the sky planes, aren't you?'

'I'm off there straight away, boss, but I thought you might want to see this chap after sacking Ronnie Biddle this morning. He's looking for a job.'

Before Solly could respond, another gaff lad arrived, panting hard from running, and blurted, 'Mr Travers has sent me ter tell yer the doors on the House of Horror are jammed. He's tried everything he can, but he can't get them to open.'

Before Solly could tell the lad that he would send over Gully Givens, the fairground carpenter, to sort it out, 18-year-old Nita Grundy, his late brother Joshua's elder daughter, bounded up and accosted him.

'Uncle Solly, Mam's asked me to find you 'cos Kevin's car won't start. Remember he's driving us to Huddersfield to hand out leaflets for when the fair's there next week, and while we're there,

Mam's taking me and Rosie shopping in the market for some material to make us a dress each. Kev's had a look but he don't know much about engines. We should have left ages ago so we're all back for work tonight. Will you come now, Uncle Solly, and sort it?' She tugged urgently on his arm.

Yet again, before he could respond, a middle-aged woman bustled up. Her face told anyone that looked at it that she was not at all happy. Without even considering that she was interrupting a conversation, she launched into a tirade.

'Mr Grundy, this is the third time I've come to see you about this matter, and if you don't deal with it I dread to think what will happen. That new bloke, Mr Packer, who you put next to us, is blatantly stealing potential customers from us and from the Pendles' stall the other side. He's also pulled his stall forward quite a bit and hung lots of his prizes on long sticks so they stand out more than ours do. And his tart of a daughter parades around like a brothel madam, shoving that big chest of hers into male punters' faces to entice them. Two weeks we've put up with this now, and if a stop ain't put to their antics then I can't promise that my Arthur and Pat Pendle won't end up taking a match or a hammer to their stall in the middle of the night. They told us they left their last fair because they'd heard this was a better one, but I reckon they were pushed out by the other stallholders for how they carry on.' She folded her arms under her ample bosom and bristled. 'Now as I said, this is the third time

I've asked yer to come and sort it out, Mr Grundy, so can yer please do it now, before war breaks out.'

Nita erupted. 'I was here first, Mrs Archer. My uncle is coming with me to fix the car, so you'll have to wait your turn.'

Solly darted a look at each of those demanding his assistance. Normally he would have quickly put each situation in order of urgency for him to deal with, but for some reason his mind seemed to have gone blank. They were now bickering between themselves, and he suddenly felt like the ground was undulating beneath him, a thick, clinging fog swirling around him, the people surrounding him like a pack of ferocious wolves making ready to pounce on him and tear him to shreds. An overwhelming need to get away from them consumed his being. How he wished a hand would come down from the sky and pluck him out of this, deposit him somewhere else, anywhere, as long as it was well away from here. Before he could stop himself, he shouted, 'Deal with your problems yourselves. I . . . I . . . need to be somewhere else.'

With that, he disappeared behind a large red and white tent housing the hall of mirrors, leaving them all staring after him bemused.

Mrs Archer looked most put out. 'What on earth has got into him?' she grumbled. 'He can't just walk off like that when he's things to deal with. Supposed to be the ringmaster, ain't he. Big Sam would never have walked away from a problem like his son just has.'

Nita wailed, 'If the car's not fixed, we won't get to Huddersfield today. I really wanted that material or me mam won't have a hope in hell of getting those dresses finished for me and me sister to wear to the local dance after we finish on Saturday night. She looked at Owen with a pleading expression. 'Do you know anything about engines?'

He shook his head. 'I know where the dipstick is and where to put water in the radiator, but that's about it.'

Tom realised Nita was now looking expectantly at him. The boss had made it clear he was far too busy to waste time on someone who was just after casual work, so he really ought to be on his way, but then a thought struck. If he could manage to get the vehicle going, then hopefully he could wangle a lift to Huddersfield with them. 'I could take a look at it for you,' he offered. 'I'm not a mechanic but I know a bit about motors.'

A bit to Nita was better than nothing, and neither was she bothered that she had never seen this good-looking man before. He was a knight in shining armour as far as she was concerned; all he was lacking was his white horse. She gratefully fell on him — 'Oh, thank you, mister, thank you!' — and herded him off before he could change his mind. Owen then departed for his own place of work too.

On her way back to her stall, the disgruntled Mavis Archer crossed paths with Gem, who was on her way to the cakewalk, where she was working in the pay booth that afternoon. As they

51

passed each other, Gem smiled a greeting at the older woman. 'Good afternoon, Mrs Archer.'

Mavis pursed her lips. 'Might be for you, but not for us having a stall next to them. Big Sam would never have told us to deal with it ourselves. Be turning in his grave at how his son is behaving.'

Her words stopped Gem in her tracks. Spinning on her heel, she called out, 'What do you mean by that, Mrs Archer?'

Mavis Archer stopped and turned back to face her. Folding her arms under her bosom, she gave a disdainful sniff before she responded. 'Just what I said. Big Sam would never have told us to deal with our own problems then run off to hide himself like a scared cat. And it weren't just me he said it to either.' She wagged a warning finger at Gem. 'I tell yer now, Mrs Grundy, with your husband not sorting out this problem I've got, well, we'll be lucky if there ain't a lynching at the end of the day. Don't say I didn't warn yer.'

With that, she turned and stomped off into the excited crowds now streaming into the area.

Gem raked a worried hand through her hair. Something definitely wasn't right with Solly. She needed to find him and ask him just what was going on. Her own work forgotten, she shot off in search of him.

The gaff lads helping out on the dodgems, where Solly was supposed to be in charge this afternoon, hadn't seen him and were wondering where he was themselves. Hurriedly thanking them for keeping the cars running during his absence, Gem tried all the other big rides, but there was no sign of him at any of those either. She was about to approach Harry Dobson in the pay booth of the House of Fun when she noticed that no one was queuing for the helter-skelter; in fact the chain was across the entrance and the Closed sign was swinging from it. Pete Jenkins, a long-standing employee, was sitting in the pay booth with his feet up on the counter, thumbing through a tattered magazine. A closed ride was lost revenue. Momentarily forgetting her quest to find her husband, Gem went over and rapped purposefully on the glass front.

Pete jumped, looking startled for a moment, then dropped his feet off the counter and sat up to attention. 'Oh, hello, Mrs Grundy, what can I do for yer?'

'Tell me why you haven't opened the skelter yet? It's nearly half two!'

'I opened at two but was told to shut it again by Mr Grundy before he went on up. Not sure what he's doing up there, though, as he'd no tools with him. Been up there ages he has.'

Frowning, Gem stood back and looked up towards the top of the garishly painted helter-skelter almost fifty feet above. There was no sign of Solly in any of the cut-out arched windows facing her way. What was he doing up there? Without further ado, she stepped over the chain and dashed up the twisting staircase, eventually arriving breathless at the top.

She found her husband sitting hunched on a pile of coconut mats on the small platform at the top of the chute, his head buried in his hands, quietly sobbing. Upset by his obvious distress, she knelt down beside him, placing her arm around his shoulder. 'Solly, what on earth is the matter?' she said softly.

Without lifting his head, he mumbled, 'Go away, Gem.'

'Oh, but sweetheart — '

He lifted his head to glower darkly at her and snapped, 'I said go, Gem. I don't want to talk to you. I just want to be left alone.' Then to her shock, to emphasise his point, he pushed her hard on her shoulder. The unexpectedness of his action made her topple sideways, hitting her head hard on the wooden floor. Shocked and dazed, she righted herself to see that he had buried his head back in his hands, shoulders slumped as though he'd the weight of the world on them.

It was agonising for her to witness her husband in such a state. As he wouldn't talk to her, she felt helpless as to what to do for him. Velda obviously hadn't yet found an opportunity to get him on his own to try and make him open up over what was ailing him. Well, he was on his own now . . . She went off to fetch the older woman.

There was a queue of people waiting patiently outside Velda's red and yellow striped tent. The flaps of the tent were closed, with a sign on the board saying a reading was in progress. To avoid a riot, she informed the waiting punters that she wasn't queue-jumping, but that management needed to talk to the fortune-teller. Then she pulled aside one of the flaps and went inside.

Velda was in the middle of dealing the tarot

cards when her unexpected visitor arrived. 'Sorry to intrude like this,' Gem said, 'but I really need you.'

The brash-looking young woman Velda was reading for looked most put out and snapped, 'So do I, and I was here first, so you wait yer turn. Madam Velda was just consulting the cards over which proposal I should accept, Geoff's or Maurice's. I can't decide which one of them is the better bet, so I'm hoping the cards will help me make the right decision.'

Velda and Gem flashed a look at each other, both knowing they were thinking the same thing. That they pitied whichever man she did decide to marry, unaware as he would be that his future had been decided on the turn of a tarot card.

Velda knew that to interrupt a reading, Gem must need to speak to her on a matter of extreme emergency. She fished in the pocket of her voluminous dress and pulled out a florin. 'Here's half your money back as you've only had half your reading. Come back another time and I'll do you another for half-price.' Then she leaned forward and eyed the young woman meaningfully. 'If I was you, I wouldn't marry either of those blokes. If one of them was the right one for you, you'd know yourself and wouldn't need to be asking the Tarot for guidance.'

The woman looked at her for a moment before she took the money and slipped it into her own pocket. 'Yeah, yer right. Geoff always puts his friends and football before me, and I can't see that changing when we're married, and

Maurice might worship the ground I walk on and would do anything for me, but he also has a widowed mother he'd do anything for, who's already hinting about how difficult she'll find it to manage on her own should Maurice get married, so I'm sure you can see as well as me where that's heading. I'll be giving them both the heave-ho. Plenty more fish in the sea, ain't there.' She beamed in delight. 'Thanks, Madam Velda.'

As soon as the punter had disappeared through the flap, Velda demanded, 'Is it Solly?'

Wringing her hands in despair, Gem told her, 'He's had some sort of breakdown. He's shut the helter-skelter and is sitting crying on the platform at the top. He won't talk to me. I tried, but he just won't.'

Velda heaved her big body up and went over to give Gem an affectionate hug. 'Well let's hope I have more luck. Can you explain to the queue that I've been called away and put my Back Later sign on the board?' With that she disappeared through an opening in the back of her tent.

When she arrived at the top of the helter-skelter, she found Solly just as Gem had described.

'Phew,' she puffed. 'Goodness, it's been that long since I've been up a skelter, I'd forgotten what a climb it is.'

At the sound of her voice, Solly lifted his head and eyed her with irritation. 'Gem sent you, I presume. Well as I told her, I don't want to talk to anyone. I want to be on my own. Now will you please go, Velda.'

If ever she had seen someone in the depths of despair, who had lost the will to live, she was looking at them now, and it distressed her beyond words. She had no intention of leaving until she had done her best to help Solly resolve whatever it was that was troubling him.

'Yes, of course I'll respect your wishes, Solly,' she said. She feigned a look of pure exhaustion before she added, 'But . . . er . . . would you mind me just resting for a minute? The climb has certainly taken it out of me. Only a few years ago I'd have had the energy to run up and down those stairs several times without stopping, but that's far from the case now.'

He grudgingly responded, 'Just a minute or so then.'

So far so good, she thought to herself. As she eased her bulk down beside him on the mats, she said lightly, 'Could really do with a cuppa right now. Pity I didn't bring a flask and sandwiches and we could have had a picnic.'

He glared at her incredulously. 'Really, Velda, I can't believe you would suggest something like that in the very place my father died. Have you no respect?'

Her words might have come across as disrespectful to Solly, but Velda had chosen them very carefully in the hope of getting a conversation going, and was relieved they had worked. 'Oh, I've every respect for your father, Solly, as you well know. He was a special man and I was very fond of him.' She spoke gently. 'Is this why you're here, to feel close to him in the last place he was alive?'

Solly looked at her blankly for a moment before he shrugged his shoulders. 'Didn't set out to,' he said defensively. 'I just found myself here.'

'And has coming here helped you?'

He frowned at her quizzically. 'Helped me?'

'When people go to places that remind them of their loved ones, it's usually to ask for their spiritual help.'

He scoffed. 'My dad is dead and I've accepted that I won't see him again. I don't believe in all that stuff about life after death and loved ones guiding us from the hereafter.'

'Yet you're here, Solly, in the last place Sam was alive, so deep down you must believe there's something in it. Many people don't believe in God, yet when they're in trouble, He is the first one they turn to for help.' She placed a hand gently on his knee. 'Are you here to ask your father's spirit to help you with something? Is the fair in financial trouble? Is someone causing you difficulties you're not sure how to deal with? Is one of your sons in bother? Is it your brother you're worried about, wondering where he is or what he's been up to since he absconded — '

He shook his head emphatically and cut her short. 'No, no, it's none of those things.' It was a moment before he spoke again, so softly Velda had a job to hear him. 'I . . . I need my father's forgiveness, Velda. I need to tell him how sorry I am.' His raised his head and settled desolate eyes on her. 'But how do I do that when he's dead?'

Her eyes widened in surprise. 'Forgiveness! Whatever would you need your father to be forgiving you for?'

58

There was a long silence before he eventually said, 'For not being the man he thought I was.' It wasn't his intention to divulge to Velda his innermost feelings, but before he could stop himself, he found himself blurting, 'I'm letting him down, Velda. I've not got what it takes to be boss of this business. It's all too much for me. Such a huge responsibility, and more than I can handle on my own. I'm frightened of letting the fair folk down, but even more terrified of letting down my family. All their futures are in my hands. I've tried so hard to deal with things how my father would have, but I'm scared of not getting it right and us all landing up on the scrapheap. I was looking forward to the start of the season, of making Dad proud of me by making it the best one we'd ever had, but then that very first morning when we set out for Grimethorpe, it suddenly hit me that he was no longer here for me to go to for help and approval, and it was like this enormous weight settled on my shoulders as I realised it was all down to me now.

'I've been trying to shove it behind me and get on with things, but it all came to a head this afternoon when it seemed to me that everyone was demanding help at the same time and I just couldn't think straight. I wanted them to leave me alone. All I could think of was getting as far away from them as I could.' Tears pricked his eyes and his voice was choked. 'I so wanted to talk to Gem about this. I know she's worried sick about me. But I just couldn't, as I'm terrified she'll think she's married a useless lump who's scared of his own shadow. No matter what was going on in my father's private life, he never let it affect his job. He would be so ashamed of me.'

Velda shook her head resolutely. 'You're wrong, Solly. Sam would have understood.'

'Understood what?'

'That you're grieving for the loss of your father, a father you loved very much and respected deeply. You might have accepted that he's gone, but you're far from over mourning him. The fact that you're still hell-bent on doing things the way he did and looking for his approval tells me that. Now you listen to me, Solly Grundy. Sam made you his heir because he knew that you would run the fair in a decent and honest manner, like he always did, but in your own way, not his. If we all continued to work in the same way our parents did, nothing would ever progress. You're Sam's son, but you're also your own man, with ways and ideas of your own that he knew you'd use to take the fair forward into the future. Stop worrying how he would have done things and instead worry about how best to do them yourself. You might not be a believer, but I do believe in the hereafter and I know that Sam is up there now, watching you with a big smile on his face.'

Solly stared at her for what seemed an eternity before his shoulders sagged and he said softly, 'I hope so. I just miss him so much. Having him for a father was like having a safety net beneath me. That net has gone now and I'm worried about who'll catch me when I fall.'

'What makes you think you will? You know as

much about running a fair as any ringmaster does. You certainly had the best teacher. And you're not the type who would do anything reckless to put Grundy's in jeopardy.' She looked at him meaningfully before she went on. 'Grief is a funny thing. It affects people in all sorts of ways. In your case, your need to prove that your father was right to make you his heir has made you doubt yourself. You need to have faith in yourself instead, like he did.'

Solly again looked blankly at Velda for several long moments before he took a deep breath and said, 'Yes, he did have faith in me or he wouldn't have done what he did.'

She patted his knee affectionately. 'You'll make mistakes along the way. You're only human after all. Sam made plenty of them. When he did, though, he owned up to them, put them right as best he could, then put them behind him, but by God he made sure he never made the same mistakes again. And while I have this chance, I need to point out that you're far more easy-going than ever Sam was, so some fair folk might think they can take liberties with you they wouldn't have dared attempt with him. You'll have to toughen up some, Solly. You have it in you to be as good if not better than your father. When it came to naming his heir, I have no doubt that had it not been for fairground traditions pulling on his conscience, he would not have had any struggle making his decision between you and Sonny. And you do have someone standing behind you ready to catch you if you fall and help you get back on your feet again. Not only

Gem, but your three children too.'

Solly sat staring into space for quite some time, digesting all Velda had told him, before he took a deep breath, sat up straight and said with conviction, 'Gem has never failed to support me through anything. How could I have treated her so badly these past weeks? I really wasn't thinking straight at all. I'll do whatever it takes to make it up to her, show her I'm still the man she married. And I'll move heaven and earth to prove Dad was right to leave the fair in my hands.'

Velda looked upwards. 'Did you hear that, Solly?'

He frowned. 'Hear what?'

'That voice from above. It said, 'That's the man I knew my son was.''

Solly looked at her strangely for a moment before he grinned and slapped her affectionately on her arm. 'You are a card, Velda.'

She chuckled. 'I have my moments. Well, come on, then, you've got a fair to run, though first I know that lovely wife of yours would appreciate a visit to let her know you're all right. Oh, but before you shoot off, could you give me a hand getting up? I think I've set solid squatted down on these mats.'

★   ★   ★

When Gem saw her husband bounding through the crowds towards the pay booth of the cakewalk with a smile on his handsome face and an aura of purpose and authority about him, she knew immediately that Velda had worked her magic and had made him deal with whatever it was that had been plaguing him. Jumping up from her stool, she came out to meet him. Before she could say anything, he had enveloped her in his arms and was professing his apologies to her for his recent behaviour. His remorse was not important to Gem, only the fact that she had her husband back. She did make him promise, though, that if ever he should feel troubled again, he would talk to her about it.

Having restored harmony with his wife, Solly then went to make amends for his unacceptable response to the fair folk who had come to him with their problems earlier. He paid a quick visit to the dodgems first to confirm that the two gaff lads were coping during his absence and to ask them to hold the fort a little longer. It was his intention to attempt to get the car running next to take Nita and Rosa to Huddersfield, but since the quickest way to get to the area where the vehicles were parked was past the section of stalls where the Archers had a pitch, he decided he might as well deal with that problem first.

From a discreet distance he watched the goings-on of the new arrivals to confirm that Mavis's accusations were justified. It didn't take long to ascertain that they were. Not only had the Packers' stall been pulled forward a foot or so and their prizes hung well over the boundary line, but their provocatively dressed daughter was accosting male punters like she was enticing them into a brothel, while Packer himself was shouting through a loudspeaker telling punters not to bother with the other stalls as his was the only one whose prizes were worth winning. Maybe other fair owners turned a blind eye to stallholders operating in an underhand manner, but here at Grundy's everyone behaved decently so that all had an equal chance to relieve the punters of the money in their pockets.

Solly felt extremely annoyed and embarrassed with himself that due to his period of self-pity, the stallholders either side of the Packers had had to endure their shenanigans, when in truth he should have dealt with it when he'd first been told.

By the time he went off to his next port of call, the Packer family were left in no doubt that their devious practices were not acceptable at Grundy's, and should they fail to put a stop to them, they would be loading up to leave. Solly was also aware that this situation had served as a warning to other fair folk that if they believed he wasn't in control in the way his father had been, they were badly mistaken.

As he walked through the fair, he did notice something that in his depressed state of mind these last couple of weeks he hadn't. There was an air of disillusionment about the fair folk, and he didn't have to think about it to know why. They had lost a leader they had looked up to and respected, and how could they have the same faith in his replacement when he had been acting as anything but a leader? Well, that was going to change.

He arrived where the vehicles were parked just as the car bonnet was being closed by a man he didn't recognise. The engine was running, so whatever the problem was had obviously been rectified. Rosa was already in the car, along with the lad Solly had commandeered to drive them, and Nita was just about to get in. On seeing her uncle approaching she called over, 'It's all right, Uncle Solly, we don't need you now. Tom managed to fix the car — something to do with the starting motor.'

Looking awkwardly at Solly, the man said apologetically, 'I hope I wasn't doing anything untoward by taking a look at the car, sir. Maybe I should have asked your permission first.'

'No, no, grateful you did, lad, saved me the trouble.' Then it struck him that he had seen this young man before. 'Oh, you're the chap that Owen brought to me after dinner at the entrance. He said you were looking for a job. Er . . . sorry I was too busy to talk to you about it then.' He was momentarily surprised that this eloquent man was seeking casual work in a fairground. But then he wasn't the first well-educated type who had fallen on hard times.

'Mind if we get off, Uncle Solly, only the printers will be shut by the time we get there?' said Nita.

Keeping his face straight, Solly replied, 'Don't you mean the market? I'm not that daft I don't know why you're so keen to go to Huddersfield and hand out leaflets. Go on, be off with you.' He turned to the driver. 'Remember, Kev, you're not driving a racing car. Make sure you bring my nieces back safe and sound.'

Nita went to get into the car, but stopped and

said to Tom, 'You still want a lift to Huddersfield, only you'd better get in if you do?'

Solly's brain whipped into action. Two men he'd let go recently needed to be replaced. This man had shown he knew his way around an engine, which would prove useful considering how much machinery there was to be taken care of. Solly wanted to know more about him before he disappeared off.

'Just a minute,' he said to Nita before turning to Tom. 'Apart from knowing about engines, is there anything else you can turn your hand to?'

'I'm reasonably good with a hammer and nails and I have a little knowledge of electrics. I don't have any problem with getting my hands dirty. I'm happy to help where I'm needed.'

Solly looked impressed. 'Then I could use a man like you if you still want a job.'

Tom smiled over at Nita. 'Thank you, but I won't need that lift after all.'

$\star \quad \star \quad \star$

After the fair had closed, Solly went home that night in a much better frame of mind. Thanks to Velda, he now realised that he was more than capable of carrying out his father's wishes. He would use the knowledge he had learned from Big Sam but would also do things his own way to keep the fair providing for all the Grundy community and take it into the future.

5

Jenny Grundy was a very pretty, slim woman of 22, her dark brunette hair cut in an urchin style. She kicked off her flat black pumps and relaxed back in the comfortable fireside chair, cradling a cup of Horlicks between her slender hands and stretching out her shapely legs to cross her bare feet on the brass fender that edged the small stove in the living area of the one-bedroom bow-topped caravan. She had opted to return straight to her own van tonight instead of joining her parents and two brothers for supper, excusing herself by saying that she was tired and an early night beckoned.

The truth was that she had wanted to be on her own to remember a woman she had loved whose birthday it would have been today.

Jenny had been born a Grundy but hadn't been known by that surname until a few months ago, when she had changed it after her discovery that the parents she had always believed to be her natural ones had in fact adopted her. The shock of this revelation, only days before her adoptive mother had died, had mentally sent her spiralling down a huge dark hole but, purely out of love and respect for the wonderful woman who had raised her, she managed to keep her true feelings on the matter to herself in order to make her passing into the hereafter as peaceful and happy as possible. It wasn't until after the last mourners had left the wake and she was on her own that she allowed herself to think about it all.

Unable to understand how any mother could throw her baby away like a bag of rubbish, she concluded that hers was indeed a monster, and vowed to track down this despicable creature and tell her in person how she felt about her. However, the life-changing shock of finding out that she was adopted was then duplicated when she discovered that her natural mother believed her to have died at birth, and in fact it was her grandmother who had given her away. She also learned that her natural father and mother were married and she had two younger brothers.

Her parents were overjoyed to find their firstborn was very much alive, although beside themselves with anger and regret at being denied the right to raise her themselves. They wanted nothing more than to cocoon her in the bosom of the family and try and make up for all the time they had lost but, unable to comprehend these revelations, Jenny had told them she needed time on her own to digest it all and decide where her future lay. Before they could persuade her otherwise, she had disappeared off.

Back in her home town, she mulled over her situation, going through every emotion in trying to come to terms with what had transpired. She had several close friends she could have confided in, but decided that she had to deal with this monumental situation alone. Weeks passed, and although she was aware that her natural family must be anxiously waiting for news from her, she was still having difficulty deciding how she felt about the whole situation. She was angry with her birth mother for allowing her own mother to dupe her into believing her baby was dead, and with her adoptive mother for not telling her the truth of her origins until she was on her deathbed.

It took the act of a stranger to make her decision for her.

It was late October and the night a cold one. She was on her way home from work, heading through town towards the bus station, when she passed a run-down public house. Huddled shivering together in the doorway were two little boys hardly more than six or seven years old. What clothes they wore were threadbare, with disintegrating plimsolls on their feet. Neither had been near soap and water for a very long time, and it was a safe bet that their matted hair was riddled with nits.

Jenny's compassion for the two little mites came to the fore, and as she approached them, she rifled around in her handbag for her purse to give them whatever she could spare; at least enough to get them some food from a nearby shop. But just before she reached them, a thirty-something woman wearing a shabby fur coat and scuffed court shoes, her face plastered in make-up, burst out of the pub in a state of intoxication. She threw two packets of crisps at the boys, slurring, 'Get yer chops around those. I'm just having a natter with Renee. Stay where yer are and don't move or I'll skin yer alive when we get 'ome.'

Without a word, the boys leapt up and scrambled for the packets of crisps as their selfish mother disappeared back inside the pub.

As she stood staring at the two youngsters ramming the crisps into their mouths as though they hadn't eaten for weeks, a realisation struck Jenny. For some children the world could be an extremely cruel one, as it was for these two young boys, all because they had been unlucky enough to be born to people who were unfit to be parents. She herself was extremely lucky to have had not just one set of parents who had chosen to look after her and treated her like she was the most precious gift, but also another set, her birth parents, who had left her in no doubt that they would love and treasure her just as much as her adoptive parents had done.

She had no doubt that those two little boys hunched in the doorway, shivering with cold, would have given anything to have the opportunity to be raised by parents who loved and nurtured them as part of a happy family, and so would many others in similar situations. If she really searched her soul, she could understand why her adoptive parents had procrastinated about telling her the truth of her background. She was happy and settled, so why disrupt that state of affairs? And in respect of her natural parents, her anger should be vented against her grandmother, the woman responsible for her coming to be with her adoptive parents in the first place.

Within a week, she had left her old life behind to begin her future in the bosom of her natural family. She would never forget the two wonderful people who had raised her, and knowing them as well as she did, she was sure they would be happy that she was now where she truly belonged. It only took a week or so for her to be calling Gem and Solly Mum and Dad, and bantering and bickering with her brothers as all siblings did.

Gem and Solly would dearly have loved her to live with them, but the van was simply not big enough, so Solly immediately offered her the use of his brother Sonny's van. Her uncle, she was later to find out, had absconded after betraying his family, and it was very unlikely he would be back to claim the van. She and Gem had cleared it out, acquiring furniture, soft furnishings and knick-knacks, and Jenny felt very much at home in it. She was immediately welcomed into the fold by the rest of the Grundy's community and quickly made a number of good friends, including Julie Otterman and Renata Shawditch, the three women all being of a similar age and sharing many qualities, likes and dislikes, and most importantly, a sense of humour.

After taking a sip of her Horlicks, she reached over to the mantel and picked up a silver-framed photograph, looking at it with deep affection. In her mind she said, *Happy birthday, Mum. I hope you're celebrating with Dad* . . .

Before she could get any further, there was a tap on the door. Wondering who it could be at this time of night, she went to answer it.

She found Gem on the doorstep. 'Anything wrong?' she asked as she ushered her inside.

'No, nothing, love,' Gem assured her. 'I just wanted to see you.' She looked awkwardly at her daughter for a moment before she went on. 'I owe you an apology. It wasn't until you said you weren't going to have supper with us as usual as you were tired that I remembered what day it is today and realised why you wanted to come back to your own van. I don't wish to intrude, so just say if you prefer to be left on your own, but if you'd like someone to share your memories of your . . . other mother with, then I'd really like that person to be me. I do owe her such a debt of gratitude for raising you to be the wonderful person that you are.'

Jenny's heart swelled with love. She was aware that many other women would never have been so generous towards someone who had done a job that should by rights have been theirs. She also knew that Gem was tired after her hard day's work and would like nothing more than to go to bed, yet she was only too willing to shove this aside to support her daughter through what she knew was an emotional time for her. She threw her arms around Gem and hugged her tightly. 'I'd really love your company, Mum. Sit down and I'll put the kettle on.'

Mother and daughter spent a very pleasant hour or so looking through photographs from Jenny's previous life and reminiscing over the two special people that had shared it with her.

As Gem left, she felt glad that she had taken it upon herself to approach Jenny with her offer. Her days were always so busy, it left her little time to spend with her daughter. Tonight's precious hour with no interruptions had helped to bring them closer together.

As she waved Gem off, Jenny felt likewise. Coming to love and respect her natural mother, as well as her father and brothers, had been easy as they were all so likeable in their own ways, and the more she got to know them, the more her feelings for them deepened. It was also of paramount importance to her that they felt about her the same way she did about them. From the way they treated her, it appeared they did; as if she'd been part of the family forever instead of for only a few months. But she was well aware that that would not be the case should they discover what she had done. As the honourable people they were, they would despise her for it, want nothing to do with her, want to see her pay the price. She wouldn't blame them either. What she had done was the very worst thing that one person could do to another. To lose the love and respect of her wonderful family would be the end of the world for her, and so she vehemently prayed that they never found out.

6

Lounging on a narrow bed, 39-year-old Samuel Grundy, a swarthy, good-looking, snake-hipped man with thick black hair, took a long swallow from a bottle of Newcastle Brown ale and looked disparagingly around the miserable damp interior of the four-berth caravan. He was angry and unhappy, and his surroundings were doing nothing whatsoever to lighten his mood.

Wind whistled through cracks in the rain-spattered windows that only a miracle was keeping in place, and Sonny felt sure that the brown damp patches on the walls were growing larger before his eyes. The whole van stank of sour body odour courtesy of the four men who shared the cramped accommodation, none of them that particular about personal hygiene, along with stale cigarette smoke, beer and chips, their staple diet due to the paltry wages they were paid for their long hours of labour. The accommodation Grundy's provided for their lowest employees could not be compared to the comfortable vans the family lived in themselves, but they would have condemned these as unfit for human habitation a long time ago.

A vision of his caravan back at Grundy's rose up like it was mocking him. His parents had bought him the warm, comfortable and cosy traditional bow-topped van when he'd announced that it was time he lived on his own. And he hadn't needed to lock the door when he had gone out, for no one in the Grundy community would ever have considered robbing him, unlike the untrustworthy types he worked amongst now. He hadn't appreciated his van; it was just somewhere for him to carry on the way he wanted without his family observing him, so he could accumulate the illicit gains that would allow him to live the life he aspired to, one far removed from the travelling funfair existence, with a woman he had loved so completely he would without hesitation have laid down and died for her.

But those dreams for his future had been shattered into smithereens. His woman had laughed in his face at his proposal, insulted that a filthy gypsy, as she termed him, would expect her to reduce herself to his primitive way of life and suffer the stigma from her own community that would be hurled her way for marrying into the dregs of society. On top of that, he had made a bad decision and fallen foul of the type of people who would skin their own grandmother alive if they could make money from it. He felt no remorse whatsoever for leaving his brother to face the consequences of his absconding; why should he have any consideration for him when Solly had managed to do the one thing Sonny himself coveted above all else: to marry the woman he loved? To add insult to injury, their father had chosen Solly as his heir, and now his brother was reaping the benefits of a business that was rightfully his.

When he had first made his escape, he'd been comforted by the fact that the money he had accumulated, along with his quality wardrobe of clothes and expensive personal items, would enable him to carry on his previous way of life and eventually resurrect his dream for his prosperous future. But then, as if bad luck hadn't visited him enough for one lifetime, it had yet another laugh at his expense when, on his way south, he left the Grundy's lorry he had purloined to have a meal in a transport café and returned an hour later to find no sign of the vehicle or his belongings, including the wad of banknotes secreted in the glove box. He was left in the dark, cold lorry park cursing to damnation the person responsible, with only the clothes he stood up in and the loose change in his pocket.

Sonny's means of earning his illicit gains had been dependent on what had been in that lorry. Posing as a successful businessman, he would visit venues frequented by moneyed folk and ingratiate himself with them in order to get invited into their homes, where he was at liberty to help himself to their cash and valuables. As an expert card player, he would also wheedle himself a chair at lucrative games and often walked away with the pot.

But now, having lost the props of his trade, the only way left open to him to keep a roof over his head was to seek work with a fair. However, the Grundys were well known in the fairground community, and word would have got around by now that Sonny was a wanted man. Not all fair folk were loyal to their own if a reward was on offer. This meant he would have to seek work under another name at a third-rate fair owned by the type of boss Sam Grundy wouldn't have associated himself with; hence the reason he was now working for Dobson's Funfair under the name of Steve Smith.

Dobson's was a tiny operation compared to Grundy's. It didn't travel, but was a fixed affair on the seafront of a run-down town called Southsea on the south coast near Portsmouth. Cyril Dobson, the owner, was a huge brute of a man, who rumour had it was an ex-binman. He owned the majority of the rides and stalls, paying people to man them for him, and those he didn't own he had no care how they were run as long as he got his pitch fee. Rides were only checked for faults and repairs undertaken when a problem occurred; Sonny knew that many of them were in a dangerous state, and how a serious accident had as yet been avoided was a mystery.

Dobson's only interest was how much money could be extracted from the pockets of the punters, and he didn't take kindly to his workers thinking they could fleece him out of even a penny of it. Sonny had heard the stories of ex-employees being found on the beach or in a dark alleyway with injuries sustained from an unseen assailant, and it was his opinion that those men definitely knew who was responsible for the attacks but were too scared to finger him. Sonny was not a coward when it came to taking care of himself, but neither was he a fool, and he knew better than to tangle with a man like his present boss, so as matters stood, his wages were his only source of income, unless he could come up with another way of obtaining any.

He had believed that this was it for him forever now, the life of a poorly paid gaff lad with a third-rate fair, living in a damp, rusting van along with three other men, but then one night a week ago, good luck had condescended to pay him a visit.

He'd been sitting on his bed as he was now, with two of his van mates, all of them eating chips out of newspaper on their laps. He had been in the process of making a sandwich on a stale slice of bread spread with margarine. As he piled the last of the chips on the bread, a photo in the newspaper was revealed. It might have been distorted by the chip grease, but nevertheless he would have known those faces anywhere. It was the boss man he was in hiding from and his main minder.

He vehemently hoped that the reason for their appearance in a national newspaper was the one he hoped it was, but as he was illiterate, he was going to have to swallow his pride and ask one of his companions to do the honours and read the article for him. Only one of his van mates could read anyway, so his humiliation wasn't that great. As he listened intently, excitement swirled in his stomach. It seemed that he no longer had to live in fear of being found by those men and made to pay, in their own particular style, for his failure to carry out a job he'd had been trusted to do, since the boss man and most of his gang were in jail and would remain there for a very long time. He stopped himself from thumping the air with joy, as his companions would be curious as to why this article had affected him in such a way, and they definitely weren't the sort you wanted knowing your personal business. He explained away his interest by telling them that it was nothing more than nosiness on his part about what these men had done to get themselves in the paper.

He had no time to consider the implications of the information as he'd had to get back to work, but that night in bed, ignoring the snoring of his van mates, his mind was filled with nothing else. He might no longer be in danger from the crime boss — such a tremendous weight off his shoulders — but he was still of interest to the police, and would serve a lengthy prison sentence if caught, so even now he wasn't free to come out of hiding and get himself a better-paid job with a more reputable fair.

The answer then was to go abroad, somewhere like Spain, where the British police had no authority and the chances of bumping into anyone who knew him were extremely remote, so that he'd be free to start again and build a new life. The idea excited him, but it was shortlived as other thoughts struck. Travel arrangements would prove a costly exercise for a fugitive like himself. How was he going to get hold of the money to fund his new life abroad?

After thinking long and hard, it seemed his only option was to approach his brother for money. He had after all been bequeathed a ride by his father and could request the equivalent in cash. Big Sam had originally purchased the dodgem ride second-hand, but as the most popular fairground attraction, it must still be worth five or six thousand. But after what Sonny had done to Solly and his family, and the danger he had left them in when he had absconded, it was doubtful his brother would hand him a penny. Far more likely that he'd tell him to go to hell and call the police on him. Gem, his wife, certainly would, Sonny had no doubt of that.

If he wanted a new life, then, he was going to have to steal the money from Solly. All he needed to do now was think of a foolproof way of doing so. And he wasn't going to settle for a miserable couple of thousand either, but as much as he could get. He had no care of the consequences for his brother. This was his one chance to get himself out of this dire mess he was in and build a future to look forward to.

For the last week, all his waking moments — his dreams too — had been filled with nothing else, but still he hadn't managed to come up with anything that he felt would succeed. He was beginning to worry he never would. To think of a plan, he needed time on his own, which was virtually impossible living in such a small space with three other men, while during work time the noise of the loud music playing and the chatter of the punters filled his head. This afternoon he'd seen his boss going out, so telling the lads he was working with that he needed the toilet, he'd gone back to his van hoping that alone inside it an idea would finally surface. But he'd hardly had time to roll himself a cigarette and prise off the top of a bottle of beer when his solitude was invaded by the arrival of one of his van mates.

Freddy Reynolds was a lumbering, slow-witted 30-year-old who was constantly made fun of by the other employees, who nicknamed him Dopey. Sonny had little time for the man as it was, and in his present mood, today was no exception. As Freddy stepped up into the van, Sonny shot him a disparaging look and snapped at him, 'For God's sake, can a man get no peace.' Only then did he notice that Freddy seemed unhappy about something. 'Who's stuck a pin in your arse?' he added.

Freddy scowled, bemused. 'Eh?'

Sonny sighed and rephrased his question in plain English. 'Who's upset you, Dopey?'

Freddy advanced into the van and perched on the bed opposite Sonny. 'Oh, that Donkey Jackson. Boss is on the rampage, 'cos he noticed you weren't manning the big wheel and sent me ter look for yer.'

Sonny inwardly groaned at misjudging how long the boss would be out for. Knowing the way Dobson operated, this was probably a ploy to find out which of his employees he could trust. Sonny had failed miserably and wasn't sure right now how to redeem himself.

Meanwhile Freddy was carrying on. 'I asked Donkey if he'd seen you and he said you was having a shag with the boss's missus in the House of Horror and I'd better warn you he was after you or you'd end up in some dark alley battered to a pulp. So I went in the House of Horror and tried ter find yer, but someone locked me in and started up the ride, and yer know how scared I am of the dark and all them

81

ghoulies in there . . . well, I started to scream blue murder. The boss let me out and gave me a right clip around the ear and told me he'd send me packing if he caught me capering around again.' He tentatively fingered the side of his head, where a bruise was ripening. 'He didn't half hurt me, blamed me for larking around instead of doing what he'd asked me to. Anyway, he told me I'd better find you and quick, or he'd give me another thump.' He paused, looking puzzled. 'Why does Donkey call himself that?'

Sonny smiled to himself. It was because he claimed his manly parts were as big as a donkey's, but feeling that Freddy's undeveloped brain wouldn't comprehend that, he said instead, ''Cos he's as ugly as an ass, that's why. Anyway, you found me, so go and tell the big man I had a headache and I'm just trying to find some Aspro to take for it. I'll be back at work in a minute.'

Freddy eyed him, bemused. 'But you ain't looking for no pills but lying on yer bed having a beer.'

Sonny scowled darkly at him and snarled, 'But that's not what you're going to tell the boss, is it? You're going to tell him that you found me raking the van for a bottle of pills.'

Freddy shook visibly. 'Oh, he won't like that, Steve. Paddy Connell broke his leg when he got it trapped in the carousel motor, and as soon as he was back from having it plastered up, Mr Dobson had him straight back ter work. Poor Paddy was in terrible pain but Mr Dobson said he either worked or could fuck off. You have to be dead before the boss will accept an excuse for not being at yer post. He'll give me another kicking if I go back and tell him you're skiving off with a headache, and you'll be out on yer ear.' He looked bothered for a moment before he offered, 'I could go back and tell him yer ripped yer trousers really badly and were just changing 'em.'

Sonny light his cigarette, pulled deeply on it and put away his baccy tin. Freddy wasn't as thick as he pretended to be. Simple excuse as it was, even Dobson couldn't risk his punters being put off by a member of his staff with his arse hanging out of his trousers.

'If it'll save you getting another thick ear, you'd better tell him that,' he said.

Freddy looked relieved. 'Ta, Steve.' Then he sighed and said forlornly, 'I wish it was Mr Walters still owned the fair. He were a nice man. Took me in when I was a kid when he found me begging on the seafront. Me mam had died and them people from the council wanted to put me in an orphanage, but I weren't going in one of them places so I'd run away. The fair was much better then and everyone who worked here was 'appy and looked out fer each other. Mr Walters was a one for making sure the rides were safe and was always getting us to paint 'em — not like they are now, all scratched and dented.'

He looked around the interior of the van before he added, 'Would have had this van set fire to long ago. Our vans weren't that new, but they were far better than these dumps. Every week on a Sunday, Mrs Walters would cook all us workers a big dinner and we'd sit around a long table and eat together. She always gave me extra pudding, 'cos she said being the big lad I am I needed to keep me strength up. She was a lovely woman, Ma Walters. It was so sad when she died. Mr Walters wasn't the same after that. It was like he'd died too. He didn't care about the fair any more and he started drinking a lot and gambling. But even then he was still kind to me. I wish he was still boss and not Mr Dobson.'

So did Sonny. Walters sounded like the sort of chap it would have been easy to fleece and get away with it. 'Did Dobson buy the fair when Mr Walters died?' he asked as Freddy stood up preparing to take his leave.

'Oh, Mr Walters ain't dead. He's in one of them old people's homes. Horrible place it is. Smells of piss and shit. The food looks like what you'd give ter pigs. I go and see him when I can. Tek him a jam Swiss roll when I've got the money as it's his favourite cake and he don't get no cake at the home — lucky if he gets an arrowroot biscuit. Anyway, he lost the fair in a card game. It was just him and Mr Dobson left in the game. I don't understand cards, but Mr Walters told me he had three cards the same and he felt sure Dobson was bluffing that he had a better set. He'd no money left so he bet the fair instead. But Mr Dobson did have better cards than Mr Walters. He had . . . er . . . ' He frowned in deep thought. 'I've forgot what it was called, but it's something to do with a king or queen pulling the lavvy chain.'

Sonny looked at him blankly for a moment before the penny dropped. 'You mean a royal flush,' he enlightened him sardonically.

Freddy grinned and nodded. 'Yeah, that's it. Anyway, Mr Walters begged Mr Dobson to give him time to find the money, but Mr Dobson was having none of it and insisted the fair was his, so Mr Walters had no choice but to sign it over. A deal has to be honoured, don't it?' He noticed that Sonny was staring at him. 'What you looking at me like that for?'

In his innocence, Freddy had given him an idea of how he could get money — and a substantial amount of it — out of his brother without him knowing he was involved in any way. The scheme seemed to be unfolding like a flower, petal by petal, inside his brain, and the more it unfurled, the more he felt it had merit. He would need to explore it further, plan it meticulously to make sure nothing could go wrong. Solly would not fall for the same trick twice, so he only had one chance at this. There was just one tricky part that he could see, and that was finding the right person to carry out the job for him. But the person he would be seeking would very likely be in need of money and would jump at the chance to earn a good sum of it, and Sonny knew just where to make a start.

The *World's Fair* newspaper was the fair owners' bible, how they kept abreast of what was going on in the wider showman community up and down the country. All stories relating to fairground matters were published in it, whether good or bad, along with births, marriages and deaths. If Sonny remembered rightly, his slovenly boss had a huge pile of them in his office, possibly dating back to when Walters had owned the fair. The first chance he got, he would help himself to some and start looking through them for the man he hoped to entice to work for him.

But then another thought struck him. His mind raced frantically for a way to overcome the problem that had occurred to him, and his eyes settled on Freddy. He knew it was a long shot, but regardless he asked, 'Can you read, Freddy?'

To his shock, the man nodded proudly. 'Mrs Walters taught me. Not great big words, though.'

It was enough for what Sonny needed. Grinning like a Cheshire cat, he jumped up and slapped Freddy on the arm. 'You're a bloody godsend, Freddy, that's what you are. That daft brain of yours ain't as daft as you make out. When I get my hands on what I'm after, I'll make sure a couple of quid comes your way as a thank you.' But in the meantime, he needed his job here, so he added, 'Come on, let's get back to work before Dobson bursts a blood vessel.'

7

After the cold winds of March, and April's endless showers, the fair folk were relieved when May arrived and the first signs of spring began to show. Buds on trees began to sprout into leaves and an assortment of early wild flowers bathed their faces under a warming sun.

Sundays were days of rest for most of society, but for the fair folk leisure time was only enjoyed when the men had finished any maintenance and repair work around the fair and on their living vans and the women had caught up with outstanding household chores. But when a move had taken place, they enjoyed very little time to themselves at all. The men would have made a start on dismantling the fair after it had closed at ten the night before, while the women began packing up their living accommodation; then, after a few hours of snatched sleep, they were all up again before the crack of dawn to finish off what they hadn't managed the previous evening. Once they had travelled to their next port of call and reinstated the fair and living accommodation, it was time for bed, any remaining jobs to be dealt with on Monday morning before the two o'clock opening.

The fair had arrived in Stockport for a two-week stay, and it was in the middle of their visit, on a warm early-May Sunday morning, that six women were sitting in a circle outside Gem's living van. Gem was darning a pile of socks, a chore she had no love for: Jenny was helping her Aunt Fran to unpick old jumpers to re-knit into something else; Ren was sorting sweets from a large sack into cones that she sold for a penny each; while the matriarchs of the group, Betty Smith and Sadie Mickleton, both in their seventies, were peeling potatoes and scraping carrots for dinner.

'No Velda today?' Betty asked no one in particular.

'She's with Emily Dunn,' Gem told her. 'They've gone for a walk to collect leaves and flowers for a nature lesson Emily is giving the children tomorrow.'

Emily Dunn was the community school teacher. She was an elderly woman who had been on the verge of retirement from her job as an assistant at a small school when she had witnessed how wickedly the teacher had treated the fair-folk children who had attended the school whilst Grundy's was playing in the town. Outraged at the teacher's behaviour and aware that this was how the children of fair folk were treated in most schools they attended during their travels, she offered her services to Grundy's. Big Sam had taken some persuading by Gem to fund a school, but finally he had relented when she told him that by offering his community a basic education he would be considered a pioneer and would stand alongside the greats in fair history who had come to revolutionise the business in some way. In the nine months Emily had been with Grundy's, she had taught the children far more than they had ever learned at outsiders' schools and was now offering lessons to any of their parents who wanted to learn to read and write.

'I was thinking of joining Miss Dunn's lessons,' said Fran.

'You should,' enthused Jenny. 'I don't know how I'd cope without my books to read before I go to sleep at night.'

Fran looked doubtful. 'Well I don't know whether I'd reach the standard of an actual book, but I'd like to be able to read some of the articles in women's magazines, and new recipes.'

'You don't know until you try, Fran. Solly is doing really well and he thought he'd never get the hang of it when he first went along,' Gem told her.

Fran thought about it for a moment before she said, 'I suppose I could go for one lesson and see how I get on.'

Silence reigned for several moments as each woman concentrated on her task. Then Betty spoke up.

'Only seems five minutes ago that we was sitting like we are now having a good old natter and next thing we know war was declared when those brainless Teddy bear idiots rampaged us last year.'

'Teddy boys, yer daft beggar,' Sadie scoffed, slapping her friend playfully on her arm. 'Yeah, yer wouldn't think it was nearly a year back. Time flies so damned quick when you're getting on. Only seems like ten minutes ago I married my Cedric, and here we are eight kids and twelve grandchildren later and about to celebrate our fiftieth wedding anniversary.'

'Fifty years married, eh, Sadie,' said Gem. 'That's some milestone.'

'Yeah, I deserve a medal for having the patience of a saint. My husband's a good man but not the easiest to live with. He's knocking seventy but still not learned that a hook is for hanging things on and the coal and water buckets don't fill themselves.'

'You'll be having a party to celebrate?' asked Jenny.

Sadie pulled a face. 'Not thought about it really, as it ain't until October. If I arrange something I'll be sure to let you all know. How's your wedding plans coming on, Fran? September seems a long way off, but it's not when yer organising a wedding.'

Fran smiled as she wound wool into a ball. 'I've finally found a pattern for my costume. It's a straight skirt with a box jacket and a lace collar and cuffs. I thought satin, but I can't decide whether to go for lilac or pale blue.'

'Definitely lilac,' said Betty with conviction.

'For goodness' sake, lilac is for old fogeys like us. Absolutely pale blue,' said Sadie.

Fran could see a row on the subject brewing, so before either woman could say anything else, she spoke up. 'Thank you very much, ladies. You've both helped me make my mind up.'

Sadie looked smug. 'Wise choice, Fran lovey, you'll look so pretty in lilac.'

Betty looked even smugger. 'Fran knows fine well that with her colouring it's pale blue.'

Fran hid a smile. 'Well, it's neither. I'm going for emerald green.'

Gem shot an approving look at her. 'I'll be making a start on the cake soon,' she said.

'Laced with plenty of rum,' added Sadie.

'Brandy,' said Betty.

'Whatever it's laced with, I can promise you that one slice will have you dancing on the table singing 'Roll Out the Barrel',' Gem told them.

They both chuckled. Betty said, 'Danced on a few tables in our time, ain't we, Sadie?'

'And fell off a few too. But them days are long gone. My legs only just about hold me up now.'

Betty nodded in agreement. 'Might not be able to dance the night away any more, but we can still tap our feet along to the music and watch all the younger ones making fools of themselves. I do love a good party.'

'I was thinking of having one,' said Ren.

Jenny looked keenly at her. 'What's the occasion?'

Ren shrugged. 'No reason. Just that we ain't had one since the season started and it's about time we did. What about this coming Saturday night after the fair closes?'

Jenny laughed. 'Oh, I like that. A no-reason party.' She leaned over and whispered in Ren's ear, 'Will everyone be invited?'

'Of course. We're a community.' Ren looked at her knowingly. 'Someone particular in mind?'

Jenny grinned coyly. 'Might be.'

The little woman scowled in thought as she mused, 'Now, who is good-looking enough for my pretty friend to be interested in? Speedy, from the Wall of Death, is a bit of all right. Then there's Charley Watson, one of the boxers. Is it either of them?'

'What are you two whispering about?' Gem interrupted.

They both shot her an innocent look. 'Nothing,' they said in unison.

'Be about a bloke then,' said Sadie.

'Most definitely,' said Betty.

Absolutely is, thought Gem. As Ren was happily in a relationship with Donny, the man under discussion must therefore be of interest to her daughter. She would like nothing more than to see Jenny happily settled with the right man, but she forced herself to stay quiet as she had no intention of becoming an interfering, overbearing mother. She trusted her daughter to know what was best for her; when Jenny wanted her to be enlightened, she would freely do so. To allow Ren and Jenny to continue their conversation without interruption, she purposely engaged the rest of the group in other general fairground topics.

Jenny might not have known her real mother for more than a few months, but she instinctively knew that Gem was restraining herself, and it told her that her mother had respect for her privacy and the patience to let her decide for herself whether to take her into her confidence. She was pleased that Gem was not turning out to be a domineering mother, but the thoughtful kind who trusted her daughter to make her own decisions. She would not hesitate to tell her just what she was discussing with Ren, but only if and when there was something to divulge. At the moment, there wasn't, though she hoped there would be soon.

Ren slapped her on the arm in a triumphant manner. 'Got it,' she whispered. 'It's that new chap that talks like he's one of them nobs with a plum in his mouth. What's his name now? Ben . . . Jim . . . something like that. Can't say as I blame you for having a fancy for him. He might not be the best-looking chap but he's definitely got something about him that makes you take notice. You'd have a fight on your hands for him if I wasn't so happy already with my Donny.'

Jenny laughed. 'Then thank goodness you are. I've noticed a couple of the other girls have their eye on him, so I've enough competition as it is without you as well. He has got something about him, but what that is I haven't a clue. As you said, there's better-looking lads who work here, but it's not his looks that attract me. It's just something about him . . . oh, I don't know. How can you have this huge need to want to know someone better after only just saying hello to them? But it was the way he stopped and took his cap off when I passed, and gave me a lovely smile, and said back to me, 'And good afternoon to you too, miss.' Fancy calling me *miss*, like I was royalty. Really respectful it was.'

'Well I hate to burst your bubble, but he called me *miss* too when he asked me for a bag of mint imperials the other day. He looks an ordinary bloke, so I wonder how he came to talk so posh.'

Jenny grinned. 'It's because his father was a head gardener for a lord or something on his estate, and he used to mix with the master's children and even had lessons with them. I overheard Dad telling Mum about him when he first took him on. I think that's what first intrigued me — to see for myself this new worker who spoke like the queen — so I went out of my way to have a look at him. I suppose I was fascinated to know how someone who grew up on a fancy estate ended up working as a casual for a travelling fair. I don't know what I was expecting.' She laughed. 'Some handsome lah-di-dah sort dressed like he was about to go on a pheasant shoot in his plus fours and brogues with a gun under his arm. But he just looked like any of the other gaff lads. Maybe not quite so scruffy. So I suppose in a way when I first clapped eyes on him I was disappointed.'

'But that changed when he doffed his cap at you and treated you like you were a lady.'

Jenny nodded. 'Yes, it did. I liked it. Made a change.'

Ren patted Jenny's arm. 'Then I'll make sure he gets an invite to the party.'

'Oh, well, aren't we forgetting that I might have a liking for him, but I may not be his type.'

Ren scoffed. 'And what is there not to like about you?' She looked searchingly at her friend. 'I'm surprised that you aren't already married. Most girls are at your age. Well, 'cept me, of course, but then it was Donny or no one, and we can't marry until we can find out where Suzie is. Still, we're as good as married anyway, so a piece of paper ain't gonna make no difference to us. So, is it that you ain't met Mr Right yet?'

Jenny flashed a wan smile. 'I thought I had a couple of times. Derek was the first one, but he got called up to do his National Service, and while he was away he met someone else and got her pregnant, so that was the end of him. The second one was Eric. I was besotted with him. He had a look of the film star Stewart Granger about him, tall, dark and . . . hell, was he handsome. He was a draftsman in a large tool-making firm and had great prospects. He was fun to be with and we talked such a lot about anything and everything. I was sure he was on the verge of asking me to marry him and I would have accepted without even thinking about it. But then my mum — my adopted mum — got ill, and that's when I realised how utterly selfish Eric was. He told me that he appreciated that I would need space to look after my mother, but what he meant was that he'd make himself scarce, and then when she was dead, we could pick up where we'd left off. I was absolutely flabbergasted. He really thought he was doing me a favour by letting me get on with it instead of assuring me he would stand by me and help me through such an awful time. Suffice to say, I don't think he realised I knew such words until I hurled them at him when I sent him packing. Would have definitely made a navvy blush.'

Ren eyed her, impressed. 'Good on you. My Donny might not win any beauty contests, but if that had been my mam, he'd have been at her bedside every spare minute, holding her hand, reading her stories, making her laugh, anything to help take her mind off what she was going

95

through, and he'd be doing all he could to look after me too whilst I was caring for her — making me cups of tea, cooking dinner, even doing the washing and cleaning, which most men would absolutely refuse to do, bless him.'

'And that's the kind of man I want for myself,' Jenny told her emphatically.

'Well then, we'd better get this party organised so you can find out if this fellow has the qualities my Donny has.' Ren noticed Julie coming out of her van nearby and heading off in the direction of the main fair. She said to Jenny, 'I've just seen Julie on her way to the Wall of Death, so I'm going to go and tell her about the party and she can help us spread the word. Really it's an excuse to have a rest from bagging up these sweets for a bit.'

Fed up herself with unpicking old jumpers and rolling up the wool, Jenny said, 'I'll come with you.'

They looked an odd pair walking alongside each other, Jenny tall for a woman at five foot seven, Ren tiny at four foot three, and they received good-humoured comments from other members of the community they passed, one in particular likening them to Laurel and Hardy.

Jenny responded laughingly, 'I hope you're not implying that I'm fat like Oliver Hardy is.'

Chuckling, Ren shouted back, 'Or that I'm as dopey as Stan Laurel.'

By the time they arrived at the Wall of Death, Julie had disappeared inside. They found her dressed in protective leathers astride a practice bike, about to rev up the engine. She smiled, delighted to see them both, waving a hand to beckon them in. 'This is a nice surprise. Come to watch me practise?'

They told her that they hadn't, but that they were inviting her and Dicky to a no-reason party next Saturday evening.

Julie didn't need to confer with Dicky first, as he never turned down an invitation to have a drink and fraternise with other pretty girls in the Grundy community. Woe betide her, though, if she had too much to drink or chatted up any of the other men. To avoid the humiliation of his behaviour, she could conveniently forget to mention the party, but he was bound to find out about it via the community grapevine, and she then risked suffering from his wrath that she had kept it from him. Acting like she was really excited about it, she accepted the invitation and confirmed that they would bring contributions of food and beer.

Ren gestured to Jenny that they ought to leave Julie to get on with her practice session, but Jenny wanted to ask Julie a question that had intrigued her since she had first been introduced to the other woman and found out what she did for a living.

'Do you ever get scared doing your stunts, Julie? They are very dangerous, aren't they?'

Julie replied without hesitation, 'Terrified.'

Ren looked at her, confused. 'So why do you do it then?'

'Because it's also so exhilarating. It's impossible to describe the feeling I have when I've finished a show and hear the crowd clapping and cheering me and know that for those few minutes I've brought them excitement.' She eyed the two girls in turn before asking, 'Have either of you ever ridden on a motorbike?'

Ren looked utterly horrified at the thought. 'Not on your nelly. I doubt my feet would reach the footrests anyway, but I know I'd take a bend and lean the wrong way and end up in a heap in a ditch.'

The other two laughed loudly at the vision Ren had conjured up in both their minds.

'I've always fancied a go but I never knew anyone that had a motorcycle to take me out on,' Jenny said.

Julie smiled at her. 'Well, now you do.' She dismounted and stood beside the bike.

Jenny looked at her aghast. 'What, you mean I should have a go now?'

'No time like the present. Just sit on it and get a feel for it, start the engine if you like. You're not really dressed for it, but if you fancy a proper go, when we're both free, I'll lend you some of my leathers and we'll go out and find a piece of straight road, like Dicky did the first time I rode a bike.'

It was too good an offer for Jenny to turn down. She dropped her handbag on the floor and with an excited gleam in her eyes stepped over to the bike, hitched up her skirt and sat astride it. At Julie's urging, she turned the ignition key, then gingerly revved the throttle. As the engine roared into life, she expected to feel fear, but instead it was a thrill of anticipation that rushed through her. She wished that a straight piece of road stretched ahead and she could kick back the stabilisers and see if she was capable of steering a straight line without falling off. She eased back the throttle until the engine died and switched off the engine, then looked at Julie longingly. 'Oh, I'd love to have a proper go if you can find the time.'

'What's going on?'

All three women turned towards the door to see Dicky looking stonily over at them. Jenny and Ren didn't notice the momentary flash of fear that blazed from Julie's eyes. Very quickly, though, she planted a smile on her face and called to him, 'This is the first time Jenny has ever sat on a bike and she'd like a proper go on one. We can arrange that for her, can't we, Dicky?'

He sauntered over to join them, giving Ren and Jenny a charming smile. 'Yeah, yeah, of course. Soon as we get time, we'll sort something out.' He fixed his eyes firmly on his wife. 'Have you practised that new stunt yet? I want to include it in tomorrow night's performance, so you will be ready, won't you, darling?'

His request might have sounded polite to Jenny and Ren, but Julie knew it was loaded with menace. Should she not be ready for tomorrow night, her husband would make his displeasure very apparent in his own particular way. The new stunt was a particularly dangerous one. While the bike was racing around the wall at speed, Julie would pull her legs up behind her until she was lying flat across the top of it, whilst still guiding it with her hands. Then after a couple of circuits she would manoeuvre her body back into a sitting position. One lapse of concentration could result in serious injury or worse, and she would have liked more time to practise it before going public, but she knew Dicky had made up his mind that it would be included in tomorrow night's show.

'Yes, of course I will. Straight onto it now,' she assured him, although her stomach was churning at the thought.

Ren and Jenny, taking this as their cue to leave, said their goodbyes and hurried out.

As soon as they had disappeared through the door, Dicky grabbed hold of Julie's arms, pushed his face close to hers and hissed, 'What do you think you're doing allowing any Tom, Dick or Harry to play around on our bikes? What will we use if they damage one, and who'll pay for it to be fixed.'

Julie froze in fear, knowing only too well what was in store for her simply because she had wanted to give a friend a bit of fun. She was married to a monster, a man who derived pleasure from causing hurt to others, and none more so than his own wife. And far worse than any of the beatings he gave her or the belittling, insulting comments he continually shot her way was the fact that as matters stood, she had no way of escaping him — until, that was, the day he went too far and killed her.

Outside the Wall of Death, Ren and Jenny had begun to make their way back to resume their tasks with the rest of the women outside Gem's van when Jenny suddenly realised she had left her handbag behind. Leaving Ren where she was, she dashed back to retrieve it. As she opened the door and made to step inside, what she saw made her freeze in stunned shock. Even from this distance she could see the gleam of power in Dicky's eyes as, gripping Julie's arm with one hand, he drew back the other, fist tightly clenched. She clearly heard him say, 'Now you know what happens when you cross me, Jules,' then he brought his fist forward with force onto the side of his wife's head.

Julie, meantime, had her eyes closed, an air of resignation about her, prepared for what she was about to receive. The pain was excruciating, making her see stars, and she let out a low groan of agony as she clutched the side of her head and stumbled backwards. Dicky watched her for a moment, a smug smile playing on his lips, before he hissed, 'Now get on that bike and don't get off until you can do the new stunt blindfolded with one arm tied behind your back. Got that, darling?'

Gazing at him with fearful tear-filled eyes, she silently nodded.

Concerned that Dicky would sense he was being watched and unsure how he would react, but more worried that Julie would suffer the humiliation of knowing there had been a witness to her husband's mistreatment of her, Jenny stepped back and let the door close silently after her.

The scene had deeply upset her. From the moment she had met Julie, she had liked the woman and instinctively knew that the pair of them would become friends. Whenever she had crossed paths with Dicky, he'd always been charming, polite and flatteringly flirtatious and had shown no sign he had a dark side to his nature. She had never had any reason to believe that Dicky and Julie's marriage was anything but a happy and harmonious one. Given what she had seen today, that obviously wasn't the case.

Sheer anger swamped her being. No woman, let alone a lovely one like Julie, should be treated by the man who was supposed to love and cherish her in the manner that she had just witnessed. She felt a huge urge to return and give that bully of a man a piece of her mind, but then what went on behind closed doors between husband and wife was their business alone and not for others to poke their noses into uninvited. She just hoped that sooner rather than later Julie would pluck up the courage to make her escape from Dicky and find herself a man who would treat her in the manner she deserved. Somehow, though, and without revealing the reason behind her offer, she would let Julie know that if ever she needed the support of another woman, Jenny would be there for her.

Despite knowing that Ren would be just as appalled and upset over what she had witnessed, Jenny didn't feel it right to tell her about it, and so when she rejoined her friend, she forced herself to appear her normal cheery self, telling Ren that Julie had been about to resume her practice session and that, not wanting to interrupt her concentration, she would collect her handbag later.

But secreted in the Wall of Death gallery someone else had witnessed Dicky's unwarranted abuse of his wife. It was far from the first time either. Their eyes narrowed darkly. Very shortly Dicky Otterman was going to pay the price for believing he could treat others in any way he felt fitting.

8

Since embarking on his journey, Tom had readily accepted any job that had been offered to him. He had humped heavy bags of coal, dug ditches, mended fences, picked fruit, grubbed through mud in trenches for potatoes, fixed roof tiles, mowed lawns and swept paths, along with many other labour-intensive manual tasks, the payment he'd received for his drudgery an insult considering the long hours and exertion he'd expended. Some bosses had treated him with respect and shown appreciation for the work he had done for them; others had been decidedly rude, expecting him to be grateful for the favour they were doing him in affording him the opportunity to eat that night. He had met a variety of people along the way, from a mixture of backgrounds, all travelling around in search of work for their own particular reasons. Some of these he knew it wise not to turn his back on, but there were also those who would have given him their last halfpenny if his need had been greater than theirs.

Here at Grundy's, he humped and hammered, fetched and carried, doing what he was asked to make sure the punters enjoyed themselves. He worked for twelve hours a day, with only two short breaks, the money he received for his labours as insulting as the pittance he had earned for all the other jobs he had done. A few of those he worked for were surly in manner and didn't show any appreciation for the job he did, but most thanked him for his contribution and treated him affably. As in all communities, there were those within Grundy's he had sussed he would be a fool to trust, but the majority he knew he could depend on for his life. And although there were some who gave him a hard time because of his upbringing, he felt welcome and comfortable with this band of fairground folk, and would certainly miss them when it came time for him to move on.

Tonight, he had been commandeered to assist Fran Grundy at the Tunnel of Love. Fran was in the pay booth whilst he installed punters safely in the swan boats before he gave the all-clear for the ride to begin. It had just started off, and with nothing to do until the train returned, he leaned back against one of the supports and looked out at the rest of the fair.

It was teeming with people of all ages, shapes and sizes, from the very poor to the well off, and it would take a better man with words than himself to adequately describe the electric atmosphere that the punters and the fairground community were creating between them. Even the most depressed person would find it difficult to remain miserable whilst paying a visit to the fair, in Tom's opinion. A momentary wave of sadness washed over him. It was a pity that his father could not have been persuaded to visit and discover what it felt like to have some actual fun. Maybe both their lives might have been different as a result.

He felt extremely honoured that despite the fact that he had only worked here for a matter of days, he had been invited to a community party after the fair closed tonight. It had been a personal invitation too, from the woman who owned the candy floss and sweet stall, who told him she had wanted to make sure he knew he was included. In truth, by the time the fair closed tonight, all he'd be fit for was downing a bottle of beer before he crawled into bed, but he would stay for a while at the party and felt sure that everyone else would be enjoying themselves far too much to notice that he had taken his leave.

After work, he returned to his van for a wash, and changed out of his work clothes into a pair of light-coloured slacks and a blue round-necked jumper. The party was in full swing when he arrived carrying his contribution of half a dozen bottles of beer. Most of the attendees were the younger members of the fairground community, apart from a couple of old men who never missed an excuse for a booze-up. Laughing and chatting together, people were sitting either on chairs or on the ground in a rudimentary circle, several dancing in the middle. Two lads were twanging on guitars and a big, muscly black man, a boxer in the booth, whose name was William White but fought under the nickname of Basher Bill, squatted beside them banging rhythmically on a pair of bongos.

Tom's van mates had already arrived at the party. Owen and Marvin had each brought a girl with them they had met earlier that evening during work, and were canoodling with them. It was obvious what they were hoping would happen before they waved the girls off on their way home later on. Roger hadn't managed to get himself a date, and his eyes were skipping over the rest of the gathering for a possible candidate amongst the fairground girls.

Tom had barely sat down on a rough patch of grass next to Roger when a young woman squeezed herself in between them, hooked her arm through Tom's, thrust out her chest at him and said meaningfully, 'You're dancing with me tonight, handsome.'

Dulcie Pickering was an attractive 19-year-old with a thick mane of chestnut hair and a shapely figure that tonight she was showing off in a tight skirt and low-cut red blouse. Her parents owned a side show, a magic act; her father was the magician and her mother his assistant, while Dulcie and one of her sisters, dressed in sparkling leotards and fishnet tights, would parade up and down in front of the booth enticing customers to watch the show and her other sister sat inside the ticket office taking the money.

Had Dulcie not been ordering Tom to dance with her, he would have been happy to oblige — for one dance at least, as although he hadn't a clue what his type of woman actually was, Dulcie definitely wasn't it — but after his father's death, he had promised himself that his days of being told what to do were over. He eased his arm out of hers and said politely, 'Thank you for the offer, but I wouldn't wish to deprive all the other men here who want to dance with you.'

But Dulcie didn't want to dance with anyone else. She had bragged to her friends that she was going to land the latest recruit to Grundy's tonight, and she wasn't prepared to return to them to face the embarrassment of having failed. She hooked her arm back through his and brazenly told him, 'It's you I want to dance with, not anyone else.'

She shifted closer so he got a better view of her breasts, a move that made Tom feel extremely uncomfortable. He again removed his arm from hers and told her, 'I don't want to dance, but again, thank you for your offer.'

She gawped at him, stupefied for a moment that this man had the audacity to refuse her advances and she now faced humiliation in front of her friends. Then she jumped up and leaned down to slap him hard across his face, sending the bottle of beer in his hand flying. 'Just 'cos you speak like the queen's yer mother, you think you're better than me,' she cried. 'Well, yer can't be if yer working as a casual for a travelling fair. In fact, it's me that's better than you as my dad is an international magician and owns his own side show.' Her father had done a season in a seaside town in Northern Ireland, but in her ignorance, Dulcie did not realise that even though they had crossed the sea to get there, they were in fact still within the British Isles. 'Now you listen here you jumped-up toe-rag. I felt sorry for you, being new to Grundy's, and was only trying ter be friendly, otherwise I wouldn't have bothered with you. You're not

108

exactly Rock Hudson, are yer?' Then with a haughty shake of her head, she spun on her heel and stormed off, leaving a stunned Tom rubbing his smarting cheek and his three van mates and the two girls with them laughing hysterically.

★   ★   ★

A few minutes earlier, Jenny had arrived with her contribution of two large bottles of Woodpecker cider and half a dozen of Babycham. As she put them on the trestle table along with the rest and began to pour a measure of the cider into the mug she had also brought with her, Ren joined her.

She looked her friend over before she said drily, 'You didn't make any special effort for the party then.'

Jenny was wearing a straight black skirt and a checked shirt, with a broad black belt around her slim waist and flat red pumps. She would have preferred to wear stilettos, but they were unsuitable for the ground the party was being held on. She playfully slapped Ren's arm. 'Cheeky. Nothing wrong with trying to look your best.'

'You look great. If the man has eyes in his head then he won't be able to take them off you. He's over there with Owen, Roger and Marvin. Oh, and I found out that his name is Tom.'

Jenny liked the name. It was strong-sounding. Her heart did a little leap of anticipation as she discreetly turned her head to look in the direction Ren was indicating just in time to see

Dulcie leap up and slap Tom hard around the face, then shout something at him before storming off.

Both girls were silent for a moment before Ren said, 'Oh well, whatever he said to her didn't make her very happy, did it? It must have been insulting to make her slap him so hard.'

Any hope Jenny had been harbouring that Tom was the sort of man she'd have liked to get to know better completely dissipated, and she sighed despondently. 'Well he might talk posh, but he's obviously not a nice man, is he?' She took a long swallow of her drink, now regretting the extra time and trouble she had taken over her appearance in the hope of attracting the attention of Grundy's newest recruit.

Forever the optimist, Ren said cheerfully, 'Thank goodness you didn't waste any time on him.' She spotted a man taking a close interest in Jenny and added with a mischievous twinkle in her eye, 'Not like you're short of admirers. Mickey Dickens can't keep his eyes off you. He's drooling that much you can almost see the saliva dripping off his tongue.'

Mickey Dickens was a thoroughly unsavoury character. He was tall and skeletally thin, his long, sharp face covered in pockmarks from a bout of chickenpox as a child, along with acne as a youth. Every other word that came gruntingly out of his mouth was of the blasphemous type, and he didn't know the meaning of the word hygiene, nor seem to realise that clothes needed to be washed at regular intervals. Unsurprisingly, no one would share accommodation with him, so he lived alone in a tiny van that the rest of the community insisted was parked well away from theirs in case they caught something nasty. Mickey himself was kept away from members of the public too. The only reason that he had not been sacked was because he worked as hard as two men put together and never complained about any task given to him. Over the time he had been with Grundy's, a few women had tried to take him in hand but had failed miserably. It was clear to everyone that he was one of those people who didn't care about the effect his personal care had on others and so it was assumed he must be happy as he was.

Well aware that Ren was poking fun, Jenny looked over at Mickey lurking on the periphery of the party, drinking beer from a bottle, and said matter-of-factly, 'I'll be generous and leave those delights for the rest of the girls to enjoy.'

The musicians started to play a popular jive and Donny bounded up and grabbed Ren's hand. ''Bout time you had a dance with me, woman.' Without waiting for a response, he dragged her off into the middle of the dance area, leaving Jenny looking longingly at them. What she wouldn't give to have a relationship that mirrored Ren and Donny's. They were madly in love and totally at ease with each other; they trusted each other implicitly and shared much in common. She would like to think that there was a man out there somewhere that she would be as happy with, and wished he would show himself, as she was getting a little fed up with waiting for him to appear. She wasn't desperate to get married and have a family, but she was twenty-two now, an age when most women had found their mates and were happily settled, so she was starting to get a little worried, though she would sooner remain a spinster than settle for second best. Not one for dwelling on matters that she could do nothing about, she put her disappointment aside to concentrate on enjoying the party.

As she sipped her drink, she watched the dancers, who now included her brother Jimmy, accompanied by his current girlfriend, while her other brother Robbie stood in the midst of a group of lads on the sidelines. She spotted Julie arriving arm in arm with her husband and was reminded of the incident the other day when she had witnessed Dicky punch her in the head. The pair now looked so happy and contented together, the perfect couple in fact, and no other onlooker would have had any idea that Julie was hiding the awful secret that she was married to a vicious bully. Jenny hated to think of her friend constantly living in fear of being on the receiving end of her husband's temper, and felt helpless that there was nothing she could do about it but support Julie should she ever decide to confide in her.

After having a few dances and chats with friends, she returned to the refreshment table for another drink. Once her glass was replenished, she leaned her backside against the table and looked around as she sipped. Her eyes reached the place she had last seen Jimmy, canoodling with his girlfriend. Now, though, there was no sign of the pair. Probably sneaked off for some private time together, she thought. Robbie was still there with his group of friends, although several girls had joined them now. One in particular was showing an interest in him, but he wasn't taking the slightest bit of notice. If she was going to get anywhere with him, then subtle hints would do her no good; she'd need to wave a big red flag in his face with *I Fancy You* written on it. Robbie was nowhere near as self-assured as his brother was. A girl had only to glance in Jimmy's direction and he would automatically believe that she was besotted with him. Jenny was going to have to give her little brother some sisterly advice of the romantic sort or she feared he would remain a bachelor forever.

Just then her ears pricked as she heard muffled giggling. She looked around, but then realised it was coming from under the table. A couple of teenagers seeking the privacy to have a kiss and a cuddle, she assumed, but then it struck her that the giggles were childish ones. She put her drink down, then stooped to take a look. Three young boys were huddled together, sniggering gleefully as one of them tried to take the top off a bottle of beer using a stick.

'You'll need a proper bottle opener to get that off,' Jenny said.

At the sound of her voice, they all jumped in shock, then stared at her guiltily. One of them blustered, 'We weren't doing nuffink, honest, Miss Grundy.'

'So, your parents allow you to drink beer then?'

They all stared sullenly at her.

'I thought so. I very much doubt that Ivy and Bert would be happy to see you coming home drunk, Col. Thank goodness for you that you couldn't get the top off.'

Ten-year-old orphan Col had joined the community last year after Solly had rescued him from a man who was using him to help him steal money for beer and cigarettes. The boy was in a sorry state at the time, but Ivy and Bert had gladly welcomed him into their home, and thanks to their love and care, he bore no resemblance to the waif he had been then. He was a nice lad, good-natured and honest, although the same couldn't be said of Olly Champion, one of his companions, who was always up to no good in some way or another and getting a thick ear for his misdemeanours from one of his long-suffering parents. It was Jenny's opinion that he was the one who had put the other boys up to this caper.

'It was only a bit of fun, Miss Grundy. We just wanted to know what beer tasted like, that's all,' Col pleaded.

'Well I'm sure you will in a few years' time, when you're old enough to drink alcohol, but until then you stick to pop. Now give me that bottle and all of you skedaddle back home before your parents discover you've sneaked out.'

'You won't tell our mams and dads, will yer, Miss Grundy?' Col asked anxiously.

'I will if I catch you doing anything like this again,' she warned.

She waited until the offending bottle was

safely in her hand and the three boys had scooted off before she had a chuckle over the incident. She herself had been guilty of one or two childhood transgressions and knew it was all part of growing up, so she had no intention of snitching on them. She put the bottle back amongst the others, although there were only a handful left now, so before all the cider disappeared, she downed what was in her own glass and poured herself another. Apart from her disappointment earlier over Tom, she had enjoyed herself. It was getting on for one o'clock and the party looked like it would continue for a long time yet, but Jenny's bed was beckoning, so once her drink was finished, she would head back to her own van.

She was just about to say her goodnights when she spotted Julie's husband Dicky acting in a way she could only describe as suspicious. He was a few yards away from her, standing well back from the rest of the partygoers, and if there hadn't been such a bright moon tonight, Jenny wouldn't actually have seen him. It was apparent to her that he'd had a few drinks just by the way he was swaying, but it was the fact that his eyes were darting searchingly around that was rousing her curiosity. She wondered who or what he was looking for. Then his eyes seemed to settle on something and she saw a smile kink the corners of his lips. It was obvious he had found his quarry.

Jenny automatically glanced in the direction Dicky was looking and saw Julie chatting and laughing with Ren and Donny by the steps of their van. So, Dicky was checking where his wife was. She wondered why. She looked back over to him, but he was gone. She searched around but could see no sign of him. Then it struck her like a thunderbolt. He had been checking that his wife was occupied so she wouldn't notice him slipping away. Her curiosity rose higher. He had to be up to no good or otherwise it wouldn't have bothered him if Julie had seen him leaving. Was he slipping away for an assignation? She dearly hoped not, for Julie's sake. But she meant to find out one way or another.

Leaving her empty mug on the trestle table, she weaved her way through to where she had last seen Dicky lurking. She looked around and deduced that as he hadn't passed her, there was only one other way for him to have gone and that was around the back of the huddle of vans. In the seconds since she had last seen him, he couldn't have gone far, so if she hurried, she could catch up with him and follow at a discreet distance. She spun on her heel and headed off.

A huge cloud suddenly drifted across the moon, plunging her into near pitch darkness save for the odd shaft of light shining through gaps in the curtained windows of the living vans. She wished she had a torch with her, but then when she had come out this evening she'd thought she'd be dancing the night away rather than playing detective.

She had sneaked her way past several vans before she caught sight of Dicky's shadowy figure, still acting furtively. She waited until he had disappeared behind the van in front of her before she crept along the side of it and peeped around the corner. A few feet away from her was an old two-berth van used by her father to provide gaff lads or labourers with living accommodation. It was empty at the moment, as it was in the process of having a hole in the floor fixed, its two occupants meantime bunking in with others. Dicky was opening its door and was about to go inside when another figure appeared to join him. Despite the lack of light, Jenny could tell it was a woman, and was near enough to hear Dicky say none too politely, 'Quick, get inside before anyone sees us.'

The newcomer giggled, leaned up and kissed his cheek before responding, 'You just hope it ain't my husband, as he'll cut off your whatsits and fry them up for his breakfast.'

Jenny recognised the woman's voice. It was Averil Hunter. Her husband was one of the labourers, a bull of a man, the sort you were wise not to mess with. She was an attractive woman in her mid-twenties; community gossip had it that she was the flirty sort, and this confirmed to Jenny that she certainly was. They were both inside the van now, and Jenny stood staring over at it in dismay. For Julie's sake she had sincerely hoped she had been wrong about Dicky cheating on her, but it appeared she wasn't, and now she had the dilemma of whether to tell her friend what was going on. She would need to think very deeply about this.

Suddenly she froze as she heard a sound behind her. It was the soft tread of footsteps.

117

Someone was creeping up on her. Panic flooding her being, she spun around to see who it was.

★   ★   ★

A short while earlier, Tom was doing his best to stifle a yawn. He had enjoyed himself much more than he thought he would tonight, making some new friends amongst the fair folk and even persuaded by a couple of the women to have a dance with them, but he was mindful that he had to be up ready for a full day's work at the crack of dawn so had been trying to take his leave for a while now. Each time, though, either someone had come up and engaged him in conversation, or Roger, not wanting to be left on his own, had persuaded him to stay just a little bit longer, and now it was nearly one o'clock. Tom didn't want to lose his job through lapses of concentration caused by lack of sleep from partying too late, and as Roger was at the moment in conversation with another gaff lad, he thought this a good time to finally make his escape.

Getting up, he put his hand on his van mate's shoulder. 'I'm turning in now. I'll see you in the morning.' Before Roger could again persuade him to stay, he hurried off.

Light from the moon was aiding his way through the huddle of vans, and in his anxiety to get to bed, his pace was brisk. He was only a short distance away from his own van when he suddenly found himself plunged into darkness as a large cloud obscured the moon. He slowed his pace so as not to fall over any discarded items other community members had left outside, and had just groped his way around a van when he suddenly stopped short.

A few feet in front of him he could see the outline of a figure. They appeared to be peering around the side of a van, observing the van beyond it. Apart from those still enjoying themselves at the party, the rest of the community would be in bed by now, so whoever this was must be an intruder from outside. Were they sizing up the van with a view to robbing it? It was the only thing Tom could think of to explain their behaviour. The robber wasn't a clever one, though, as the area he had chosen to line his pockets was where all the gaff lads and labourers lived, and poorly paid as they were, none of them owned anything worth taking. Regardless, he wasn't about to turn his back on a potential thief and leave them at liberty to roam around the rest of the vans, helping themselves to whatever they wanted.

He realised that the figure had obviously sensed his presence, as they were turning around. He had no idea whether they were armed or not, but he wasn't going to wait to find out. Taking a deep breath, he launched himself forward, rugby-tackling the figure to the ground and straddling them to keep them pinned down, his intention then to grab their wrists to fully restrain them before he yelled for help.

Jenny had just been in the process of turning around to see who or what was approaching when she found herself on the ground. Fearing what her attacker was about to attempt to do to her, her survival instincts flooded in. If he thought her easy prey, then he had another think coming. She raised her knees and brought them up as hard as she could, at the same time flailing her arms wildly to stop him grabbing her wrists, then balling both fists and punching him in the side of his head and then his face. Her efforts did the trick, and he yelped and toppled off her.

As soon as she was free, she made to scramble up and run off whilst shouting for help, but Tom managed to gather himself together enough to grab her ankle, pulling her over. As she hit the ground again, she cried out, though it was in shock more than pain, as thankfully the thick couch grass the vans were parked on provided a cushion.

At her exclamation, Tom sat bolt upright and stared down at her in astonishment. 'You're a woman!'

Jenny struggled to get up, rubbing her elbow where it had struck the ground, glaring at the dark outline of her attacker a couple of feet away from her. 'Do men wear skirts and have long hair?' she snapped angrily.

He stuttered. 'Well . . . it's . . . it's just that usually burglars are men.'

'Burglars!'

He retorted accusingly, 'Well that's what you are, isn't it? What else could you be up to, sneaking around the vans at this time of night?'

She snorted in indignation. 'If I was a robber, I hope I'd have more sense than to be sizing up an empty van to steal from. And anyway, thieves don't rob their own.'

He gawped at her for a moment before her words registered. 'Oh! You work here? Oh . . . well. I'm sorry, but obviously it's dark, and from the way you were acting I assumed . . . ' He added defensively, 'I'm sure if the roles had been reversed you would have assumed the same thing. It seems I was wrong to judge you as I did. Please accept my apologies.'

Although she now appreciated how he had come to mistake her for a robber, she wasn't sure if she had forgiven him enough yet to accept his apology. Then it suddenly struck her just who he was. It was his voice that gave him away. Ren had told her his name was Tom.

'You're the new man that started here a few days ago, aren't you?' she said.

He answered warily. 'Yes, I am. We haven't met before, have we, so how do you know that?'

To Jenny, Tom spoke with the same cultured tones of the privileged as the consultant at the hospital who had dealt with her adopted mother, but whereas the consultant's voice had had a superior clip to it, this man's was far softer, with no hint of superiority at all. She wanted to tell him that she found his accent fascinating and could listen to him speaking forever, but she was far too angry to say anything complimentary. Instead she snapped, 'I heard you spoke like you have a broom stuck up your backside, and it was a good description because you do.'

To her shock, he burst out laughing. 'Well I shall have to try and be more un-bristle-like then, won't I?'

She found herself laughing too. Then she

suddenly stopped as a memory of earlier struck and she said tartly, 'Seems you have a habit of upsetting women. I'm the second to my knowledge tonight.'

He frowned quizzically. 'What do you mean by that?'

She snorted. 'Well whatever you said to Dulcie Pickering upset her enough to make her slap your face.'

He sighed. 'I have the right to decide who I would like to dance with, and Dulcie didn't take kindly to my polite refusal of her offer and reacted rather violently.'

Jenny's lips clamped tight. She knew Dulcie well enough to be aware that the girl wouldn't be at all happy to have her advances rebutted. It seemed she had misjudged this man.

Just then a light came on in the van beside them, the window was thrust open and a dishevelled head shot out. 'What's going on 'ere? We're trying to sleep, goddammit. Go and have your bit of hanky-panky somewhere else.' The head disappeared and the window slammed shut.

They both sat in silence for a moment in embarrassment that the man in the van believed he'd caught them in a compromising situation. Jenny prayed that he hadn't recognised her; the last thing she wanted was rumours going around the fairground that the boss's daughter was a trollop.

Eventually Tom scrambled up, then extended a gentlemanly hand down to her, saying, 'Again I apologise for jumping to the wrong conclusion. I hope I didn't cause you any damage when I tackled you.'

She opened her mouth to tell him that she was going to suffer a sore elbow at least for a couple of days thanks to him, but then he really did seem genuinely sorry that he had misread the situation. And after all, hadn't she herself misread the situation she had witnessed him in earlier that evening? Instead she said curtly, 'I'm made of strong stuff, so I'll live.'

Tom, though, hadn't come off as lightly from their tussle as she had. Now that she was standing before him, she could make out that he had a bloodied nose and lip. She was sorry for the damage she had caused him, but then she was only trying to protect herself. She lightly quipped, 'I didn't realise I had such a good left hook. I should think about taking up boxing in the booths.' Then her tone of voice became serious. 'You really need those cuts seeing to.' She was about to ask him if he had antiseptic and plasters in his van, then thought better of it. Although gaff lads were always cutting and bruising themselves during the course of carrying out their jobs, they would generally seek out an obliging female member of the community to administer to their injuries. 'If you come back to my van, I'll clean them up for you,' she said.

She saw him hesitate and assumed that was because he would sooner risk his cuts turning septic than spend any longer in her company. To her surprise, she realised she felt hurt by that. But having caused his injuries, if they did fester from lack of attention then she didn't want to be responsible. 'Come on, I won't bite,' she said as she brushed down her skirt and turned to head off back through the huddle of caravans to where her own was parked.

In fact, Tom's hesitation had been because he had been searching for the right way to accept her invitation back to her van without appearing too eager. For some reason he couldn't at all fathom, given that his introduction to this woman hadn't been in the best of circumstances, he was finding himself intrigued by her and definitely wanted to find out more. He was surprised he hadn't noticed her before now, as he'd gone about his work around the fairground, as she was certainly very attractive, but then all his attention had been concentrated on learning his job and making sure he kept it. As it was, she didn't give him the opportunity to respond to her invitation before she'd set off, expecting him to follow. So he did, before she became lost to him amongst the huddle of vans.

★ ★ ★

'Oh goodness, that smarts!' Tom exclaimed a short time later.

Jenny chuckled. 'Is that a posh way of saying 'Ouch'? I did warn you it would sting.' She screwed the top back on a bottle of witch hazel, then cut a length of plaster, put a smear of Germolene on it and placed it over the cut on his nose, firmly pressing down the sticky ends. She stood back and admired her handiwork. 'Maybe

I should have been a nurse. I've made a good job of that.'

Tom hid a smile. It was the least she could do considering she had been the one to cause his injuries in the first place. 'Thank you. I shall be eternally grateful to you for saving my life.'

Jenny smiled at his quip.

He was sitting at her small pine kitchen table, and as she put the medical supplies back in a wall cupboard, he said, 'I'll leave you so you can get to bed.' He stood up and pushed his chair back under the table, taking a quick glance around. 'It's a nice place you have.'

Jenny knew it must seem like a palace compared to the van he would be sharing with the other gaff lads. She didn't feel she owed him an explanation, but found herself telling him, 'It's not mine, it belongs to my uncle.' She wasn't about to divulge Sonny's criminal history to an employee, so she just said the first thing that came into her head. 'He's emigrated to Australia to work on a sheep farm.'

Tom looked surprised. 'A little different to fair work. Is he enjoying the life?'

'Err . . . well he's not come back, so I assume he is. Not a great communicator, my Uncle Sonny.' She looked at him enquiringly. 'You grew up on a lord's estate, so rumour has it. What was that like, having all that space to run around and play cowboys and Indians in?'

Tom would have given anything when a boy to be allowed to play such games. He said shortly, 'Fun. Yes, lots of fun.' He shot her a smile. 'Well, thank you for patching me up.' He made to turn, then a thought struck and he asked her, 'Just as a matter of interest, what were you actually doing when I mistook you for a burglar?'

She looked at him blankly. To tell him the truth would mean having to divulge Julie's personal business, which she wasn't even sure she was going to tell Julie herself about yet.

'I'd had a couple of drinks too many at the party and was walking it off before I went to bed. I was just resting by that van when you saw me.'

'Well, next time I see someone lurking by a van late at night, I'll not be so quick to assume the worst of them but make sure of my facts first.' He stood looking at her for a moment, as though there was something he wanted to say, but then he seemed to change his mind and flashed her a smile. 'Thank you again for your nursing services. I hope you sleep well.'

★   ★   ★

As Jenny readied herself for bed, her thoughts were all on the man who had just left. She had never met a man of her own age before who was so polite and well-mannered, and although not handsome in a film-star way, his face was a very pleasant one. For a gaff lad, young men who weren't known for their strict attention to hygiene, he was very clean, as were his clothes, and when she had leaned in close to attend to the injuries she had caused to his face, she had smelt expensive aftershave.

She liked a man who took care of himself. And he was a protective, conscientious sort of man

126

too, who when he believed he'd stumbled across a potential burglar hadn't turned his back and walked away but had tried to prevent that burglar from doing his worst. He was definitely of interest to her. She sighed despondently. But then he hadn't shown the slightest hint that he found her attractive in return, so she was wasting her time thinking about him as a possible boyfriend.

Forcing all thoughts of Tom from her mind, she turned over and tried to get to sleep.

* * *

In his own van, attempting to get comfortable on the thin, lumpy mattress on his narrow bed, Tom couldn't seem to get the woman he had unwittingly attacked tonight out of his head. Why hadn't he asked her name? She had a pretty face, and was sparky too. It was obvious that she was quick-witted, with an intelligent mind, and she could certainly look after herself. He'd like the chance to find out what other qualities she possessed. Perhaps she'd agree to go for a walk with him one evening, or sit and talk over a drink or suchlike . . . Abruptly he stopped his thoughts from running away with him. With her looks and personality, she more than likely already had a boyfriend. He'd been an idiot to consider asking the likes of her out; thank goodness he had come to his senses in time and saved himself the humiliation of her refusal.

Forcing all thoughts of Jenny from his mind, he turned over and tried to get to sleep.

9

Councillor Ernest Dunster, leader of Huddersfield council, buttoned up his trousers, tucked in his shirt, straightened his tie and put his jacket back on, never for one moment taking his piggy eyes off the shapely blonde dressing herself close by. It was only a few minutes ago that he had virtually ripped her clothes off her before they had had rampant sex on the thick carpet before the large marble fireplace over which hung a picture of the young Queen Elizabeth II.

Ernest looked at the clock on his desk, part of an expensive jade and silver art deco writing set he had treated himself to when he had first been elected three years ago. His eyes almost bulged out of their sockets when he saw the time.

'Hurry up and sort yourself out, Lena. I've a meeting with Booth from Planning in his office at eleven, and it's five minutes to.'

Lena's skirt was pulled up around her shapely thighs and she was snapping a popper on her suspender belt. Pulling the skirt down, she began to do up the buttons on her white blouse. 'Five minutes to talk to you then, lover boy,' she said casually.

Her tone of voice made him look at her sharply. 'What about?'

She walked around his desk to where he was standing and perched her backside on the edge, fixing him with her gaze. 'Us, Ernest. Me and you.' She leaned over and ran a hand down his arm in a seductive manner. 'You told me you loved me. Lots of times you did. I don't want to be your bit on the side any longer. I want to be your wife.' Her eyes gleamed a steely grey as she paused for a moment before demanding, 'So I want to know when you're going to tell your wife about us and get a divorce so we can be together.'

Ernest's eyes bulged, and he gulped and grabbed hold of his tie to loosen it. He hadn't been expecting this at all. Lena had seemed more than happy with their office fling, which had been going on now for over three months. She had been the one to instigate matters between them only a week or so after she had come to work here when his previous secretary, a thin, humourless spinster, had retired.

Ernest had been married to Gertrude, a formidable, matronly woman in her early fifties, for nearly thirty years. For the last ten of them, they had slept in separate rooms, his wife no longer of sexual interest to him now her once-shapely body had thickened and spread through childbirth and age, though his excuse had been that her restlessness and snoring kept him awake at night so he was unable to function properly at work the next day. But just because he was no longer interested sexually in his wife didn't mean he was prepared to go without. So, he had satisfied his needs with discreet visits to prostitutes, over the years building up a list of those he favoured most.

He was quite happy with things as they were

now, but the thought of his looming retirement, when he would be stuck at home with Gertrude, no longer at liberty to live his secret life, filled him with dread. Consequently, he had come up with a plan, in which he was going to sell his house without Gertrude's knowledge, empty their bank accounts, and, with the money that was accumulating nicely through backhanders from grateful businessmen who'd gained lucrative council contracts, abscond abroad like a thief in the night to somewhere warm like Spain where Gertrude would never find him. The fact that he would be leaving her destitute caused him no sleepless nights.

He'd thought his Christmases had all come at once when Lena was announced as his new secretary and made her feelings clear from the moment they shook hands. At first he couldn't believe that such a good-looking young woman actually fancied him, given that he was a portly, bespectacled middle-aged man with a toothbrush moustache, who had never had the women flocking even when he was younger, and so he had assumed he was misreading her innuendoes and provocative body language. But she had made her intentions clear one dinner time when the rest of the staff had left to go home or to the canteen, locking his office door and having wild sex with him over his desk.

After that, they had sex whenever possible, and he'd felt smug that he had landed such an attractive mistress, only sorry that he was unable, for obvious reasons, to brag to anyone about his conquest. She had never made any demands on him before, seeming happy with the little presents he bought her now and again, so this mention of marriage was totally out of the blue and an utter shock. Should his wife even get an inkling that he was having an affair, he was in no doubt that he would be lucky to end up keeping the clothes on his back after her lawyers had finished with him, and his exploits with his secretary would see the end of his job as head of the council too.

His face the colour of beetroot due to a sudden rise in blood pressure, he blustered, 'Now . . . now, look here, Lena. I thought it was just a bit of fun we were having. You knew I was married. I never said anything about leaving my wife.' He wagged a fat finger at her. 'It wasn't me that started all this, it was you.'

The corners of her lips kinked as she again stroked her hand down his arm. 'I can't remember you making any protests when you were taking advantage of me across your desk, or on the carpet, or anywhere else in this office you've had your wicked way with me, honey bun.'

'I . . . I bought you presents,' he stammered, like it justified him committing adultery with her.

She looked down at the silver bracelet he had given her just before they had had sex that morning. 'Yes, and very nice they were too. Made me a nice few bob at the pawnbroker's, the same as this one will.'

He gawped at her. 'You sold the jewellery I bought you?'

131

She smiled and nodded. 'It'll help me pay for my bottom drawer.' She paused for a moment, her eyes glinting maliciously. 'You can take that look off your face. I'm not serious about you asking your wife for a divorce so we can get married. Did you really believe that I would want to saddle myself with a fat, ugly old pervert like you?' She sniggered before she went on. 'I am getting married, though. To my fiancé Billy. We've been saving for the last six years but neither of us gets paid that much. You know what my wages are here, and by the time I've paid out my board money to my mother and bought my essentials, there isn't much left over for saving. Billy's a joiner for a little firm down by the gasworks, and his wages aren't anything to shout about either. We could just about afford to rent a small flat in a back-street area, but we both want kids and a flat's no place to bring up a family, is it? I want a house, and not a rented one either. And Billy's fed up with working for someone else and wants to start his own business. A thousand should be more than ample.'

Ernest frowned, bewildered. 'A thousand?'

She flashed a look at him as though to say, 'Are you stupid?' and said sardonically, 'Pounds, Ernest. We can get a decent house for about four hundred, one of them three-bedroom pre-war semis in a nice area. Couple of hundred to furnish it. As I told you, I've already got most of my bottom-drawer stuff, and we've both got big families, so there'll be plenty of wedding presents. That would leave four hundred to set Billy up in his own business.'

Ernest's thoughts were beginning to turn somersaults as it slowly struck him what she was saying. He ventured, 'Are you . . . er . . . asking me to loan you the money, Lena? Now look here, you must know that I'm not a rich — '

'Loan!' she scoffed. 'No, of course not, Ernest. We could never hope to pay that huge amount back. I'm asking you to give it me as a present.'

His already bulging eyes almost popped out of his head and his jaw dropped. 'What?'

She eyed him warningly and spoke to him like she was a nanny scolding a naughty boy. 'Now don't get yourself in a tizzy, Ernest. Remember your blood pressure. I'm not expecting you to hand it over right this minute — you'll need a bit of time to get it all together — but I want it tonight. Best not risk anyone catching you handing a wad of money over to me and wondering what it's for; I'll come back here after work when most people have gone home, tell the security guard I forgot my purse or something. Shall we say about eight? I'm sure you won't have any trouble convincing that dear wife of yours that you've got to work late; after all, she's used to it, isn't she?'

She saw him about to protest and snapped, 'Don't try and tell me that you haven't got it, because I know you have. I know all about your little sideline in helping local businesses win lucrative council contracts, and the back-handers you get from them for your help. You keep the money locked in a cash box in your bottom drawer until you can get to the bank and deposit it in your private account, and the bank book's taped under your desk. I know how much you've got in it too. More than I'll earn in a lifetime. I'm your secretary, remember, and secretaries know everything about their bosses.

'Like last week, for instance, Mr Granger of Granger Homes called in to invite you and your wife to a party to celebrate him landing the contract to build new council houses that you obviously had a hand in him getting, and I heard him say to you, 'This should pay for a nice bit of jewellery for your wife.' And you laughed and said, 'What my wife doesn't know won't hurt her.' What would your help in winning a huge housing contract be worth to Mr Granger? A few hundred at least, I'm sure. Not bad for putting a good word in for someone in the right ear. Maybe it's about time Mrs Dunster knew what her husband was up to behind her back, as it's my guess you're not planning to let her in on it until you retire and she gets up one morning to find you gone, leaving her high and dry.'

His face turned a deep dark purple and he furiously blurted, 'Now look here — '

She again cut him short. 'Oh, don't bother to deny you're on the make, Ernest. Virtually everyone who works for the council suspects you of being crooked. You're just lucky you haven't been caught at it yet. That's maybe because the majority of the council are at it too in one way or another, so you cover each other's backs. That's why I applied for the job in the first place, because of what I'd heard about you when I was working in the typing pool. I knew that if I got it, I'd be in a position to find out if you really were on the make and work out how to get my hands on some of it.

'I hadn't a plan then of how I was going to blackmail you into giving me money, but it became clear to me the minute I was introduced to you. You couldn't take your eyes off me.' She sneered at him in disgust. 'The thought of letting you have your way with me made me feel sick to my stomach, but if it gets me and Billy a better life, then a woman's got to do what a woman's got to do. You didn't need any persuading to drop your trousers, did you; couldn't get them down quick enough once I let you know I was willing.'

She smiled slowly before she went on. 'Well, Ernest, I'm sure your wife will be very interested to know that her husband has been regularly shagging his secretary. If she accuses me of lying, I've got all the times and dates listed in my diary that she can compare to the times you told her you'd be late home from a council meeting or one of those male-only do's at your club. And how would I know you've got a mark at the top of your thigh that's shaped like a star unless I'd seen you with your underpants off, or that hideous mole just under your belly button?

'I dread to think what'd happen to your job if I went to Mr Musson and told him that you'd been blackmailing me into having sex with you by threatening to get me sacked without a favourable reference if I didn't. Of course, that would be my word against yours and who's going to believe a lowly secretary against a bigwig like you, but it would still damage your reputation and have people wondering if there was any truth in my allegations.' She scowled at him darkly. 'And you can stop looking at me like I'm the scum of the earth. I'm only doing what you are — making people pay for my services. I'm doing this to give me and Billy a better life, just the same as you are for when you retire.' She smirked maliciously. 'Oh, and just in case you're wondering how I'll explain the money away to Billy, I'm going to tell him I found it wedged down the seat on the bus home. I believe in finder's keepers. Billy will be far too excited thinking what we can do with all that lovely dosh to be bothered how we got it anyway.'

She eased herself off the edge of the desk and stood facing him. 'You'll be glad to know that once you give me the money, that's the last you'll see of me. I've a new job I start tomorrow. I typed out my own glowing reference for it on your personal headed notepaper and forged your signature. Really lovely boss I'll be working for too, a gentleman, not a pig like you.' She rubbed her hands gleefully. 'Oh, I've just remembered that the fair arrived today and Billy is taking me tonight, and with all that money in my hands I think I can spare a couple of quid for us to really enjoy ourselves and celebrate our good fortune.' She leaned over and patted his arm. 'I'll see you tonight at eight. Now I'd best leave you to get ready for your meeting. You don't want to be late, do you, Councillor Dunster?'

His meeting could go to hell for all he cared. As soon as Lena had left, he shot over and locked the door, then returned to his desk, where he put a call through to the planning office, apologising for not being able to attend the meeting as something urgent had come up. Then he collapsed shaking into his chair and cradled his head despairingly in his hands.

What a complete idiot he had been not to once question why a pretty young girl was throwing herself at a man old enough to be her father. He was going to pay dearly for his arrogance. He would have to cough up, because otherwise the consequences didn't bear thinking about.

He knew without looking, as he'd only counted it the other day when he'd got his backhander from Granger, that he had seven hundred and eighty pounds in his tin in the drawer, the proceeds from the last three favours he had done for local businessmen that he had not yet deposited in his secret bank account. He would have had eight hundred had he not spent twenty pounds on the bracelet for Lena. But that meant he was still two hundred and twenty pounds short of her demand. He had to give notice of at least five days to take money out of his secret bank account. He knew there was five thousand in his and his wife's joint savings account, but again he needed to give notice to withdraw it, and when his wife checked the balance in the bank book that was kept in his desk drawer at home, she would want to know why he had taken out two hundred and twenty pounds without her knowledge, and what he had done with it.

There should be about three hundred pounds

in their current account, which his wife used to pay their household bills. He could go to the bank and withdraw the money he needed and then replace it in five days with money from his secret account. But what if Gertrude needed to pay bills in the meantime and the cheques bounced?

His brain whirled, trying to think of any colleagues or acquaintances who might have as much cash as he was after lying around. Thankfully there were a couple. He was very optimistic that one of these two would come up trumps after all the favours he had done for them in the past, but as he replaced the phone receiver back in its cradle after the second call ended, he was plunged into a deep dark hole he could see no way out of. His first contact was out on business and wouldn't be back until after six; his second, who owned a factory making cushions and curtains, had just lost a major contract and so had money worries of his own.

He slumped back in his chair, wringing his hands, his life and the future he had planned shattering into smithereens around him. A vision reared up in which he was dressed like a tramp, ragged and filthy, sleeping rough. He gave a violent shudder. The thought of ending up like that terrified him. He had to get hold of that shortfall of money; he just had to.

His thoughts whirled again, but with no one else he could think of to ask for a loan at such short notice, and no one who owed him any money, it seemed that it was all over for him. But then something Lena had said resonated in his brain. She had mentioned that the fair had come to town today and she was planning a visit with her fiancé tonight. At once, all the anger he felt towards her for her despicable blackmailing plot was pushed aside. He was far too jubilant about the fact that she had unwittingly given him an idea of how he could make the money he needed to pay her off. Then a greedy smile kinked his fat lips as an idea struck of a way to make himself a few pounds on top. The only thing that niggled away at him was that he might be too late and the money he was after getting his hands on had already been handed over.

Without further ado, he grabbed up his telephone receiver and made a call.

10

The move from Stockport to Huddersfield, a distance of 27 miles, might be a leisurely couple of hours' drive for most people, but for the fair community it was a major undertaking. The huge assortment of vehicles carrying their equipment and living accommodation had to travel a warren of narrow roads, many in poor condition, their surfaces uneven and peppered with potholes. As usual, lorries developed mechanical faults and drivers got lost, arriving hours late at their new destination. This could have put the erection of the fair ready for opening on Monday afternoon in severe jeopardy had not all the fair folk pulled together, most of them working an eighteen-hour day on the Sunday and snatching a couple of hours' sleep before they were back at work at six on the Monday morning. It was important to ensure that the fair opened on time, as not only would Grundy's reputation have suffered, but valuable takings would be lost.

At just after midday, Solly was about to breathe a sigh of relief that all was in order and he was safe to leave the rest of them to it so that he could go to the town hall to settle the fees due to the council for the fair's seven-day stay when it came to his attention that the dodgems ride had lost its electrical supply and needed his expert attention. It wouldn't do for the fair's most popular and profitable attraction to be out of action. It seemed his visit to the town hall would have to be postponed until later.

Anticipating that he might need help resolving the issue with the ride, and bearing in mind that time wasn't on his side, Solly dispatched the gaff lad who had come to tell him of the problem in the first place — who happened to be Tom — to seek out the community's Mr Fix-It, Gully Givens, and ask him to meet him at the ride.

Ten minutes later, Tom returned to inform him that Gully was nowhere to be found. Probably, thought Solly, because the crusty middle-aged bachelor, thinking all was in order, had taken himself off down to the local pub for a much-needed pint, pie and chips.

After assessing the situation, it seemed to Solly that there was a break in the electrical circuit somewhere on the ride, a big task for one man to locate. He needed help to resolve it, but there was no telling what pub Gully was in, so he would just have to tackle it himself and hope he could find the break in the cable and fix it before the punters started arriving.

It had been a long time since breakfast, and Tom was by now ravenously hungry. There was bread, chips and a huge mug of tea waiting for him back at the van courtesy of Roger, who had fetched the chips from the local fryer. But it was obvious that the boss had a major problem on his hands, and it wasn't in Tom's nature to turn his back and walk away from anyone in need.

'Would you like me to help, Mr Grundy?' he offered.

141

Solly was up a ladder, minutely inspecting a length of cable that looped around the roof skirting and helped to feed the current of electricity running through the metal pads lining the roof of the dodgem ride that made the cars run. He looked down at the younger man. 'You never mentioned you were a sparky when I interviewed you for the job or I'd never have just had you labouring. I'd be delighted with your help.'

It took Tom a moment to work out what a sparky was. 'I'm not an electrician, Mr Grundy, but I'm sure I could spot a break in a wire. Where would you like me to start?'

Solly was impressed by the young man offering to forgo his break in order to assist him. He had observed Tom quite a few times going about his work, and whenever he had seen him he was always busy, never idling or larking about, which was the case with most of the other gaff lads, who needed constant supervision and keeping in check. And if he or Tom could just find the break in the wire, he might still have time to enjoy his dinner before opening time.

They had only been working away for a couple of minutes when another young man approached. This wasn't one of Solly's employees, but an outsider, with an official air about him, wearing a suit and carrying a briefcase.

'Been told the boss man is around here somewhere,' he said.

Solly stopped what he was doing and looked down from the ladder. 'That's me. What can I do for you?'

'I've come to collect the council dues.'

Solly eyed him, surprised. As far back as he could remember, in this town the boss of the fair visited the town hall to pay the fee. Obviously, the council had changed its rules. Saved him time paying a visit, though. 'As you can see, I've my hands full at the moment,' he said. 'You'll need to see Mrs Grundy about payment. Head off into the living area and ask someone there to point you in the direction of her van. She'll sort you out.'

The young man nodded, then set off towards the living vans.

It was Solly who found the break in the cabling ten minutes later. Just a small cut; impossible to fathom how it had happened, but enough to break the electrical circuit. The whole length of cable would need replacing, but for now gaffer tape would suffice as a temporary measure.

He thanked Tom and was about to tell him to go and enjoy what was left of his dinner hour when a thought struck. The least he could do was offer him a proper home-cooked meal, something the gaff lads only got on moving day, when the community women banded together to provide a vast spread sufficient to feed all of them. It never occurred to him that he should consult his wife before surprising her with a dinner guest. Gem would welcome the lad, and even if she hadn't got enough food in, she would make it go around.

Tom was taken aback by the boss's offer to sit at his table. If the other gaff lads got to hear, he'd be in for a lot of ribbing for hobnobbing with the hierarchy. They'd suspect he must have been brown-nosing to get the invite. But his mouth watered at the thought of a home-cooked meal rather than the now-cold chips and two-day-old bread that was waiting for him back at the van. Besides, it would be very rude of him to refuse. He smiled. 'I would be delighted to accept your very generous offer, Mr Grundy.'

Solly did a double-take at Tom's response, still not used to dealing with such a well-mannered employee.

As Solly knew she would, Gem enthusiastically welcomed their guest and hurriedly set a place for him at the table. She had heard all about Grundy's latest recruit, who spoke like he'd been born with a silver spoon in his mouth, but hadn't as yet come across him in person, so now was her chance. She had held dinner back for as long as she could so that the whole family could eat together, but time went on and Solly had not appeared, and she had just been about to start serving when he had arrived with Tom. She had made a huge pot of stew — whatever remained would make a pie for dinner tomorrow — so there was more than enough to go around.

Already acquainted with Tom through work, Robbie and Jimmy both fell into easy conversation with him. As Gem started to pile food on their plates, her husband asked her, 'Where's Jenny?'

'She had something to do,' Gem said. 'She didn't say what, but she's already eaten. Say when for potatoes,' she told Tom as she spooned a pile onto the plate before him.

Picking up his knife and fork, Sonny looked appreciatively at his plate. 'This is a sight for sore eyes, my lovely,' he said. 'I'm that hungry I could eat a rabid scabby dog.'

Just about to tuck in herself now, Gem gawped at him mortified and hissed, 'Solly, we have a guest, remember.' She was glaring at him in a way that told him Tom was not their usual sort of gaff lad.

'Actually, Mrs Grundy,' said Tom, 'I was thinking exactly the same as Mr Grundy.'

They all laughed then.

As the men chatted amicably whilst they ate, mostly about work, Gem appraised her visitor. He was coming across as a very personable young man who took pride in himself. Solly was obviously impressed enough to invite him into their inner sanctum. He had told her when he had first taken Tom on that his father had worked for a titled gentleman, and she wondered why he wasn't using his education to do better for himself. But she supposed all sorts of people arrived at the fair looking for work, for all sorts of reasons, and it was Grundy's good fortune that he had come to work here.

'How are you finding working and living in a travelling fair, Tom?' she asked.

He politely finished a mouthful of food before responding. 'I like it well enough, thank you, Mrs Grundy. I've learned quite a lot since I came here. I do particularly like helping out on the rides and seeing people enjoying themselves.'

'Glad to hear that, as that's what we're here

for. The more fun punters are having, the more money they'll spend, which keeps us going,' said Solly.

'So, do you plan to stay with us for a while?' Gem asked.

Tom hadn't really given it any thought, just living from day to day. The work was hard, though it wasn't anything he wasn't capable of, but now, being faced with the question, it surprised him to realise that if he did move on, he would very much miss the community spirit and the friends he had made. 'I've no plans to leave just yet, Mrs Grundy. Well, of course providing I'm still required here, that is.'

Solly smiled at him. 'Always have a need for a lad like you, Tom, so I've no objections to you sticking around for a while.' He looked at him searchingly. Tom had said that he had no intention of leaving at the moment, but what if he saw a job advertised in the town that would suit him better? Conscientious sorts like him needed encouragement to stay with the fair. Gully Givens was in need of a mate. Solly had been on the lookout for someone who had some experience of carpentry and electrical work, but Tom seemed to be the quick-learning sort, so what harm would it do to give him a try and see how he got on? 'If you're interested, there's a job going with Gully. His last mate left us a week or so back and Gully has been nagging me to find a replacement. A lot of the job would be fetching and carrying and general labouring, but he could teach you a lot about carpentry and electrics. If we were short-handed, though, you'd still be needed to help out on the rides in the evenings.'

Tom hadn't been expecting his offer to help the boss fix the dodgems to turn out like this. He felt honoured that Mr Grundy thought him worthy of a try-out for this job. 'I like the sound of that very much, Mr Grundy. I promise you that I will try my best not to let Mr Givens down.'

Solly looked pleased. 'Good, then I'll introduce you to Gully as soon as we finish dinner, providing he's back from the pub by then. He's very choosy who he has for his mate, but I'm sure he'll take a liking to you, and if he does, I don't see why you can't start with him as soon as you've finished any outstanding jobs you were given this morning. Oh, and you'll be pleased to hear that your new job comes with a pay rise and better accommodation. Trevor's room — that's Gully's old sidekick — is still empty in the van he shared with another two lads, so you can move in there and at least now have a room to yourself.'

Tom would miss sharing accommodation with Owen, Roger and Marvin. They might be the rough-and-ready sort, but they had welcomed him into their circle and couldn't have treated him more fairly. Regardless, it had been cramped living on top of one another, and none of them ever had any privacy, so he did like the sound of having his own room, even if it was a tiny one. It all depended now on whether Gully Givens liked the look of him and was willing to give him a try. He would do his best to convince him.

A nudge in his ribs jerked him out of his

147

thoughts. The culprit was Jimmy.

'You were miles away, mate. I was asking if you'd got yourself a girlfriend yet. I heard that Dulcie had her eye on you. That's what my girlfriend Katie told me . . . well, she's my girlfriend for the moment, at any rate, until a better one comes along.'

Gem's jaw dropped, mortified for the second time in the space of a few minutes by a comment one of her family had made in front of their guest. She flashed an apologetic look at Tom before scolding her son. 'Jimmy, that's no way to treat women. Your father and I have not brought you up to behave like that.'

'No, we haven't, son,' snapped his father. 'That attitude will earn you a reputation as a love-'em-and-leave-'em sort, and you'll end up an old man on your own, as no woman worth her salt will go near you, no matter how good-looking you are.'

'I've tried to tell him he's getting a bad name with the girls, but he won't listen,' Robbie said. He loved his brother and didn't like the thought of him making a reputation for himself.

Jimmy just shrugged his shoulders. 'I can't help it if the girls flock around me. I don't ask them to. Who am I to turn a girl down if she fancies me, even if I am seeing someone else at the time? Not like I'm engaged to be married to any of them, is it?' He turned his attention back to Tom. 'So, you and Dulcie. Did she manage to get her claws into you on Saturday night like she bragged she was going to do?'

Tom replied matter-of-factly, 'She found

herself a better proposition.'

Jimmy laughed. 'Well, if a bloke's got a penny more in his pocket than the bloke that Dulcie is with, then he's a better proposition to her. It's a wise man that steers clear of her. She tried it on with me but I soon put her straight. So, any of our other girls take your fancy?'

Having cleared away the dirty dinner plates, Gem was dishing out apple crumble topped with thick creamy custard. She snapped at her son, 'Jimmy, stop embarrassing Tom. If me and your father try and quiz you on your love life, you tell us to mind our own business.'

He gave an innocent shrug. 'That's different. I ain't daft, Mam; I know you're being nosy so that if you don't like the girl I'm seeing you can stick your oar in to try and break us up. I was just going to offer to put a good word in if there was a girl Tom fancied, him being new with us.'

Gem tightened her lips. Her son knew her better than she'd realised.

'So, is there any girl you like the look of, Tom?' Jimmy asked again.

There was: the girl he had believed was a burglar on the night of the party last Saturday. He hadn't been able to get her out of his mind since. He hadn't thought he'd stand a chance with a girl like her, him a mere gaff lad, but now he was going to be Gully Givens' mate, well, it was a different matter. If he described her, Jimmy would probably know her, as he seemed to know all the community females, particularly the eligible ones in their age group, but he felt foolish admitting he was interested in a girl whose name he didn't even know, and then Jimmy might ask how he'd met her and he'd have to admit he'd mistaken her for a burglar and ended up on the receiving end of her fists. Besides, while she was repairing the damage to his face in her van, she certainly hadn't given him any sign she was interested in him in the same way.

He shook his head and said lightly, 'I've been too busy making sure I do my job properly so I don't get the sack to give women a thought.'

Solly chuckled. 'That's what I like to hear from my employees: that they put work before their social life. You'll do, lad, you'll do.' He scraped back his chair. 'Right, come on, boys. We've a fair to open.'

His last remark reminded Gem that she had something to tell him; the fact that he had brought home a guest for dinner had made her temporarily forget about it. 'Before you go, Solly, can I have a quick word?'

From her face he knew it was something of importance, and as soon as the three lads had left he asked her, 'What is it, love?' He laughed. 'Not going to tell me you're leaving me for another man, are you?'

She playfully slapped his arm. 'You should be so lucky. Just that the man from the council called for the payment.'

'Yes, I know. He came to see me first and I pointed him in your direction as I was too busy fixing the fault on the dodgems to come and get the money from the safe myself. I was grateful they'd changed their rules and sent someone to collect it themselves, as it saves me a trip into town.'

'But you should know that the fee has gone up. And by a lot too.'

Solly frowned. 'By how much?'

She paused for a moment before she broke the bad news to him. 'A hundred pounds.'

He gawped, astounded. 'How much? A hundred pounds on top of what we already pay? I can understand a small rise, but to almost double what we paid last year . . . ? How can they justify charging us two hundred and fifty pounds for the use of a bit of waste ground for seven days with just a standpipe on it? That's daylight robbery. If all the councils do the same, we'll end up bankrupt.' He scraped an exasperated hand through his hair. 'This means we'll have to put the price of the rides up while we're here, and the punters aren't going to like that. Though even that won't benefit us. They won't have any more to spend than they were going to, so all it means is that they'll go on fewer rides.'

He lapsed into silence for a moment before he announced, 'I'm going to go and see the council and tell them that they either reconsider this ridiculous price increase or it won't pay us to continue coming to Huddersfield in the future. This was one of the first places that Dad secured when he first started up, so he's been coming here forty years at least to my knowledge, and I doubt they'll get another fair to replace us at the price they're charging. The council had better prepare themselves for a backlash from the

151

locals, as they ain't going to like the fact that they're no longer going to get the fair coming, and all down to the greed of the fat cats.'

He went over and grabbed his donkey jacket from the back of the van door and began to put it on.

Gem looked him over. 'You're not going to the council dressed like that, are you, Solly?'

He glanced down at his dirty working clothes, then back at her. 'They can think of me what they like. I haven't got time to spruce myself up. I need to deal with this now, Gem. If other town councils get to hear that we accepted this price hike without so much as a murmur, they could do the same.'

He was just about to open the door when a loud rap came on it. Intending to tell whoever it was that they'd have to deal with Gem or wait to see him after he returned from his errand, he pulled the door wide. At the bottom of the van steps stood a tall, thin man with sparse grey hair topping a long face with sharp features, wearing a shiny grey suit and carrying an old briefcase. Solly asked him what he could do for him.

The man replied, 'I'm from the council — '

Before he could say any more, Solly blurted, relieved, 'Oh, come to tell us of the mistake you've made and give us a refund.'

The man looked puzzled. 'I am at a loss to understand what you're talking about. I'm looking for Mr Grundy. I'm here to collect the fee. The rules are that if the fee isn't paid then the fair isn't allowed to open and you must immediately vacate. In addition, your right to operate in this town in future will be revoked. I have to say, I am very surprised about this state of affairs. This is the first time I can remember in all the forty-odd years Grundy's fair has been coming to town that Mr Grundy hasn't presented himself at the town hall prompt at eleven o'clock to settle up.'

A cloud of sadness momentarily crossed Solly's face before he said quietly, 'My father died last year so that's why he hasn't visited you himself this morning.'

The man looked genuinely regretful when he replied. 'Oh, I am very sorry to hear that. I always found Mr Grundy a fair man to deal with. He certainly was a character. You have my sincere condolences.'

Solly nodded his thanks, then said, 'I was on my way to pay the dues this morning but had a couple of major problems to deal with that delayed me. I was saved the visit, though, by your man coming to collect the money, so really I can't understand why you're here. It was a while ago he came, so he should have got back to the office before you left it. But anyway, now that you're here, this rise in the fee . . . well, how can you justify more than doubling it? People might think fairs make a fortune, but I can assure you we don't, Mr . . . err . . . '

'Barroclough. I'm the chief accountant for the borough council.'

Solly politely held out his hand. 'Pleased to meet you, Mr Barroclough. Solly Grundy. I'm the boss of the fair now.' The men shook hands whilst Solly carried on. 'As I was saying, we

153

don't make a fortune and you hiking the fee up a ludicrous amount . . . well, after paying that and covering all our other costs, it will hardly be worth us playing here. If the other councils follow your lead, it'll see us out of business.'

Mr Barroclough was frowning, bewildered. 'Again, Mr Grundy, I haven't a clue what you're talking about. No man from the council has been sent to collect the fee, and we certainly haven't put it up. A visit to the fair is the highlight of most of the townsfolk's year, and it's not the council's intention to put that in jeopardy and more importantly lose votes when election time comes. This man who called . . . what was his name?'

Solly's thoughts were tumbling and he didn't like the way they were heading 'Err . . . I was busy when he arrived . . . a young man he was, early twenties, looked official enough. I sent him to see my wife. Look, come inside, and she'll tell you more.'

Mr Barroclough followed Solly into the caravan, where Gem, having finished clearing away after dinner, was readying herself to go to work in the pay booth for the hall of mirrors.

Solly introduced their visitor to her and explained why he was here.

Gem smiled a welcome, but then frowned as what Solly had told her registered. 'But the money has already been collected by the young man who called earlier from the council.'

Mr Barroclough's face had taken on a grave look. 'As I told your husband, Mrs Grundy, we haven't sent anyone along to collect it.'

154

'Then, who . . . ?' The truth hit and she exclaimed, mortified, 'Do you mean we've been had? Oh, how stupid of me to let someone fool me like that. I thought it was odd that someone had been sent to collect the fee when we've always had to visit the town hall before to pay it. But he seemed such a nice young man and I had no reason not to believe he wasn't who he said he was.'

'Did he give you his name?' Mr Barroclough asked.

Her frown deepened. 'Yes, he did. Err . . . Smith. John Smith.' She groaned, annoyed with herself. 'Smith, Brown, Jones, those are the names people usually use when they don't want to give their own. Why didn't even that twig something in my brain?' She looked at her husband. 'Oh Solly, I'm so sorry. I can't believe that young man took me for such a fool.'

Solly placed a hand on her arm. 'There are people genuinely called Smith, Brown and Jones, love.' He was thinking of his brother and how he had been duped by him when he said, 'You won't be the first or the last to be taken in by a con man.'

This didn't seem to mollify her in any way. Then a memory struck and she crossly exclaimed, 'Even more stupid of me, I asked for a receipt for our books and let him fob me off with the excuse that he'd left his receipt book back in the office and would get it sent to us.'

'Stop blaming yourself, Gem,' Solly said. 'If I hadn't been busy, I would have taken this lad at face value and handed over the money myself.'

He thought for a moment and then turned to Mr Barroclough. 'It was obviously someone who knew we were due to pay our fee for the rental of the land today. So, it must have been someone from your office that called on us.'

Mr Barroclough looked thoughtful. 'You said the man who called on you was young, in his twenties, Mrs Grundy. Four of my accounts clerks fit that description, but I can assure you that none of them have left the office this morning.'

Solly suddenly realised something and raked an angry hand through his hair as he said, 'I suppose this means that we still have to pay the council, don't we?'

Mr Barroclough nodded solemnly. 'I'm afraid so.'

Solly went over to the small safe that was hidden behind one of the easy chairs by the stove, opened it up and counted out the required amount of money, which he then handed over to Mr Barroclough, who placed it safely in his briefcase and wrote out a receipt.

As he departed, he said, 'I do hope you manage to find out who impersonated one of my employees and get your money back.'

Both Solly and Gem thought there was little chance of that. They wouldn't have a clue as to where to look for him, and only an idiot would return to the scene of his crime.

Solly did his best to console his wife, but she was far too cross with herself for not having seen through the man to forgive herself for the loss of such a large amount of money. She vehemently prayed that their stay here would be heavily attended by the local population, and that they were all in a spending mood to help recoup at least some of their loss.

11

A short while earlier, Jenny had been standing outside Velda's living van, hesitating before she knocked on the door. She really wasn't happy about calling on the older woman during her dinner, but having agonised over her problem now for several days, she really felt she needed advice over how to handle it.

If Velda was put out that her meal was being disturbed, she didn't show it. When she opened the door of her small traditional-style van, she beamed in delight on seeing who her caller was.

'Jenny, what a nice surprise.' Her kindly eyes then grew troubled and she clasped her large hands together over the mound of her stomach as she said gravely, 'Mmm, I can tell by your face you're bothered about something. Come on in, dear, come on in.'

'I'm not interrupting your dinner, am I?' Jenny asked in concern.

'Wouldn't matter if you were. You're welcome in my home at any time. Actually, I wasn't enjoying my meal anyway. I cooked liver and onions, but God knows what I did wrong. The liver was as tough as old boots and the gravy was lumpy, so I was just about to scrape it all in the bin and make myself a slice of bread and dripping when you knocked on the door.' She wasn't being truthful — she had actually been enjoying her food — but the last thing she wanted was for Jenny to feel guilty when it was obvious that she was worried enough about something as it was. She would cover the remains of her meal and reheat it later for her tea.

Jenny normally would have found it extremely amusing that Velda had a large tea towel covering the front of her voluminous dress, which she had obviously draped there to catch any dribbles of gravy, but at the moment her thoughts were clouded by far more important matters.

A few moments later, she was sitting in a comfortable armchair opposite the fortune-teller by her small cast-iron stove. Both of them were nursing mugs of hot tea.

Velda didn't need her psychic powers to tell her that the young woman was struggling with her conscience over whether to divulge what was obviously deeply bothering her. She said softly, 'What you say to me won't go any further, lovey. What anyone says to me is in complete confidence. We clairvoyants have a code of conduct. We aren't like hairdressers, you know; you tell your innermost secrets to them while they're crimping your hair and the next minute those secrets are all around the town. I'd not even tell your mother, who's my closest friend. It must be something you don't want your mam to know, or it'd be her you were sitting with now.' She took a deep breath before she ventured, 'You've not gone and got yourself in trouble, have you, love? 'Cos if you have, let me tell you, your mother is the last person who wouldn't be understanding after what happened with her over falling for you.'

Jenny urgently insisted, 'No, no, I'm not having a baby, Velda.' She gave an ironic chuckle. 'Gracious, it would be a miracle if I was, as I haven't had a boyfriend for over a year now, and anyway, I'm not that kind of girl. I plan to marry because I'm in love, not because I have to. No, I've come to ask your advice about a friend.' She lowered her head and began to twist the silver ring on the middle finger of her right hand that she had treated herself to from her first wage packet on leaving school. 'This friend has no idea I know what I do. I think she'd be mortified if she did.'

She paused, gnawing her bottom lip anxiously for several moments before she took a deep breath and went on, careful not to mention any names, 'I thought she was happily married, but after what I saw . . . ' She paused again, her face screwed up in distress as the horror of what she had seen replayed in her mind. 'From what I heard him say, she had annoyed him by offering to do something he didn't like, and he was so nasty when he was telling her off for it, but if that wasn't enough, he . . . he then thumped her on the side of her head. I don't know how much he hurt her as I couldn't stay and watch any longer, but I wouldn't be surprised if he hadn't knocked her out with the force he used.' Tears pricked her eyes and her voice was choked when she added, 'It's not right, is it, a man using his fists against a defenceless woman?' Before Velda could express her own views on the matter, Jenny continued, 'But it's not just that. I think — no, I know, because I saw it — that her husband is cheating on her as well.

'It was at the party last Saturday night. I was just thinking of leaving when I saw my friend's husband acting . . . well, suspiciously. I just knew he was up to no good, and then I realised he was making sure that his wife wasn't watching him so he could slip off, so I followed him . . . I just couldn't help myself. He made his way to one of the empty vans, where he met . . . a woman and they disappeared inside together. It doesn't take a genius to guess what for, does it?'

Solemnly Velda shook her head. 'No, I don't suppose it does.' She looked at Jenny for a moment before she said, 'And your problem is whether you tell your friend what you saw?'

Jenny eyed the older woman imploringly. 'Well, do I, Velda? I mean, he's hurting her. From what I heard him say, it was definitely not the first time. She can't be happy living with a man she's frightened of, never knowing when he's going to beat her for something she says or does just because he feels like it. Maybe she stays with him because she's too scared to leave him, but if she knew he was cheating on her as well as abusing her, it might give her the motivation to get herself away from him.'

It hadn't taken Velda long to deduce who this friend was that Jenny was in turmoil over. Two couples were top of her mental list. Ren was number one. The girls were very good friends, but Ren wasn't actually married to Donny yet. Besides, the mild-mannered Donny would never lift a hand to his beloved Ren in any other way

161

than a caring one, or cheat on her either. Second on the list was Julie Otterman. She was married to Dicky, and all Velda's instincts told her that beneath his charismatic surface was a rather unpleasant man. It was her guess that it was Julie Jenny was concerned about.

Looking pensive, she sighed. 'It's a difficult situation you're in, Jenny, and a difficult decision you have to make. But there's far more to it than just clearing your conscience. If you stay quiet about this, then you'll feel guilty every time you're with your friend for keeping the knowledge from her. Yet if you don't tell her and she finds out about it and the fact that you knew and didn't tell her, then it will also damage your relationship with her. But then if you do tell her, she's very likely going to be utterly humiliated that you are aware she's been allowing her husband to treat her as he has been and done nothing about it. She might suspect that her husband is cheating on her but has no proof. You giving her proof will mean she has no choice but to accept it and do something about it, because if she doesn't, she will be losing your respect as well as her own. There's also the fact that she might not believe you; might accuse you of wanting him for yourself and trying to split them up. Ending a marriage is not an easy thing to do, Jenny. When your friend married her husband, she had all these hopes and dreams for her future with him, and despite his brutality and infidelity she might be clinging onto the hope that he might suddenly change his ways and she will have that happy-ever-after. He might be a terrible husband but, regardless, she might still love him and not be ready to leave him.'

Jenny was gawping at her, horrified. 'Oh God, I never thought of all this. Oh, I wish I had never seen what I did. But I did and I can't forget it. What am I going to do, Velda?' she beseeched.

Velda looked helplessly at her. 'This is one of those times when you're the devil if you do and the devil if you don't. I can't advise you, lovey. This is a decision only you can make.'

Jenny left Velda's caravan in more of a turmoil about what to do than when she had arrived.

★   ★   ★

Solly's efforts to convince Gem not to blame herself for handing over such a large amount of money to a conman fell on deaf ears. She couldn't shake off the guilt that her actions had put a huge dent in the fair's finances that was not going to be easy to mend, or the humiliation of allowing that young man to make a fool of her. At least she hadn't had to suffer the gossip and snide remarks of the less than charitable types amongst the community — she was a very popular member but there were those who enjoyed nothing more than capitalising on another's misfortunes for their own amusement — as Solly had insisted that the incident be kept between the two of them. The fair's finances were the owner's affair alone, unless they came to affect the community, which wasn't the case, thank goodness. Had they been fleeced of a

163

larger sum, things might have been different. Regardless, it was a glum Gem who was slumped in the pay booth of the helter-skelter that evening.

Her sister-in-law, Fran, was her helper that night, handing mats out to the punters and generally making sure they behaved themselves whilst on the ride. Gem was usually a joy to work alongside, but tonight she had hardly said a word to Fran, or to any of the punters either as she took their money from them. It struck Fran that something was deeply upsetting her sister-in-law, and being as fond of her as she was, she wanted to offer her help.

During a lull in the queue, she went into the pay booth.

'I give up,' she said. When she received no response, she repeated it more loudly: 'OKAY, I GIVE UP.'

Gem turned her head distractedly. 'Sorry, I didn't catch what you said.'

Fran sighed. 'I said, okay I give up.'

Gem looked at her blankly. 'Oh, all right. Before you go back to your van, though, can you stop by Solly on the dodgems and ask him to send me a gaff lad to replace you. Hope you feel better soon.' She turned away and stared out of the window again.

Fran grimaced, bemused. 'What? No, I'm not giving up for the night because I feel poorly. It's you I'm giving up on, guessing who's died. Well, someone must have, judging by the mood you're in tonight. You're not acting like yourself at all. What's the matter, love?'

Gem bristled. 'Nothing. I'm perfectly fine, thank you.'

Fran eyed her like a headmistress would a naughty schoolgirl. 'You'll get painful spots on the end of your tongue for telling lies. You ain't fine. You're far from it. Spill the beans, Gem. What's ailing you?'

Gem was not a natural liar and was not feeling at all comfortable over not being truthful with Fran, who she knew was only asking because she was genuinely concerned about her. Sighing heavily, she said, 'I want this going no further. I feel bad enough about it already without being gossiped about by the community busybodies.' She took a deep breath. 'Oh Fran, I've been such a bloody idiot and my stupidity has cost the business a lot of money.'

Fran looked surprised. 'Not like you to make a mistake. How did it happen?'

'The mistake I made was taking someone at face value and not making certain they were who they said they were. You see, Solly was delayed from going down to the town hall this morning to settle the payment for using the council land for the fair, only we thought he'd been saved a trip because a young lad who said he was from the council came to collect it. I should have asked him to prove who he said he was, show me his credentials, but he came across as so genuine that I just handed over the money. I never even suspected anything was amiss when I asked for a receipt and he said he'd left his receipt book back in the office. I did say that it wasn't right when he told me the council had upped the

165

price, but he just told me that we'd need to take that up with the treasury department as he was just the errand boy. Solly was furious when I told him about the price rise, and was just about to go and tackle the town hall when the real man from the council turned up demanding payment, and that's when it came to light that I'd been conned. I feel such a fool, Fran, and so humiliated and embarrassed. I'll wring the little blighter's neck if I ever cross paths with him again. Though it's unlikely he'll have the nerve to revisit the scene of his crime. It just maddens me that he got away with so much of our hard-earned money.'

Fran knew there was nothing worse than being made a fool of. She appreciated fully how Gem felt, but she wasn't about to make her feel any worse. She leaned over and clapped her shoulder, saying jocularly, 'Good God, love, you ain't on your own in being taken for a mug. It's happened to me loads of times over the years. I got took right in once by a pedlar that enticed me to buy a set of pans for a guinea. He swore blind they'd last me a lifetime, but they broke the first time I used them. I still feel ashamed about it to this day.'

Fran's story hadn't made Gem feel any better, though. 'A guinea is a far cry from two hundred and fifty quid, Fran,' she said tersely.

'I grant you it is, but just be thankful that was all he swindled you out of. What's happened has happened, Gem, and wallowing in self-pity won't change it. You being miserable is making everyone else miserable too. Best thing you can do now is try to make that money up, and you're not doing that by putting customers off with your grim reaper look, are you?'

Gem smiled wanly at her. 'I suppose not.'

'Well get that smile back on your face, and quick, as there's a group of young 'uns coming over to us now.'

Fran was right. What was done was done and moping over what had happened was achieving nothing. Gem planted a huge smile on her face and said. 'That better?'

Fran grinned back at her. 'Much.'

The crowd that arrived was a boisterous one, joking and teasing each other good-naturedly. One of the lads, an extremely good-looking boy and he knew it, flirted outrageously with Gem in a bid to let him ride for free, but whereas previously she might have waved him good-naturedly through just for his cheek, now she was conscious that they couldn't afford to lose any more revenue, so he paid the same fare as the rest of his crowd. The last of the group was a young man and his girlfriend. As soon as he appeared before her to pay for their tickets, she recognised him. How she kept her composure as she served him she had no idea, but as soon as he had pocketed his change, and he and his girlfriend had started to make their way up the steps, she flew out of the booth and accosted her sister-in-law, grabbing her arm and giving it a frenzied shake.

'That was him, Fran. That was him.'

Fran looked bemused. 'Him?'

'Yes, him.' Gem pointed across to the entrance

to the skelter. 'The one who pretended to have been sent from the council this morning.'

Fran turned her head to see the man's legs disappearing up the steps, then turned back to look at Gem. 'The chap who robbed you, you mean?'

Gem nodded. 'Yes. Absolutely it is.'

'He's some brass neck coming back here,' Fran said incredulously.

Gem spoke urgently. 'We've no time to discuss his cheek, Fran. He'll be back down in a minute and I mean to make sure he doesn't leave the fair without giving us our money back. I'm going to go and round up a couple of our boys to grab him when he comes down. If I'm not back in time, do whatever it takes to keep him here.'

Leaving Fran staring at her open-mouthed, Gem sped off. The ride nearest to the skelter was the sky planes. There was a crowd around it several deep and she had to push her way through to get to the front, much to the displeasure of some of the punters, who thought she was queue-jumping. The ride was in progress and she found Owen leaning against one of the support posts smoking a cigarette as he waited for it to finish. He didn't question why she wanted him to go with her; she was the boss's wife after all and her commands were to be obeyed.

En route to the next nearest ride, the dive bomber, to commandeer another of the gaff lads, she bumped into Tom. He had started his new job as Gully's assistant and hadn't been required that night to help out on the rides, so not having anything better to do, he was wandering around watching the punters enjoying themselves. For the same reason as Owen, he did not ask the whys and wherefores when Gem requested him to come with her.

Meanwhile, back at the skelter, Fran was frantic for Gem to return with help to apprehend the young man who had fleeced her. She prayed that this group of youngsters would linger around at the top of the slide, but unfortunately, within a matter of only a minute or so, the first of them started to arrive down. Gem still hadn't returned by the time the young man appeared, laughing as he jumped up and rejoined his girlfriend, who had slid down in front of him. Most of his group had started to move away by now, and Fran watched in panic as the couple joined the rest of their gang, her thoughts racing frantically. There was only one way she could think of to stall him.

Running over to him, she grabbed his arm as though she was about to tell him something, then screamed piercingly and did a very theatrical slow faint to the ground. Stunned by what had transpired, the group stared down at her for several moments, all unsure what to do. Then one young woman knelt down beside her to take a closer look, feeling Fran's forehead and trying to find a pulse on her wrist, announcing to her friends that she had seen it done this way on the television programme *Emergency — Ward 10*. Having no medical training, she declared that she thought Fran was dead until another of her friends pointed out that she couldn't be as her chest was still going up and down. How Fran stopped herself from bursting out in laughter she would never know, but she wished that Gem would come back, because she wasn't sure how much longer she could keep up her play-acting.

12

When Gem arrived back to find three young men and the same number of young women gathered around the prostrate figure of Fran on the ground, a surge of panic immediately seized her that something terrible had happened to her sister-in-law during her absence. But then it struck her that Fran must have pretended to faint in order to keep the young man here. She would thank her later for her cleverness and no doubt have a laugh over it, but right now she had a far more important matter to deal with. Quickly she instructed Tom and Owen that she wanted them to apprehend one of the young men so she could bring him to task for a grave injustice he had done against the fair. It was apparent they were both intrigued as to just what that was but knew it wasn't their place to question her.

Without a word they seized the man Gem had singled out, each grabbing an arm and pulling them up his back.

His cry of shock alerted his friends to his predicament, and whilst the girl crouched next to Fran jumped up to join her two girlfriends in a frightened huddle, the two other men immediately went to tackle the pair strong-arming their mate, one of them lunging for Owen whilst the other tackled Tom, crying out, 'We ain't about to let you rob us without a fight, you thieving gyppos.'

Owen was too quick for his attacker, kicking him hard in the shin and sending him falling to the floor crying out in agony. Tom wasn't so lucky and received a hefty punch on the nose from the other man. Although it hurt like hell and was pouring with blood, the blow wasn't enough to make him release his grip on his prisoner. Instead he balled the fist of his free hand and, as the man went to thump him again, managed to smack him in the face, hard enough to topple him backwards to land awkwardly on the ground.

Gem meanwhile urgently shouted at Fran to get up and run to fetch Solly. Then she spun to face the men on the ground and snapped angrily at them, 'For your information, you ignorant flatties, we aren't gypsies, we're showmen, and we work hard for our money, unlike your mate here.' She then turned to face the man being held captive by Tom and Owen and snarled at him, 'It's you that's the thief. And a stupid one at that if you thought us fair folk wouldn't recognise you.'

As his friends looked over at him in stunned astonishment at Gem's accusation, the man cried out, 'What the hell are you going on about? I'm no thief.' He looked appealingly at the girl he was with. 'I ain't, Sandra, honest. These people have me mixed up with someone else.'

Gem placed her hands on her hips and thrust out her chin. 'So, your name isn't John Smith and you didn't come to the fair this morning and take two hundred and fifty pounds from me on the pretence it was the council fee you were collecting?'

Looking bemused, he nodded. 'Yeah, my name is John Smith and I did come here this morning . . . Oh, I recognise yer now. You're the lady I collected the money from.'

So, he was admitting stealing the money from them! Something was amiss here, or else the man was just brazen, believing there was nothing they could do about it. But before Gem could say anything more, a panting Solly arrived with Fran, equally out of breath, followed by Jenny and Robbie. Jenny, who was working on the House of Fun, had happened to spot her father and aunt as they belted past on their way to the skelter and immediately realised something was wrong. Summoning her brother, she'd ordered the gaff lad working alongside them to take care of things and run after Solly and Fran to see if she could help.

Locking his eyes on the man Tom and Owen were holding onto, Solly said, 'That's him, is it?'

Gem nodded. 'Yes. He's admitted coming here pretending he was from the council and stealing the money from us.'

Looking wild-eyed, John Smith cried out frenziedly, 'I didn't steal no money off anyone.' He glanced over at his friends, who were gawping back at him, bewildered and appalled at what he was being accused of. 'You all know I'm no thief.'

Solly grabbed his collar, pushed his face close and snarled, 'The game's up, matey. You admit coming here this morning claiming you were from the council and walking away with two hundred and fifty quid in your pocket. Well you're a liar, because the real chap from the council turned up a bit later. Your mistake was taking us for mugs and thinking you wouldn't be recognised, otherwise you'd have got away with it.' He shook his head incredulously. 'And what a bloody nerve you've got, coming back here to spend some of the money where you stole it from. Now hand it over or I'll just have to take it back myself.' He added grimly, 'And that won't be none too gently. Your choice.'

Jenny said to her mother, 'This man stole off you? I saw you at dinner time and you never said a word.'

'Yeah, Mam, why didn't you tell us?' Robbie demanded.

Gem cast down her head in embarrassment. 'Because I was far too ashamed of myself for allowing that man to con me out of fairground money.'

They both put their arms around her and held her close. Jenny told her, 'You've nothing to be ashamed of, Mum. Con people are clever.'

Robbie said ruefully, 'Yeah, they are. Remember the bloke who sold me that wallet in the pub? Swore blind it was good-quality leather. I thought it would make a great present for Dad at Christmas. The one he showed to me and all the other people that bought a wallet off him might have been leather, but the one he sold me was nothing more than cheap plastic. A whole quid I paid for a wallet that wasn't worth half a crown. By the time me and the others realised, the man

174

was long gone. So, don't feel bad, Mam, 'cos you ain't the only one that's been fooled by someone like that.' He nodded his head in John Smith's direction.

Smith's girlfriend spoke up in tones of disgust. 'I thought you were honest and decent, John. I thought you were the one for me. I was going to ask you to come and meet my mam and dad. I can't believe you're just a common thief. Shame on you robbing off these people just to line your own pockets.' With that she stormed off and the rest of them followed suit.

John shouted after them. 'But I'm not a thief, I'm not. You have to believe me.' When none of them turned around but continued on their way to be swallowed up by the crowd, he pleaded with Solly, 'I was just doing a job for someone. Honest I was. I thought it was all legit. I got a fiver for it.'

'Who? Who were you doing it for?' Solly demanded.

'Well, I . . . Look, if I tell you then he won't put any more work my way. I'm employed by a taxi firm and don't earn that much, so these little jobs I do on the side now and again come in handy. My firm doesn't know I do them and they'll sack me if they find out.'

Gem spoke up. 'If you don't tell us who paid you to do this job, you'll not be in a position to accept any more because you'll be in jail.'

John Smith's face paled. The threat of jail was enough to loosen his tongue. He blurted, 'Ernest Dunster. Councillor Ernest Dunster. It was him I did the job for. He called the taxi office and said he wanted a lift somewhere and told them it was me in particular he wanted to drive him. I often drive him to places when he doesn't want to be seen in his own car. Usually when he visits a certain brothel. He's well known in Huddersfield, being the leader of the council, and he wouldn't want to be noticed coming and going from a place like that. Sometimes he asks me to collect packages for him and deliver them to him. I know it's money inside those packages. Backhanders most likely from favours he's done for people. He pays me well for these jobs so I never ask questions. I didn't ask questions this morning when I arrived at his office and he told me what he wanted me to do, not when there was a fiver involved.' He eyed Solly pleadingly. 'That's the truth, honest it is.'

Gem was conscious that members of the public had begun to take an interest in the proceedings, so she hurriedly pulled Solly aside. 'We're starting to get an audience, Solly, and I don't like the look of some of them. They're the types that would use their fists first and ask questions later. It must look to them like we fair folk are setting on one of theirs.'

He looked over at the gathering crowd and nodded. 'Yes, I see what you mean. I can't get to grips with what this man is telling us, though. If this Ernest Dunster is leader of the council, what is he doing paying someone to collect the dues from us that he knows the accounts department deals with? And why didn't he hand the money over to the accounts department after he'd had it collected? Then there's the fact that he made us pay double to what was actually due. Well, I can only see one way of getting to the bottom of this.' He stepped back over to face John Smith. 'Whether you like it or not, you need to take us to see this Ernest Dunster and get this matter cleared up, or it's you I'll be looking at to pay back the money. I trust as you admitted driving him about that you know where Ernest Dunster lives?'

John Smith's whole body sagged as he saw his little earner coming to an abrupt end. He replied dejectedly. 'Yeah, I know where he lives.'

As a precaution in case John Smith decided to try and make a bid for escape, Solly asked Tom to accompany him and Gem, and whilst the others went back to work, they all clambered up into one of the fairground lorries and set off for Ernest Dunster's house.

Jenny had watched closely as Tom helped her father escort Smith to where the vehicles were parked. Her emotions were playing havoc with her. Despite Tom's assurances to Solly that the injury he had suffered to his face was just a scratch, she knew it must be extremely painful and needed attention, yet he had opted to suffer in silence in order to assist her father. She hardly knew this man, yet she was having to fight an overwhelming need within herself to rush to him now and minister to his injuries. Why? She didn't need to ask herself that question, though, as the answer was glaringly obvious to her. She fancied him and wanted the chance to get to know him better. She made a plan to begin the process. She would keep an eye out for his return and offer to attend to his injury, and hope that by the time she had finished, she would have made a good enough impression for him to ask her out on a date.

13

The lorry drew to a halt in front of a house in a leafy suburb of the town where only professional people could afford to reside. It definitely wasn't the sort of area where fairground people would be welcome. The red-brick double-fronted three-storey Victorian villa was set back off the road, with a short shrub-lined gravelled drive leading up to the three stone steps that accessed the front door.

Tom and Solly closely shepherded John Smith between them up the steps, Gem bringing up the rear. They were playing safe just in case he did try to escape. The subdued man seemed resigned to his fate, though, and had told them that he was desperate to clear his name in order to regain the trust of his friends and his girlfriend. He couldn't bear the thought of them believing him a criminal when he'd thought he'd simply been doing a favour for a prominent public figure.

The door was answered by a large matronly woman dressed in a tweed suit and brogues, her greying hair expertly coiffed. She was heavily jowled with small grey eyes. She obviously wasn't amused to find that her visitors were not the sort she'd like her neighbours to witness calling on her, and hurriedly snapped, 'What is it?'

In her previous life as the daughter of a prosperous businessman, before she had married into the fairground community, Gem had come across women like this one on many occasions, including her own mother. They were all lucky enough to have married ambitious men, but then chose to forget their own lowly beginnings and instead replace them with a self-imposed superiority because they now had the money that enabled them to move amongst those whom previously they would have served.

It was Solly who responded. 'It's urgent we have a word with Mr Dunster.'

The woman snorted with derision. 'Councillor Dunster doesn't conduct business at home and especially not at this time of the evening. Call at the offices tomorrow, where I am sure one of the clerks will deal with whatever it is.'

She made to step back inside and shut the door, but Solly stopped her. 'It's only Mr Dunster that can sort this matter out, as according to this young man . . . ' he gave John Smith a slap on his shoulder, 'it was the councillor himself who hired him to do the job in question.' He paused, then added, 'But if this man is lying to cover his own back, then — '

John Smith erupted. 'I ain't, honest I ain't. It was Mr Dunster that hired me.'

Gertrude Dunster's brow furrowed quizzically as her eyes settled on John Smith. 'Just what job did my husband hire you to do?' she demanded sharply.

'Collect the fee due from the fairground folk for the use of council land. Easy fiver for me, so 'course I jumped at it.'

Mrs Dunster puffed out her chest and

snorted. 'My husband is the leader of the council and doesn't get involved with day-to-day matters like that. There are council clerks who attend to that sort of thing in any case, so why would he need to hire you to do it?' she challenged.

'That's what we'd like to know, Mrs Dunster.' Gem spoke up. 'Something isn't right, is it? Either your husband or the chap from the council that came calling after John here has money of ours in his pocket that we can't afford to forget about.'

Gertrude Dunster looked momentarily shocked to hear Gem's genteel accent. She'd believed that all travellers were ignorant illiterates, but obviously she was wrong, as this woman had certainly been educated to a high standard. She gazed at them all blankly, her brain whirling as she tried to figure out just what was going on. Then a spark ignited in her eyes and a look that could only be described as excitement beamed from them. 'I agree,' she said. 'Something isn't right. Mr Dunster is working late in his office, or that's what he informed me when he telephoned earlier and said he wouldn't be home for his supper, so I suggest we all go to there to speak to him.'

'Oh, but there's no need for you to have your evening disturbed, Mrs Dunster,' Solly said politely.

Her lips twisted into a secret smile. 'This might turn out to be the opportunity I've been praying for, and I'm not about to let it pass. Anyway, at this time of night the general public are not allowed into the town hall unless they've been specifically invited, so you'll need me to get

181

you past security. Wait for me in your vehicle while I get my coat and bag and you can follow me there.'

They all wondered what she had meant by her comment about an opportunity, but they knew better than to ask. The four of them went back out to the lorry to wait for her, and five minutes later she pulled out of the drive in a Morris Minor. Bemused at how she had managed to squash her large bulk inside the little car, they started the engine and followed her.

★　★　★

Inside Ernest's office, the councillor was sitting in his chair, while Lena, her skirt hitched up to show a good portion of her shapely thighs, was perched on the edge of his desk. She really should just collect her blackmail money and leave, but she couldn't resist goading him one last time about his gullibility over her plan to extort him.

Seductively licking her lips, she smirked at him as she gave her breasts a jiggle. 'Gonna miss these, ain't you, Ernest? Couldn't keep your eyes or your hands off them the minute we were alone, you dirty old man. Or the rest of me either.' She shuddered violently. 'Ugh. At least I haven't got to suffer you slobbering all over me any longer. Having sex with you was like having a fat walrus on top of me. And you've got bad breath.' Her tone changed to that of a mother scolding her errant young child. 'But next time you eye up your secretary, or any other woman come to that, I'd think twice about it if I was you, as you'll never know if they're setting you up like I did. Now I've got my future to be getting on with, with the man I love, and a wonderful future it is too, thanks to you, so hand over my money and I can get off.'

He was shaking with anger, knowing he had no choice but to part with an amount of money that would have substantially added to his retirement escape fund. What an idiot he had been not to see through her ploy. He had learned a valuable lesson, though. He'd only five years to go before he retired and collected his substantial golden handshake and pension, and this situation had made him realise how close he had come to losing all that, not to mention what his wife would have done to him had Lena blabbed.

Opening the top drawer of his desk, he took out a bulky envelope, which he looked at for several long moments, loath to be parting with it, before he resentfully held it out to Lena. She made to snatch it, but he pulled it back out of her reach and snarled, 'If I hear one word about how you got this money . . . '

'And just how *did* she get the money, Ernest?'

At the sound of the unexpected voice, and the very last one he wanted to hear considering the circumstances he was in, Ernest jumped up from his seat and stared frenziedly over at his wife. He had been so consumed with anger at having to part with such a large sum through his own stupidity that he hadn't heard her arrive.

Stuttering, he blustered, 'Err . . . err . . . hello, dear. What are you doing here?' It was only then he noticed that she wasn't alone. He looked bewilderedly at Gem, Solly and Tom behind her in the doorway, all strangers to him, but when his eyes settled on John Smith, they widened in alarm and he demanded, 'What's going on? Why have you brought these people here?'

Impatient to get to the bottom of the matter and back to the fair, Solly spoke up. 'It's about the — '

Gertrude Dunster interjected. 'Would you please allow me to deal with this business first, Mr Grundy. We will address your problem as soon as this is resolved.'

Gem too had heard what Mrs Dunster's husband was saying to the woman perched on his desk and knew that something else, apart from the business over the fairground money, was badly amiss here. She slapped a hand on Solly's arm, and when he looked down at her quizzically, she shot him a look that told him to accede to Mrs Dunster's request. Knowing his wife would have good reason to ask him to do this, he nodded his agreement.

Gertrude Dunster flashed him a look of gratitude before she turned and made her way across the spacious room. Lena, meanwhile, slid her backside off the desk and stood up, looking decidedly uncomfortable at the unexpected arrival of her boss's wife.

Arriving in front of the desk, Gertrude snapped, 'I will answer your question when you've answered mine, Ernest. So . . . why are you paying money to your secretary and warning her not to tell anyone how she came by it?' When

184

he didn't immediately reply, her deep baritone voice boomed, 'WELL, Ernest?'

Beads of sweat were visible on his forehead, starting to trickle down the sides of his face. He whipped a large handkerchief from his pocket and gave his face a wipe before venturing, 'Lena . . . Miss Richards . . . well, she asked me to loan her some money. I was telling her not to breathe a word in case others started asking too. You know what people are like. Do one person a favour and they all come calling. That's right, Miss Richards, isn't it?'

Lena vigorously nodded her head. 'Yes, absolutely, Mrs Dunster. Just a loan. Look, I'd best be off as my boyfriend is waiting for me.' She snatched the envelope out of Ernest's hand, but then, to her shock, Gertrude whipped it from hers.

'So how much is this loan, then? Not just a few pounds judging by the weight of this envelope.' She slit open the sealed flap with a fingernail and ran a thumb over the top of the notes. 'Without counting it, I'd estimate there's a good few hundred in here, maybe even a thousand. I didn't realise we were so rich that we could afford to lend such a huge sum, and anyway, shouldn't you have discussed it with me first, given that it's *our* savings?' She frowned thoughtfully. 'What does your secretary earn? Three . . . four pounds a week at the most? Take her a lifetime to pay this off, so you and me will be long dead before she does. Why are you lending her such a large amount?'

Face beetroot red and sweating profusely now,

Ernest blurted, 'Now look here, Gertrude — '

'I asked you a question, Ernest,' she barked. 'It's polite to answer.'

His red face paled alarmingly to an ashen grey and he stared blindly at his wife. It was apparent that he was fighting to find a plausible reason to justify what she had caught him doing.

Meanwhile, Lena too was looking decidedly worried. If she hadn't wasted time satisfying a malicious need within herself to goad Ernest for his stupidity, she'd have had the money safely in her handbag and been on her way to meet her fiancé by now. Well, she was certainly paying for that. Blackmail was a criminal offence, and if Ernest Dunster decided to tell his wife the truth, Lena could kiss goodbye to her wonderful future and instead look forward to a term in jail. Her honest, down-to-earth family would never forgive her for trapping her boss even though it was to fund a better life for herself, and should her fiancé find out she'd been having sex with another man, he would never forgive her either. Her thoughts whirled frantically. If she didn't think of a way out of this mess, she could lose everything. Then an idea struck. What if she got in first and told Mrs Dunster a version of the truth that would wipe out any accusations of wrongdoing on her part? She would lose the money, but at least her family and fiancé wouldn't disown her.

Without further ado she blurted, 'I'll tell you the truth, Mrs Dunster. Mr Dunster was forcing me to have sex with him; has been since I first became his secretary. He threatened that he'd have me sacked if I didn't, and make sure I never got a decent job again.'

Ernest erupted. 'She's lying, Gertrude. Nothing she is saying — '

Gertrude rounded on him. 'Shut up, Ernest. Let Miss Richards finish.'

Lena flashed a brief look at Ernest and he didn't miss the malicious glint in her eye as she went on. 'Well, today I'd finally had enough.' Wanting to be seen as the victim, she forced tears to her eyes and a false wobble into her voice. 'I couldn't stand the thought of him pawing me any more and having to do what he told me. I was frightened he'd ruin me and I told him that I was going to tell the police. He saw I meant what I said and this money is to shut me up.'

Despite his wife's warning to let Lena finish her side of the story, Ernest couldn't contain himself and leapt up to wag a fat finger at the girl. 'You . . . you . . . ' He looked at his wife. 'For God's sake, Gertrude, she's lying. None of this is true. I never laid a hand on her.'

'Yes, you did!' Lena cried. 'How else would I know about that horrible hairy black mole next to your belly button?'

Gertrude rounded on her husband. 'I told you to shut up, Ernest, and let the young woman finish. Carry on, Miss Richards,' she commanded her.

Lena lowered her head and spoke meekly. 'Well, Mrs Dunster, when Mr Dunster first offered me money to keep my mouth shut, I told him what he could do with it, but then I don't earn much, and me and my fiancé are saving to get married. With what we earn between us we'd be lucky to afford the rent on a flat in a slum area, so please don't think badly of me, but getting my hands on a sum like that could change my life. It was too much of a temptation. I convinced myself that I had earned it in a way. Besides, Mr Dunster told me that if I did go to the police they weren't going to take the word of a humble secretary again the leader of the council. And he's good friends with the chief constable.' She squeezed more fake tears out of her eyes. 'I don't expect you to believe me either, but it's the truth I'm telling you, honest it is. I'm so sorry you had to find out like this that Mr Dunster is not the lovely husband you think he is.'

She steeled herself, waiting for the outburst of verbal abuse from Gertrude Dunster in defence of her husband, and was shocked to the core when it never came. When she lifted her head, her shock escalated when she saw a look on the older woman's face that could only be described as triumphant.

Gertrude fixed steely eyes on her husband. 'I don't care whether Miss Richards' story is true or not. Whether she was willingly sleeping with you or you forced her makes no difference to me. Either way you were having sex with her.' She eyed him disgustedly. 'You portray yourself as an upright, solid citizen, above reproach, when you're nothing but a fornicating crook. It's common knowledge that you take bribes from local businessmen to push their plans through or see they're awarded lucrative contracts for council work. Do you know how humiliating it's been for me, catching the milkman and our daily woman whispering on our back doorstep about the rumours they've heard, or overhearing the wives of businessmen gossiping in the ladies' powder room about your underhand dealings?'

'How can you accuse me of such despicable things?' raged Ernest. 'This is all preposterous — '

'Save your lies for the jury. How else do you fund your private life? Visits to prostitutes don't come cheap.' She smiled. 'Yes, I know all about those. You should have been more careful where you hid your contact book. You were getting ready for a civic do one night and were having a fit as you couldn't find your best cufflinks. I had a quick rummage in the drawers of your tallboy just in case they were in there and I found a little black book hidden at the back of your underwear drawer. Rightly or wrongly, I couldn't resist having a look through it. What did I find but a list of ladies' names and telephone numbers. Other women might have been outraged at their husbands using prostitutes, but not me. I was just glad I didn't have to put up with you slobbering all over me any more. You thought you were being so clever using the excuse of my snoring to move out of our marital bed, but it saved me trying to find a reason to get you out.'

She flashed him another look of disgust before she went on. 'And while we're at it, I also know about your plan to move abroad when you retire, which I assume doesn't include you taking me along with you. How do I know about that? Well,

189

you can thank the estate agent who mistakenly sent a brochure to our house instead of your office just to give you a taste of the sort of overseas properties they sell, along with an accompanying letter saying that they'd be glad to help you purchase a suitable property in due course. I was shocked at first, I must admit, thinking you were planning for us to move abroad after you retired, but when I casually asked whether you would ever think about moving to a warmer climate, you said that as far as you were concerned England was your home and you'd no intention of ever leaving it. That's when I realised just what you were up to.'

The sound of Solly stifling a sneeze reminded Gertrude that she hadn't arrived alone. She eyed her husband suspiciously. 'Tell me something, Ernest, why did you feel the need to fleece these good people out of their hard-earned money? What you took from them is a trifling sum compared to what you must have stashed away from the bribes you've accepted over the years. And don't deny it. Mr Smith has already come clean over the fact that you paid him to pose as a council official to collect the fee.'

Ernest stared wild-eyed at her for several long moments before he slumped dejectedly in his chair, resting his elbows on his desk and cradling his head in his hands. All his hard work towards his new future had been for nothing. There was no point denying what he'd done to those fairground people Gertrude had brought with her, given that the man he'd hired to do the deed was present. 'I had no choice. Lena . . . Miss

Richards was demanding I pay her the blackmail money tonight or she'd go to the police with her trumped-up story, and I hadn't enough in cash — '

Gertrude cut in. 'So, you came up with an idea to save your own skin but gave no thought to whether these people could afford to lose that money.' She laughed sardonically. 'What a pity for you that Mr Smith went back to the fair tonight and was recognised.'

She took a deep breath and clasped her hands across her front. 'I've been no more than a housekeeper to you for years, and for all that time I've prayed that you'd find someone else you wanted to marry and divorce me so I could be free of you. When that didn't happen, I prayed that I might discover evidence to divorce you, but apart from the rumours I heard about your crooked dealings at the council, and the book with the prostitutes' names in, I couldn't find anything concrete that would stand up in court. But when these people came looking for you at our house earlier and told me why they wanted to see you, all my instincts told me that something suspicious was going on, so I decided to accompany them. How glad I am that I did. Walking into this situation . . . well, it's all I could ever have hoped for. Finally I have got what I've prayed for so long. You can be assured, Ernest, that I intend to get every last penny out of you that I can, and I don't give a damn if that leaves you with nothing.'

She turned to face Lena. 'As I told Ernest, I don't care whether you willingly slept with my husband or were coerced. What I want to know is if, in exchange for the money in the envelope, you'd be willing to stand up in court and swear that he was paying you to keep quiet about the fact that he was forcing you to have sex with him.'

On hearing this, Ernest was jerked out of his self-pitying stupor and cried out in anguish. 'If she does that, it will ruin me, Gertrude. I'll be sacked from my job. I won't get my pension or my golden handshake and I could go to prison. And what about you? You'll never hold your head up in this town again. Look, I'll give you your divorce . . . anything you want . . . '

'What I want is to see you pay for your crimes, and the years of misery you've caused me. I've lived with people gossiping and sniggering about you for years, so what's to come will be water off a duck's back to me. I shall be free to live my life without you in it, and that's all I care about. So, what's your answer, Miss Richards?'

Lena's mouth went dry as she looked blankly at Gertrude. This was the last thing she had expected. Her thoughts whirled. Lying to Mrs Dunster to excuse away the situation she had caught her in was one thing, but to stand up in court and lie under oath was another. But then if there was a thousand pounds at stake . . . Her parents would be horrified to learn that her boss had been abusing her, but they would stand by her nevertheless, and if she lost her fiancé through this then he wasn't the right one for her. She was already planning in her mind how she was going to spend the money when she answered. 'Yes, I will, Mrs Dunster.'

A loud groan of despair came from Ernest's direction.

'Then as soon as you've given a statement to the police, I will make sure you receive the cash.' Gertrude placed the bulky envelope safely in her own handbag.

From over by the doorway John Smith spoke up angrily. 'I've lost my friends and my girlfriend because they think I'm a thief, thanks to Mr Dunster, so anything I can do to help, you can count on me, Mrs Dunster.'

She looked gratefully over at him. 'Thank you. I will be taking you up on that offer. In return, if you bring your girlfriend and other friends to see me, I will explain to them that whatever jobs you did for my husband you did in all innocence.' She turned to Solly. 'Mr Grundy, I will personally make sure that your money is refunded to you. I will visit the bank tomorrow and have the cash brought to the fair. I can only apologise to you all for my husband's despicable behaviour.'

She cast a derisory glance at Ernest, who was still slumped despairingly behind his desk. 'Find somewhere else to live. I don't ever want to see you darken my doorway again. First thing tomorrow I will be speaking to my solicitor and also to the police, so you can expect a visit from them.' She smirked triumphantly. 'Once this starts to get around in a day or so, then it will be *you* who won't be able to hold your head up.'

With that, she spun on her heel and marched out, the rest following after her, leaving Ernest

Dunster rueing the day he decided to fleece the fair folk to save his own skin.

Outside in the street, Gertrude climbed into her little Morris Minor. Solly offered John Smith a lift home, but he declined, wanting to visit his girlfriend to tell her of Mrs Dunster's offer to help him clear his name. Gem told him that she felt sure that would put his relationship back on track, and to bring his girlfriend and friends back to the fair and seek her out and she would give him some free passes for the rides.

Gem, Solly and Tom walked silently over to the fairground lorry, all reeling from this turn of events. They had set out tonight to clear up the simple mystery of why they had paid the council twice for the fair's stay and to get the overpayment refunded; who could have foreseen that it would result in the downfall of the crooked leader of the council and freedom for his long-suffering wife.

★   ★   ★

Back at the fair, Jenny had managed to do a staff swap and was now helping Ren on her candy floss and confectionery stall, which was sited just inside the entrance. Ren was no fool and was intrigued to know why her friend was so keen to be her assistant tonight. So far, all her probing questions had reaped no believable results, but the tiny woman wasn't going to give up easily. Whilst serving customers, she said to Jenny, 'Come on, tell me why you really swapped jobs with Katie Bishop tonight. Keeping your patience with kids who keep changing their minds about what sweets to spend their pennies on can't compare to dealing with dishy blokes on the rides. And you seem to be very interested in the front entrance. Are you looking for someone to arrive? You might as well tell me, because I'm not going to give up until you do.'

Jenny tutted. 'What a nosy bugger I have for a friend.' Then she sighed resignedly. 'If it'll stop your nose from twitching, I'm waiting for my mum and dad. They had to scoot off quick on private business and I just want to know that they've got back safe and the business is sorted out. That'll be thruppence,' she said to a little girl as she handed her a quarter of aniseed balls in a paper cone twisted at the top and held out her hand for the money. She then went on to add a scoop of sugar and strawberry flavouring to the basin of the candy floss machine at the request of her next customer.

Ren was separating a toffee apple that had become stuck to another and said tartly, 'Couldn't you have told me that in the first place instead of letting me think there was a juicy reason behind it, like it was a man you were looking out for?' She glanced towards the entrance and saw a Grundy's lorry approaching. 'I think this is them now.'

Jenny spotted the lorry as crowds coming and going parted to allow it passage. Just before the entrance, it veered to the right to make its way to where all the fairground vehicles were parked. 'Yes, that's them.' She hurriedly pulled off her protective apron, which she balled up and thrust under the counter, saying, 'You can do without me for a bit.' This wasn't a question, but a statement. Then she ducked under the gap in the counter and hurried off, leaving Ren with no choice but to manage without her.

A smile spread over Ren's face as she watched her friend squeeze herself through a gap between two stalls, part of a row that edged the horseshoe-shaped fairground. Jenny had been economical with the truth. Yes, she might be anxious to see that her parents were back safely, but it was the passenger Ren had spotted sitting in the front of the vehicle with them that she suspected had brought the twinkle of excitement to Jenny's eyes. Jenny had told her that her interest in Tom had dissolved when she had seen Dulcie slap him at the party the other week. Obviously, something had happened meantime to change her mind. As soon as Jenny returned, Ren meant to find out what, and wouldn't relent until she had.

Solly, Gem and Tom were climbing out of the lorry when Jenny arrived. 'Did you manage to get your money back?' she asked breathlessly.

It was her mother who answered. 'Yes, thank goodness, but it's a long story.'

Before she could say any more, Jenny pretended to notice Tom for the first time and, pulling a concerned face, said to him, 'That cut on your nose needs disinfecting before it goes septic. Come to my van and I'll clean it up for you. I'll come and see you after, Mum, and you can tell me the whole story then.' She spun on her heel and headed off in the direction of her van, obviously expecting Tom to follow her.

Gem could tell that the young man was in a dilemma. She had told him that she would minister to the cut herself as soon as they got back, and it was obvious that he didn't want to hurt her feelings as she had offered first. She smiled at him. 'Go on, she won't bite. I need to get back to the skelter anyway. My sister-in-law will be desperate for a break by now.'

Tom was relieved that Gem had resolved the matter for him, but overriding that emotion was the shock he had received at hearing Jenny calling her Mum. Well, that scuppered any hope of him ever getting the chance to know her better. The daughter of the owners of the fair wouldn't spare a glance for Mr Fix-It's assistant, any more than she would have done for a gaff lad.

As she watched Tom hurry after Jenny, Gem smiled to herself. Her daughter might have thought she had disguised her feelings, but that look in her eyes when she had glanced at Tom had been unmistakable. So, she had a fancy for the young man. She could do a lot worse. He came across as a nice fellow, and Gem would have no objection should they get together. How did he feel about her daughter, though? Gem didn't see how any young man could find fault with Jenny. But then she was biased, wasn't she? She saw Jenny through the eyes of a loving mother. Tom would see her through the eyes of a man looking for the qualities that would make her a good wife and mother to his children. So she would just have to keep her fingers crossed that Tom liked what he saw in Jenny as much as she obviously did in him.

★　★　★

'OUCH!'

Jenny laughed. 'Oh, you baby. Ten-year-old Davie Cotting made less of a fuss when he broke his leg falling off the back of his dad's lorry last week. He shouldn't have been larking about on it at the time, but that's beside the point.'

Tom's hand was cupped protectively over his nose. 'Did you have to twist it so hard?' he moaned.

She wished she knew just what it was about this man that was making her heart race and her legs feel weak. 'I hardly touched it,' she admonished him. 'I had to give it a little wiggle just to check if it was broken or not. I watched Wally Wilson, the manager of the boxing booth, do that to one of our boxers after a battering. If the bone moves, it's broken. Yours didn't. Now,' she warned, 'it will sting when I put antiseptic on the cut.'

He wished she would hurry up and get this over with so he could make his escape, as he was having great difficulty stopping himself from taking her in his arms and kissing her. He was glad to hear his nose wasn't broken but not so pleased to hear that more pain was about to come his way. Fearfully eyeing the wad of cotton wool soaked in antiseptic that she was holding between her thumb and forefinger like it was a handful of sharp pins she was about to stab him in the nose with, he steeled himself. 'You do know what you're doing, don't you?'

She feigned insult. 'Excuse me, but you're looking at a girl guide who came top in her group in the first-aid badge exam.'

'Glad to know I've only got the best attending to me,' he quipped.

A few minutes later, she stood back and inspected her handiwork. 'That's as good as any professional job, if I say so myself.' She picked up a bottle of aspirin, unscrewed the top and shook out six tablets, which she handed to him. 'Take two now to help with the pain, and the others are for later if you need them.'

He took them from her, swallowed two with the help of the glass of water she passed him and put the other four in his pocket. 'Thank you. I appreciate what you've done. It's beginning to feel much better.' That was a lie, but he felt sure it would improve once the painkillers started to do their job. With no excuse to linger any longer, he got up from his chair. There was no point in staying anyway now that he knew his feelings for her were futile. 'I'd best get back to work.'

Jenny groaned inwardly. There hadn't been any opportunity during their time together to steer the conversation on to social matters in the hope that it would lead to him asking her out. He might be showing no interest in her, but all her instincts were telling her that he liked her, his eyes holding that spark of attraction when they settled on her. Had he not seen the same expression in her eyes? Other men would have chanced their luck by now. Unfortunately for her, Tom obviously wasn't the forward, conceited type who thought every woman fancied him. But then that only served to make her like him more. Her thoughts tumbled. Whenever she came across him, one or other of them was always with other members of the community, not the ideal situation for him to ask her out on a date. There was no telling how long it would be until another opportunity like this one arose, and she didn't want to wait any longer to find out what his lips would feel like on hers. Before she could stop herself, she blurted, 'So what do you get up to in your spare time?'

Tom wasn't sure where this was leading. 'Erm . . . well as you know, we don't get that much time to ourselves the hours we work. I will get the odd night off now I'm Gully's assistant, if I'm not needed to help on the rides or the stalls.'

Jenny had never been the one to do the instigating in getting a man to ask her out before, and she couldn't believe she was doing it now. 'So what will you do on those odd nights off you'll get?'

He pursed his lips. 'Read in my van, perhaps, or have a walk around the fair watching people enjoying themselves. Nothing more exciting than that.'

She inwardly quaked with nervousness, aware that she was either just about to make a huge fool of herself or hopefully have her wish granted. She took a deep breath, and before she could change her mind, which she knew she'd regret, said, 'The next time you get a night off, if you want company, let me know and I'll wangle the night off myself.' She smiled. 'Not that I'd ever abuse it, but being the boss's daughter does have its benefits.'

A shocked look clouded his face — was that horror at the idea of spending time alone with her? Humiliation flooded through her at the thought that she had made an idiot of herself after all, and she snapped tartly, 'I wasn't asking you to marry me, just offering my company if you wanted it, but I'd have to be blind not to see that the notion terrifies you. I need to get back to work, and I expect you have better things to be doing too.'

Tom was horrified. 'Oh . . . oh no, no,' he blustered. 'I don't think that at all. It's just that . . . ' His voice trailed off.

'Just that what?' she demanded.

He shuffled his feet uncomfortably. 'Well . . . you're the boss's daughter and I'm just a casual worker.'

She gawped at him, aghast. 'You think I'm a snob?'

He scraped an exasperated hand through his hair. He wasn't expressing himself very well. 'No, not at all,' he assured her.

'Well, what then?'

He hesitated for a moment before he responded. 'I thought I wasn't good enough for you.'

'Well you've judged me wrong,' she snapped. 'To me it's the person who matters, not how much money they have.'

Shame filled his face. 'Maybe I shouldn't have

assumed to know how someone thinks. I am sorry, truly I am.'

Her anger subsided and she smiled. 'I'll forgive you this time.'

His face lit up. 'Does that mean that your offer to accompany me out when I next have a free night still stands?'

Absolutely it did. Tom was different to any man she had met before. There was something special about him that singled him out from the crowd, and she was thrilled that she would get the chance to find out what that was. She was well aware that this relationship couldn't lead to anything permanent. Tom was a casual worker, and when the end of the season came — if he even stayed that long — he would move on like all the rest of them did. It would be nice to have a boyfriend for the summer, though. But she was getting ahead of herself. He might not want to see her again after the first date, nor she him.

Despite her eagerness for their date to happen, she didn't want him to know she was keen, so she slowly nodded her head and said matter-of-factly, 'Yes, why not.'

Despite his nose still throbbing, Tom almost skipped back to his van. Hopefully none of the other gaff lads would fall ill or suddenly up sticks and leave, which often happened for varying reasons, and he'd be free again tomorrow night. He was well aware that a serious relationship with Jenny would never happen. He was only a casual worker and, same as all the rest, he would have to move on at the end of the season. By that time, though, he would really need to be making decisions about his future. Did he extend his travels or return home to the life that awaited him there? But that was all in the future. Right now, he had a date with Jenny to look forward to, and that was what he would concentrate on.

★   ★   ★

As soon as Jenny returned to help Ren on her stall, the little woman accosted her. 'Did you get him to ask you out then?'

Jenny did a double-take. 'Eh? Get who to ask me out?'

'Oh, no games, Jenny,' Ren snapped. 'You might have been wanting to find out if your mam and dad got their business sorted out, but it was Tom you were more interested in. I saw your eyes light up when you spotted him sitting in the van. I might be lacking in the height department, but there's nothing wrong with my eyesight. So, what's happened to make you change your mind about him after seeing Dulcie wallop him at the party?'

'I bumped into him later that night and found out Dulcie slapped him because he refused to dance with her and it made her look a fool in front of her friends.' Her eyes glazed dreamily. 'There's something about him, Ren . . . oh, you know what I mean, like you saw in Donny. He's special, I know he is.' She sighed forlornly. 'But then any relationship with him can't go anywhere, can it, as come the end of the season he'll move on with the rest of the casuals while we go off to our winter lodgings.'

'Yeah, well, that's the downside of falling for a casual, but isn't it better to have loved and lost than never to have loved at all? Anyway, will you bloody well put me out of my misery and tell me whether he asked you out or not?'

Jenny smiled broadly. 'It was me that asked him.'

Ren gasped. 'You didn't! Oh, you hussy.'

'Well it was obvious he wasn't going to make the first move, although I could tell he wanted to. I just thought it was because he was shy and couldn't pluck up the courage, but I found out it was because he thought he wasn't good enough for me, me being the boss's daughter and him just a casual. I soon put him straight on that. Anyway, he's going to let me know the next time he gets a free night. Hope it's soon. I can't wait,' she said excitedly.

Ren pulled a face. 'Pity he's a casual or we could have had a double wedding.'

Jenny almost choked on the jelly baby she had popped in her mouth. 'God strewth, I've not even had a date with the man and you have me married off to him. Well you never know, one day that wedding might happen, but the groom isn't going to be Tom. Anyway, while Donny is still married to Suzie, marriage for you isn't even on the cards.'

Ren sighed heavily. 'Yeah, yer right. Before I go to sleep every night, I pray that she meets someone she wants to marry and gets in touch to ask Donny for a divorce. Eh, and will you stop eating my profits. You've eaten at least a pound of jelly babies tonight.'

Jenny scoffed. 'Hardly. I've had three at the most. Make that four,' she chuckled, popping another in her mouth.

'Well if you continue stuffing your face with sweets, you'll be that fat for your date with Tom you'll not be able to get into any of your clothes and you'll have to borrow one of Velda's enormous dresses.'

Jenny burst into hysterical laughter at the thought of Tom's face if she turned up in one of Velda's shapeless creations. 'Point taken.' Then a thought registered and she exclaimed, 'Oh, what the hell *am* I going to wear? You're going to have to help me decide, Ren. My relationship with Tom might only last a short while, but I still want to make him proud to be with me.'

Ren sighed. It looked like she was in for a marathon styling session tonight as soon as the fair closed. She'd better warn Donny not to expect her home until the early hours.

14

The crowd in the gallery were cheering, clapping and stamping their feet in appreciation of the exciting display they had just witnessed. Dicky should have been pleased with this response, but instead, seething anger was raging within him, because the thunderous show of approval wasn't primarily for him but for Julie. He was the leader of the daredevil riding team and it was his name the crowd should be chanting, not his wife's. Admittedly Julie had performed several impressive tricks with perfect precision, including a couple that she had only just mastered, but regardless, it was his persistence and bullying of her that had made her reach performance standard, so it should be him receiving all the accolades now. He wouldn't show his displeasure in public, but he would certainly be doing so to Julie in private as soon as they got back to their van.

Julie should have been elated as she took her bow, waving happily up at the crowd for their appreciation of her performance, but instead she was wishing vehemently that it was her husband they were showing their praise for. He was standing behind her, also waving and bowing at the crowd, but she could sense his inner fury oozing from him and knew that as soon as they were alone he would vent it upon her. She was dreading it.

She was still recovering from the pasting he had given her a couple of weeks ago. He'd come in in the early hours of the morning, drunk and in a foul mood, dragged her from her bed complaining that she should have waited up for him with food ready, then taken his wrath out on her for her lack of wifely duties, despite the fact that he had told her that he was having a few drinks and a game of cards with several of the booth boxers and not to wait up. The nasty tirade about women in general that had spouted from his mouth as he had carried out his beating had made her come to the conclusion after-wards, as she lay silently weeping in their bed with him snoring in a drunken stupor beside her, that there had never been any card game; only an assignation with a woman that must have gone sour in some way.

She could try and avoid him, go and visit Jenny or Ren on the pretext of having a catch-up and keep out of his way until the next show was due to start, or take a walk to the shops saying that she needed a pair of new nylons or toiletries, but that would only be delaying the inevitable and also giving Dicky more time for his mood to worsen as he brooded over what had come to fuel it in the first place.

The audience had all left to enjoy themselves on other rides and stalls and she was alongside Dicky, wheeling the display motorbikes to the repair van where they would be checked over and refuelled ready for the next show at four o'clock. The other two riders who had accompanied them in the show had already done that and gone off to enjoy their free time. As they dropped the bikes off, Speedy came to the back door of the large van decked out as a workshop, wiping his hands on an oily rag. Smears of grease covered his cheeks and forehead. He smiled at his visitors good-naturedly and addressed Dicky.

'Great show, boss.'

Dicky scowled at him and growled, 'When you're not riding, you're supposed to be maintaining the rest of the bikes, not sneaking off to watch the show.'

Julie flinched at her husband's nasty tone. She had to suffer his manner because she wasn't in a position to walk away from it, but the rest of the team didn't; they'd get jobs easily with another fair or speedway track, and he was lucky that none of them as yet had told him what to do with the job and gone off to find a boss who appreciated their loyalty and hard work. Speedy might still be wearing his congenial look, but his eyes told her a different story. He was inwardly fuming at the way Dicky had spoken to him — and in front of her, too. He didn't speak out, though, as he valued his job too much, but one day Dicky would go too far and Speedy wouldn't be able to hold his tongue.

'I only watched from the gallery for a couple of minutes during my break, as I wanted to know how the show was going. Won't happen again, boss.' Speedy seemed to be deliberating, as though he had something to tell Dicky and wasn't sure whether to speak up about it or not. Eventually he said, 'I've made some adjustments to one of the practice bikes. I've enlarged the sprocket to give better acceleration speed and improved the suspension to make it more stable when circling the wall. I've test-run it and I can really feel the difference, but you're the boss and I need your approval before I make these modifications to the performing bikes. I'll bring the practice bike through to the wall, shall I, for you to trial?'

Dicky lit a cigarette and blew a plume of smoke in the air before he said offhandedly, 'Another time.' He cast a sly look at Julie before adding, 'I've something I need to do.'

'Oh, well what about you then, Julie, if you've nothing else important on just now?'

Julie felt honoured that Speedy thought her capable enough to give her opinion on the improvements. 'No, I haven't, and I'd love to — '

Dicky cut across her, shouting at Speedy. 'What the fuck are you asking her to do that for? She might be a passable rider but she knows nothing about the workings of a bike. Wouldn't know a fuel pipe from a brake pipe.'

This was untrue. Julie might not be mechanic standard, but even before she had learned to ride she had picked up quite a lot about the workings of the bikes through watching Speedy and the others tinkering with them when she brought them mugs of tea. Sometimes when Dicky wasn't around she would stay and talk to the lads, feeling it would be wise to learn more about the bikes since she was putting her life at risk on them.

'Bring it to the wall, and I warn you these modifications better be good,' Dicky told

Speedy. He looked knowingly at Julie. 'You needn't think you're sloping off anywhere while I'm testing the bike. You're coming too, then we've unfinished business, haven't we?'

An icy shiver shot down her spine and she solemnly nodded.

Inside the wall, Dicky sat astride the practice bike that Speedy had wheeled in and was just about to rev it up when Jenny appeared. He impending date with Tom might have been all-consuming to her, but there had still been room for her conscience to prick her over the worrying matter of her friend's husband. Wise woman Velda had had no answer to offer her other than that this was a decision that only she could make, so after much soul-searching she had finally decided that the right thing to do was to tell Julie what she had witnessed and offer her support should she need it. To Jenny, friendship was based on truth and honesty, and she wasn't being a friend to Julie if she kept a secret of such magnitude from her.

She smiled over at her and called, 'Time for a cuppa and a catch-up before your next show, Julie?'

Before Julie could respond, Dicky called back. 'No, she can't. I need her to help me test out some new modifications I asked Speedy to do.'

Julie sighed inwardly. Dicky had had no hand in the modifications and had no right to claim them as his, but that was typical of him, declaring that he was responsible for any new idea a member of the team came up with to better their performance. Only moments ago he

210

had insulted her in front of Speedy, saying that she was inept when it came to the workings of a motorcycle, but now he was stating that she was expert enough to help him test the new modifications in order to stop her going off with her friend. She smiled apologetically at Jenny. 'Another time?'

Jenny smiled back. 'Yeah, sure.' She left reluctantly. She had wanted to get the problem dealt with and off her conscience, but it seemed she was going to bear the burden of it for a while longer.

Glaring at Julie standing alongside Speedy in the middle of the well of the wall as though it was her fault Jenny had disturbed them, Dicky snapped, 'Not expecting anyone else, are you? I want to get this over.'

Kick-starting the engine, he twisted the throttle until the bike was revving at its highest and let go of the brake. The wheels squealed as the machine hurtled forward up onto the sloping part of the wall. After only two circuits of the vertical sides, Julie could already tell that the bike had reached its speed much faster than normal and appeared more stable, and she was just about to tell Speedy what she thought when suddenly the back wheel abruptly stopped spinning. The engine stalled, and the bike seemed to hang in mid-air for a second before it plunged thirty feet into the basin below with a loud thud.

Stunned at what she had unexpectedly witnessed, and for the second time in only a few weeks, Julie momentarily froze before her wits returned and, letting out a shriek of horror, she ran over to the crumpled figure of her husband lying under the wreckage of the bike, parts lying scattered around him. Speedy, though, had reached him first and having heaved the remains of the wrecked bike off him was squatting down beside him checking for vital signs.

Julie stared down at him frenziedly, her thoughts rolling one way then another. How many times had she longed to be free of her husband's tyranny, but she had believed it would be on her own death or from some other miracle that came to part them. Never would she wish anyone to die in such a terrible way, even Dicky. 'He's all right, isn't he, Speedy?' she cried fervently. 'Please tell me he is.'

Speedy looked up at her. 'I can't find a pulse. Go and phone for an ambulance.' She seemed rooted to the spot, so he shouted at her. 'Now, Julie. Don't waste time stopping to tell anyone; you need to make that call as quickly as you can.'

His order brought her to her senses. 'Yes, yes, I'll be as quick as I can.' Kicking up her heels, she dashed out of the small door in the side of the wall and out of the fairground, ignoring fair folk she belted past who tried to stop her and ask her what was wrong. She didn't stop until she had reached the red telephone box on the corner of the street a quarter of a mile away from the fairground site.

Fifteen minutes later, she was back, to be greeted at the door by an ashen-faced Speedy.

A great fear washed through her as he laid a hand on her arm and said gravely, 'I'm so sorry,

Julie, there was nothing I could do.'

She gasped, horrified as the significance of his words sank in. 'You mean . . . Oh no, you can't mean he's dead?'

He nodded his head. 'I'm afraid so.'

Her eyes filled with confusion. 'But . . . but what caused the bike to stall like that? I mean, you'd just finished doing the modifications, and I know you'd have given it a thorough check before you allowed Dicky . . . any of us to ride it.'

'I don't know, Julie. I'm as stumped as you are. That bike was mechanically sound. It must have been rider error. Dicky must have taken his hand off the throttle . . . Look, there's no point us trying to guess; we'll have to wait for the police report.'

Julie stared blindly at him for several long moments before she whispered, 'I should be with him until the ambulance arrives.'

Word had obviously got around that something dreadful had happened inside the Wall of Death, as several worried-looking fair folk had arrived. One of them asked, 'What's up?'

Speedy told them there'd been an accident and that they were waiting for the ambulance to come. Mr Grundy ought to be informed, and would one of them find and tell him.

A volunteer shot off to do the deed as the clang of the ambulance bell sounded in the distance.

Whilst Speedy had been enlightening the fair folk about the accident, Julie had slipped back inside the Wall of Death. When the two

213

ambulance men arrived, they found her squatting dazed by Dicky's crumpled body. Whilst one turned his attention to Dicky, the other, a kindly middle-aged man, placed his arm around Julie and urged her to her feet. 'Is there anyone who'll make you a cuppa while we attend to your husband?'

'I will,' Jenny replied, running in and dashing over. As she led Julie gently outside, she said to Speedy, 'My dad's on his way. Nobby Jessop was fetching him when he bumped into me and told me there'd been an accident, so I came on ahead to see what I could do. I heard the police siren as I came in, so they'll be here too in a minute. I'll take Julie to my van and make her some sweet tea to help with the shock — when the police need to speak to her, they'll find her there. You're in shock too, Speedy, but are you all right to stay here to tell them what happened?'

He nodded.

'When they've finished with you, come and find me and I'll have tea or a stiff drink ready for you.'

Jenny was desperate to find out herself just what had happened, but that would have to wait. Dicky might be beyond help, but Julie wasn't. She eyed her friend worriedly. It was like she was frozen; as though her husband's death hadn't yet sunk in, but soon it would and then she was going to need all the support Jenny, Ren and the rest of the Grundy community could give her to help her through this dreadful time.

15

Julie still hadn't said a word all the way to the van and was sitting now like a puppet who had lost its strings, slumped on a chair at the kitchen table. She even hadn't replied when Jenny had offered her tea, coffee, water or a stiff drink, so she made her all four, but they remained untouched on the table in front of her.

Having lost her adoptive mother after a long illness, Jenny was well aware of the pain the death of a loved one brought, but then she had had time to prepare for the inevitable. To lose someone you loved without any warning, though, no time to say goodbye . . . She couldn't imagine the level of pain and devastation, the emotional turmoil that Julie was suffering now. From experience she knew that nothing anyone said or did would ease her pain — only time did that — so all she could do was let Julie know she was there for her as a shoulder to cry on, someone to talk to, get drunk with, while she travelled through her grief.

Pulling a chair to Julie's side, Jenny sat down and tried to coax her. 'Try and drink something, it will make you feel better.' When she still received no response, she picked up the cup of tea and placed it in Julie's hand, then put her own hand under Julie's and guided the cup to her lips, saying, 'Please, Julie, just a sip.' But still Julie didn't utter one word or move a muscle.

Resigned, Jenny put the cup back down in its saucer, then turned her head as she heard the door opening and saw her mother entering. Gem looked worried. She walked over and pulled out another chair parked under the table to sit next to her daughter. She whispered, 'Your dad is at the Wall of Death, so I thought I'd come and let you know what's going on and see how things are here. Not so good, going by the look of her. Anyway, the ambulance men have left.' The way she said this indicated to Jenny that they had taken Dicky's body with them, she presumed to the mortuary. 'The police are still questioning Speedy over how the accident happened. Poor Speedy is beside himself, as he did all the modifications to the bike that Dicky was testing out when the accident happened, but he's adamant they won't find anything wrong with it and that it was Dicky who caused the accident himself. We'll have to wait for the results of the police examination of the bike and see what they decide. Has Julie said anything about it?'

Jenny shook her head. 'She's not said a word. It's like she's not in, if you know what I mean.'

Under normal circumstances Gem would have laughed at her daughter's description of someone who was so consumed in their own thoughts that they were unaware of anything going on around them. 'She's in shock. Poor girl. I can't imagine what's she's going through, losing her husband so young and actually witnessing him die. They seemed such a happy couple.'

They might have appeared it, but Jenny knew that things weren't all they seemed behind closed doors in the Otterman household. The only consolation for Julie — not that she would ever know it — was that there was no reason now for Jenny to tell her that her husband had been cheating on her. She was suffering enough emotionally without bearing that on top.

'I can't get her to drink anything, Mum. Hot sweet tea is supposed to be good for shock, but she won't even take a sip.'

'She will when she's ready.'

'I expect Ren will be here any minute. The news of this must have reached her by now. She might have an idea of how to get Julie to start facing up to things.'

'Ren's not here, love. She came to tell me she was leaving Betty and Sadie in charge of her stall while she went to the wholesaler's, as her stocks were running low. She won't be back until six. I happened to pass her stall about an hour ago and saw Sadie and Betty sampling all the sweets. I'm just hoping they leave enough for customers until Ren gets back with the new stock.'

Jenny didn't comment as she herself had been doing likewise yesterday whilst helping Ren. 'Oh, I remember now. When I saw her last night she did tell me she was going to the wholesaler's today, and whilst she's got the chance she's buying Donny a present as it's his birthday next week.'

Gem laid a hand on her daughter's and gave it an affectionate squeeze. 'It's not surprising you forgot, given what's happened.' She sounded concerned when she asked, 'What about you, love? Julie is your friend, so this is bound to affect you too.'

Jenny sighed heavily. 'I'm okay, Mum. I just feel so sad for Julie. I wish I could wave a wand and magic her into the future, so she doesn't have to go through this.'

'Well you can't, dear. All you can do is be there for her. Now, I'd best make myself visible in the fairground, make sure everything is running smoothly there while your father is helping the police. The inspector asked me to tell you that he'll be along to speak to Julie after they've interviewed Speedy.'

Jenny turned her head to look at Julie, then turned back to her mother. 'Whether they'll get anything out of her at the moment . . . '

Gem look sadly at Julie, then kissed her daughter on her cheek before she got up. 'I'll pop back later to see how she is. I know she's in safe hands with you.'

The hot drinks were now stone cold and the cold drinks tepid, and still Julie was sitting slumped in the chair, her head hung low, chin almost touching her chest. She hadn't uttered one word. Jenny was becoming increasingly worried that the shock of her husband's death had affected her mentally. She was wondering if they should try and locate a local doctor who wasn't against giving medical aid to fair folk, as many were, when without warning Julie lifted her head and said matter-of-factly, 'I need to talk to the police. You have to take me to them. I need to tell them that I am responsible for

Dicky's death. It was me that killed him.'

Jenny gawped, astounded by this unexpected and shocking admission. 'You caused the accident?' she spluttered. 'But how? Oh my God, did you do something to the bike, Julie? Did you sabotage it?'

Julie looked aghast. 'What? Deliberately kill Dicky, you mean? No, no, of course I didn't. I wouldn't do such a thing.'

Jenny frowned, bemused. 'Well, how do you think you're responsible then?'

Julie heaved a deep breath. 'You know that saying, that if you wish for something enough times it comes true? Well it does, Jenny.' She hung her head and wrung her hands. 'I wished Dicky dead, you see, many times, after . . . after . . . '

Jenny laid a hand on her arm. 'It's difficult for you to say out loud what he did to you, but I know, so you don't have to say it.'

Julie gasped. 'You knew? But, how could you?'

'I saw him.'

Tears of distress and humiliation sprung to Julie's eyes. 'You saw him . . . you saw Dicky beating me?'

'Oh Julie, none of it was your fault. Thinking you're responsible for Dicky's death just because you wished it is silly and you know it. Either something was wrong with the bike or Dicky made a mistake while he was riding it, and the police will confirm this once they've done their investigation.'

Julie stared at her for several long moments before she whispered, 'Yes, I know I was being stupid. It's just that I feel so guilty for wishing him dead.'

'I'd be wishing my husband dead if he was doing to me what Dicky was doing to you. How long had he been hurting you, Julie?'

The grief-stricken woman's eyes glazed distantly. 'It started nearly as soon as we got married. If something didn't go his way, he'd take it out on me. I should have left him, but I'd no money and nowhere to go except back home, but my parents were against me marrying Dicky in the first place and I couldn't bear them going on and on about how I should have listened to them and this proving them right.' She heaved a miserable sigh. 'At first, he was always sorry when he beat me, begging me to forgive him and promising he'd never do it again, but then he changed and stopped apologising and instead insisted that it was something I'd done that had caused him to lose his temper. I won't blame you for thinking I was pathetic, but despite what he was doing to me, I still loved him, Jenny. Well, I loved the man I thought I had married, not the one that I actually did.'

'I wish you'd told me, Julie.'

'I couldn't. I couldn't bear the thought of anyone knowing and pitying me and thinking me weak for staying with him.' She looked at Jenny directly. 'You know about the other woman too, don't you?'

Jenny heaved a breath and spoke remorsefully. 'I was going to tell you what I'd seen straight away, but I knew how much it would hurt you so I agonised over it, but friendship is all about trust and honesty and that's what made me decide. That's why I called in at the wall earlier to ask you to have a coffee with me. I was going to tell you then.'

Julie laid a hand on her arm and looked at her encouragingly. Jenny continued.

'It was at Ren's no-reason party. I saw him acting suspiciously, and I could tell he was checking that you weren't watching him. Then he disappeared behind a van. My curiosity got the better of me and I followed him. I saw him meet a woman outside one of the empty caravans and they went inside together.'

Hands clasped in her lap, Julie said quietly, 'Obviously not for a cup of tea.'

'So, you already knew Dicky was cheating on you?'

'I suspected he was but I had no proof, he was too clever for that. I could have tackled him but he would only have denied it, and then he would have got in a fury because I was accusing him of cheating and that would have been an excuse for him to take his fists to me.' She smiled wanly at Jenny then. 'I can appreciate you agonising over telling me; I would have felt the same in your shoes.' A shudder shot through her and her face crumpled, miserable fat tears gushing down her face. 'I can't believe he's dead. Knowing what you do now, you'll be thinking I should be glad because he can't hurt me any more, but I will miss the nice side of him. You saw yourself how charming and funny he could be. I just wish I hadn't been there when the accident happened, because when I think of him now it will be him lying there with the wreck of the bike on top of him and wondering if he was still alive and in pain and if he knew he was going to die — '

Jenny interjected. 'Stop torturing yourself, Julie. At least he died doing something he loved.'

Julie sniffed back snot and wiped tears from her face with the back of her hand. 'Yes, he did. He told me that his dad took him to the local race track when he was about eight years old, and after that all he dreamed of being was a top speedway rider. He could never raise enough money to buy a proper racing bike, though, and he couldn't find a backer willing to take a chance on him either, so he had no choice but to abandon that dream and join a fair as a Wall of Death rider, which to him was the next best thing. His dream then was to own his own Wall of Death ride. Every spare penny we had went into saving towards it. I have no idea how much is in the cash box, as Dicky never told me and he kept it locked and the key on him, but hopefully there's enough to give him a decent funeral.

'I shouldn't speak ill of him now he's dead, but he craved the limelight; nothing made him happier than hearing the crowd cheer and clap in praise of his skills as a rider, and I know he'd have sooner been riding his favourite performing bike, going out in a blaze of glory in front of an audience instead of on an old practice bike with just me and . . . ' Her voice trailed off and she exclaimed, 'Oh!'

'What is it, Julie?' Jenny urged.

'What! Oh . . . er . . . You know when something flashes into your mind and then it immediately goes; that's what just happened to me.' She frowned in thought. 'It was to do with the practice bike he had the accident on, but what it was I — '

She was interrupted by a knock on the van door. Jenny said. 'That'll be the police. Are you up to talking to them?'

Julie nodded solemnly. 'I don't suppose I can tell them any different from what Speedy did, though.'

★ ★ ★

A while later, Jenny saw the two policemen to the door and returned to sit by Julie. She looked worriedly at her friend as she took her hand and rubbed it between hers. Reliving the events that had resulted in her husband's death had been a terrible ordeal for her, and she looked haggard and exhausted. A good sleep was what she needed, to be released from her pain for a few hours at least. That might prove a problem, though, with all that she had on her mind. Maybe Gem had a sleeping remedy she could give her; Jenny would ask her later. But in any case, Julie shouldn't be on her own at a time like this, and Jenny told her, 'You're staying with me tonight. No arguments. And you can stay as long as you want, that goes without saying.'

Julie smiled her appreciation at Jenny's offer, then a look of worry flooded her already strained face. 'I hope the new lead rider your father takes on treats the team better than Dicky did. None of them liked him and I can't say as I blame them. He treated them like they were his slaves and I never once heard him praise any of them. I'm surprised no one walked out while he was in charge; I can only assume it was because they're loyal to Grundy's.' She paused for a moment, her face clouding worriedly. 'Your grandfather, who first took me and Dicky on, was very open-minded and saw me as a draw to bring the crowds in — the first woman rider in the country — so I hope the new leader is of the same mind and gives me a slot in the shows. If he doesn't, I suppose I'll have no choice but to go home and get a job in an office, which is what I doing when I met Dicky.' She sighed heavily and wrung her hands together. 'I know I haven't been here for that long, but I shall miss Grundy's terribly. The community has made me feel such a part of it, which none of the other fair communities we worked for before we came here did, and I can't tell you how much I'll miss you and Ren.'

Jenny would miss Julie very much too if she left. She would speak to her father, see if he'd agree to finding a lead rider who was receptive to having a woman on his team. If that proved difficult, then surely he could offer Julie another job in the fair? It would be a come-down and a lot less money — not that it seemed she received any of her share of the takings, as from what she had said, Dicky had pocketed it all to save up to buy his own ride — but at least it would mean she wouldn't have to leave.

She decided not to tell Julie of her plan and build her hopes up only to have them dashed if it didn't work out the way she hoped. Instead she stressed to her, 'You don't need to be thinking about anything like that yet.' She picked up the glass of brandy that she had poured earlier and held it out to her, insisting, 'Get that down you, then I'm going to make you something to eat.' She saw the look on Julie's face and added, 'Just something light, and you'll eat it or I'll pin you down and force it into you. You need to keep your strength up.'

But the food had to be put on hold for a little while, as just then the door opened and Ren charged in. Seeing the two women sitting at the small kitchen table, she dashed straight over and threw her arms around Julie. 'I've just got back from my trip into town and heard the news. Julie, I'm so sorry, really I am.' She released her hold on her friend, pulled a chair out at the table and sat down, laying a hand on Julie's arm. 'If there's anything I can do, you just have to ask. You shouldn't be on your own at a time like this, so you're welcome to come and stay with me and Donny.'

'That's good of you, Ren, but it's already been agreed that she'll stay with me,' Jenny told her.

Ren replied matter-of-factly. 'Maybe that's best, as I don't expect you snore as loud as my Donny does. I'm sure that sometimes it's forceful enough to lift the roof off the van.'

'I don't snore at all,' Jenny snapped indignantly. 'Ladies don't snore; they just breathe heavily.'

Ren giggled. 'Oh well, that rules me out of being a lady then, as Donny has told me that when I've had a few too many bevies, my snoring could be mistaken for a trumpet voluntary. And you were *breathing heavily* enough for me and Donny to hear you as we walked past your van the other night, so if things do get serious with you and Tom, then you have to hope he's a heavy sleeper.' She laughed at the mortified look on Jenny's face. 'I'm having a joke with you. We never really heard you snoring as we passed your van.'

Julie started laughing too then. 'Oh, you two are so funny.'

Simultaneously they realised how thoughtless they had been to be happily bantering together, completely forgetting that their friend was in deep grief and shock from the terrible tragedy that she had suffered earlier, and they both looked at her, mortified at their unforgivable behaviour.

'Oh, you must think we're so disrespectful,' Jenny said. 'We're so sorry, aren't we, Ren, for — '

Julie cut in. 'For acting as you normally do. Teasing each other. I'm so glad you did, because for a couple of minutes I managed to forget what happened today. I don't want you to pussyfoot around me. I want you just to be yourselves. I've done nothing but cry since the accident, and it was so good to laugh. My grandmother used to say a good laugh was better than any medicine the doctor could give you, and she was right. Now please help me take my mind off it again for a while. I want to know what Ren meant when she said 'if things do get serious with you and Tom'. Is he the lad that talks so nicely who is

226

now Gully's assistant? Have you got a date with him, Jenny? Come on, tell me everything.'

Ren stayed for another hour before she needed to go and put away her new stock and relieve her two helpers on her stall. Before she left, Solly and Gem called in separately, Solly to pay his respects and offer what help he could to Julie, and Gem to check on Julie's welfare after the desolate state she had found her in earlier. Both were astounded to find her sharing a joke with Ren and Jenny. Some people would deem it inappropriate behaviour, considering her husband had met an untimely end only hours before, but both Solly and Gem were of the same mind as Jenny and Ren: that people dealt with grief in their own individual ways, and whichever way Julie felt was right for her, they were fully supportive.

As soon as Ren left, Jenny made it her business to ensure Julie ate something. The scrambled egg on toast along with another large glass of brandy she managed to coax Julie into consuming took away the need for a remedy to help her drop off, and by eight thirty she was tucked comfortably in Jenny's bed, sound asleep. Hopefully she would stay that way until the morning, able to better face what was in store for her after her rest. Praying that her dreams were pleasant ones, not nightmares about the accident, at ten thirty Jenny checked that her friend was still asleep, then slipped out to visit her parents.

Her father and two brothers were still working, along with the other men, securing the fair for the night, but her mother wasn't alone, as Velda and Ren were paying her a visit. Ren called on Velda every night to check if the older woman, whom she considered her second mother, needed water fetching or coal bringing in, and had come with her to Gem's caravan in order to find out the true facts of Dicky's death. Velda didn't trust that the gossip that had come to her via the community had not been embellished as it had passed from mouth to mouth.

As always very pleased to see her daughter, Gem ushered her to sit with the others at the table and poured her a mug of tea. The three women were very keen to hear how Julie was faring and gratified to learn she was in bed asleep, all sharing Jenny's belief that a good rest would help her in what faced her tomorrow. Jenny had just finished updating them when her father and two brothers arrived. They were all sombre, which wasn't surprising, as a death in the community always hit everyone hard. They congenially greeted the other women as they all took seats in the living room area to take off their working shoes. Gem meanwhile immediately got up and mashed a fresh pot of tea and took a cloth off a plate of cheese and pickle sandwiches she had prepared earlier for them.

As he gratefully accepted a mug of tea and took a sandwich off the plate Gem offered him, Solly told her, 'I won't be sorry to see the back of this day. I know they're only doing their job and we all want to find out what caused Dicky's accident, but police crawling all over the place is really bad for business. But that's not what's really got to me. You know we put a sign up on the Wall of Death explaining why it was closed, yet punters were still complaining that they'd come specially to see the show and couldn't understand why we didn't start up again once the police had finished their investigation, like the death of a showman was of no consequence.'

Robbie piped up through a mouthful of food. 'Yeah, well it's the same as when an actor dies on stage; people still expect the show to go on, don't they?'

Solly reached over and took a second sandwich. 'Any chance of another cuppa, love?' he asked Gem. He paused thoughtfully. 'I need to place an advert in the *World's Fair* for a replacement for Dicky so it will run in next week's edition. I've asked the team if they'll do their best to put the shows on until we get a new leader, and they all agreed . . . once I told them I'd make sure they were compensated accordingly. Now, about Julie . . . '

Jenny thought this was a good opportunity to ask her father if he would consider keeping Julie on as a team rider, or if not, find her another job in the fair. 'Yes, about her, Dad. Would you — '

Looking at her astounded, he interjected, 'Would I consider making her leader in her husband's place? You can't be serious. For a start, she's a woman.'

The four women at the kitchen table gawped at him in astonishment.

'You've shocked me, Solly,' Velda said disapprovingly. 'I believed you a man who had a great respect for women.'

He looked taken aback. 'I have.'

'As long as we keep to our place in the kitchen, eh, Dad,' Jenny snapped, appalled.

Flippantly Jimmy piped up. 'That's where you belong, ain't it?'

Gem erupted. 'I hope you're not serious, son.'

He was, but he saw the look on his mother's face, and those of the other three women, and muttered, 'No, no, 'course I wasn't.'

Gem turned on her husband. 'So, in your opinion, because Julie's a woman she isn't capable of leading the Wall of Death riding team?'

He shifted uncomfortably in his seat. 'Well, you can't put a woman in charge of a team of men. They'd run rings around her. And she only partnered Dicky anyway, so she's not skilled enough to be lead rider.'

'Have you watched her ride, Dad?' Jenny challenged him.

'I have,' said Robbie. 'She's really good.'

Solly said defensively, 'So have I, and admittedly she's not bad at all . . . ' He was about to add 'for a woman', but stopped himself in time.

Jenny snapped, 'Not bad! She's better than all the rest of the team put together and she would have proved that had her husband given her the chance, but he wouldn't because he was scared a woman would prove to be better than he was.'

Gem stood up, placed her hands on her hips and looked stolidly over at Solly. 'Am I understanding right that you don't think women are good enough to be in charge? So, Solomon Grundy, when you were sick with the flu for two weeks last year, who took over the running of the fair meantime? When you were under the weather at the start of the season because you didn't think you were up to following in your father's footsteps as ringmaster, who took over then? And when you have to go off to sort out fair business, who do you turn to to take your place while you're away? Who is in charge of all the fair's finances? Well, Solly? WELL?'

He shifted again in his seat, feeling he was facing a firing squad. He looked at his wife, then at each of the other three women in turn, and shuddered to see them all staring back at him questioningly. Finally he admitted, 'You, love.'

'And what am I, Solly?'

He blew out his cheeks and stared blankly over at her for several long minutes before mumbling, 'A woman.'

'And have you ever left me in charge and come back to find I haven't done a good job, as good as you would do?'

He reluctantly shook his head.

'And while I was keeping the fair running smoothly on all those occasions and far more besides over the years, my family didn't suffer. You had hot meals on the table, clean and ironed clothes to wear, and this van was kept spotless. Show me a man who would cope with all that without ending up in the mental home, and then you can tell me that a woman isn't capable of being in charge of a team of six motorbike riders — and without even giving her a try at it!'

Jenny piped up. 'And Julie would treat them far better than Dicky did. Apparently, he wasn't a nice boss and was always threatening them with the sack if they didn't do as he told them.'

Not wanting to be left out, Ren chipped in with, 'I manage my own stall by myself and I'm a woman.'

'So am I a woman, and I manage my own fortune-telling business.' Velda spoke up proudly, flashing a quick look at Gem with a twinkle of amusement in her eyes.

Solly held up his hands in mock surrender. 'Okay, okay, you've all made your point.' He heaved a sigh. 'I have to admit that I never liked Dicky Otterman myself. Even though I'm the boss, I always felt he thought I had no right to be calling on him to check things were okay or see if he needed any help with anything. I found him rather arrogant. Julie is a completely different kettle of fish. Very likeable.' He wanted to add that she was very attractive too, but thought better of it. His wife was annoyed enough with him already. 'I always got the impression that she was embarrassed by her husband's manner towards me.'

He paused, looking anxiously at each of the women in turn. What a quandary he was in. If he did agree to give Julie a trial as leader of the riding team, he would not be at all popular with the male members of the community, who would accuse him of giving their own women ideas that they too were capable of much more than running their homes and playing second fiddle to the men. But if he didn't agree to it, he risked the wrath of the women for openly showing that he perceived them as inferior to men. They would band together to formulate a plan of campaign against what they saw as a grave injustice to their sex, withdrawing their labour and possibly marital rights too, and whatever else they thought would win them the war. Without the support of the womenfolk, the fair would grind to a halt, and could even go under. 'Look, maybe I've been a bit hasty . . . ' he blustered.

Jenny jumped up from her seat and clapped her hands together excitedly. 'You'll give Julie a chance at the job of leader? She'll make a great boss, I know she will. You won't regret this, Dad. Oh, it will give her such a boost, as she was worried there wouldn't be a place for her in the team once the new leader started.'

'It's just a trial,' he hurriedly reminded her.

'Oh, she'll fly though it,' said Jenny confidently. 'Pity she's asleep, or you could go and tell her now, but you will first thing tomorrow, won't you?'

Solly nodded reluctantly.

Gem smiled at her husband as she sat back down at the table. 'I'm proud of you, Solly. It might turn out that Julie isn't up to the job, but at least you're giving her a chance to prove whether she is or not.'

The women exchanged glances that said that Solly had really had no choice if he didn't want a female uprising to deal with. The men had got to start moving with the times. Women were making inroads into positions in the workplace that previously only men had been allowed to occupy, and were proving themselves just as capable, and fairground women were not going to allow their menfolk to keep them stuck in the dark ages because of their antiquated attitudes.

16

Julie was so overwhelmed by Solly's proposal that it took him a while to convince her it wasn't just a trial for a place in the team he was offering her, but the chance to be in charge. But then she was still struggling to come to terms with the shocking demise of her husband less than a day ago, and wasn't completely compos mentis.

Out of respect for Dicky, he would have preferred to wait a while before appointing someone in his place, but Jenny had told him that Julie was worried there would be no job for her once the new leader started, and he felt she had enough to contend with without worrying about her future as well. He told her he wasn't expecting her to take up her new role until after the funeral, and in the meantime the rest of the team would manage the shows.

Despite his reservations about putting a woman in charge of a team of men, as the fair-minded man he was, he sincerely hoped she succeeded. After being cajoled into agreeing to her trial, he had given the matter much thought and had come to the conclusion that this could prove a fortuitous move on his part. Julie had proved a novelty as a rider and helped to swell the audience for the Wall of Death, so as leader she could expand it even more, especially by attracting more females to the shows. A woman succeeding in a man's world was more than a novelty; it was a phenomenon. How the team would react to having a young, attractive female as their leader remained to be seen, but Solly reminded himself that he was overall boss of the fair, and if they decided to walk before giving her a chance, then that was their choice.

As soon as Solly had left, Julie tackled Jenny with her concerns.

'I can't believe your father is giving me this chance. I'm determined to make sure he doesn't regret it. But what if the lads aren't happy with me as their leader?'

Jenny shrugged nonchalantly. 'Then they can leave and my dad will take on riders who will be.'

Julie heaved a worried sigh. 'But I've never been in charge before and have no idea how to go about it.'

'Well to start with, you definitely don't have the attitude that your husband had or they will all be walking. Think of how you'd like a boss to treat you and be like that. When I worked in an office before I came here, I had a couple of jobs where it was like working for the Gestapo. What the bosses said went and you didn't speak until you were spoken to. Woe betide if you were a minute late or started packing up your desk a second too early. But one office manager I had when I worked for a printing firm was wonderful.

'Miss Almond, her name was. She looked after her elder brother who was an invalid and that's why she never married. But she appreciated that those she was in charge of had brains in their heads and she used to encourage us to put forward any ideas we had for improving how we worked, and if she thought them good, she'd put them into practice. She used to have an awards ceremony at tea break on the last Friday of the month and give out prizes, bought out of her own pocket — just things like bath cubes and chocolates and bars of nice-smelling soap — for things like the typist who had typed the most letters, or the best timekeeper that month. She never told us off for laughing and chatting together as long as we did our work to her high standards. She believed a happy office was a productive one. I was sorry to leave that job, but that was when my adopted mum was very ill and needed looking after full time.'

Julie had been listening intently. 'That last boss you had is the type I want to be,' she said resolutely.

Jenny smiled at her. 'And you're going to be a great one, Julie. Just start as you mean to go on and don't take any nonsense from the lads. Remember you're the boss.'

Good advice. Julie just hoped she could put it into practice.

★   ★   ★

Having been given leave from work for a couple of days to support her friend through this dreadful time, something Julie was extremely grateful for, the next day Jenny accompanied her to a local funeral parlour to make arrangements for Dicky's funeral. After deliberation, Julie decided not to have him buried, as it seemed wrong to leave him in a town he had no associations with. Instead she opted for cremation, with the idea of scattering his ashes when she felt she'd found a suitable place. The ideal one would be the track at a motorcycle stadium, but she doubted any owner would give consent.

Unfortunately, the fair was due to leave for its next destination in three days' time: a small town called Brig-house, fifteen miles away from Huddersfield. So once the police released Dicky's body after they had finished their investigation into his death, the undertakers would keep it until the funeral, which Julie and the mourners would travel back for. Usually the whole community would have attended the funeral of one of their members, but due to the travelling involved — and after all, none of them could afford to lose a day's earnings — only Julie, Jenny, Ren, Gem and Solly together with the Wall of Death riders would be attending. There would be food and drink afterwards in a nearby pub.

Having lived for the last eight years with Dicky's unpredictable moods, never knowing when she would say or do something to ignite his temper, these last two days staying with the good-natured Jenny had been pure bliss for Julie. Regardless, she did not want to abuse her friendship or overstay her welcome, so reluctantly she returned to her own van.

There were reminders of Dicky everywhere, and it seemed insensitive to clear them out so soon after his death and make the van her own. But being reminded of him did not conjure up happy memories for her; rather, it brought back years of living in fear. If she wanted to put those miserable times behind her and build a new and happier future for herself, those reminders needed to go, whatever people thought of her. She would never forget Dicky, though. Despite his ways, she had loved him and there would always remain a piece of her heart that belonged to him, though if she ever met a man in the future that she felt was possible husband material, she would make sure that he possessed none of the bad character traits that Dicky had had.

She knew that Jenny would understand her need to cleanse the van of him so she could begin afresh, so she asked her for her help. Her friend was only too happy to oblige, and also assured Julie that in the meantime she could stay with her for as long as she needed. She had thoroughly enjoyed her company, and in fact had the van had two bedrooms she would have seriously considered asking Julie to share with her permanently.

★   ★   ★

It was two evenings later that Tom tapped on Jenny's van door.

The two women had spent a couple of hours that day making a start on disposing of Dicky's belongings, bagging them up to take to a local men's hostel, which they felt sure would be grateful for them. Dicky had dictated where the furniture was placed in the van, so they had rearranged it as much as possible in the small space in an effort to give it a different look. He hadn't liked ornaments or pictures, but had agreed to Julie displaying a photograph of the two of them on their wedding day, which stood in a silver frame on the mantel. After putting that away, they had stood and thought about what Julie could buy to make the van homely and to her taste rather than his. Pleased that they had made good progress towards giving Julie her fresh start, they had then gone over to Solly and Gem's to have dinner. They had not long returned to Jenny's van, and she was in her bedroom sorting out some washing she needed to do when the knock on the door came.

She called out to Julie in the living area, 'Will you answer that for me?'

Julie willingly obliged. She laughed when her caller looked surprised to see her and told him, 'It's all right. If it's Jenny you're after, you have got the right van. I'm just staying with her at the moment.'

As she was speaking, Tom realised who she was and said, 'I'm so sorry for your loss.' He felt awkward, as he hadn't had anything to do with her before now, just seen her around the place in her motorbike leathers.

Julie smiled her appreciation for his sentiment. 'I'll get Jenny for you,' she said.

Jenny's eyes lit excitedly when Julie went to tell her. She quickly checked her appearance in the mirror, wishing she didn't look such a mess in old clothes she had put on to help Julie clear out her van. She just hoped he didn't notice, as there was no time to make improvements.

Tom's eyes too lit when she appeared in the doorway. 'Hello, Jenny.' He looked decidedly nervous as he went on. 'I've . . . er . . . come to see if you're still interested in accompanying me out. I've finished my work with Mr Givens for the day and your father has told me that my services won't be required tonight, so I have it free.' He paused before quipping, 'I do wonder if he would have given me the night off had he known I was going to be asking his daughter to join me.'

Jenny's face was a mask of seriousness as she responded. 'If he did know, he'd be shadowing us armed with a shotgun to make sure you don't try anything funny.'

He looked aghast. 'Oh, I wouldn't dream of . . . ' Then he chuckled as he realised she was joking. 'So are you free tonight?' he asked hopefully.

'I'd really love to come out with you, Tom,' she began ruefully, 'but — '

She was cut short by a call from behind her. 'Have you got a minute, Jenny?'

She frowned, wondering what Julie could possibly want her for, and said to Tom, 'Sorry about this. I won't be a moment.'

Inside the living area, Julie grabbed her arm. 'Don't you dare turn down a date with him because of me,' she hissed. 'You've not left my side since Dicky's accident and I am really grateful, but to be honest, I could do with a few hours' break from you. So, you ask him what time he wants to meet and I'll help you get ready.'

Jenny smiled and gave her a hug. 'Thanks, Julie.'

'Now don't keep him waiting any longer or he'll think you're giving him the brush-off and leave.'

They arranged he would call for her at seven thirty and he told her he was happy to do whatever she wanted. On the drive to the site last Sunday, Jenny had noticed a pub about a mile away that had a garden by a river. He was most amenable to her suggestion to visit it.

Julie helped her pick out a navy-blue skirt with netting underskirt, and a short-sleeved boat-necked blue and white spotted blouse with a broad navy belt emphasising her trim waste. She wore black stilettos on her feet and styled her hair in a becoming French roll. Julie assured her that Tom couldn't fail to be proud to be seen out with her. His eyes told her that that was indeed true when she opened the door to him at the appointed time. Her eyes too lit up when she saw him looking casual but smart in a pair of light-coloured trousers and a white shirt under a blue crew-necked jumper.

They fell into step beside each other, talking easily about a range of subjects, from what they had done that day to their tastes in music, and that continued throughout their whole time together and didn't stop until Tom saw Jenny back to her van steps at just after eleven. Somewhere on the mile walk home, their hands had become joined together. Jenny was delighted when Tom asked her if she'd like to have another evening out soon. There was no hesitation when she told him she'd be pleased to.

Julie only had to look at Jenny's face when she entered the van to see that she had thoroughly enjoyed Tom's company and was very much looking forward to a repeat. She laid down the novel she had been reading and said knowingly, 'No need to ask if you had a good time; it's written all over your face that you did.'

Jenny plonked herself down on her small sofa and said dreamily, 'I've never known time to pass so quickly. He's a lovely man, Julie. Just . . . well, nothing like any man I've ever met before. We got on so well together. I can't wait to go out with him again.' She heaved a deep sigh and eyed her friend regretfully. 'I'm heading for trouble, I know I am. A broken heart is what's in store for me. But I couldn't stop myself if I wanted to. It's like when you know you're going to be sick if you eat too many sweets but you can't stop yourself because they're just too yummy.'

Julie reached over and placed a hand on her knee. 'Enjoy it while it lasts, Jenny. I don't like to think of you having a broken heart, but me and Ren will be there to help you.'

Just then there was a tap on the door and the little woman herself, dressed in her nightclothes, burst in to throw herself down next to Jenny on the sofa. 'I was watching out for you coming back and had to come over to find out how it went,' she blurted. 'Donny tried his hardest to persuade me to wait until tomorrow, but I knew I wouldn't sleep from wondering. Oh, I do hope it went well. So, come on, chapter and verse and nothing less.'

Julie laughed. 'You've arrived just in time, as she was just about to give me all the details.'

Jenny smiled, only too happy to oblige her two dear friends.

$$\star \quad \star \quad \star$$

Tom also knew he was heading for trouble. Jenny was unlike any other girl he had met before. Humour, intelligence and sincerity were just three of the traits he had learned she possessed, and they were more endearing her to him the longer he spent in her company. He already knew that when the time came for him to leave the fair, it would not be easy; that more than likely he would be nursing a broken heart. But he couldn't stop himself from seeing her. It was like she was a magnet and he a nail being drawn towards her. He would deal with what was in store for him when the season ended, but meantime he was going to savour every minute he could spend with Jenny.

$$\star \quad \star \quad \star$$

The police came to visit Julie the next day to inform her that their investigation into Dicky's death was now complete. The bike had been thoroughly examined by their experts and nothing was found that could have caused the engine to suddenly stall. Nothing had been found wrong with the wall either. Dicky's death was declared accidental due to rider error. His body would be released so his funeral could take place.

Although no one had expected the verdict to be anything other, they were still relieved to have it confirmed.

The funeral took place the following Wednesday, which Julie and the rest of those attended travelled back for, and once it was over, Julie felt it was time she got on with her future by taking up her new responsibilities. Despite Jenny and Ren's reassurances that she was more than capable of doing a job that previously had only been deemed suitable for a man, she was extremely nervous the first morning she faced the team as their boss. She knew it wasn't going to be easy proving her worth to them, gaining their respect, but she was determined to do it; to show Solly Grundy too that he had been right to give her this opportunity.

They were all awkward with her when she arrived that morning, especially Ray Jenkinson, a veteran rider in his early forties who wasn't at all happy that this chit of a girl was going to be ordering him about and was determined he was going to make life very difficult for her until Solly saw the error of his ways and brought a man in to lead them. Julie, though, took the wind from his sails by informing the team that she appreciated that they all knew their jobs and what was required of them, and as far as she was concerned, they would all work together to bring the best shows they could to the public. Any ideas they had to improve the shows would be most welcome, and if they had merit, she would implement them and make sure that the contributor got fair recognition. Every man, even Ray Jenkinson, went off to start work both surprised and impressed by their new leader's attitude and feeling it only fair they give her a chance.

17

Jimmy Grundy took after his father in many ways, inasmuch as he was a good-natured, very congenial young man, hard-working and loyal, but he'd also inherited traits of his Uncle Sonny, very aware of his good looks and the charm that had never failed to attract any woman he took a fancy to. Every girl that caught his eye, albeit aware of his Casanova reputation, regardless still believed she'd prove to be that special one who'd claim his heart, only to be left desolate when he tired of her as quickly as he had of his previous conquest. He was, however, about to learn a hard lesson that women were not always swayed by good looks, but by what lay beneath.

It was a Sunday afternoon in mid-June. A warm sun shone down from a bright blue sky, fluffy cotton-wool clouds lazily drifting across. The fair had just arrived in Keighley, a small town near Bradford. The move had not been without its share of problems but, as always, the community pulled together to ensure the fair was ready for opening at two o'clock the next day. Whilst the women were clearing up after the communal dinner and catching up on household chores, all the community men were employed seeing to any last-minute repairs to the rides and stalls.

21-year-old Jimmy was sitting with his younger brother Robbie on the steps of the carousel having a break from painting duties — touching up chips and cracks on the brightly painted horses and the rest of the ride. Placing a roll-up cigarette between his lips, he lit it, took a long draw and blew out a plume of smoke. 'I'm looking forward to the party tonight,' he said. 'Be fun having it in the clearing in the woods down the road. That way we can make as much noise as we like without the old folk bellowing at us to keep the noise down. Hopefully that new girl, Zena, will be coming.' A smile kinked his lips before he added meaningfully, 'She'll be glad if she does.'

Robbie had a splinter in his thumb and was trying to get it out with the blade of his penknife. So that was her name, he thought as he poked and prodded. Zena. It was a pretty name for a pretty woman. No, she was more than pretty; she was the most beautiful woman he had ever seen, and the minute he had clapped eyes on her perched on the back of her father's flat-bed lorry as they had driven into the living area just over a week ago to join the community, he was instantly smitten. He had seen her a couple of times since, helping out on her father's donkey derby stall, and his feelings for her had only heightened.

According to community gossip he'd over-heard, she was a nice girl too, very amenable and friendly. Apparently, she had been excited to learn that Grundy's had its own school and was keen to have the chance to learn to read and write proficiently, so she obviously had a brain in her head that she wanted to expand. He liked a girl who took an interest in more than film stars and the latest fashions, who he could have a decent conversation with. But he'd known from the start that hankering after a girl like her hoping she would fancy him was futile. She could attract any man she wanted — and now he knew that Jimmy was interested in her, his chances were even slimmer.

Other young men with an older brother better-looking and far more charismatic than they were themselves might have been insanely jealous and extremely resentful, but not Robbie. He loved his brother, admired and respected him, and he knew that Jimmy felt the same about him. Rivalry didn't exist between them, each happy with the other's successes and willing to do what was necessary to help bring those triumphs about. Their parents had seen to that, nipping any potential brotherly trouble in the bud right from them being babies together. Robbie knew that if he told Jimmy of his feelings for Zena, then without hesitation Jimmy would step aside and aid him in his aim to get a date with her. But he couldn't see the point, for even if Zena agreed to go out with him, all the time they were together he would know that really it was Jimmy she wanted to be with.

He stopped what he was doing and shook his head at Jimmy. 'No wonder you've got the reputation you have, looking at another woman when you're already got a girlfriend.'

Jimmy laughed. 'Not me, brother. I've been free and single since I ended it with Tessa the other night. She was starting to hint about engagement rings. Marriage ain't for me for a long time yet. I'm having too much fun finding the right girl. So, are you coming to the party?'

Robbie pulled a face. 'Everyone is paired off at the moment so I'm about the only one that'll be going who hasn't got anyone. I don't fancy playing gooseberry, so I might give it a miss.'

'I'll be on my own.'

'Not as soon as Zena arrives you won't.'

Just then two young women passed by arm in arm, giggling together. Spotting Jimmy, one of them stopped, flicked her hand through her long hair and said coyly, 'Hello, Jimmy. Going to the party tonight?'

He shrugged and replied nonchalantly, 'If nothing better comes up.'

Her eyes lit up. It was obvious that was just the news she'd been hoping to hear. 'Oh, I might see you there then.'

He shrugged. 'Yeah, yer might.' As the girls carried on their way, heads bent together giggling again, he said to Robbie, 'Nice to have a backup if Zena doesn't come. Anyway, why don't you get yourself a date for tonight? What about Joannie Hopgood? She's not got a boyfriend at the moment since that gaff lad she was seeing upped and left. I've seen her looking at you more than once. You don't have to marry her, it's just a date.'

Joannie was a nice enough girl and Robbie wouldn't say no to a date with her, but he didn't think it fair to take a girl out when he really wanted to be with someone else. He needed to get Zena out of his system first. He made his excuses. 'She's pretty friendly with Billy Cocker.

I saw her talking to him during the community dinner today.'

'They could have been talking about anything. Why don't you ask her anyway? Go on, go and do it now, while we're having a break.' Jimmy couldn't fail to see the look on Robbie's face. 'Are you afraid to for some reason?' he asked.

Robbie felt the red of embarrassment rush up his neck. 'No, no, it's not that,' he blustered.

'What then?'

He heaved a sigh. 'It's . . . well . . . I've only ever asked one girl out before and that didn't go well.'

Jimmy looked shocked. 'But you must have asked out more than one; you've had three girlfriends to my knowledge.'

'Four, actually, but it was them that asked me out. Two of them I didn't actually want to go out with but I didn't like to say no.'

Jimmy burst into fits of laugher and slapped him on the back. 'Oh Robbie, sometimes you're too nice for your own good.'

'It's not funny, Jimmy. It's all right for you, you've only got to look at a girl and she's putty in your hands. The one time I tried to ask someone out I got all flustered and ended up making a right fool of myself, and the girl and her friends took the mickey out of me for weeks after. I ain't going to risk that again.'

Jimmy smacked his hand down on Robbie's leg. 'Asking a girl out is easy. Just do as I say and you'll have them desperate for a date.'

Just then Jenny arrived. She eyed them both scathingly. 'This what you call working?' she scolded. 'If Dad catches you, I wouldn't like to be in your shoes.'

Jimmy replied defensively. 'He won't know, he's right over the other side of the fair working with Gully and Tom fixing a fault on the waltzer. Anyway, we're allowed a break, sis.'

'You only had your dinner break an hour ago.'

'Well it don't look to me like you're working either, strolling around the fairground like you are.'

She placed her hands on her hips. 'I've just helped wash and dry a mountain of pots after the community dinner and now I'm on my way to help Ren put some new bunting up around her stall, so put that in your pipe and smoke it. Anyway, you two look like you're plotting something. What are you up to?'

'Don't tell her, Jimmy, please,' Robbie pleaded with his brother. 'What I told you was private between me and you. Jenny'll think I'm a right idiot if you say anything.'

She looked hurt. 'I would never think you an idiot, Robbie. Why do you think I would?'

Jimmy nudged him in the ribs. 'You'd better tell her. She's like Mum, she won't give up until you do.' Before Robbie could respond, he turned to Jenny. 'Our little brother is shy when it comes to asking girls out, so I was offering to show him how it's done.'

'And you've had plenty of practice the amount of girls you go through,' Jenny said with a twinkle in her eye. 'I've only been on the scene less than a year and you've had six girlfriends — and that's just the ones I know about!'

He grinned. 'Blame Mum and Dad for having such a good-looking son.'

She tutted disapprovingly as she sat down between her brothers and challenged Jimmy, 'Well come on then, I'm interested in seeing how you charm a girl into going out with you.' She noticed a young woman approaching, heading over to the stalls edging the fairground. She was slim and very good-looking, with long blonde hair that she had protected by tying a colourful scarf pirate fashion around it. She was wearing fashionable fitted black pants and a baggy knitted jumper that covered her shapely backside, and was weighed down by a heavy holdall she was lugging. 'She's pretty, just your sort,' Jenny said. 'Show us how you'd go about getting a date with her.'

She was indeed Jimmy's sort, and unfortunately Robbie's too. It was Zena.

Whilst Robbie's heart sank at the prospect of watching the woman he had been fantasising over since the moment he had seen her agree to go out with this brother, Jimmy jumped up and swaggered over to waylay her, saying, 'A beautiful woman like you shouldn't be carrying such a heavy load. Here, I'll help you.'

He tried to take the bag from her, but she pulled it out of his reach. 'So, if I wasn't beautiful, in your opinion, then you'd just let me get on with it?'

He looked taken aback, used to women giving in immediately. 'Eh? Oh, no, course I wouldn't. I was just . . . er . . . just . . . '

She finished for him. 'Trying to chat me up.'

He shrugged sheepishly. 'Okay, you got me.' He shot her one of his practised winning smiles and said cockily. 'It's your lucky night tonight. After all the offers I've had, I've decided it's you I want to take to the party tonight. Eleven suit you? That should give you plenty of time to tart yourself up after the fair shuts. You just say where and I'll be there.'

She shook her head. 'No,' she said flatly. 'Thanks for asking, though.'

He looked absolutely flabbergasted. 'What! You're turning me down?'

She nodded. 'Yes. I've heard about your reputation and I don't intend becoming another notch on your bedpost, thank you very much.'

He glanced round at his audience. If he failed in the task that he had so blatantly bragged was a foregone conclusion, he was going to look a right idiot and would never live it down. 'Now listen,' he said. 'What you heard about me . . . well . . . yes, I've had a few girlfriends, but you're different — '

Zena cut in. 'I bet you tell all the girls that when you ask them out. But you're right, I am different. I don't fall for men's claptrap. Anyway, I'm sure you've a list of other women who'll jump at the chance to go to the party with you, and I wouldn't like to stand in their way.' She turned and smiled at Robbie sitting a few feet away, then returned her attention to Jimmy. 'Now if your brother asked me, that would be a different matter.'

Jimmy gawped, astounded. 'What, you'd sooner go to the party with Robbie?'

'Absolutely I would.'

He sulked. 'Why? What's he got that I haven't?'

'From what I've found out about him since I first saw him, he's got everything that I like in a man.'

Robbie was staring, stunned, not believing what he was hearing.

Jenny nudged him hard in the ribs and hissed urgently, 'Do you want to take her to the party, Robbie?'

'Want to! I'd give my eye teeth to, sis. She's everything I've ever dreamed of.'

'Then don't just sit there like a clot; go and make arrangements with her before she thinks you're not interested. She might not give you another chance.'

He didn't need another telling.

Jimmy was reeling. He didn't begrudge his brother his good fortune in having a girl like Zena set her sights on him, and he dearly hoped their date went well for Robbie's sake, but regardless, he felt so stupid and embarrassed in front of his sister and brother for failing to pull off what he had boasted was a done deal. He wished the ground would open and swallow him up.

He realised his sister had joined him and steeled himself for her ridicule. He was shocked when instead she patted his arm and said sympathetically, 'You can't win 'em all, Jimmy.'

He grunted, shuffling his feet uncomfortably. 'No, suppose not.' He just wanted to get away and nurse his humiliation. 'I need to fetch something from home,' he muttered, and without waiting for a reply, he hurried off towards the living van area.

Jenny smiled to herself as she watched him go. Until short of a year ago, she'd had no idea she had a brother, let alone two, but she had grown to love them both as much as she would have had she known them all her life, and she knew by the way they treated her that they felt the same. She didn't like to see either of them upset, but it didn't hurt for Jimmy to be knocked off his perch for once and realise that good looks weren't everything. Maybe in future he might not be so complacent. Knowing her brother, she felt sure that he would soon shrug off his hurt pride and be back acting like it had never happened.

She watched as Robbie and Zena headed off towards her father's stall. Robbie was now carrying the holdall and their heads were close together — making their arrangements for the evening, she assumed. They looked well suited and Jenny had a feeling that this was not going to be a one-night stand, though time would tell on that score.

★　★　★

Living in a community of eighty or so people did have its benefits. No one was ever lonely; there was always someone around to have a chat or share a triumph or trouble with. But when solitude was craved, which was what Jimmy wanted now — just a few minutes on his own to lock away his disgrace and return to his usual self — that could prove difficult. He did have a place in mind, though, and that was where he was heading now. Through sentimental reasons his father had been unable to decide what to do with his grandfather's living van, so for the time being, it was parked on the periphery of the living area. The empty van was just the place Jimmy needed to recover his equilibrium.

At the back of the van was a small straggle of trees, and leaning his tall, lithe frame against a trunk covered in crawling ivy, Jimmy rolled himself a cigarette. As he placed it in his mouth and lit it, his eyes settled on his grandfather's van and immediately memories of the old man flooded in. Big Sam had been seventy and riddled with arthritis when he had accidentally fallen from the top of the helter-skelter, but he had still been a commanding figure, parading around with the aid of a stick, surveying his domain, checking all was running smoothly and to his exacting standards. He'd had a gruff manner and stood no nonsense, even with his beloved grandchildren, but nevertheless he was much admired, respected and loved, and still keenly missed by all the community.

Looking down the side of the van now to the door, Jimmy could almost see his grandfather emerging from it, dressed smartly as usual in his trademark striped blazer, ready to face anything that came his way. He knew that Big Sam would have shown no outward sympathy about what had happened, but would have told him in his blunt, matter-of-fact way that it was his own conceitedness that had caused his humiliation, and to man up and learn from the situation. He smiled ruefully. That was just what he'd do. And next time he fancied a girl enough to ask her out, he wouldn't assume that he was making her dreams come true.

He realised he'd better get back to work. It wouldn't do for his father to find him absent; he'd demand an explanation, and the whole mortifying episode would quickly become the topic of conversation around the dinner table, not to mention the entire fairground. Taking a last draw from his cigarette, he threw it down and ground it out with the heel of his shoe. He was just about to set off when a movement over at the door of his grandfather's caravan caught his eye. He froze when he saw that a head had popped out and was furtively looking around, its features hidden by a wide-brimmed hat. His immediate thought was that someone was burgling his grandfather's van, and fury filled him.

'Oi, you!' he bellowed angrily as he straightened up and made to dash over to apprehend the robber.

At the sound of his voice, the head spun to look at him; then, before Jimmy could react, the intruder, wearing a belted mackintosh with the collar pulled up, bolted down the steps and raced off. Jimmy went to make chase, but found that the heel of his shoe had become entangled in the roots of the ivy and instead fell flat on his face. By the time he was on his feet again, he knew the intruder would be well on his way, so there was no point trying to pursue him. The man had appeared to be empty-handed, so hopefully he hadn't found anything in the van worth taking; nevertheless, Jimmy ventured inside to have a quick look around.

The van hadn't been lived in for many months, but his mother made sure it was kept clean. Jimmy was gratified to see that nothing seemed to have been touched. Hopefully he had disturbed the man before he'd had the chance to rifle around for anything of any value. None of the community ever locked their doors, but maybe his father would decide to keep this van locked in future in light of this incident.

18

Julie smiled to herself as she put away the breakfast dishes and gave the small kitchen table a wipe. She couldn't remember the last time she had felt so happy and contented. Even when she'd been living at home before she had met Dicky, life hadn't felt this good.

She might only have been in her job as lead rider for a matter of weeks, but already she felt that the men, even bigoted Ray Jenkinson, were impressed with her. They certainly seemed far happier going about their work than they had been when Dicky was in charge. The name of the ride had been changed so that it was no longer Dicky's Daredevils; after consultation with the team and a vote on the names they had put forward, it was now called Wheels of Death, implying to the audience that what they were about to see was death-defyingly dangerous.

The whole team had a say in the way the shows were run, what tricks were performed and by whom, and Julie had rotated the slots so they all had an equal share of riding time and took it in turns to open and close the show. She had successfully overseen the packing up and unpacking of the ride and their equipment twice now as the fair had relocated, and none of the members of the team had even showed a sign they were thinking of leaving. So, although never complacent, she believed she was proving to

Solly Grundy that he hadn't made a mistake in promoting her. She heard only praise for what she was doing when he regularly came to check how things were. She hoped that continued.

Her living van was now feeling more homely and she had added some feminine touches in the form of scatter cushions, with a couple of pictures from a second-hand shop breaking up the bareness of the walls. She hadn't yet got around to buying any ornaments, as concentrating all her efforts on her new job left little time for shopping except for essentials.

She had found time for friends, though. Since Dicky's death, she had grown particularly close to Jenny and Ren, and the three of them made a point of getting together as often as they could, even if it was just for a few minutes' catch-up. But the two women weren't the only ones Julie had grown close to. Speedy had been especially supportive after Dicky's death, playing a major part in getting the rest of the riding team to give her a fair chance of proving herself to them, and when he sensed she was floundering, never failing to do what he could to buck her up.

Speedy was as different in both looks and personality from Dicky as it was possible to be. He was fair against Dicky's darkness, five foot ten to his six foot one, slim-built where Dicky had been broad and muscular. Speedy was not at all aggressive or egotistical, but very easy-going and good-natured. When he had shyly asked Julie to accompany him for a drink at a local nightclub a few nights ago, she had found herself agreeing, despite worrying that it wouldn't look right her going out with a man so soon after her husband's death. She was far from ready for another relationship, but it was such a revelation being out with a man who was concerned only for her that she had thoroughly enjoyed herself. She knew how fond Speedy was of her, as he'd never kept that secret, and she knew that in time she could grow very fond of him.

It was around eleven o'clock in the morning and Julie was practising in the Wall of Death with a couple of lads from the team. She was sitting astride her practice bike when she noticed that the handlebars seemed a little stiff and needed attention. She told the others she was off to the maintenance van to deal with it, then she got off the bike and wheeled it outside and across the grass to where the large brown van was parked. She could see Speedy inside, standing with his hands on his hips, surveying a bike that was propped on a stand. Leaning her own bike against one of the open van doors, she walked up the ramp and went inside.

The van had been kitted out like a workshop on wheels. Down one side were shelves and drawers filled with all manner of tools, a number of spare parts and other paraphernalia required to keep the practice and performing bikes in peak condition. Along the other side was a workbench. Underneath it were brushes, cans of oil and tins of paint, while above it were shelves also filled with tools and equipment. Speedy was standing at the far end, by the wooden partition that separated the workshop from the driving cab. As always when working in the van, he was wearing oil-stained brown overalls.

Usually on seeing Julie his face would crease into a broad grin of pleasure but, to her surprise, on this occasion he didn't appear at all pleased to see her.

She frowned at him. 'You all right, Speedy?'

'Eh? Oh . . . er, yes . . . yes . . . I just wasn't expecting you. I thought you were practising in the wall with Jake and Ray.'

She laughed. 'Do we need to make an appointment to visit the van to make sure you're expecting us?'

He smiled at her quip. 'What can I do for you?'

She glanced at the bike on the stand and her face paled. 'Is that . . . is that the bike Dicky was riding when he . . . '

He put his hand on her arm and nodded. 'I haven't had a chance to look at it since the police returned it after their investigation. I was just seeing if it was repairable, or if not, what parts could be salvaged. Look, if you prefer, I'll just scrap it . . . '

Julie was looking at the bike, bemused. 'But that's not the one Dicky had his accident on.'

Speedy looked taken aback. 'Of course it is, Julie.' He tried to steer her away from the bike, saying, 'Come on, I'll take you back to your van and make you a cuppa. This is bound to be distressing for you.'

She agitatedly shook herself free and snapped, 'But that isn't the bike, Speedy. Something about it isn't right. I wish I could remember . . . '

'It is the bike, Julie,' he assured her. 'It's the same one the police took away and brought back. Maybe they did something to it during their investigation that makes it appear different; after all they would have had it apart looking for anything that could have caused the accident before they reassembled it.'

She stared again at the bike for several long moments before she conceded, 'Yes, that must be it. I'm sorry, Speedy. Seeing it has shaken me up a little. I think I will go back to my van for a cup of tea. Meantime, could you have a look at the handlebar on the bike I've left outside. It seems a bit stiff; might need a squirt of oil or something.'

'I'll have it done by the time you get back.'

A few minutes later, she was sitting at her small kitchen table, nursing a mug of sweet tea between her hands. She wished she could shake off the feeling that the bike in the maintenance van wasn't the same one that Dicky had had his fatal accident on, but she just couldn't, and neither could she pinpoint why she suspected that. By the time she finally gave up and admitted to herself that she was wrong and it was the same bike and in fact couldn't be any other, her tea had grown cold.

If she wanted to get some practice in this morning, she had no time to make and drink another cup. And Speedy would have resolved the problem with her handlebars by now. As she thought of that, something twigged in her brain. That was it. That was the difference between the bike in the maintenance van and the one that

Dicky had been riding when his accident had happened.

After the bike had stalled then plummeted to the ground, taking her husband with it, the shock had frozen her rigid and she had stood staring stupefied at his crumpled figure only feet away from her. The fall hadn't actually thrown him clear, and he was lying sideways on the wooden floor still astride the bike, hands gripping the handlebars. The one nearest the floor had bent on impact, and she could distinctly remember thinking that if the bent bar had damaged Dicky's hand, it could affect his grip, which would end his career as a stunt rider. That had all shot through her mind in the split second before her faculties had returned and the seriousness of what had just transpired had fully sunk in. She had dashed over then to aid Dicky, though by that time Speedy was pulling the bike off him to check for any vital signs whilst commanding her to go and call for an ambulance.

Both handlebars on the bike in the maintenance van were straight.

How could this be? The police wouldn't have straightened the bent handlebar; all they'd been interested in doing was examining the bike for faults that could have caused the accident. Speedy had only been surveying the bike to ascertain whether it was in a repairable state but he hadn't started work on it, so he hadn't straightened the handlebar either.

Julie frowned, perplexed. Whichever way she looked at it, the bike in the maintenance van was not the one Dicky had had his accident on. Then her thoughts began to churn. The only explanation she could come up with for this state of affairs was that the bike Dicky had had his accident on must have been swapped with an identical one that had also been damaged in a similar accident. But all the other practice bikes were accounted for. So where had this bike come from?

The two bikes could only have been swapped while she was away calling for an ambulance. When she had arrived back, word that a serious accident had happened inside the wall was only just getting around the rest of the community, and Speedy was still on his own with Dicky. So, the only person who could have swapped the bikes over was Speedy! Why would he do such a thing? He had obviously lied to her when she had first mentioned her doubts to him and then made a great effort to persuade her she was wrong. Her frown deepened. Speedy was such a nice man, honest and trustworthy, and would surely have a simple explanation for why he had swapped the bikes over then made her believe she was mistaken. She would go and see him, get this matter cleared up so she could put it to rest.

19

Jenny was jauntily making her way back to the living area to help her mother with the family midday meal. She had been up to her elbows in soap and water all morning, washing the seats on the sky planes, and after scrubbing off all the grime that had accumulated since they had last been cleaned just a week ago and scraping off globs of hardened chewing gum that people had stuck under their seats, she felt in need of a good wash herself before the fair opened at two. The dirty job of the morning, though, had not done anything to dampen the happy mood she was in. After work finished tonight, some of the younger community were getting together and she was going with Tom. They had enjoyed time with each other on several occasions now, and each time she had found her feelings for him growing. Although he hadn't said as much, she suspected just by the way he was with her that he felt likewise, or else he was a good actor. The terrible wrench that she knew was coming when the season ended was rapidly approaching, but she decided not to think that far ahead and instead just enjoy the time she spent with him. She would deal with the consequences when it happened, same as many women in the community had to do when they fell for a seasonal worker.

She was just passing the second-hand and

bric-a-brac stall when a small porcelain bowl with colourful flowers inside it caught her eye. It was such a pretty little ornament and her immediate thought was whether Julie would like it as a present to sit on her otherwise bare mantel. She picked it up and examined it. There was a tiny chip in one of the flowers, hardly noticeable unless you closely examined it, but the bowl also had a hairline crack running from the rim down one side to the base. The fair wasn't due to open for another hour and a half, but the couple that had owned the stall for the last fifty or so years were sitting behind it. Although they knew her, both were eyeing her suspiciously, as they did anyone who approached their stall, having over the years had their fair share of thefts.

Jabez Cobbler looked to be in his eighties, his gnarled face wizened, his eyes sunk into their sockets and his skin a dirty grey. Long grey hairs grew out of his ears and nose. His hands, crippled with arthritis, resembled claws, and one of them was resting on top of a wooden walking stick that he had a reputation for using as a weapon on anyone who tried to pocket an item without paying for it. He was dressed in a shabby 1930s-style pinstriped three-piece suit, a thick gold chain across its middle, a large pocket watch clipped at the end tucked into one of the pockets. A worn bowler hat perched on top of his grizzled grey hair and he had a clay pipe clamped between toothless gums.

Beside him, sitting legs wide apart, her skirt filling the gap between, was his wife of over fifty

268

years, dressed in a worn black full-length woollen dress edged around the neck and long sleeves with white lace, thick knitted stocking on her varicose-veined legs. She had a long black coat on top. Her white hair was scraped up into a bun on the top of her head, over with she wore a black felt hat with a bunch of plastic cherries pinned on one side. She too had a clay pipe clamped between her lips. Jenny always had trouble not laughing whenever she saw the couple, as they reminded her of caricatures of Dickens characters, or a joke salt-and-pepper set bought from the seaside as a cheap souvenir for a relative you didn't like.

The items on their stall were mostly bought for a pittance from local musty-smelling junk shops, lying discarded and forgotten for decades on shelves right at the back. Jabez Cobbler would bring them back to his van and fix them up, then place them for sale on his stall at a price far higher than he'd paid for them. The couple's two sons went out every day to prey on the poor or elderly of the town the fair was playing in, giving them a few pennies for items worth much more that then appeared on the stall for their real value.

Jenny wouldn't insult Julie by giving her an ornament that was so badly damaged, and replaced the bowl where she had found it. The Cobblers also did a trade in carnival glass, which Gem had a penchant for, owning quite a few cherished pieces, some gifted to her at Christmas and birthdays and some passed down from her mother-in-law, and it was a piece of carnival glass that now caught Jenny's eye. It was a large dessert bowl, in a marigold colour, with a fluted edge and engraved with grapevines and six smaller matching dishes. Jenny hated it on sight — she had no love for carnival glass — but knew her mother would be beside herself to own it. If it was affordable, she would buy it for Gem's birthday in a couple of months' time.

She pretended not to appear too keen when she asked Jabez, 'How much for the dessert set?'

He eyed her as though she was stupid and spoke through his pipe. 'Price is on the ticket.'

She hadn't seen that. Having a quick scan for it, she found it stuck underneath. The price was twenty-five shillings and ten pence. She thought that a bit pricey, so decided to haggle. 'How much will you take for it?'

'The price it says on the ticket.'

She pulled a face. 'It's a bit steep. It's not like it's Crown Derby; just an old piece of carnival glass. I'll give you seventeen bob for it,' she braved.

In his cracked voice he growled, 'Is that the price it says on the ticket?'

'No. It says twenty-five shillings and ten pence.'

'Then that's the price I'll tek for it.'

If she hadn't bought a new dress the other day to wear for the party tonight, she could just about have scraped the money together, but she didn't quite have enough. She really wanted the dessert set though, so she tried again. 'It's a present for my mum's birthday. Surely you'll take something off as I work here.' Her parents were both against any of the family using their status as the owners of the fair to gain favours for themselves from the rest of the community, so she didn't try that tack.

'Price is the price whoever you are.'

Miserly old bugger, she thought. She sighed in resignation. Seemed she was going to have to save up, and hopefully they wouldn't sell the set in the meantime.

She was about to continue her journey when a voice reached her ears. 'Hello, Jenny.'

She spun round and stared in surprise. 'Nurse Robertson. How good to see you. But . . . but what are you doing here?'

Gwendoline Robertson was 34 years old, plump, a mop of dark curly hair framing a homely-looking face. She wore a flower-patterned belted dress, a short box jacket in cream over the top and cream kid gloves on her hands. Her handbag was cream too. She was the district nurse who had visited daily during the last couple of months of Jenny's adoptive mother's life. Jenny would never have got through that terrible time without Gwen's support, and after her mother's death she had given her a brooch by way of a thank you — only costume jewellery, but her mother had treasured it as it has been bought for her by her husband on her twenty-fifth birthday. Gwen had been very touched by the gesture. Jenny hadn't seen her since the funeral, and here in the fairground, many miles from her home town, was the last place she expected to.

'I was looking for you,' Gwen told her. 'I

found out from your old neighbour that you'd found your birth family and were now travelling with them. Took me a while to discover where the fair was, but anyway . . . here I am.'

Jenny smiled warmly at her. 'It's lovely to see you, Gwen. But why would you go to all that trouble to find me?'

'I need to talk to you. Not here, though, somewhere private. You never know who's earwigging, do you, and I don't think you'll want anyone overhearing what I have to say to you.'

She frowned, puzzled, wondering what on earth Gwen could possibly have to say to her that she wouldn't want anyone else to hear. 'Er . . . well . . . we could go to my van.'

Inside the van, she offered her visitor a seat on the sofa and sat down opposite in the armchair. Desperate now to discover why Gwen was here, she said, 'I'll make you a cuppa, but first can you just tell me what it is you've come to see me about?'

Gwen was looking around. 'You've got it nice in here. It's bigger than I thought it was from the outside. It's still small, though. Don't you find it claustrophobic?'

'It was hard to adjust when I first came here, but I'm used to it now. I find it very cosy and couldn't imagine living in a house or flat again and being stuck in one place. It's fun travelling around to different towns I'd otherwise never get to visit. Anyway, you were going to tell me what you want to see me about?'

'I'm emigrating to Australia on the Ten Pound Pom government scheme. I go at the end of

August. They need qualified nurses. I've a sister that went out there five years ago, so I have family there to help me get settled.'

Why Gwen had gone to all the trouble to tell her that, Jenny couldn't fathom. They had become friends during her mother's illness, but not friendly enough to warrant her doing this. 'I'm really pleased for you. Sounds very exciting. I'm sure it will all go well.'

'Yes, well it might only cost ten quid to travel, but I still need other things, like a few new clothes, and of course money to put down on a place to live. I draw the line at living in a nurses' home and possibly sharing a room with another nurse at my age. Since my own parents died when I was twenty, I've been fending for myself, and a nurse's wage doesn't go that far, so saving hasn't been possible.'

Jenny was beginning to twig the reason for her visit. 'Oh, you've come to ask me for a loan?'

Gwen smiled. 'Not a loan, Jenny. A couple of grand would do nicely.'

Jenny's jaw dropped. '*Give* you two thousand pounds! Well apart from the fact that I'd have a job to raise two pounds at the moment, why on earth would I give you two grand?'

Gwen looked at her for several long moments before she said quietly, 'I know what you did, and if you don't pay me to keep quiet, then I'll go to the authorities about it.'

Jenny frowned. 'What I did? What do you mean?'

'I know that you killed your mother.'

She gawped, stupefied. 'I did no such thing!'

'Oh, you might not have put your hands around her neck, but what you did was tantamount to the same thing. Did you know that your mother asked me to help her die? It was about a month before the end. She was in so much pain, unbearable most of the time by then, and it was only going to get worse. As much as I sympathised with her, I'd taken an oath to nurse people, not help them die. She said she understood and never broached the subject with me again; just told me how extremely sorry she was to have put me in that position. I'd nursed quite a few patients in the latter days of the sort of terminal cancer your mother had, and I did really feel for her, as I knew she had a few weeks still to go before the end would finally come.

'A few nights later, I was back at the surgery checking my medical bag and getting it ready for the next morning when I found one of my bottles of morphine was missing. I'd been to a dozen or so patients that day, including your mother, and at every visit I'd left the bag for short periods of time while I went to wash my hands or get a drink for my patient. At most of those visits a relative or neighbour was present, and so any one of them could have taken it, but when it came down to it, I was responsible for all the medication I was carrying and would be in serious trouble for the loss, so although it was wrong of me, I told my boss that I had accidentally broken it. I did get a very serious reprimand, but thankfully my boss decided to take no further action against me as nothing like that had happened before.

'The next day, I arrived to see your mother only for you to tell me she had died in the night. I was surprised, as I wasn't expecting this for another few weeks at least, but the doctor didn't appear to show any concerns. Then I was busy helping to arrange for your mother to be laid out, so it wasn't until later that I remembered the missing morphine and realised that you must have taken it and given her an overdose. I couldn't do anything about it, though, as I'd already lied to my boss that I'd broken the bottle.

'I can't say as I blame you for doing what you did. Watching someone you love die is not easy. Day after day, week after week, seeing them in agony, slowly withering away . . . well, it's enough to break the most caring person. And during that time you have no life of your own, having to be at the beck and call of the person who is ill.' She paused for a moment to look stolidly at Jenny before she added, 'Did you reach the stage where you'd had enough, Jenny, and just wanted it all to stop so you could get on with your own life?'

Jenny jumped up from her seat. 'How dare you accuse me of killing my mother!' she cried. 'How dare you! I did no such thing and you can't prove I did. Any one of those other patients or their relatives could have taken that morphine, as you've already said. If anyone is in trouble, it's you for covering up the fact that you lost a bottle. Now get out. GET OUT, I said.'

Gwen didn't move a muscle. 'Yes, you're right,' she said evenly. 'If I went to the police with this I would be in trouble, not only with them but also with my superiors for lying over what happened. I could even get struck off. But how would your new family react to hearing that their long-lost daughter could be a murderer? Would they still want you around them? You've probably got a boyfriend, a pretty girl like you; if he was thinking of marrying you . . . well, he'd think twice once he learned you might have killed your mother.'

Jenny stared at her, horrified. 'You're that desperate you would blacken me in front of my family and wreck my future with them?'

Gwen nodded. 'Yes, I am. If there was any other way for me to get the sort of money I need to start my new life, then I would. It's not personal, Jenny. I like you. Obviously, I can't force you to give me the money, and if you don't, I will just have to manage without it, but before I leave here I will see your parents and tell them what I've told you, and that's a promise. Even if they say they believe you didn't take that morphine, there would always be that doubt in their minds that you just might have, and they will never completely trust you again. Can you bear that, living for the rest of your life knowing that every time any of your family look at you, at the back of their minds they will always be wondering . . . did she or didn't she? And if she did, could she do it to one of us?'

She paused for a moment before she added, 'Don't try and fob me off by saying you can't get your hands on such a sum. Your family own a fair; they must be loaded. Two grand will be petty cash to them. I don't care how you get it — that's your problem — but I want that money or else I will pay them a visit.'

Jenny's whole body sank in despair. If she didn't get Gwendoline the money, then her future with her real family — whom she had grown to love so much she couldn't imagine her life without them in it — would be ended. Her relationship with Tom was only temporary, but the thought of him thinking she had hastened her mother's death just so she could get on with her own life was unbearable to her.

That amount of money and probably more besides would be in the safe in her parents' van, as her father only went to the bank once a week. She knew where the key was kept; they had allowed her this knowledge by way of letting her know how much they trusted her. Later this afternoon the whole family would be working in the fair and the van would be empty. She could make it look like there'd been a robbery so no suspicion would fall on her. But would she be able to live with herself afterwards, knowing that she had stolen from her own family, regardless of the reason?

20

Julie waited until lunchtime, when she knew Speedy's habit was to sit on a stool in the maintenance van and read the newspaper while he ate a sandwich he had made before leaving for work earlier that morning, washed down with tea from a Thermos. They wouldn't be disturbed, as the rest of the team would either be in their own vans having a meal or paying a visit to a nearby café or pub.

His unwrapped sandwich on his knee, Speedy was just pouring tea from the flask into an enamel mug when she entered the van. He smiled at her as she clambered over discarded spare parts on the floor on her way over to join him.

'You didn't come back to pick your bike up after I'd seen to it for you. It just needed a bit of grease around the handlebar where it slotted into the frame.'

She perched her backside against the workbench. 'I borrowed one of the other ones to practise on. But thank you. I much appreciate you sorting it for me.' She took a deep breath before she continued. 'Look, Speedy, I know that the bike the police returned is not the one Dicky had his accident on. The handlebar on that one was bent. The bar on the bike the police returned wasn't. That can only mean that the bike Dicky had his accident on must have been swapped with the one the police took away.' She paused momentarily. 'The only person who could have done that was you, Speedy. Why on earth would you do such a thing? And you took a lot of trouble to convince me I was mistaken when I told you that I knew the bike the police returned wasn't the one Dicky was riding.'

He looked at her blankly for several long moments before he turned his head away and in silence continued pouring out his tea. The mug filled, he asked, 'Would you like a cup? I've enough for another left in the flask.'

She shook her head. 'No thanks. I just want answers to my questions.'

He screwed the lid back on the flask and put it down, then picked up the mug and took a sip of the hot liquid before cradling it between his hands and sighing heavily. 'If I hadn't swapped the bikes over, then the police would have found that the one Dicky was riding had been deliberately tampered with.'

Julie gawped at him, astounded, as she processed what he had told her. Eventually she said, 'You meddled with Dicky's bike? You . . . you meant to harm . . . to kill him? But why, Speedy, why?'

He took another sip of his tea before he responded. 'Yes, I meant to kill him. As payback for killing my brother. Like for like, Julie.'

She was utterly stupefied by his admission. She had expected a simple explanation for him swapping over the bikes, but not this, never this. So stunned was she, all she could do was listen to him as he went on.

'As if it wasn't bad enough how he treated us in the team, like we were imbeciles, it became even more important to me to deal with him after I found out how he was treating you, Julie. The bully just had to be stopped.' He eyed her sorrowfully. 'I knew he was abusing you. I saw him once through your van window. I'd come to ask his permission for something — well, you know we weren't allowed to do anything without his say-so for fear of the sack — and as I went to knock on the door I heard him having a go at you. He was accusing you of flirting with one of the customers who had asked for your autograph after a performance. He was obviously furious as the bloke hadn't asked for his. But him accusing you of flirting was a joke when he was playing around behind your back with any woman he could get his hands on.'

He noticed the look on her face. 'So that's not news to you. You knew about his cheating. That man didn't deserve you, he really didn't. Anyway, then I heard you cry out, so I went to the window and peeped though. He had you in an armlock and was punching you in the ribs. How I stopped myself from bursting in and attacking him myself I don't know. It was only down to the fact that I was no match for him and all it would have achieved was me getting the sack and losing the chance to avenge my brother.'

A lone tear fell from his eye; he hurriedly wiped it away with the back of his hand and spoke distractedly. 'I adored my brother. Kenny was four years older than me. He'd always been my hero. My father died from influenza when I was seven and my brother took his responsibilities as head of the household very seriously, even though he was only eleven years old. My mother didn't earn that much from her job in the hospital laundry, but Kenny did anything he could to help her out. His odd jobs kept us off the streets.

'He'd always been into motorbikes, right from a young age, when our Uncle Brian used to take him for a spin on his old Norton sixteen horsepower. It was pre-war, but my uncle kept it in immaculate condition. From the first time Uncle Brian took him out on it, Kenny was smitten, and from then on, any spare time he had, he was always around Brian's house helping him look after it. He got so good he only had to listen to the engine noise to know if it was running at peak performance or if something was off, and he'd know just how to put it right.

'When Kenny was sixteen, my uncle taught him to ride. After that, all he lived for was being allowed to take the bike out for a spin. Idolising my brother like I did, anything he did I wanted to do, and he was so chuffed when I asked him to teach me motorbike maintenance. Seemed I had as much of a gift for it as he did, and soon local riders were bringing their bikes to our house for us to fix. Of course, we were cheaper than a garage, and the money we earned really helped my mother.

'I was about fifteen at the time, so Kenny would have been nineteen, when one night one of his mates from work asked him if he'd go to the speedway with him as his friend had let him down. Kenny couldn't afford it, but the mate said he'd stand him the ticket sooner than go on his own. It was a special meeting, with famous riders from all around the country. Kenny was full of it when he came home. From then on, all he craved was to be a speedway rider. It became an obsession. Good money could be made, the sort that could change our lives, allow our mother to cut back on her workload. But it wasn't just the money with Kenny; he was determined he was going to be up there with the best in the country, if not *the* best. He would have done it, knowing my brother, had not . . . ' he paused for a moment, and it was obvious that it was very difficult for him to utter the name, '*Dicky Otterman* made sure he didn't.

'But anyway, from then on, Kenny worked all hours fixing bikes for locals. I often woke up in the middle of the night to find him in the yard using the light from an oil lamp to see by. Some of the money he earned he kept to buy parts with, until he had all he needed to build his own bike. The day he put the final touches of paint to it and it was ready for its trial run was one that I will never forget. Four years it had taken him to build that bike, and I've never seen anyone so proud of what he'd managed to do. He then spent as much time as he could practising on it on a large piece of waste ground near where we lived until he felt he was good enough to apply to the manager of the speedway track for a place in the team. He was lucky, as there was a place going at the time, but he was up against it as a dozen or so others had applied for it too. Dicky Otterman was one of them.

'The manager held elimination races, two riders against each other, until eventually the two left were Kenny and Dicky and the winner of that race would get the place on the team. My brother was by far the better rider and he knew that, but he wasn't the big-headed sort by any means and tackled this like it was the ride of his life. I'd gone with him to the trials to cheer him on. When the final race came, I so wanted to go and wish him good luck, so although I wasn't allowed in the back, I sneaked in to try and find him. I searched everywhere and eventually found myself in a small lean-to-like structure behind the main building. There were a few bikes in there, and one of them was Kenny's. There was a man with his back to me squatted down at the side of it. He seemed to be doing something to the front wheel. He was dressed in riding gear like Kenny wore, so I obviously thought it was him.

'When I called out his name, the man jumped up and spun around to face me and I realised that it wasn't my brother but the bloke he was racing against — Dicky Otterman. When I asked him what he was doing with my brother's bike, he told me he wasn't doing anything, just admiring it, wishing his own bike was as good. You knew Dicky better than anyone, Julie; he had a way with him that made people believe everything he was saying. Knowing how proud Kenny was of that bike, I was so chuffed to hear another rider praising it and I couldn't wait to tell him, but at the time I knew the final race would be starting very soon so all I had on my mind was to find him so I could wish him the best of luck. I asked Dicky if he knew where Kenny was and he told me he was around somewhere but as spectators weren't allowed in the back he'd pass the message on for me and I'd better get back outside as I didn't want to do anything that might cause my brother to be disqualified, did I. That was the last thing I wanted, so I scarpered off quick.

'The race started very shortly after that. At first it was neck and neck, but then soon my brother was ahead and it was obvious that Dicky didn't stand a chance of catching him. I was jumping up and down in excitement, screaming out Kenny's name, and then there was just two laps to go and Dicky was yards behind Kenny by now and it would have taken a miracle for him to overtake him. Then it all seemed to happen in slow motion. Kenny was heading down a straight towards a bend when the front wheel started to wobble and I could see he was having trouble steering the bike, then the front wheel flew off and he came flying off too, tumbling across the track to crash against one of the fencing posts. I just froze and my mind went blank. I could see the track officials and the other spectators rushing over to him, but I couldn't move. It was like I was at the pictures watching a film. Then what had happened suddenly hit me and I vaulted the fence and raced over to my brother, screaming out his name. Just as I got there, some of the other spectators who had arrived before me stopped me and held me back. It was then that I knew Kenny was dead.

'What happened after that is all a daze. I can't tell you how devastated I was that my brother, my hero, was gone. The police came, and after they'd done their investigation, they put it down to an accident, saying that the wheel bolts either hadn't been tightened properly or had worked loose during the ride and caused the wheel to come off. I couldn't understand it. My brother had checked the bike over meticulously before we set off for the trial races — I'd helped him, in fact — and I knew he'd have checked it after every elimination race too. But who was I to argue with the police mechanics?

'My mother was inconsolable. It was bad enough when she lost my dad, but now her eldest son . . . well, it was like her life's blood had just drained out of her. After Kenny's death, it was me now that was head of the house and I needed to step up to help my mother. Thankfully, through Kenny's teaching me mechanics when I left school, I'd managed to land myself an apprenticeship with a local garage and had just a few months left before I received my indenture papers. Money was very tight, but we managed.

'About six months after Kenny died, the owner of the garage where I worked told me he wanted me to strip down a motorbike a client wanted rebuilding. It was a 1940s Triumph 3T 350cc, a beautiful bike I'd have given my right arm to own. I was unbolting one of the wheels when suddenly the memory came back of me going to look for Kenny before the last elimination race on the day he died and finding Dicky Otterman squatting down beside it. That was when I remembered that when he'd jumped up and spun round, he'd slipped something into his pocket, and I realised it must have been a spanner. He wasn't admiring Kenny's bike; he wouldn't have needed to be squatting down by the front wheel to do that. He was squatting by the wheel because he was loosening the bolts. Whether he meant to kill Kenny or just scupper his chances of winning . . . '

He paused and swallowed his now tepid tea before he went on. 'So, the very next night, as soon as I'd finished work, I went to the speedway track to accuse Dicky of tampering with my brother's bike and tell him I was going to the police. When I asked for him in the office, pretending to be a friend, I was told that he no longer worked at the track and they had no idea where he was. They had heard through the grapevine that he had worked at several tracks since but hadn't lasted long, and there was a rumour that he had left speedway riding to join a travelling fair as a stunt rider on the Wall of Death.

'This news was a blow to me as it meant Dicky could be anywhere in the country. I had realised by then that going to the police was a waste of time as I had no physical evidence of what he'd done to Kenny's bike, so it would be my word against his, but I was determined I was going to find him and make him pay somehow for what he'd done to my brother and the

286

suffering he'd caused my mother and me. I had to put it on hold, though, as I couldn't leave my mother. As I mentioned, she took my brother's death badly, and by this time she was hardly able to drag herself out of bed. She started to miss shifts at work so of course she was eventually sacked, which meant the burden of providing for us fell on me. Money was even tighter then, just my wage keeping us both and what I could earn on the side fixing motorbikes for the locals, but we got by.

'Three years later, I discovered my mother's body one morning when I took her a cup of tea before going off to work. She was hardly forty-five yet she looked years older, just a shadow of her once happy self. She'd taken an overdose of sleeping tablets. She'd left me a note telling me how much she loved me but saying that no matter how hard she tried, she just couldn't get over Kenny's death and life didn't have any meaning for her any longer. Dicky Otterman might not have personally killed her, but he was responsible all the same. I made a vow then to avenge both her and my brother's deaths. I wanted no less than like for like. Until Dicky Otterman was dead and was no longer around to hurt anyone else to get his own way, then I wouldn't rest.

'Cut a long story short, it took me several weeks and hundreds of miles of travelling and I lost count of the number of fairs I visited, but finally I met someone who knew where Otterman was working, at a fair called Grundy's. My plan was that I would get a job with them as a casual worker so that I'd be able to keep a close eye on him and work out how I was going to get my revenge. I wasn't worried about Dicky recognising me when I did finally come face to face with him, as he'd only seen me for a couple of minutes when I'd caught him by Kenny's bike, and since then I'd grown from a skinny nineteen-year-old lad into a man.

'I couldn't believe my luck when I approached Sam Grundy for a job to hear he'd a vacancy for a mechanic and also a stunt rider if I was willing to learn — which of course I was — on the Wall of Death team under the very man I was seeking revenge on.'

He eyed Julie searchingly for a moment before he said, 'You'll have realised by now that it was me that caused the other two accidents Dicky had before his fatal one. I thought it'd be ironic justice if he met his end the same way as he had brought about my brother's, only I didn't quite loosen the bolt on the front wheel enough for it to come off the first time, so he was able to steer it further down the wall before he fell off and only dislocated his shoulder. It was me that greased the wall too, only miraculously he again escaped with just cuts and bruises. The man seemed to have nine lives. But the third time I was determined to succeed.

'I knew that putting sand in the petrol tank would cause the engine to suddenly seize, but I also knew that the police would soon discover it during their investigation and realise it was no accident, and that as it was me who took care of most of the maintenance, the finger would soon be pointed, especially if they checked my background and discovered what had happened to Kenny. So, knowing Dicky always used the same practice bike, I decided to make a replica, without sand in the tank, of course, which I could use as a replacement for the one Dicky had been riding. All I had to do was make sure that only I was present at the time, so that I could swap the bikes over unobserved. I planned to hide the bike Dicky had been riding under a tarpaulin on the back of my trailer, and get rid of it at the first opportunity. I was sure this plan couldn't fail, and I would have got away with it too if you hadn't happened to notice the bent handlebar.'

He paused for a moment and looked at her apologetically. 'I'm so very sorry that you witnessed what you did, but it wasn't often that all the other lads were off elsewhere at the same time, so it was either do it then or wait God knows how long for another opportunity to arise.'

He wrung his hands, shaking his head sadly. 'I thought that finally avenging my brother and mother would bring me some kind of peace, but it hasn't. It hasn't lessened the pain of missing them one iota. I will go on missing them until the day I die myself.' He raised his head and spoke with conviction. 'But I'm not sorry that arrogant swine is no longer around to blight any more lives. I don't suppose many people who knew him shed a tear when word got around of his death. The rest of the team have never been happier since he's been gone. I even heard that miserable bugger Ray whistling a merry tune the other day as he was cleaning his bike ready for a performance. I've never seen you as happy as you are either, and if you're honest you'll admit that.' He heaved a deep sigh and looked steadily at her for several long moments before he said. 'Well, now you know I purposely killed your husband. No matter how much he deserved it, I can't expect you to turn a blind eye. I'll turn myself in to the police.'

Julie was utterly overwhelmed by Speedy's story and in turmoil as to how she actually felt about it. Part of her condemned him for deliberately planning to take someone's life, no matter what the reason; the other part sympathised with him. Wouldn't she herself feel like murdering the person who had purposely brought about the death of her beloved brother and been responsible for the early demise of her mother? Dicky must have realised the damage that could be caused by loosening the front wheel of Kenny's bike, given the speed it would be travelling. Knowing him as well as she had come to over their eight years together, she didn't doubt that he was capable of doing what Speedy was accusing him of. But then was it right that a man who had deliberately planned to murder another be let off scot free? If Speedy told the police what he had done, he'd go to prison for at least twenty-five years.

She shut her eyes tight, her whole body sagging. She had never faced such a difficult decision in all her life, and in truth she never wanted to again. She sat for an age debating the whys and wherefores, the rights and wrongs, feeling she was damned if she didn't and damned if she did. Still unsure, she finally opened her eyes and looked hard at Speedy. She saw a nice, polite, unassuming man, a man she had considered might become a serious fixture in her life in the future, who had been driven to do what he had because Dicky would never have been brought to justice otherwise and would have been left at liberty to blight others' lives if he so chose. Hadn't she herself feared for her life at times when his rage had seen him lose control of his mind?

Whether what she was about to do was right or wrong, she had made her decision.

Taking a deep breath, she spoke quietly. 'I don't want you to go to the police, Speedy. I'm not condoning what you did to my husband in any way whatsoever, but no purpose would be served by you going to prison. I know you're not a danger to anyone else.'

He looked at her in astonishment for several long moments before his body sagged in relief. 'Oh Julie,' he choked, 'I don't know what to say. Thank you doesn't seem enough for what you're prepared to do for me.' He heaved a deep sigh and said sorrowfully, 'It will be best all round if I leave Grundy's, won't it?'

She nodded. 'I wasn't happy with Dicky,' she said. 'For most of our married life I was living in fear of him, but he was still my husband and I can't work alongside the man who killed him, carrying on like normal.'

He nodded in agreement. 'I can appreciate that.'

He was now looking tenderly at her and she knew that he was about to declare his love for her, and that she couldn't bear to hear, knowing that had she not discovered the part Speedy had played in her husband's death, then she could have ended up unwittingly married to his killer. She said hurriedly, 'I'll explain to Mr Grundy and the rest of the team that you had to leave suddenly for private reasons and ask him to see about getting someone to replace you. I'm going now, to leave you to pack up. I do wish you well, Speedy.'

His voice was loaded with regret when he responded. 'You too, Julie.'

She went back to her van, her heart breaking, though she wasn't actually sure who her tears were for. For Dicky, whose arrogance and greed had got him killed? For Speedy, and what he had experienced at the hands of her husband that had made him turn to murder himself? Or perhaps for herself, for the losses she had suffered: firstly Dicky, not the man he had turned out to be but the man she had believed she was marrying and the wonderful life she had thought was in store for her; and secondly Speedy, and the loss of the life she might have had with him had she not discovered he had murdered her husband.

21

While Julie was sobbing her heart out in her own van, only yards away Jenny was in her parents' van, about to confide in her mother and terrified about what the outcome would be.

As soon as Gem realised that whatever her daughter had come to talk to her about was something deeply concerning, she abandoned the dinner preparations and sat Jenny down at the kitchen table. For the last couple of minutes she had been sitting opposite her, worriedly watching as Jenny, her head bowed, nervously twisted her hands together.

'You're really worrying me now, love,' she said eventually. 'Come on, tell me what's troubling you.'

Jenny heaved a deep breath. 'It's just so difficult. I know that once I tell you, you're going to hate me and never want to see me again.'

Gem looked stunned. 'Nothing you tell me will ever make me hate you,' she said emphatically. 'Mothers love their children no matter what. Now, what it is? Have you pocketed some of the ride takings for that new dress you bought for your date tonight with Tom and now can't live with yourself?'

Jenny raised troubled eyes to her mother. 'I wish that was it, believe me I do.' She took a deep breath, still nervously twisting her hands together, and falteringly began. 'I've had a visitor today. Gwendoline Robertson, her name is. She was the nurse who called in every day to see to . . . my other mum when she was nearing the end. It was such a dreadful time. Knowing that there was going to be no miracle cure and all she had to look forward to was her pain getting worse, leading to an agonising death. I just prayed that she wouldn't linger and death would come quickly.'

She paused for a moment, and it was clear to Gem that reliving this awful time in her life was causing her great grief.

'I had no idea until Gwen told me this morning that Mum had begged her to put her out of her misery. Gwen told her that although she really did sympathise with her, it was against the oath she had taken when she had begun her nursing training. Anyway, a few days later she was getting her medical bag ready when she noticed a bottle of morphine was missing. She had visited quite a few patients that day, all terminally ill and suffering as much as Mum was, and any of the people present when she visited could have taken it. She would have been in trouble for allowing that to happen, so she told her boss that she had accidentally broken the bottle. That night Mum died, and I hadn't seen Gwen since the funeral so was surprised when she turned up out of the blue today.

'She'd come to tell me she was emigrating to Australia. I couldn't understand why she had taken all the time and trouble to find me and tell me that. But I soon found out. She needs money to help her get settled when she arrives. Two thousand pounds. I told her that I hadn't money like that to loan her and couldn't understand why she would think I had. It was then she told me that if I didn't give it to her, she would tell you and Dad that it was me who had stolen the bottle of morphine and used it to kill my mother. She said you wouldn't want a murderer living amongst you and wouldn't want anything more to do with me. So I either gave her the money or she'd make sure I lost my family.'

Tears of misery fell from her eyes and she wrung her hands. 'To lose you all now . . . I can't bear the thought of it, Mum. I love you all so much. I have to be honest and tell you that it did cross my mind to take the money from the safe and make it look like we'd had a robbery, but I couldn't do that to you and live with myself afterwards. I could have let Gwen come here and tell you all this herself, but then I worried that even if you sent her packing, it would be like she said, that you'd always be wondering whether I really was a murderer and might do it again to one of you. I can't live like that either.'

Gem reached a hand across to lay it on top of Jenny's and said quietly, 'It was you who took that bottle of morphine, wasn't it, love?'

Jenny nodded slowly. 'Yes, it was. After Gwen refused to help her put an end to her misery, my mother's only option was to ask me. She begged me, in fact. At first I refused. I was beside myself that she would think I could do such a thing, but then she made me see that if I truly loved her, I would. We'd have put a dog down by then for being in less pain than she was. She was on the highest doses of morphine that she could safely be given, but it was hardly taking the edge off her pain. It was so distressing for me to watch her fighting not to scream out in agony every time she had an attack, which by then was often, so in the end I agreed. It was the least I could do for her.

'Gwen was coming in four times a day to give Mum her medicine, and stood over her while she took it, so it wasn't possible for us to put those doses aside to make up one final fatal one. Besides, she needed all the morphine Gwen was giving her. So I came up with a plan that while Gwen was occupied with Mum the next time she called, I would take a full bottle of morphine from her bag, empty it into another bottle, then fill it up with glycerine mixed with water and replace it. I never thought about the poor person who wouldn't be getting their pain relief; all I cared about then was helping my mother end her suffering. Only I never got the chance to replace the bottle, as when I came back from the kitchen ready to slip it back into Gwen's bag, she was already closing it up and making ready to leave. All I could do now was deny stealing it if I was ever accused and hope that Mum's death so soon after its disappearance was put down as a coincidence. When nothing happened — no visit from Gwen herself or the police about the missing bottle — I thought somehow she hadn't noticed it had gone from her bag and that I'd got away with it.'

A faint smile settled on her lips, her eyes glazing distantly. 'Knowing that she was finally going to be released from her terrible suffering, that day my mum was at peace with the world. As much as her pain would allow her to talk, she told me how much she loved me and how much joy I had brought into her life, my father's too. She had missed Dad so much since he'd died and firmly believed that she was going to join him again. Gwen made her visits as usual that day and we acted normally so as not to give her any hint that something was afoot. Mum was eating very little by then, but I made her some of her favourite soup and she enjoyed the couple of spoonfuls she managed. We spent the rest of the day talking over the good times we had shared and looking at old photographs.

'We hadn't settled on a time for the deed; I knew she would tell me when she was ready, and just before nine, she did. I fetched the bottle and helped her place it to her lips to drink it, then I lay on the bed beside her, holding her in my arms, talking softly to her, telling her how much I loved her and to tell Dad the same when she met up with him very soon, until I knew she was gone. She looked so at peace and she had a smile on her face. Funny, but I didn't cry, not then, as this was what Mum had wanted and I was just glad I'd found the strength to grant her final wish to bring her suffering to an end.'

Her story finished, Jenny lifted her eyes and look at Gem, but she couldn't tell from her expression whether she was disgusted, appalled, horrified by what her daughter had done, or whether she felt it had been the right thing.

She started to ask, but Gem stopped her by

holding up her hand in a warning gesture. 'Where is this woman now?'

'Woman? Oh, the nurse, Gwen. She's in my van, waiting for the money.' She thinks that's what I'm doing here, getting it from your safe. But Mum — '

Gem held up her hand again, then scraped back her chair and stood up. 'I'd like a chat with her.'

Jenny froze, heart hammering painfully in her chest. Was her mother going to ask Gwen to go to the police with her and have Jenny arrested for murder?

Gem had already left the van, and prepared for her fate, Jenny went after her.

Gem didn't knock on Jenny's van door but marched straight in. Gwen jumped up off the sofa and blurted, 'If you're looking for Jenny — '

Gem cut her short. 'Your name is Gwen?'

The woman frowned, perplexed, and said warily, 'Yes.'

'Then it's you I'm looking for. Let me introduce myself. I'm Gemma Grundy, Jenny's natural mother.' She looked Gwen up and down before she went on. 'So . . . you're trying to blackmail my daughter out of two thousand pounds. You do know that that is a criminal offence?'

Neither Gem nor Gwen noticed Jenny arrive and hover just inside the door, filled with trepidation that either she would shortly be taken to the nearest police station to be charged with murder, or told by her mother to pack her bags and never darken her door again.

Gwen looked agog at Gem. She had expected Jenny's natural mother, despite being married to the owner of a fair, to be an ignorant, down-at-heel gypsy sort, but this woman was anything but. She was presentable and articulate, and it was clear that her schooling hadn't been a courtesy of the state. She blurted, 'Blackmail! No, certainly not. I was . . . I . . . er — '

Gem interjected, 'Well I don't know what it's called where you hail from, but as far as I'm concerned, threatening to ruin someone's life if they don't pay you money is called blackmail.' She folded her arms across her shapely chest, looking fixedly at Gwen. 'Jenny has told me you're accusing her of murdering her adoptive mother with an overdose of morphine that went missing from your medical bag. Did you personally witness Jenny taking that bottle of morphine out of your bag?'

Gwen looked uncomfortable. 'Well . . . no,' she stuttered. 'But it was a bit of a coincidence that her adoptive mother died that night when she was expected to live for a few more weeks yet.'

'Then why didn't you go to the police and tell them your suspicions at the time?'

The nurse shuffled even more uncomfortably. 'Well . . . I . . . er — '

'You didn't go to the police because there was absolutely no suspicion that Jenny's mother had died from anything other than the cancer that was ravaging her body, and it only struck you that you could use this to blackmail her with when you decided to emigrate and needed to get your hands on a sum of money to help you settle in Australia. Besides, you had already covered up the missing bottle to your bosses by telling them you had broken it. To then admit that you lied . . . well, you could be struck off for that and your career as a nurse ended.

'Let me tell you something for nothing, Nurse Robertson. Had Jenny done what you're accusing her of doing, then considering the unbearable agony her mother was suffering, which was only going to get worse before she eventually died, to me that was an unselfish act of mercy, and should I ever, God forbid, find myself in the same situation, I hope she would do the same for me.' Her eyes darkened warningly. 'Now I'll give you two seconds to get yourself out of this van and off the fairground, or I am calling the police to have you arrested for blackmail. And be warned, I'd better not ever see your face again, or I won't be responsible for my actions. That clear?'

The woman snatched up her handbag and rushed out, nearly knocking Jenny over as she pushed past her in the doorway in her haste to leave.

Gem immediately crossed to her daughter, put her arms around her and pulled her close. 'I meant every word I said, love,' she murmured.

'You . . . you don't think I'm a murderer then? You're not afraid I might — '

Gem snapped, 'Stop that. What you did for your mum was an act of love. Her life must have been purgatory for her, and she asked for your help to end that. You could have taken the money from the safe and made it look like we'd had a robbery, but you didn't; you came clean to me, ready to take the consequences, and that shows to me what an honest, loyal person you are.' She kissed her cheek before adding, 'As if I didn't know that already. Next time we're back up that way, would you take me to your mother's grave? I'd like to put some flowers on it and thank her for raising you to be such a wonderful young woman.'

Jenny's whole body sagged in relief. 'Yes, of course I will, Mum.'

Gem pulled away from her daughter and held her at arm's length. 'I don't keep secrets from your father — well, not after the mistake I made in not telling him about you — so I will tell him about this, but don't worry, he'll see it in the same way as I do: that what you did was an act of kindness and certainly not what that diabolical woman accused you of. No one else needs to know, not even your brothers, though I have no doubt they would agree with me and your father. That time was a bad one for you, and it needs to be put to rest so that you can get on making a good future for yourself.'

Jenny heaved a deep sigh. 'I'm glad you now know what I did, and I can't tell you how relieved I am that you understand why I did it.'

Gem smiled tenderly at her. 'I'm so blessed having you for a daughter. Now, I have a serious problem on my hands I need your help with. I've three hungry men about to arrive any minute expecting their dinner on the table, and I've hardly made a start on it.'

Jenny chuckled. 'Then we'd better hurry and get cracking, hadn't we?'

As they made their way back to Gem's van, she couldn't believe that twice in a very short space of time, two individuals had tried to blackmail fair folk in order to line their own pockets. Thankfully, both had discovered they had made a grave mistake.

22

Solly Grundy lived and breathed the fair. It had always been his first love — that was, until he met Gem. Despite being the owner, there was no job he felt was beneath him, nothing he would expect any of his employees to do that he wouldn't: digging holes to house support posts for the rides; fixing a broken engine; helping to push a lorry that had become stuck in squelching mud . . . There was only one job he couldn't bear, and that was to sack someone.

He treated every member of the community — from the old retainers of many years' standing to newly joined gaff lads who might only be with Grundy's for a matter of weeks — in the same congenial manner. Unlike many other fair owners, who dealt with their employees like they were ten a penny and easily replaced, Solly believed, as his father had done, that if you looked after your staff and trusted them, they would be loyal to you. Those in his direct employ might not receive top wages for their labours, but he paid them as much as he could afford to. The vans he provided for their living accommodation might not be in the best of condition, but he made sure they were well maintained. He treated all the stall and sideshow owners equally fairly, rotating their businesses around so that no one could complain that a favourite few were getting the best positions, and any trouble that arose between them he would deal with impartially, in as fair and just a manner as possible.

Therefore, if he found out that a member of his staff had acted inappropriately in any way, risked harm to another member of the community or done anything that could damage the good name of the fair, he took it personally.

It was just before dinner break on a Wednesday in the middle of July when he found himself confronting a lad of eighteen who had only been with them for a few weeks. The young man had been reported to him for not doing a job properly and putting at risk not only his fellow workers but members of the public too. The previous night, as he'd been having a bottle of beer and a chat with Gem before they retired to bed, Solly had been telling her what a good lot of lads they had at the moment, all hard workers, not one he could find any fault with, only to discover the very next morning from Toby Gittings, one of his longstanding and very diligent labourers with several gaff lads under his charge, that this wasn't entirely the case.

It seemed Gittings had asked one of the lads to check the ghost train and report any problems he found. The young man in question, Rod Mathers, returned a short while later to say he'd found nothing amiss. It was niggling at Gittings that the lad hadn't been inside the ride long enough to have inspected it thoroughly, so he went and had a look for himself and immediately spotted that a bolt securing one of the support struts had somehow worked loose. Had it been left unattended, the vibrations of the carriages rattling past could have loosened the bolt further, eventually bringing the strut down and possibly part of the roof with it. Had a carriage been passing at the time, the passengers inside could have been seriously hurt, even killed.

Solly immediately went to find and confront the lad concerned. He had been told that he was washing down the carriages of the waltzer, but when he found him, he was flicking water from a bucket with a sponge at another lad who was trying to get on with washing down another carriage nearby by. Rod Mathers was a good-looking, Jack-the-lad sort, tall and muscular. Solly immediately assessed that he belonged to a group of lads who perceived working for the fair as an easy life, away from their parents' rules and regulations, with a steady supply of women with whom to sow their wild oats. What the staff did in their spare time, providing it didn't bring disrepute to the good name of Grundy's, was their business as far as Solly was concerned, but what they did during work time was most certainly his concern.

Solly had to call his name three times before Rod stopped his shenanigans, almost leaping out of his skin when he realised just who it was that was summoning him to join him on the steps of the waltzer.

As he arrived next to Solly he said jocularly, 'Sod's law, ain't it? Been working like a navvy all morning and the boss catches yer just as yer letting yer hair down for a couple of minutes. So what d'yer need me to do, Mr Grundy?'

Solly eyed him blankly. 'Before I tell you what

I want you do to, I just want to satisfy myself that you did thoroughly check over the ghost train this morning as Toby Gittings asked you to do?'

Rod looked insulted that he was being asked such a thing. 'Yeah, course I did, boss. Every nook and cranny.'

'Every nook and cranny, eh? So, in that case, how come you never spotted that a dirty great bolt in a support structure had worked loose a few feet inside?'

Rod's eyes darted wildly as the significance of what Solly was saying registered. 'Er . . . well . . . it weren't loose when I checked, Mr Grundy. It must have happened after I'd done me inspection.'

'How?'

'How?' repeated the young man.

'Yes, how? The bolt had obviously worked loose through the vibrations of the carriages, but the ride hadn't been in operation between you supposedly checking it and when Toby went in to re-check, as he was worried that you hadn't been in long enough to do a proper inspection. When he went in, he found it straight away. So, this is what I think, Mr Mathers. You just stood inside the entrance, flashing your torch here and there, saw the ride was still standing and then skived off for a fag somewhere you couldn't be seen.'

The lad shuffled his feet awkwardly. That was exactly what he had done.

Solly went on. 'Thank goodness Toby takes his job far more seriously than you obviously do and put a stop to a possible major accident.

Customers and staff could have been badly injured, not to mention the damage done to the good name of Grundy's.'

Rod looked visibly shaken. 'It . . . it won't happen again, boss, I promise.'

Solly said flatly, 'No, it won't. While my employees are working, I need to know I can trust them to do what is asked. Obviously, you're not the type I can rely on. I'd like you to pack your stuff and leave. I'll give you ten minutes to be out of the fairground.'

Rod went to plead again for another chance, but by now Solly had had enough and held up a warning hand to stop him. He'd only been having a quick check around before going back to his van for a spruce-up. After dinner, he was due to set off for another fair fifty miles away where he had arranged to inspect a second-hand ride called the Cage, a giant wheel with compartments for punters to stand in while it whirled around at great speed, which he had spotted advertised for sale at a very good price in the *World's End* newspaper.

This outing was proving emotional for him. It would be the first time since his father had died that a ride he had wanted to buy had come up for sale. Big Sam had always taken charge of buying rides and suchlike, and had proved a formidable opponent when it came to haggling. He had been known to walk away from buying a ride he was desperate to own because the seller was demanding a shilling more than he was prepared to pay for it. Big Sam was a hard act to follow, but Solly was determined to give it a go.

He had conferred with Gem about how much they could afford to pay without causing any damage to the fair's finances, and was taking Jimmy and Robbie with him, not just for company but to expand their knowledge about managing the fair, which hopefully both would do when the time came for Solly to hand over the reins. He meant to leave it to them jointly, whilst providing for Jenny in other ways.

Lying in bed the previous night, he and Gem had had a discussion about Tom. It had not escaped their notice that their daughter was becoming very attached to the young man. This did not displease either of them. They both liked Tom very much, seeing the qualities in him that had attracted their daughter. He was definitely several cuts above the usual type of casual fair worker, most of whom had petty criminal records and couldn't get jobs easily anywhere else. He had proved himself to be dependable, willing and conscientious, and a thoroughly pleasant young man to be around. He had certainly impressed Gully, who was not the easiest of men to get on with. In turn, Tom did not hide the fact that he was becoming attached to Jenny.

But when all was said and done, he was a temporary worker, and come the end of the season, he would move on the same as all the others would. They both suspected this would devastate their daughter, and Tom too. He could return the following year, but being parted for four months would seem like a lifetime to a couple in love. And there was the possibility that he might find a permanent job during the winter, and perhaps ask Jenny to marry him, and then Solly and Gem would see little of her or any children they might have. Considering they had been deprived of her for the first twenty-two years of her life, they certainly weren't willing to miss any more if they could help it.

They were both aware that they might be jumping the gun, but nevertheless, they decided that if by the end of the season Jenny and Tom were still as attached as they were now. Solly would offer him a job over the winter during their lay-up. There was always plenty of work to do on the rides and vehicles that couldn't be done during the summer, and the stall and sideshow owners who rested up along with them were glad of help with repairs on their own equipment. They would keep this to themselves for the time being, though, for fear of being thought interfering.

Gem had suggested that by way of showing Tom, and Jenny in turn, that they approved of him, Solly should invite him to accompany them on this afternoon's jaunt. The young man had been delighted to be asked and readily accepted. Jenny showed her appreciation with a hug for them both.

Solly said with meaning to Rod now, 'Ten minutes. Any longer and it'll be my boot up your arse kicking you out.'

The lad realised that no amount of pleading or persuading was going to make the boss change his mind, and head hung low, he hurried off to do his bidding.

Solly returned to his van, arriving at the same time as Jimmy and Robbie. Gem was busy finishing off preparations for the meal, and as soon as Tom had freshened himself up, he would be joining them along with Jenny, who at the moment was helping Fran clean the skelter and get the coconut mats out ready for opening at two.

Solly was knotting his tie when he came out of his bedroom to join his sons in the living area, both of them dressed casually but smartly in black trousers, Robbie in a red jumper and Jimmy a grey one. Jimmy took one look at his father and quipped, 'You look like you're off to a funeral in your suit, Dad, not a jolly to another fair.'

Solly looked hard at him. 'It's a business meeting I'm going to, not a jolly. How do you expect the seller to believe I've got the money for the ride if I turn up looking like a ragbag?'

Gem glanced over at him then, a warm tingle shooting through her at the sight of her handsome husband, and said jocularly, 'I'd marry you if I wasn't already married.' She added worriedly, 'We've gravy with the pie.'

Solly licked his lips. 'Lovely. You'd win prizes for your gravy . . . well, since Velda gave you her recipe anyway.'

Robbie chuckled. 'Dad, what Mam's getting at is should you be wearing the shirt you're going out in while you're having your dinner? You know how you dribble sometimes.'

Solly glanced down at himself. 'Er . . . oh, that's a thought.'

Gem suggested, 'Save you changing again, why don't you do what Velda does when she's having gravy with her dinner, and drape a towel around the front of you. She's a dribbler too.'

He nodded. 'Good idea, love.' He went back into the bedroom and came out again with a hand towel tucked into the neck of his shirt and spread across his chest, the bottom tucked into his waistband.

Gem said, 'Dinner will be a good twenty minutes yet, so — '

She was interrupted by a tap on the door. It was open in this warm weather and they all looked across expecting to see either Jenny or Tom arriving in, but instead it was the face of a stranger that greeted them.

'Can I help you?' Solly asked.

The newcomer was a man in his early thirties, clean-shaven with a shock of unruly black hair, dressed in cheap black trousers, black waistcoat and a white shirt open at the neck, showing a scattering of dark chest hairs. He had a black pork pie hat pushed back on his head. He smiled at Solly, showing a row of uneven yellowing teeth. 'I was told to enquire here for Samuel Grundy. Is he here, as I need to speak to him?'

'Samuel was my father. I'm afraid he died last year. I'm Solly Grundy. Maybe I can help you?'

'I'm sorry to hear that.' The man hesitated. 'Well, it's rather difficult. Don't know where to begin really. It's about the fair . . . your father and my grandfather and the deal they made.'

In the kitchen, Gem carried on with her meal preparations whilst listening to the conversation going on in the living area.

Solly frowned, puzzled. 'What deal? Look . . . er, you'd better sit down and explain what this is all about. Oh, these are my sons, Jimmy and Robbie, and my wife Gem.' He nodded over at the kitchen area.

They all said hello, and the man sat down in Gem's armchair. 'My name is Barry Topper. My grandfather was Nev Topper.'

Solly frowned thoughtfully. 'Nev Topper,' he mused. 'That name rings a bell. Oh, is he the Topper of Topper's fair that operates down south?'

Barry nodded. 'He was. He died five years ago and my dad inherited. Within four years he'd gambled and drunk everything away, leaving me and my mam without a penny. I work for another fair now and support me mother as best I can. Thankfully we did manage to keep hold of the family van, so at least we have that to live in.'

'Yes, I remember hearing about it now. It was a very sad affair, Topper's going under like it did. At one time it must have ranked with the best.' Solly realised that he still had the towel draped over his front and whipped it away to stuff it down the side of the chair before asking. 'But what's this deal you mentioned between your grandfather and my father?'

'We knew nothing about it until last week. You see, my father had always been a gambler and a drinker. Grandpa should have left the fair to me, but he was a showman through and through, so to him the eldest son was his heir no matter what. When he died, all Dad was interested in

312

was finding the will and claiming what was his; the rest of Grandpa's paperwork was packed away to be sorted out later. I'll cut a long story short, but watching my dad ruin the business Grandpa had built up from scratch was awful for me and Mam, and to be honest, it was a relief to us when he died too. But by then it was too late to save the business. Most of the old stall owners who'd been with Grandpa for donkey's years had already left and found pitches with other fairs, and the rides were so badly maintained they were hardly worth the price as scrap. We were lucky that anyone was interested in buying it. The bloke who did had his own successful fair and was looking to expand. Topper's had the rights to play in forty or so additional towns and villages, and that clinched the sale.

'After Dad's debts were paid off, we were left with just a couple of pounds. We've managed to survive so far, but last week water started to come through the roof of our van and we hadn't the money to repair it, so Mam was looking through our stuff to see if she could find anything worth pawning. She found a few bits of old jewellery in a handbag that would hopefully go some way towards paying for the repairs, but she also came across the box containing Grandpa's old papers. There were lots of old bills and suchlike in there — even a receipt for the secondhand suit he'd bought to marry my grandmother in — but then Mam came across this.' He pulled a long yellowing envelope from inside his waistcoat and flapped it against his other hand. 'Mam can't read, so she gave it to

313

me to tell her what it said.'

'And what does it say?' Solly urged, a fear beginning to niggle at him that whatever it was, he wasn't going to like it.

Barry Topper paused for a moment before he announced, 'It's a deal made between my grandfather and your father, about forty years ago. In exchange for the sum of six thousand pounds, my grandfather got thirty per cent of your father's business. The partnership could be dissolved at any time if the six grand was paid back with the appropriate interest. If your father died, Grandpa would get thirty per cent of what his business was worth at the time; if my grandfather had already died, that money would go to his estate. It's all in here. My grandfather obviously never asked for the loan to be repaid when he was alive; he never had need of the money as his own fair was giving him a good living.

'When my grandfather died, as I've already told you, my dad didn't go through his papers properly because all he was interested in was claiming his inheritance, so we didn't know about this deal. But now that we do, I'm here to ask you to settle it. We sorely need the money, I can tell you.' Anger entered his voice as he continued. 'Anyway, what's more to the point is why your father didn't honour his obligations when he heard that my grandfather had died, and why you didn't when your father died.'

Solly had grown pale by now, and Gem had stopped what she was doing to stare blindly over at their visitor. Jimmy and Robbie sat in silence, understanding the significance of what this man had told them.

Solly said, 'We didn't do anything because we knew nothing about this. When my father died, I went through his papers and I can assure you I found no agreement between him and your grandfather.' He stood up and looked at Gem. 'Do you want to offer Mr Topper a drink while I go and check the paperwork again, just in case I missed something before.'

Barry smiled at her. 'Cuppa would be lovely, thanks. Three sugars and plenty of milk.'

The atmosphere in the van was strained until Solly returned a good ten minutes later looking grave. 'Same as before,' he said. 'I found nothing at all about any deal made between my father and your grandfather.'

Barry shrugged. 'Maybe over time it was lost somehow, but that doesn't change the fact that it was made. I have the proof here.' He held out the envelope to Solly. 'You'll want to see it for yourself.'

Taking the envelope, Solly opened it and removed the contents. It was just a single piece of paper, and thanks to the lessons in reading and writing that Gem had persuaded him to take with the community teacher, Miss Dunn, he could see that it was exactly as Barry had said. Either Nev Topper or someone else must have written the document out, as Big Sam had been able to read and write only a very few words, but he could sign his name, and the signature on the document was definitely his spidery scrawl. Nev's signature was written next to Sam's. Both had two witness signatures underneath them.

Solly heaved a deep breath and said solemnly, 'Looks genuine.'

He turned his head and beckoned Gem over, handing her the piece of paper. As soon as she had read it, a worried look clouded her face. 'Yes, it does,' she said. 'That's definitely your father's signature. I've seen it enough times whenever he had to sign cheques or letters to do with fair business. But best we make certain.' She went to the safe and opened it, then knelt down and rummaged through until she found what she was looking for. 'This is a copy of the bill of sale for a ride your father sold last year before he died,' she told Solly. 'His signature is on the bottom. We can compare it to the one on the document Mr Topper has.'

The two signatures were placed side by side and they all scrutinised them thoroughly before unanimously agreeing that they appeared to be identical.

Jimmy looked worried. 'Does this mean we could lose the fair, Dad, if we can't raise the money?'

Solly gnawed his bottom lip anxiously. That was exactly what he was beginning to fear would happen, as he had no idea how he could come up with thirty per cent of the value of the fair without having to sell up. Something was niggling at him, but he hadn't time to explore it as Barry reached over to retrieve the document.

'Well, I hope for your sake it don't come to that, but when all's said and done, a deal is a deal and this one is in writing, signed, dated and witnessed. If you still have doubts, then we could always take it to the Showmen's Guild and let them decide. Unless, of course, you can provide paperwork to say that your father paid my grandfather back the money he was owed, though we never found nothing amongst Grandpa's papers to say that was the case.

'I had a look around your fair when I first arrived and what I'm due has to be at least thirty grand, if not more. It's a good-sized fair so must make good money. A proper valuation will decide that, though. It's not really my problem how you raise what I'm owed, but I'd like this settled quick, as I really need the money.' Barry Topper got up. 'Look, I can see this has come as a great shock to you and I suspect you'll need time to go back through your dad's papers to see if you can find his copy of the deal. I'll give you a couple of weeks to get the fair valued, then I'll be back to see how you're getting on. I'll let myself out.'

He was gone before any of them found their voice to stop him.

Gem clamped her hands to her head in dismay. 'Oh Solly, how on earth are we going to find a third of the value of the fair in a fortnight?'

They all stared at her worriedly.

Just then Jenny came through the door, followed by Tom. Jenny was saying breezily, 'Hope dinner's ready as I'm starv — ' Her voice trailed off as she saw the looks on her family's faces. 'Oh God, what's happened? Has someone died?'

Solly sighed heavily. 'If we lose this fair, it will certainly kill me.'

Tom spoke up. 'Had I better leave if this is family business?'

Solly shook his head. 'You're part of the family at the moment, son, you courting our daughter, but what you're about to hear I trust will go no further. If the community get wind of it, they'll start panicking. No need for them to know unless the worst happens.'

It was apparent that whatever they were about to hear was very bad news. Tom took Jenny's hand in a protective gesture and replied with conviction, 'Of course, sir, no one will hear a word from me.'

'Thanks, Tom.' Solly then proceeded to enlighten the pair on what had just transpired. When he had finished, they both looked at him horrified.

It was Jenny who spoke. 'And this document looked kosher to you, Dad?'

He nodded. 'And to your mum it did too.'

Gem nodded her agreement.

Robbie, who had not said a word since Barry had left, suddenly piped up. 'Then this means that Grandad lied to us. Six grand was the amount he told us he got by selling his two stalls along with money he had saved to buy his first ride from a place he called the old ride graveyard. Grandad could be a cantankerous old bugger, but one thing he wasn't was a liar. If he had borrowed money to buy that first ride, he would have been honest and told us.'

It hit Solly then just what had been niggling at

318

him earlier. 'You're right, Robbie,' he exclaimed. 'Dad never borrowed a penny in his life. He would never consider buying anything unless he had the cash. I remember badgering him to borrow some money when we first had the chance to buy a dodgem ride, as it was a real bargain at the time and I knew it would bring in the crowds and boost our takings, but he dug his heels in and flatly refused; said he wasn't prepared to put himself in hock to anyone and we'd get the ride when we had the money.

'And he certainly wasn't a liar. If he had borrowed money to start the fair with, he'd never have told us that he'd built it himself from scratch without borrowing a penny from anyone. And that would mean that my mother was a liar too, as she was always telling us she didn't know how she stopped herself from taking her rolling pin to him when he first came and told her that he'd sold their two stalls and emptied their Christmas savings pot to pay for that wreck of a carousel and not breathed a word to her about it as he knew she'd have flatly refused to agree to him taking such a risk.'

Gem said, 'I knew your mother well, Solly, and as much as she loved your father, she would never have lied for all those years about something like that just to make him look like a hero to his family.'

Solly jumped up from his seat and began pacing the small space in front of the range. 'Dad making that deal with Nev Topper . . . well he didn't, or he'd have told us . . . but then his signature . . . I'd swear it was identical to the one

319

we compared it to that we know he did sign. It wasn't just me; we all did, didn't we?'

'Or it's an excellent forgery,' said Tom.

They all stared over at him, astounded.

'Well it must be if you're adamant that your father never lied to you about how he started the fair up.'

Gem said, 'But how? To forge a signature you'd need one to copy first. How did Barry Topper get hold of Big Sam's signature in the first place?'

They all looked at Jimmy as he issued a gasp. 'Do you have any idea of how he could have got it, son?' demanded Solly.

'Well I might. A couple of weeks ago I happened to be at the back of Grandad's van having a fag . . . I just wanted to be on my own at the time to think about something.' He flashed a quick look at Jenny and Robbie to see if they realised that it was his embarrassment after Zena had refused his offer to escort her to the party that had taken him there. 'Anyway, I was just about to leave when I saw this man's head appear out of the van door, obviously checking the coast was clear before he scarpered. I didn't get a good look at him as he had the collar of his mac pulled right up and his hat pulled right down.' He didn't want to make himself look foolish by admitting that when he tried to apprehend the interloper he'd fallen flat on his face. Instead he told them, 'I tried to catch him but he was too quick for me. Anyway, he didn't seem to be carrying anything, and when I checked inside the van nothing seemed to be missing. I meant to tell you about it so that in future the door was kept locked, but I forgot.'

Solly shook his head at him disparagingly. 'Because all you were thinking about as usual was who you were lining up for your next girlfriend. But that bloke must have been Topper, and that's how he got hold of Dad's signature, from his old paperwork. He's either a damned good forger himself or he paid someone a lot to do it, but then if he does get a third of what this fair is worth, it'll be money well spent.'

Gem was frowning. 'But how did Topper know which van was Big Sam's without making enquiries? You all know what the community are like if they catch outsiders sniffing about; soon make short shift of them. And anyway, why pick on us to pull this swindle on?'

Tom said, 'With respect, Mrs Grundy, when everyone is working it's easy to have a sneak around the living van area. Topper might have apprehended one of the children to tell him which was Mr Grundy's father's van and given them sixpence to keep quiet. And when he came up with this plan to make himself some money, he obviously checked out a fair that could produce the amount he was after, and Grundy's fitted the bill.'

Solly scraped a worried hand through his hair. 'If none of us could tell that signature was a forgery, then neither would the representatives of the Showmen's Guild if we took it to them, or any solicitor either, so how the hell do we prove it? Knowing my dad would never have lied about how he got the money to start the fair with just

321

isn't enough, and if I can't prove this man's claim isn't genuine, then the only way I can raise what he's demanding is to sell up. It's an utter nightmare.'

'Then we need to find a way to prove that document is a fake,' cried Jenny with conviction. When they all looked at her for a suggestion as to how, she shrugged and said, 'I've not thought of any way we could try yet, though.'

Gem piped up. 'What about the witnesses? What if we found them and showed them a photo of Sam and asked them if this was the man they saw signing the document?'

Solly shook his head. 'If the document was genuine then it's most likely that those witnesses are both dead by now, and if it's a fake, then whoever Topper got to sign it will have been paid enough to keep quiet; maybe even threatened with death if they don't, considering the amount of money involved.' He went over to his chair and slumped dejectedly into it, heaving a deep sigh. 'Well if no one else can come up with a plan as to how we can prove this document is a fake, then I think we're done for.'

Jenny was looking thoughtful. 'Dad, did Barry Topper tell you what fair he was working for at the moment?'

He shook his head. 'Why? I don't see how knowing that will help us.'

'Well, he hasn't met me, has he? What if I went to the fair and spoke to him? I could make out I was desperately searching for a friend who used to work for Topper's before it went under and that someone told me to contact him as he might know where she was. I could get talking to him, pretend I fancy him, wheedle him into taking me for a drink after he finishes work, then get him drunk, and you know how drunks can't keep secrets to themselves so he might let — '

Tom cut in. 'I don't like the sound of this, Jenny.'

She liked the fact that he was obviously jealous of her making up to another man, but before she could tell him he'd nothing to fear, Jimmy piped up.

'Yeah, and what if he's married or has got a girlfriend? She isn't exactly going to stand by and watch you chatting up her fella, is she?'

'Mmm, I never thought of that.' Then her eyes sparked. 'Oh, but the mother. What if I went to her with the same story and managed to get her talking about her son? You know how mothers love to brag about their kids, and she might let something slip . . . something like how proud she is of her son for having a plan that's going to make them a fortune. Of course I'd make sure that Topper wasn't around first. But if I could just pull that off, then at least we'd be positive it was a swindle. Then we'd just have to put our heads together to plan our next move to put a stop to it. Okay, so I know it's clutching at straws, but if none of you have any ideas, then it's better than sitting around doing nothing. I won't be in any danger, as the worst she can do is decide I'm a nosy parker and send me packing.'

'Jenny has a point, Solly,' Gem told him. 'There's nothing I like to talk about more than my children, and I don't need any encouragement to do so. I've told strangers things about ours that I haven't told anyone else because it doesn't matter them knowing as you're never going to see them again.'

'Such as what, Mam?' asked Robbie.

'Oh, just things like when you've done something you shouldn't that I didn't want friends to know because I didn't want them to think you're not the angels I make you out to be. All mothers do it. Anyway, Solly, Jenny's idea has got to be worth a try.'

Solly sat in thought for a moment. 'As we've nothing else, anything is worth it, I suppose,' he said at last.

'I'm coming with you, Jenny,' Tom insisted. 'I know you said there's no danger attached to what you're about to do, but even so . . . Oh, if that's all right with you, sir?'

'Of course it is, Tom. Me and Gem will be happier letting her go off on this hare-brained jaunt knowing she's got you with her. Now, whoever bought what was left of Topper's fair might know where Barry and his mother went to work. He might even have kept them on as a goodwill gesture. That would be a bit of luck if he did and save you lots of travelling around trying to find their whereabouts. I'll go to the telephone box and put a call through to the Showman's Guild. As a member they'll tell me who it was that bought Topper's and where they're playing at the moment.'

Gem said, 'While you're away, I'll finish off the dinner. I just hope the pie isn't ruined by now.

I'll be happier sending Jenny and Tom off with a good meal inside them. Oh Solly, what about your appointment to view that ride this afternoon?'

He sighed. 'Well we can't exactly go off buying rides when we might not even have a fair left to put them in. Jimmy, I'll give you the details of the chap we were going to see and you can go to the post office and send a telegram saying that something unexpected has come up so we can't make it this afternoon. I was looking forward to that trip out as well.'

Gem said positively, 'There'll be other rides to go and view, love.'

He flashed her a wan smile. 'Let's pray you're right.'

23

It transpired that the man who had bought the bankrupt Topper's fair along with its charters and council contracts was called Jerry Morgan. Solly didn't know him personally, as his fair operated around the south of England so didn't cross paths with Grundy's, but he had heard of him through the fairground grapevine and knew that he was a decent, honest ringmaster in the same mould as Big Sam and Solly himself. His fair at the moment was playing in a town called Andover in Hampshire. It would be there for another week. Allowing for a couple of short breaks, it would take Jenny and Tom at least ten hours to journey the distance. To keep them well fed on the journey, Gem made a pile of sandwiches and a flask of tea, and wrapped up slices of Miss Dunn's fruit cake, which the elderly teacher had kindly brought around the day before.

They didn't set off until after two that afternoon, and the drive was long and tedious, most of it through the night, though they both consoled themselves with the fact that they were spending time together they wouldn't normally be able to. It was a young policeman on the beat who pointed them in the direction of the fairground when they arrived in Andover at four in the morning. Parking the garishly painted Grundy's lorry down a side street well out of sight of the fairground entrance, they finished the last of their food and drink and settled as comfortably as they could on the long bench seat for a much-needed sleep.

Given that she was about to present herself to first Jerry Morgan and then hopefully Mrs Topper as a casual fair worker in search of a friend, Jenny had chosen her outfit very carefully, and was dressed in a pair of close-fitting black trousers and a baggy knitted jumper, items she would normally wear when on cleaning duties at Grundy's.

She waited until after ten o'clock to make her enquiries of Jerry Morgan, reasoning that if the Toppers were working for him, Barry would be out in the fairground by this time, helping to set up ready for opening at two, while his ageing mother would be in their van dealing with chores and preparing the midday meal.

As she made to leave the lorry to embark on her task, she could see in Tom's eyes that he was deeply worried about her tackling this on her own. She reached over and patted his hand. 'I'll be fine, Tom. Any sign that Mrs Topper suspects I'm not who I say I am and I'll be out of there like my tail's on fire.'

'You promise me, no heroics?' he demanded.

'Yes, promise. Now I'd best get off before I lose my nerve.'

She started to slide her bottom over the bench seat to the door, but he caught her arm, pulling her back. Then before either of them realised what was happening, they were in each other's arms, their kiss long and passionate.

The nearest they had come to kissing previously had been a shy peck on the cheek as they had said their goodbyes after spending time together, and when Tom finally released Jenny, she blew out her cheeks and mouthed, 'Phew! Well that was worth waiting for.' Then she quipped, 'Don't you dare go anywhere. I'll be back for more of that.'

He grinned at her. Their first kiss might have been a while coming, but like Jenny had said, it was well worth the wait, and he was desperate for more.

With Tom's kiss still lingering deliciously on her lips, Jenny clambered out of the lorry and set off towards the fairground, fired up with determination to return to her family with information that would help to expose Topper as the conman he was. But as she approached the entrance, her nerves began to jangle and it felt like she was about to enter a lion's den with no weapons of defence. She spun on her heel and started back the way she had come, then suddenly stopped as it hit her that if she didn't at least attempt to do what she'd promised her family she would, she was not only letting them down but herself too. Only cowards ran, and she was no coward. With renewed resolve, she spun back and ran into the fairground before her nerves got the better of her again.

No members of the public were allowed in any fairground outside of opening hours, so almost as soon as Jenny entered she was accosted by a worker. Before he could order her to leave, she told him she was there to see the ringmaster on a private matter, and he pointed her in the direction of Jerry Morgan's caravan.

Morgan was a large, florid man with a shock of wild ginger hair, mutton chop sideburns and a bushy walrus moustache waxed into points that curled around his bulbous nose. She found him sitting behind a cluttered desk in a modern but cramped caravan. There was so much furniture in it that there was hardly room to move around. He was wearing a loud Prince of Wales checked suit and a garishly patterned tie, and was smoking a foul-smelling cigar.

His eyes lit up and quickly appraised Jenny as she entered the van, and before she could offer a reason for her visit, he told her in a loud, booming voice, 'You've got the job, lovey. Start straight away. Go and ask for Bonnie, tell her I've set you on and she'll introduce you to Master Zane, who you'll be working for. She'll sort out your living arrangements too.'

'Er . . . I'm not here about a job, Mr Morgan.'

His face fell. 'Yer not after the job as one of the hostesses in the illusion side show? Oh that's a shame, pretty girl like you would've drawn in the punters. So what *are* you here for then?'

'I need to find out if you've a Mrs Topper working for you, or if you might know what fair she's working for now. I understand you bought her family fair when it went up for sale. My friend used to work for Topper's, you see, and we lost touch, but I desperately need to find her and I'm hoping Mrs Topper might be able to help me.'

'Oh, I see. Yes, I kept Bessie Topper on when I

took over what was left of Topper's. Least I could do for the poor soul after that wastrel of a husband left her and her son with hardly a copper to their name. We fair folk look after each other. You'll most likely find her in her van at this time of day. Someone will point out which one.' He looked regretfully at her. 'Sure you don't want a job?'

She smiled. 'Sure, Mr Morgan, but thanks for the offer.'

She found Bessie Topper hanging out washing on a line strung between her van and a tree behind it. She was a small woman, thin and scrawny, aged before her time, looking nearer seventy than her actual fifty-five, and was dressed in shabby clothes with an old black shawl draped around her shoulders and holey slippers on her feet. Her van was the old-fashioned bow-top type, the same as the Grundy family all resided in, but whereas theirs were kept in pristine condition, Mrs Topper's was in dire need of repair and a lick of paint.

She eyed Jenny warily and snapped at her. 'What do yer want?'

Here goes, Jenny thought. She suddenly realised that women tended to talk more when they were relaxed. She needed to get this woman seated. She noticed two shabby Lloyd Loom chairs beside a small table outside the van, and an idea came to her. 'Would you mind if I sat down so I can shake a stone out of one of my shoes?'

The woman hesitated before she said, 'Help yourself.'

330

Jenny pretended to limp over and sat herself down in one of the chairs, where she proceeded to take off one of her pumps and shake out an invisible stone. Meanwhile, much to her relief, the older woman had sat down in the other chair. Jenny smiled at her as she replaced the shoe. 'That's better. You wouldn't think such a small piece of grit could cause such pain.'

'Are you going to tell me what you're here for?' Mrs Topper asked. 'I'm a busy woman.'

Jenny took a deep breath. She wasn't happy about having to lie, but then she reminded herself why she was having to. 'I'm looking for a friend, Mrs Topper, and I was hoping you would have an idea where she might be.'

The older woman looked bemused. 'Why would you think I would know?'

'She worked for you before Mr Morgan took over.' Jenny adopted a sympathetic expression. 'It's so sad what happened to Topper's; great fair it was. Paula loved working for you and that's how I ended up working for you too, as she persuaded me to join her. We were at school together and really close. Paula Jones was her name and mine is Jenny Richards.' She used her adoptive name for obvious reasons. 'Paula worked for Topper's for about four seasons but I only did two. We both loved our jobs. You were great people to work for. You must remember us?'

Mrs Topper was frowning, bemused to hear this young woman proclaim that the Topper's had been great people to work for. Maybe they had been when her father-in-law had been ringmaster, but certainly not after her bully of a husband had taken over after his death. She studied Jenny's face for a moment before she responded. 'No, can't say as I do remember you. Sure it was Topper's you and your friend worked for?'

'Yes. We only left because . . . well, things got bad, didn't they, and some weeks us casual workers weren't getting our wages, so we had no choice but to find work at another fair. Well, Paula did, because she had no home to go back to. Her parents had disowned her for running off to work for a fairground and had told her they'd not speak to her again until she gave that life up. I went home for a while, but I couldn't settle back in civvy street and so I decided to join Paula again. Only when I arrived at the place she told me she'd got a job, she'd already left and I've not been able to find out where she's gone.

'But you see, although she's not in touch with her family, I still am. They might be dead set against Paula working for a fair, but they still love her. When her mother found out I was going to be joining Paula again, she asked me to let her know on the QT how she is. Paula's mum and my mum are friends, so when I ring home my mum passes messages on. But last week when I phoned, that's when I got the news that Paula's mother is seriously ill. It looks like she's going to die, so I need to find Paula to tell her.'

Bessie Topper grimaced. 'Oh, I see. I'm sorry, I can't help you, lovey. I've no idea where any of the people that used to work for us are now. A few of them did join Morgan's when he took over, but they've all moved on 'cept me and my son.'

Jenny sighed. 'Oh well, at least it was worth a try.' She could see the older woman was about to excuse herself to get back to hanging out her washing, but Jenny hadn't yet got what she'd come for. 'Er . . . your son . . . Barry, his name is, isn't it?'

'Yes, that's right.'

Jenny smiled. 'Me and him had a fling for a couple of weeks when I was working for Topper's. I was really cut up when he finished with me to go out with another girl. All the girls were after him; he was such a good-looking man.'

How right Gem was that mothers never missed an opportunity to talk about their children, whether it be to complain or praise. Mrs Topper was no exception. At the mention of her son, her eyes lit up, a tender smile kinking her thin lips. 'I was blessed with Barry. He's a good lad. He should be running a successful fair in truth, had his father . . . ' She sighed and carried on distractedly. 'I thought I'd landed the golden ticket when I married Arnold, him being heir to a fair as successful as Topper's, but I wasn't happy for long. I soon discovered that he loved his drink more than me and was addicted to gambling. His father managed to keep a bit of a rein on him when he was alive, but after he died, Arnold was free to do as he liked and spent more time down the bookie's than he did running the fair.

'When Mr Morgan took over, he was kind

enough to keep us on, Barry running one of the rides and me in any of the booths I'm asked to work in. The pay we get between us just about keeps our heads above water. It was hard for us both going from owning the fair to just being workers, but we had no choice but to grin and bear it.' She suddenly realised that she was speaking to a stranger. 'Sorry, love, I got carried away. You came here to ask after your friend, not listen to my woes.'

Jenny laid a hand on the other woman's and said sympathetically, 'I'm a good listener, Mrs Topper. It's healthy to get things off your chest. You can tell me what you like and it'll go no further. I think it's terrible what's happened to you, to be left in such a dreadful financial state through no fault of your own.' She took a deep breath. 'I suppose you've had a good look through all your husband's family papers to make sure neither he nor his father left an insurance policy or anything else that might reap a few pounds for you . . . maybe an IOU from an old friend he'd loaned money to that you could call in?'

The older woman scoffed. 'My husband's father was like Scrooge, wouldn't give you the drippings off his nose. Every penny he had went on building his fair up. He wanted to go down in fairground history as having the biggest and best operation in the country, only he died before he could achieve that. Any money my husband could get his hands on, as I've already told you, went down his throat or over the bookie's counter. He even hocked my jewellery. All he left me with was debts.'

Jenny thoughts whirled. So the story Barry had told them of his mother finding the contract between her father-in-law and Big Sam while searching for old jewellery to pawn certainly wasn't true. But how was she going to find out whether it was Bessie or Barry who had come up with the idea of forging the document?

All she could think of to say was, 'You never know, a miracle might happen and you might come up with a way to make some money, enough to work for yourselves again maybe.'

At this the woman threw up her hands and exclaimed, 'Well how strange you should say that. A miracle has indeed happened that is going to change our lives for the better.'

Jenny's eyes sparked. Was this the break-through she'd been hoping for?

'Really? I'm so pleased for you. Oh, you must tell me what this miracle is. If you don't, I shan't be able to sleep for wondering about it.'

The woman looked hesitant for a moment before she said, 'Well, I don't suppose it will hurt to tell you about it. You're a stranger and I'll never see you again and I'd love to tell someone as it's so exciting.' She took a quick look around to check that no one was in the vicinity to overhear what she was about to say, then lowered her voice and began.

'A couple of weeks ago, a bloke turned up out of the blue. Said he'd come across the story in the *World's Fair* newspaper about us losing the fair because of my husband's drinking and gambling . . . so ashamed I was when it was all published for the fairground community to read about, and of course the *World's Fair* reporter is no better than the national newspaper ones and made sure all the gory details and some made-up ones too were written. Me and my Barry had to keep a low profile for weeks afterwards to avoid all the gossip and sneers from people we once thought of as friends. Anyway, getting back to what I was telling you . . . Having read the story, and knowing the two of us were on our uppers, this bloke had a proposition he hoped Barry would be interested in that would see him well rewarded. He introduced himself as Steve Smith. Such a handsome man, he was, bit of a gypsy look about him, and so very charming. And, of course, Barry was interested in listening to his proposition because of the money involved.

'A thousand pounds Steve Smith was willing to pay him just to help him carry out a plan to get money back from a man who owed it to him but was refusing to cough up. He'd tried all sorts to get the man to pay, but nothing had worked and he was beginning to think he'd never get the money back when he read our story in the *World's Fair* newspaper and it gave him an idea. All my Barry had to do was visit the man with a forged document for a deal that was supposedly made many years ago between my father-in-law and the father of the man who owed all the money. As the man would not be able to prove it wasn't a genuine document, he would have no choice but to settle the debt. It's a very clever plan, don't you think? If anyone came enquiring as to where I had found this document, I had to swear blind that it was amongst my late father-in-law's papers, or else the whole plan would be scuppered and we wouldn't see a penny. For the money we'll be getting, I'd swear to the Lord himself that black was white.

'It meant though that Barry would have to go and stay with Steve Smith so he could make sure he was word perfect on what he was to say when he visited the man, and again when he went back to collect the money. Steve Smith is in a worse state than we are financially and has been reduced to working for a fair himself because of this unpaid debt, and that was where Barry would be staying with him. The fair was in Southsea. It's not a travelling fair but a fixed one on the seafront, though I can't remember the name of it. I can't say as I was happy about Barry leaving me on my own while they put this plan into action, as we've never been parted before, and besides, he sees to all the heavy work that I can't manage any longer, but still, sacrifices have to be made when the rewards are so great.

'Barry had been away for several days and I was beginning to wonder if something had gone wrong, but late last night he came by to tell me that he was just on his way back from a trip up north to carry out the first part of the plan. It had all gone just as Steve had said it would. The man who owes him money couldn't find any fault with the document and saw he had no way out of settling the debt. Obviously, he needs time to raise the money, but it won't be long before Steve gets what he's owed and we'll be paid for our part in helping that come about. So, it's certainly is a miracle for us that Steve Smith read our story and approached us to help him get his money, don't you agree?'

Jenny's thoughts were racing again. So, a man called Steve Smith was paying Barry to do his dirty work for him. At least she had discovered where to find this Steve Smith, thanks to Bessie Topper's need to brag about her stroke of luck, though she wasn't sure what good knowing this would do them. They had nothing physical they could take to the police to prove that Steve Smith was involved in the scheme to defraud her parents. She needed to get back to Tom, tell him what she had learned and see whether he had any ideas.

She smiled at Bessie and patted her hand. 'Absolutely I do,' she enthused. 'I hope the plan works out and you get your money. I really do. After all you've been through, you deserve some luck, Mrs Topper.' Though she suspected that this Steve Smith had no intention of parting with a penny of his ill-gotten gains. The likelihood was that as soon as he'd got his hands on the money, he would disappear off and they'd never see him again. She got up from her chair. 'I've really enjoyed talking to you, but I need to carry on looking for my friend.'

'Wish I could have helped you, dear. Oh, do you want me to remember you to Barry when I next see him?'

'Oh yes, please do. Tell him I still haven't found a bloke who kisses better than he does.' That should please the old dear, she thought.

Bessie smiled proudly. 'I certainly will. Best of luck finding your friend before her mother passes on.'

Tom was relieved to see her back safe and sound. He gave her a hug and kissed her hard before he said, 'How did it go? Find out anything we can use to prove this is definitely a con?'

She said gravely, 'Oh, it's a con all right, Tom.' She proceeded to tell him what she had gleaned from Bessie Topper.

When she had finished, he was frowning. 'Like you said, it's a really clever plan this Steve Smith has come up with, but we still can't prove that document is a fake.'

She scowled angrily. 'Maybe we need to kidnap Barry and his mother and wring the truth out of them,' she snapped.

Tom shook his head. 'They're never going to admit it considering what's at stake for them — enough money to start a new future with. What are the chances of another opportunity like this ever coming their way again? We'd better get back to your father and tell him what you've found out and see what we can do about it. If anything, that is.'

He made to start the engine but she laid a hand on his arm to stop him. 'We can't be that far away from Southsea, Tom. Can't we just go and pay a visit to the fair there? I'd like to see this Steve Smith for myself.'

'Why? What good will that do?'

She shrugged. 'I don't know. I just want to get a look at the man who's trying to ruin my family. Just a thought. Do you think Barry Topper and his mother might be open to bribery from us? Dad could offer to pay them more than Steve Smith is promising, on the understanding that Bessie admits she never found that document amongst her father-in-law's papers.'

Tom nodded. 'That's worth mentioning to your father to consider.' He thought for a moment. 'But while it would put a stop to Steve Smith's plan, it would still leave him free to try another scheme to extort money out of your father, or some other innocent businessman. We need to stop him from conning money out of people, but how we do that when he's getting others to carry out his schemes on his behalf? If it hadn't been for you getting Mrs Topper to talk, we'd never have known Steve Smith was the one behind all this.'

'I still want to get a look at him. I just need to see the face of the man who's trying to ruin my family.

He smiled at her. 'Then you shall.'

★   ★   ★

Dobson's fair, on the seafront at Southsea, was dilapidated to say the least, the rides poorly maintained and rubbish and weeds abundant. How the local council hadn't condemned the place as a danger to human life was a mystery. After snooping around and making discreet enquiries, Jenny had managed to find the man who was attempting to con her father out of a substantial amount of money — and as matters stood, looking like he was going to succeed.

Dressed in black trousers and a grubby white American-style T-shirt, he'd been lounging against the support post of a swing boats ride, smoking a roll-up cigarette. He was just as Bessie Topper had described him: in his early forties, slim-hipped, with muscular shoulders, and extremely good-looking in a dark, brooding kind of way. As soon as Jenny set eyes on him, she instantly got the feeling that she had seen him before somewhere, but however hard she tried, she just couldn't remember where that had been, and it was really annoying her.

Now that she had satisfied her curiosity, they were well on their way back home. Tom took his eyes off the road for a second to flash a quick look at Jenny cuddled next to him before he returned them to the road. 'Penny for them,' he said. 'Or shall I save myself the money and tell you I know you're still trying to remember where you think you've seen that man before. Maybe you haven't. Maybe he just reminds you of someone you know and that's why you think you've seen him.'

She sighed. 'Yes, maybe you're right. But now I'm left with the problem of who he reminds me of.'

Tom laughed. 'The best way to remember is to forget about it and let it come to you naturally.' He sighed himself. 'I just wish we were returning with better news to tell your parents, at least something that would help us prove that document is fake.'

When she didn't answer, he flashed another quick look at her and smiled tenderly as he saw

341

she was asleep. The whole experience had obviously taken its toll on her.

Hours later, at just after two in the morning, Tom drew the lorry to a halt inside Grundy's fairground. The jolt of the vehicle stopping woke Jenny.

'Why are we stopping?' she asked sleepily.

'Because we're home.'

'What! I slept all the way back?'

He laughed. 'You certainly did.'

She yawned loudly and stretched before issuing a deep sigh. 'Mum and Dad will be anxious to hear whether we found out anything useful, so we'd better go and tell them the bad news.'

★   ★   ★

A while later, Solly was standing with his back to the stove looking worriedly at his daughter. 'So it's not the Toppers who are behind all this. Who is this Steve Smith? Out of all the fairs operating in the country, why did he pick on Grundy's to swindle?'

It was Tom who responded. 'Shouldn't we be concentrating all our efforts into coming up with a way to put a stop to this conspiracy?'

Solly nodded. 'Yes, you're right, Tom. But it boils down to us being able to prove that signature of my father's is a fake — in fact that the whole document a fake — and I still can't see a way of doing that.'

Feeling useless, Gem got up from the armchair she was sitting in. 'I'll put the kettle on.

Unless anyone wants anything stronger?'

'I could down a bottle of whisky, but that won't solve anything, will it,' Solly said dispiritedly.

'I wish you'd let me loose on this Steve Smith. I'd soon beat the truth out of him,' snarled Jimmy.

Slouched next to him on the sofa, Robbie gave his brother a hefty nudge in his ribs. 'Yeah, and then we'd be visiting you in jail for murder, wouldn't we.'

'If you haven't anything useful to say, then don't say anything,' Solly scolded. He heaved a despairing sigh. 'I suppose there's nothing else for it but for me to find out the value of the fair. I'll organise for an agent to come tomorrow.'

'Oh Solly.' Gem's voice was choked. 'I can't bear it, I really can't. We can't give up so easily.'

He shook his head sadly. 'What's the point of prolonging the agony, love? This Steve Smith has us over a barrel. He knows as well as we do that the only person who can dispute the signature on that document is my father himself.'

Squashed at the side of Robbie on the sofa, Jenny was again racking her brains to try and remember who the man reminded her of. She absently watched her father lean his back against the tall cupboard beside the stove and take a tin out of his pocket to extract a roll-up cigarette. He put it in his mouth and struck a match, then tilted his head slightly over as he lit it. At this action, Jenny gasped. 'That's it!' she exclaimed. 'That's who Steve Smith reminded me of. You, Dad. He has a look of you about him.'

Solly looked stupefied at his daughter. 'Me! This Steve Smith looks like me?' Then, as the horrible truth dawned, his face turned a deathly grey and he looked over at Gem to see that she was thinking exactly the same thing. 'It can't be him, Gem, surely it can't?' he blurted.

'Oh my God, Solly, of course it is. Your father might not have left him the fair, but that hasn't stopped him believing he was robbed, and he's obviously determined to get his revenge no matter what.'

Solly's whole body sagged dispiritedly. 'We should have known we hadn't heard the last of him. He knew it was unlikely he would get any money out of me if he came and asked, and there was always the fear that we'd report him to the police, so he must have decided that the only way to get what he felt he was owed was to swindle it out of us. It was Sonny that Jimmy saw slinking out of Dad's van. He must have found something amongst Dad's old papers with his signature on it so he could practise forging it.'

'Uncle Sonny!' Jimmy exclaimed. 'It's him that's behind this?'

At the mention of Sonny's name, Tom leaned over the back of the sofa and whispered in Jenny's ear. 'You told me the night we met that your Uncle Sonny had emigrated to Australia to work on a sheep farm and that's why you were living in his van.'

She shrugged. 'Not something you brag about to someone you want to impress, is it: that your uncle is a villain on the run from the police.'

He gravely shook his head. 'No, I suppose it isn't.'

'We need to stop Uncle Sonny ruining us, Dad, we just have to,' cried Robbie.

'Yes, we do, Dad. What are we going to do?' Jimmy demanded.

Solly held out his hands in a helpless gesture. 'I have no idea yet, but I won't lose the fair through him, I just won't. Now all of you go to bed. Me and Gem need to sit down and decide what we're going to do about this, and we still have a fair to run tomorrow.' For how much longer, though? he thought worriedly.

He waited while they all reluctantly obeyed his order before making his way over to the kitchen table, where he sat down with his head in his hands. Gem sat opposite and laid a tender hand on his arm.

'So, love, now that we know it's Sonny behind this, we can threaten him that we'll tell the police where he is if he doesn't drop his plan to swindle us. They're still looking for him to charge him with working for those criminals.'

Solly sighed forlornly. 'He's my brother, Gem, despite all he's done to us. I still love him and I can't do that to him. Anyway, Sonny believes he should have been Dad's heir, and he won't stop until he gets his hands on what he believes is his by rights. A prison sentence will only halt him temporarily; as soon as he gets out, he'll try again. If we don't sort this out now, we'll always be worried about when he's going to strike next. We can't live like that, love.'

Suddenly he knew what he was going to do to

put a stop to Sonny once and for all. He pushed back his chair and stood up.

Gem eyed him, puzzled. 'Where are you going, Solly?'

'To do the only thing I can do. To give Sonny what is rightfully his.'

24

Lounging back on the lumpy mattress on the narrow bed in his dilapidated accommodation, Sonny took a long draught from a bottle of beer and smiled smugly to himself. Thanks to his ingenious idea — well, really it was that imbecile Freddy who deserved the credit for sparking it in the first place, but then he himself had come up with the rest — very soon he'd be waving this miserable life goodbye for one a damned sight better. Somewhere hot, where the police couldn't touch him.

He didn't care one iota where Solly got the money from to settle the fictitious deal he'd concocted between his father and Topper's grandfather — burn down Grundy's and claim off the insurance, sell it or hock himself up to the eyeballs — as long as he got it. He knew his plan was solid and couldn't fail, but still, the waiting to get his hands on the money, feel it between his fingers, was hard. Patience had never been one of Sonny's virtues — if indeed he possessed any virtues. Still, he was sending Barry Topper back again in a couple of days to find out how Solly was progressing. Hopefully he would come back with good news.

Having Topper around was getting on his nerves, so to give himself a bit of a break, he'd sent him off for a walk along the front with enough money to buy himself some chips, warning him not to come back until later tonight. He really should be working himself, but the boss had gone out, so leaving a gaff lad in charge of the ride he was running, Sonny had taken the opportunity to come back to his van for a rest.

He was just about to take another swig of his beer when a tap came on the door and the huge, lumbering figure of Freddy appeared.

'Oh for God's sake, Freddy,' snarled Sonny. 'Can't a man have a few minutes' peace without you disturbing it?' Then he sat bolt upright and asked worriedly, 'Boss not back, is he?' He needed to keep this job for a while longer, just till his plan came to fruition.

Freddy shook his head. 'No. Just come to bring a bloke who's looking for yer. You weren't at the waltzer, so I knew you'd be here skiving as the boss is out.'

Sonny frowned. Apart from Topper, the only other people he knew around these parts were fellow workers, and none of them would need Freddy to show them where he lived. 'What bloke?' he asked.

'Me,' announced Solly, pushing past Freddy into the caravan.

Sonny's face was wreathed with a mixture of confusion and bewilderment at the arrival of this unexpected visitor, and it was a moment before he managed to find his voice. 'How did you — ?'

Solly interjected. ' — find out you were the mastermind behind Barry Topper trying to swindle me out of the fair?' He smiled. 'You can blame Mum and Dad for having two sons that resemble each other for that.'

'Eh?'

'Do you really want this man to hear what a nasty piece of work you are?' Solly asked him.

Sonny flashed a look at Freddy hovering just inside the doorway. 'Sod off,' he ordered.

As soon as he'd left, Solly went over and sat down on the bed opposite Sonny's. He looked hard at his brother. 'I can't believe how low you've sunk, Sonny.'

Sonny smirked and flashed a look around before bringing his eyes to rest back on Solly. 'You can see for yourself how low I've sunk, brother. But not for much longer, eh, once you settle that deal our dad made with Topper's grandad.'

'We both know that document is a forgery.'

Sonny snorted sardonically. 'You've still got to prove it. I spent hours and hours practising Dad's signature after finding one amongst the papers in his van. Even an expert wouldn't be able to tell the real one from the fake.'

'So, it *was* you Jimmy saw coming out of Dad's van?'

'Certainly was, brother. Thankfully I was quicker than him and managed to scarper before he could catch me.'

'You did a good job forging that signature. I believed it was genuine and so did Gem. I have to say, I can't find a fault with your plan, Sonny. Very clever.'

'Yeah, it is,' agreed Sonny smugly.

'Well, apart from the fact that you forgot one thing when you planned out your grand scheme.'

Sonny frowned, bewildered. 'What's that then?'

'That our dad never borrowed a penny in his life, was always bragging about how he started the fair from the sale of the two stalls our grandfather left him and money he'd saved up himself. That was what got us thinking that the document couldn't be genuine.'

Sonny shrugged nonchalantly. 'Makes no difference. You still can't prove that Dad's signature is a fake. So how are you getting on with raising my money?'

Solly scowled darkly at him. 'It's not your money and I've done nothing about raising it, nor am I going to either.'

It was Sonny's eyes that darkened thunderously now. 'Then it'll be a judge that makes you pay up.'

Solly smiled. 'And you've got the money it will cost to see me in court, have you? That's providing you can persuade Barry Topper and his mother to stand up and lie for you under oath. They believe that you're carrying out this scam because a man owes you money and is refusing to pay it. They have no idea that in truth you're swindling your own brother out of money you're not entitled to. They'll run a mile when they realise they've got themselves involved in something that could land them in jail.'

Sonny gawped, startled. 'How do you know all this?'

'You can thank your niece.'

He looked bemused. 'What niece? I haven't got a niece. You had two boys.'

'A daughter too, but I'm not here to discuss that with you. You gave up your right to know anything about my family when you left us to the mercy of those thugs and facing jail for crimes you were guilty of committing. Your plan is dead in the water, Sonny, so give it up. And be warned, if you try anything like this again, you won't get off so lightly.'

Sonny froze as the realisation that his carefully planned scheme was not going to come to fruition sank in. Then a great rage filled him, and if he hadn't been wedged in the small space he would have reared up, but instead he just balled his fist and swung his arm back, his intention to land a blow under his brother's chin. But Solly was too quick for him and grabbed his wrist mid-air.

'At one time I was no match for you, Sonny,' he declared. 'But since you left the fair you haven't done so well for yourself and are far from the man you used to be. Unlike you, I have never believed that problems are resolved by violence.' He released his grip on Sonny's arm before adding. 'But go ahead and give me a hammering if it'll make you feel better. I won't humiliate you further by putting up a defence, but it won't make any difference to your plan. As I said before, that is dead and buried.'

Fist still raised, Sonny stared wildly at his brother for several long moments before he hissed, 'I wish you knew how much I fucking hate you. You'd fall into a cesspit and come up smelling of expensive soap.'

Solly shook his head sadly. 'Still bearing that

351

grudge, eh, Sonny? Once and for all will you finally accept that it wasn't my fault that Gem accepted my proposal while Belinda belittled yours to her, and Dad made me his heir over you?' He thrust his face towards Solly, eyes hard. 'Belinda was a nasty piece of work, and instead of you seeing her for what she was, you chose to allow your resentment to fester and sour you against your own family. You got yourself involved in criminal activities because you wanted to turn up at her door in a fancy car, dressed in a hand-made suit and shoes, with a wad of banknotes in your pocket, and make her see what a fool she'd been in turning you down. Had you managed that, I very much doubt that she would have regretted her choice; she would have been relieved instead that she hadn't saddled herself with such a bad lot.

'And why should Dad have made you his heir when you hardly showed any interest in Grundy's but instead concentrated your efforts on your criminal activities? Besides, you told me yourself that you intended selling the fair once you got your hands on it, and didn't give a damn what happened to your family or the rest of the folk that worked for us. If you're honest with yourself, you'll admit that Dad was right to leave me as ringmaster. And it's not like he disinherited you, which he was perfectly entitled to do given the way you were with him. Since the night you suddenly changed which we now know was because of how badly you took it when Belinda turned down your marriage proposal you hardly spoke to dad, let alone treated him like a son should. You might have come to greatly disappoint him, but he never stopped loving you, or he wouldn't have left you a ride to do what you wanted with.'

Solly reached inside his jacket pocket and pulled out a bulky envelope, which he held out to his brother. 'You left so quickly after Dad died and never claimed your inheritance. This is more than any of our rides are worth. Before I came here to see you, I got Gem to work out how much we could afford to give you in cash without risking the fair's future. She wasn't at all happy about you getting a penny of it, and she's right really, after what you did to us, but she's my wife and backs me in any decision I make. Now you either take it or leave it, but what's in this envelope is all you're going to get.'

Sonny was staring blindly at his brother as he blasted out his tirade of home truths, and suddenly a great surge of regret swamped his being. Solly was right. What an utter fool he had been to allow the spiteful words of a woman to shape the way his life had gone. Had he seen her for what she was, then instead of the dire situation he was in now, he could be in Solly's shoes and in essence have all he'd ever wanted before she had come into his life: a good woman by his side, the means to earn a decent living to support them both, and a loving family in the wings. It was too late for remorse, though, and besides, he wasn't prepared to humiliate himself any more than he already had done. In any case, Solly would more than likely believe that any show of repentance was just part of the plan to get his hands on the fair, and after his past behaviour, he couldn't blame him for thinking that way. He took the envelope and slit open the flap, then flicked his finger over the wad inside.

'There's just under ten grand there,' Solly told him. 'Enough to get you abroad and start a little business.'

It was far from the amount he had hoped to be getting, but if he was honest, it was a lot more than he deserved when all was said and done. He had no doubt his brother meant business; either he accepted this offer or he'd get nothing.

The fact that Sonny put the wad of cash into his pocket indicated to Solly that he was accepting the deal. 'Good. This is goodbye, then.'

As he walked out, both men knew that they'd never see each other again.

25

Gem heaved a deep contented sigh. 'Oh, this is the life, eh, Velda? Sitting in the sun on a lovely Sunday afternoon with nothing else to do today as Jenny has offered to cook the tea. Just listen to that silence . . . pure bliss.' The words had hardly left her mouth when a loud commotion filled the air. Sitting bolt upright, she screwed up her face and snapped, 'Goodness me, do they have to make such a racket? I thought it was a friendly game they were having, not a brawling match.'

Velda laughed. 'One side has obviously scored a goal and their supporters are showing their delight. Hope it was our team that scored. It was a good idea by the farmer whose field we're camped on: a match between the fair and the locals as a way to bring us all together. There's at least fifty of the townsfolk have come to watch, and most of our community have turned out too.' She frowned thoughtfully. 'Don't you think we should show our faces to cheer them on?'

Gem scoffed. 'Be my guest. I hate football. Grown men chasing a ball around a field, kicking hell out of each other, isn't my idea of Sunday afternoon entertainment.'

Velda got up and went over to the hedge behind them. She stood on her tiptoes to peer over the top before returning to her seat outside Gem's van. 'I don't know that much about football, but I do know there are only supposed to be eleven players in each team. There appear to be at least twenty per side over there. They all look like they're having fun, though, and that's the main thing.'

'Fun! It sounds like they're killing each other to me.' Yet another loud commotion rent the air, followed by prolonged shouting and cheers, and Gem added, 'I'd better get the medical box ready to tend to any casualties.'

She returned with the box just in time to see Tom limping over to her. He sat down on the grass before her chair and pulled down his sock to show a nasty gash on his shin, blood flowing from it.

Gem looked at him in horror. 'Oh, don't tell me the locals are playing nasty? That wasn't the aim of the match at all; it was supposed to bring us all closer together.'

'This wasn't caused by one of the locals,' Tom assured her. 'It was Mr Grundy . . . Solly. He went to kick the ball but missed and kicked my leg instead. I need to get back. We're losing eight — nil. So, if you could just put a quick plaster on it to stop the blood, I'd much appreciate it. Oh, and Solly asked if you could send over the oranges and drinks for half-time in about ten minutes.'

'I'll do a quick patch-up for now,' Gem said, 'but after the game is finished you'll need a proper job doing on it.'

Temporary dressing applied, Gem smiled as she watched Tom limp back to the hole in the hedge he'd come through to rejoin the match on the other side.

'He's a nice lad,' Velda commented. 'He and Jenny seem to be very fond of each other.'

'Mmm, yes, they are. I'd go so far as to say they're in love. Me and Solly both like him very much and think he'd make her a good husband.'

'It will be hard for them then when the season ends and Tom leaves along with the other seasonal workers.'

'Well, if they're still together when that time comes, Solly is going to ask him to work for us over the winter. We haven't told either of them as we don't want to be seen as interfering. Do your special talents tell you that Jenny and Tom have a future together?' Gem probed.

Velda lapsed into thought. Her gift for sensing things far more acutely than most people was telling her that something didn't ring true about Tom. She didn't believe he was lying; just not being as open as he could be. She had a strong feeling that he was hiding something, something that he feared wouldn't go down well with others should they discover it. Perhaps he had been in prison, although he was still young, so it couldn't have been a lengthy sentence. Or was it something else entirely? Was he a famous actor or singer, a celebrity in some way, and sick and tired of being in the public eye, his private life under constant scrutiny? He might be hiding out inside the fair to rest up for a while before he returned to the limelight. Or maybe he was already married and afraid to own up to Jenny for fear of losing her. Velda sincerely hoped that wasn't the case for the sake of the lovely young woman.

She supposed she could go on thinking of endless possibilities over what Tom was hiding, but when all was said and done, unless he himself decided to reveal whatever secret he was harbouring, it would remain just that — secret. She had no doubt, though, that at heart he was an honest man, and when the time was right, he would make his confession. She just hoped that whatever it was wasn't bad enough to break the pair apart, as they were obviously well suited together.

She realised that Gem was speaking to her and gave herself a mental shake. 'Sorry, dear, I didn't quite catch that.'

Gem clicked her tongue in frustration. 'I was saying that I don't want to waste my time hoping for a wedding that isn't going to happen, do I?'

Feeling as she did towards Tom at the moment, Velda wasn't prepared to make any predictions about his relationship with Jenny. She said evasively, 'Jenny is far too pretty to remain a spinster for the rest of her life.' Then, wanting to change the subject, she looked concernedly at her friend and asked, 'I know a few weeks have gone by, but have you and Solly got over the shock of nearly losing the fair because of Sonny?'

Gem heaved a sigh. 'I continually thank God that we managed to stop him, or I dread to think where we'd all be now. I can't pretend that the thought of never seeing him again causes me sleepless nights, but despite all he's done to us, Solly will never stop loving and missing his brother.'

'You have yourself a good man, Gem. He didn't need to give Sonny that money to start afresh.'

'To be honest, Velda, I begrudged Sonny every penny, but it was something Solly needed to do, and for that reason I didn't cause a fuss when he told me what he'd decided. I just hope Sonny uses the money wisely, as it wasn't like we could afford to give it away. It was meant for two more rides to bring the punters in, and a new entrance arch, as the one we have is getting a bit shabby.'

Velda and Gem's attention was caught by Julie and Ren, giggling together arm in arm as they approached the hole in the hedge that led into the field.

Gem said sadly, 'Such a shame for Julie to be widowed at such a young age. She and Dicky seemed so happy together.'

Velda snorted with derision. 'Shame! It's the best thing that could have happened to her, in my opinion. That husband of hers was nothing but a fornicating bully, and I still suspect that he used to beat her. She's better off without him. I'm not saying he deserved to die, but I'm glad he's no longer around to blight Julie's life. The Wall of Death riders are definitely a far happier bunch since she took over as their leader.'

'Yes, they certainly are. And the takings have gone up too. I'm so glad we managed to persuade Solly to give her a chance at the job. She's more than proved that she's worthy of it.'

Velda laughed. 'Between you, me, Jenny and Ren, we didn't give him any choice, did we?'

Gem laughed too. 'No, we didn't.' She paused

thoughtfully. 'I can't believe that we're only four months into the season and already we've had to deal with Solly having a breakdown because he got it into his head he wasn't up to being ringmaster; Dicky's death; nearly being fleeced by a crooked council leader, then by Solly's own brother; feuds between stallholders, and other things I've forgotten about now — and that's as well as doing all it takes to keep a fair this size running smoothly. I dread to think what could be in store for us for the rest of the season.'

Although she spoke gravely, a merry twinkle of humour sparked in Velda's eyes as she said, 'I fear you will be dealing with a riot next if we don't get those refreshments over to the field before the half-time whistle blows.'

'Oh crikey, I forgot about that. Come on, you slice the oranges while I make up the jugs of cordial.' Gem gave an ironic chuckle. 'So much for a peaceful Sunday afternoon, eh?'